EX LIBRIS

VINTAGE CLASSICS

THE MYSTERY OF EDWIN DROOD

Charles Dickens was born on 7 February 1812 in Landport in Portsmouth. His father was a clerk in the Navy Pay Office who often ended up in financial trouble. When Dickens was twelve years old he was sent to work in a shoe polish factory because his father had been imprisoned for debt. In 1833 he began to publish short stories and essays in newspapers and magazines. *The Pickwick Papers*, his first commercial success, was published in 1836, the same year that he married Catherine Hogarth. Many other novels followed and Dickens became a celebrity in America as well as Britain. He also set up and edited the journals *Household Words* (1850–9) and *All the Year Round* (1859–70). Charles Dickens died on 9 June 1870 leaving his last novel, *The Mystery of Edwin Drood*, unfinished.

He is buried in Westminster Abbey.

ALSO BY CHARLES DICKENS

CHARLES DICKENS

The Mystery of Edwin Drood

AND

Trial of John Jasper

WITH AN INTRODUCTION BY
Matthew Pearl

ILLUSTRATED BY
Luke Fildes and Charles Collins

VINTAGE BOOKS
London

Published by Vintage 2009

4 6 8 10 9 7 5

Introduction copyright © Matthew Pearl 2009

The Mystery of Edwin Drood was first published in 1870

Vintage
Random House, 20 Vauxhall Bridge Road,
London SW1V 2SA

www.vintage-classics.info

Addresses for companies within The Random House Group Limited
can be found at: www.randomhouse.co.uk/offices.htm

The Random House Group Limited Reg. No. 954009

A CIP catalogue record for this book
is available from the British Library

ISBN 9780099518891

The Random House Group Limited supports The Forest
Stewardship Council (FSC®), the leading international forest
certification organisation. Our books carrying the FSC label are
printed on FSC® certified paper. FSC is the only forest certification
scheme endorsed by the leading environmental organisations,
including Greenpeace. Our paper procurement policy can be found
at www.randomhouse.co.uk/environment

Printed and bound by
CPI Group (UK) Ltd, Croydon, CR0 4YY

GENERAL CONTENTS

INTRODUCTION

How was this book to end? This question has been asked since Charles Dickens died in early summer 1870 and left only the first six of the planned twelve installments of *The Mystery of Edwin Drood* complete. A few weeks after his death, the magazine *Public Opinion* promised that Dickens's private notes were forthcoming and would 'enable the reader to arrive at a partial solution of the mystery', while the *American Literary Gazette & Publishers' Circular* reported even more optimistically that Dickens had in fact finished the whole book. But the prefatory note in the first edition of *Drood*, containing only the six installments, responded indirectly to this wishful thinking and, in the tone of an affidavit, stated categorically that there were no pages, clues or notes left by the author about the second half of the novel:

> All that was left in manuscript of EDWIN DROOD is contained in this volume . . . The only notes in reference to the story that have since been found concern that portion of it exclusively, which is treated in the earlier part. Beyond the clews therein afforded to its conduct or catastrophe, nothing whatever remains.

However, even this did little to quiet readers. More than for any other unfinished book, we are incorrigible in our demand for an ending to *The Mystery of Edwin Drood*. After all, the title promises a mystery and a mystery, at least in the tradition of fiction, promises a solution. But – here I tread sacrilegious ground – are we certain Dickens himself knew the ending?

The novel's set up is swift. A few chapters in, we navigate our way around claustrophobic 'chattering old Cloisterham' – a stand-in for Dickens's own rural village of Rochester in Kent. In part because the plan for twelve installments invited a smaller canvas than Dickens's usual twenty, the cast of characters is more focused and single-minded than in most serialized Dickens novels. At the center of it is a provocative figure named John Jasper simmering an obsession over the pretty and starry-eyed Rosa Bud, who is engaged to marry Jasper's nephew Edwin Drood. What is no mystery is that Jasper desires to remove his unsuspecting nephew 'Ned' as an obstacle and rival. Whether he has succeeded in doing this by the end of the existing fragment provides that burning question we wait in perpetuity for someone clever enough to answer.

The longstanding assumption that Dickens knew how the novel would end – and the vague guilt that it is our own deficiency that we haven't deduced his wishes yet – emanates from two primary sources. First, there seems to be an unspoken fantasy about Dickens, because of his great mastery and consistency as a storyteller, that the novels emerged more or less complete from his head. Second, despite some excellent scholarship on the subject, the process behind writing in the serial-novel format of the nineteenth century is still not widely understood.

At times an inspiration, at other times a burden, publishing a novel in serialized installments usually meant *composing* in installments. Dickens might be a few months, weeks or just days ahead of each installment deadline while writing. We need not speculate whether this could have led to him changing significant parts of the machinery of his stories midstream; there are striking examples on record. The final scene of *Great Expectations*, for instance, was scrapped and rewritten, based in part on feedback from one of Dickens's friends, in a way that changed the fates of Pip and Estella. Four installments of *Martin Chuzzlewit* had already been published before Dickens decided to send the title character on an excursion to the United States. This surprise geographical plot shift, which introduced the scathing critique of American manners and ideals for which the novel is primarily remembered, was in part vengeance against the ongoing negative coverage of his recently published *American Notes* in the States. It is equally intriguing that Dickens changed Miss Mowcher in *David Copperfield* into a more noble figure after receiving a letter of complaint from Jane Hill, on whom the character was based. Hill was not an editor or Dickens insider, she was simply following the serialized installments with the rest of the reading public.

Even Dickens's original 'number plans' suggest fluidity and flexibility rather than fixed intentions. The surviving plans show the novelist's practice of outlining primary plot points and character arcs under chapter headings for each installment of his serial work. However, evidence strongly suggests that the number plans were not filled out until after he had written the installment itself. Rather than being intricate blueprints, Dickens apparently logged the chief developments of his plots as he wrote in order to have a handy reference for purposes of continuity. In fact, the number plans for the fifth and sixth installments of *Drood*, the last two sections Dickens completed before his death, are blank except for chapter headings. His work while in progress really was a work-in-progress.

None of this is meant to suggest that Dickens flew by the seat of his pants when creating *Drood* or that he didn't know where he thought John Jasper and Edwin would end up by the close of the book. However, it should be recognized that Dickens – wisely – allowed his writing to be influenced by factors as external as the comments of a reviewer in another country and a letter from a reader, and as close to home as simple inspiration or advice from a friend. It is worth noting, too, that Dickens paid close attention to the sales reports for the installments, each of which was released in London on the last day of the month, on 'Magazine Day'. This meant he could adjust quickly according to a market success or disappointment. In other words, Dickens, who frequently complained of the pressures of the serial format, took advantage of its unique hybrid state – wherein a book is printed and still fluid at the same time – in ways that helped keep his texts alive, marketable, fresh and surprising.

If we could perform an impossible experiment and squirrel away the second half of, say, *Bleak House*, and ask scholars and enthusiasts to prognosticate before the actual ending were unveiled, I am certain we would not try it so readily on *Drood*. Perhaps the unfinished state of a novel like *Drood* unnerves because it reminds us, despite all our dissertations and annotations, how little we can possess the creative mind of one of our great writers. In a sense, the lack of an ending for *Drood* – the frustrating lack of the expected resolution of all the loose ends – meant the end of the nineteenth-century novel. On the other hand, *Drood* fossilizes the serialization process from which we've become so far removed in an 'on demand' age: it preserves forever the sensation of suspense inherent in installment reading. Almost a hundred and fifty years later, we appreciate the anticipation Londoners of the mid-nineteenth century felt lining up on Paternoster Row on Magazine Day.

Sending along *Drood*'s first installment to Buckingham Palace in the spring of 1870, Dickens did offer to tell the Queen of England 'a little more of it in advance of her subjects'. The novelist was more tight-lipped in two other recorded exchanges about *Drood* that took place as the novel was being published. Here is an account by son Charley:

Charles Dickens, Jr.: 'Of course, Edwin Drood was murdered?'
Charles Dickens: 'Of course; what else do you suppose?'

And another, of a separate conversation, by Georgina Hogarth, Dickens's sister-in-law and confidante:

Georgina Hogarth: 'I hope you haven't really killed poor Edwin Drood?'
Charles Dickens: 'I call my book the Mystery, not the History, of Edwin Drood.'

The first exchange calls to mind the phrase 'The Loss of Edwin Drude' one of Dickens's early scribbled title choices, and the second evokes another title in the same list, 'Edwin Drood in Hiding'. What these flashes of reflected memories give us are not answers but important indications that, in whatever detail Dickens had worked out his story, he wanted it to be a surprise even to those close to him. That he had offered a preview to Queen Victoria – though in language suitably gradual ('a little more of it in advance'), rather than suggesting a full revelation of the ending – should remind us what a commodity surprise was to Dickens.

Rather than asking 'how was this to end?' of a book that might have been asking itself the same thing, we may enjoy a more fruitful reading of *The Mystery of Edwin Drood* by asking 'how was Dickens building up to a surprise?' Armed with this lens, we can concentrate more on what's there instead of what's not. The book contains an interconnected network of destinies and memories that captures the familial spirit and suffocation of the kind of English village that gave rise to Dickens's talents and many of his anxieties. For example, in a conversation with Jasper, Dickens has

Durdles the stonemason refer to an event that occurs a year before Edwin's disappearance in order to prepare his readers to delve more deeply into the characters' pasts as much as their futures. Elsewhere, we have mentions of the death of Edwin's parents, buried in Cloisterham, with his father referred to only as Drood (or, as Crisparkle breaks the name down, 'D-r-double-o-d'). Is his first name withheld purposefully? Like the two Barnaby Rudges (one of whom is presumed dead) and the two Martin Chuzzlewitzes, not to mention the two Charles Dickenses, was Dickens tipping us off to learn about another Edwin Drood? Could the title's mystery have been about the senior Drood, as much as the younger one?

When Dickens began *The Mystery of Edwin Drood* in 1869 he was an increasingly ill man who tried his best to hide or deny his physical deterioration. John Forster, Dickens's executor, claimed incorrectly that the clause in Dickens's contract for *Drood* establishing compensation in case he died before finishing was a unique one. In fact, an equivalent clause appeared in the contract for *Our Mutual Friend*, the novel directly preceding *Drood*. There was nothing academic about this clause. After all, Dickens did almost die in a calamitous train accident during *Our Mutual Friend*'s serialization, and, in what was an eerie experience, had to climb into a train compartment dangling over a river in order to retrieve the manuscript of the latest installment of that novel. After work on *Drood* had begun, in what may have felt an ominous turn, Dickens's chosen illustrator, his son-in-law Charles Collins, became too ill to finish the job, after drafting only the kaleidoscopic cover design. Dickens must have been apprehensive about the novel reaching completion, particularly because it had been five years since *Our Mutual Friend*, the longest break he had ever taken between books. 'If please, I live to finish it,' Dickens wrote of *Drood* to his daughter Katey, Charles Collins's wife, 'I say *if*, because you know, my dear child, I have not been strong lately.'

The stakes were raised higher by *Drood*'s special status in America. Still twenty years before the United States Congress passed legislation that would recognize copyright protection for foreign authors, Dickens had agreed that Fields, Osgood & Co., a Boston publishing firm, would be named his authorized American publisher and that royalties would be provided based on sales.

Previously, under the Harper Rule, the practice had been to pay a sum up front for advance proof sheets but nothing beyond that. The new structure, while commonplace to modern eyes, sparked a firestorm of debate in the trade and in the press, which called it 'The Dickens Controversy'. Fields and Osgood, standing firm, proudly labeled each installment as authorized by Dickens. All eyes were on *Drood* to see if it would change a longstanding and destructive American system that took advantage of unprotected English publications.

It is no surprise that some of Dickens's fears about finishing his work seep into the text of *The Mystery of Edwin Drood*. As we begin the novel, Rosa and Edwin wrestle with completing their respective parents' arrangements for their marriage, and then with their incomplete plans to undo them. The sanctimonious Sapsea's wife could only ever speak to him in 'unfinished terms'. Mr. Grewgious, Rosa's guardian, uses a fragmented 'guiding memorandum' – strongly reminiscent (and perhaps self-consciously parodic) of Dickens's number plans – to help resolve his long obligation to Rosa. Grewgious's clerk, Bazzard, has written a play but cannot manage to get it staged. In some ways, the book was already structured through the anxiety of completion before Dickens's death ever passed that anxiety on to its readers.

The most immediate mystery for first-time readers of the novel – before reaching all the questions that plague the end of the fragment – might be how to approach Edwin Drood himself. In Chapter III, we see him as something of a celebrity at Miss Twinkleton's school for girls; in fact, one female pupil is 'making his acquaintance between the hinges of the open door, left open for the purpose' which is exactly what had happened to Dickens at his Boston hotel on a visit to America not long before he began *Drood*. But Edwin, charming from afar, is hard to like, or even tolerate, closer up. 'An insufferable bore', as tagged by George Bernard Shaw, he is careless without being free-spirited, fanciful without any romance – perhaps best captured by his 'provoking yawn'. He is irritatingly obtuse when Rosa breaks down at the piano under fear of Jasper's attention. 'Pussy's not used to an audience, that's the fact', he comments. Nor is his remark to the swarthy Neville that 'you are no judge of white men' particularly ingratiating.

Of course, Edwin's exasperating traits serve a very basic purpose in the plot – to provoke the short-fused Neville enough that he will seem guilty to the townspeople of harming Edwin. Jasper goads Neville on about Edwin, knowing just which buttons to push because of his own long-standing bitterness toward his freewheeling and unreflective nephew:

> See how little he heeds it all . . . It hardly is worth his while to pluck the golden fruit that hangs ripe on the tree for him. And yet consider the contrast, Mr. Neville. You and I have no prospect of stirring work and interest, or of change and excitement, or of domestic ease and love. You and I have no prospect . . . but the tedious unchanging round of this dull place.

Jasper's words could easily have been Dickens complaining about his own sons. Like Edwin Drood with his airy plans to travel to 'undeveloped countries', by 1869 all but one of the six surviving Dickens boys had been, or were, involved in exotic colonial pursuits. Most of Dickens' sons would have likely joined Edwin in claiming to be about 'doing, working, engineering' and in 'contempt' of reading. Theirs were flighty, unfocused, and wastefully expensive lives, at least in the eyes of their famous and inordinately successful father. There was danger, too. When Frank, the third son, arrived in India to join the British civil service, he found that his brother Walter, who had been in the army there, had died on the last day of the previous year – though the news did not reach Charles in England until February.

Despite flashes of pride, Dickens's private comments about his sons more often sound notes of disappointment and Jasper-like resentment: 'I never sing their praises, because they have so often disappointed me.'; 'My boys with the curse of limpness on them.' Dickens, flipping his dynamic with his own irresponsible father, at times felt a virtual orphan of his own children: 'Why was I ever a father! Why was *my* father ever a father!' About his son Sydney, born in 1847, he ventured into even darker territory. The diminutive Sydney, called the Little Admiral by his family but known as 'Little Expectations' by his messmates after the publication of *Great Expectations*, was a sub-lieutenant in the Royal

Navy – on his way to being like *Drood*'s noble naval character Tartar – but the gold-garnished uniform could not blot out compulsive debts and financial straits. Dickens banned him from Gadshill, the family estate. 'I begin to wish,' he says of twenty-year-old Sydney, 'that he were honestly dead'. This contrasts with his comment a few months prior, when checking up on the latest pages of *The Mystery of Edwin Drood*, that 'the safety of my precious child is my sole care'. In this case the novel is his child, one he could perfect and control.

Whether Dickens was playing out the fantasy of wishing Sydney dead through John Jasper, or reconciling himself to the earlier disappearance of Walter through Edwin, one need not delve into psychoanalysis to notice the emotional parallels with Dickens's own family life carried by *Drood*. These parallels are not necessarily straightforward, and it is likely that the book would have had a less cathartic feeling than a novel like *David Copperfield*, which restaged Dickens's youth. Still, Dickens's regrets about a youthful marriage and its ultimate incompatibility are poignantly reflected in the anxieties of Rosa and Edwin. Jasper, Edwin's uncle, meanwhile, cannot fail to remind us of Dickens's own children's uncles – his rather unscrupulous, backbiting and lecherous brothers Augustus and Frederick.

There is a surprising amount of Dickens in the shadowy Jasper, as well. Like Jasper, Dickens burned his diaries at the end of each year, along with his letters. In his final years he relied on medical opiates to ease his ailments, surely an experience he channels into Jasper's drug use. He also kept up hypnotism (or mesmerism) as a hobby, and this description from his eldest child Charles Jr. suggests a carryover to everyday life also seen in Jasper: 'the mere intense gaze of those keen and luminous eyes, even without any of the passes and manipulations which form so much of the stock in trade of the ordinary mesmerist, had astonishing influence over many people, as you will read in all sorts of descriptions of him, and to my mind always seemed as if it could read one's inmost soul.' Dickens's wife Catherine, before their separation, suspected that Dickens's mesmerism was wrapped up in a romantic obsession and emotional liaison with at least one woman. Whether Dickens also felt himself the older man wedging himself into the life of young actress Ellen Ternan we cannot say, but at the very least he was obliged to keep their relationship as secret as possible, and some of his surely conflicted feelings about this may be on display in Jasper's destructive and clandestine pursuit of Rosa. The dark secrets of abandonment and resentment in family life – and by extension the life of an incestuously small village – are more key to an understanding of *Drood* than any one character in the cast.

The characters in the novel may be divided between the writers and the men and women of action. Edwin, with his contempt for 'you readers', heads up the latter category. Jasper is the primary writer figure. His diary, a crucial object in the plot, is called 'A Diary of Ned's Life', which sounds more like a novel, and could be an alternate to 'The Mystery of Edwin Drood'. In fact, the Dean of the Cathedral makes Jasper's position as writer explicit and repeats the sentiment: 'You are evidently going to write a book about us, Mr. Jasper . . . to write a book about us. Well!' Other characters also fall somewhere in the spectrum of authorship. Like Bazzard the playwright, Sapsea is a parodic example of the writer who has – adding another trace of completion anxiety – 'an Author's anxiety to rush into publication' the inscribed monument for his late wife. Stonemason Durdles, who speaks of himself in the third person as though narrating his own book, is described among his tombs as 'surrounded by his works, like a popular Author'. The naval Tartar, who takes pride in growing a garden, and the amateur pugilist Crisparkle fall in line more with action than text. The mystery of what has happened to Edwin becomes, by the end of the unfinished book, a competition among variously aligned characters between storytelling about it – Jasper's response – and action around it – which the quasi-detective Dick Datchery represents, whose own writing amounts to 'illegible' chalk marks on a cupboard door.

Datchery, who shows up in Chapter XVIII after the novel has leaped forward six months, is the character lavished with the most attention by Droodists. By the time we reach the end of the fragment, we still do not know where this man came from or his motivation, all we do know is he is surreptitiously investigating Jasper and the strange events of Christmas Eve. As a result, Datchery becomes the vehicle – the lost hope – for how the book would have ended. Interestingly, many of the theories involve some disguise on Datchery's part, despite little to no textual support for it – Datchery is Neville Landless, Datchery is Helena Landless, Datchery is Bazzard – in short, Datchery is not Datchery, he is a mere proxy for anyone else we want.

Not unlike these responses to Datchery's open-ended status, with Dickens unable to provide us with an answer, the yearning for some other figure to step in and solve the mystery for us arose quickly. Dickens's body had hardly been laid to rest at Westminster Abbey by the time a rumor spread that his sometime-collaborator and rival Wilkie Collins was undertaking the completion of *The Mystery of Edwin Drood*. That rumor was untrue, in fact Collins dismissed *Drood* as 'the melancholy work of a worn-out brain', but many other people – including Charles Dickens Jr., in the form of a later play – eventually tried their hand. Those who have attempted to 'complete' what happened to Edwin – whether through fiction or scholarly speculation – call to mind the scene in Chapter IX of the novel when the girls at Miss Twinkleton's school recreate the fight between Edwin and Neville Landless using a paper mustache and silverware as weapons. One American attempt to finish *Drood* even put out the public claim – which was taken rather seriously – to have been dictated by Dickens's ghost.

Of all the sequels and completions – Don Richard Cox lists thirty-six of them in his annotated bibliography of the novel – the 'Trial of John Jasper for the Murder of Edwin Drood' is perhaps the most unusual and ingenious. When it was staged in 1914 in London, intense interest from the public meant the venue had to be moved to King's Hall in Covent Garden, where proceedings lasted from six-thirty until almost midnight. The trial brought together important Dickens scholars – J. Cuming Walters, B. W. Matz, and Cecil Chesterton – with prominent editorial and publishing figures like Arthur Waugh (father of Evelyn) and writers G. K. Chesterton, who served as the trial's judge, and George Bernard Shaw, a late addition as foreman of the jury.

The result is an enjoyable and somewhat bizarre blend of scholarly analysis and cultural commentary, of debate and dramatization, that ends up edging into a postmodern paratext of the unfinished book. The setting must have been made more striking still by the period costume of the participants juxtaposed with the contemporary dress of the jurors. The format works well because intrinsic in the idea of the trial is the absence of a single resolution as to how to read *Drood*. No one voice triumphs, and all voices must compete with rivals and arbiters. When literary analysis turns esoteric, humorous interjections are made from Judge Chesterton or Shaw. Such antics prompted complaints for months after the trial (and a retrial of sorts in Philadelphia) that it had not been serious enough and the rules hadn't been followed.

At the end of the 'Trial', a surreal satisfaction comes when Judge Chesterton is faced with a cacophony of somber literary analysis and prejudgments by the jury. Chesterton, himself a famed mystery writer influenced by Dickens, decides to hold everyone in the crammed courtroom (except himself) in contempt of court – turning the tables so the readers are as answerable for *The Mystery of Edwin Drood*'s fate as its characters.

Matthew Pearl, 2009

No. I.]   **APRIL, 1870.**   [Price One Shilling.

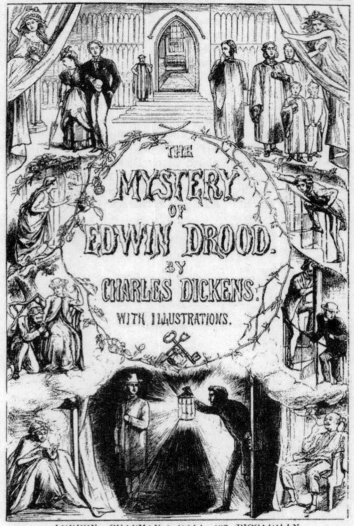

THE MYSTERY OF EDWIN DROOD.
BY CHARLES DICKENS.
WITH ILLUSTRATIONS.

LONDON: CHAPMAN & HALL, 193, PICCADILLY.

Advertisements to be sent to the Publishers, and ADAMS & FRANCIS, 59, Fleet Street, E.C.
[*The right of Translation is reserved.*]

Cover design to original part issue

CONTENTS

LIST OF ILLUSTRATIONS

———

CHARACTERS

MR. BAZZARD, *clerk to Mr. Grewgious.*

THE REV. SEPTIMUS CRISPARKLE, *one of the Minor Canons of Cloisterham Cathedral; a model clergyman, and a true Christian gentleman.*

DICK DATCHERY, *a mysterious white-haired man.*

DEPUTY ('Winks'), *a young imp employed by Durdles.*

EDWIN DROOD, *a young man left an orphan at an early age, and now studying engineering.*

DURDLES, *a stonemason, chiefly in the monumental line.*

MR. HIRAM GREWGIOUS, *Miss Rosa Bud's guardian.*

MR. LUKE HONEYTHUNDER, *Chairman of a Philanthropic Committee.*

JOHN JASPER, *a music-master, and also choir-master in Cloisterham Cathedral; uncle to Edwin Drood.*

NEVILLE LANDLESS, *a pupil of the Rev. Septimus Crisparkle.*

MR. THOMAS SAPSEA, *an auctioneer, and Mayor of Cloisterham.*

LIEUTENANT TARTAR, *a retired officer of the Royal Navy.*

MR. TOPE, *chief verger of Cloisterham Cathedral.*

MRS. BILLICKIN, *a lodging-house keeper, a widowed cousin of Mr. Bazzard's.*

MISS ROSA BUD ('Rosebud'), *an orphan, a pretty, childish young lady, the ward of Mr. Grewgious.*

MRS. CRISPARKLE ('The China Shepherdess'), *a bright old lady; the mother of the Rev. Septimus Crisparkle.*

HELENA LANDLESS, *a ward of Mr. Honeythunder's.*

MRS. TISHER, *a widow, employed at Miss Twinkleton's Seminary.*

MRS. TOPE, *wife of the chief verger of Cloisterham Cathedral.*

MISS TWINKLETON, *mistress of a boarding-school for ladies.*

Vignette from original title-page

THE MYSTERY OF
EDWIN DROOD

CHAPTER I

The Dawn

AN ancient English Cathedral Town? How can the ancient English Cathedral town be here! The well-known massive grey square tower of its old Cathedral? How can that be here! There is no spike of rusty iron in the air, between the eye and it, from any point of the real prospect. What IS the spike that intervenes, and who has set it up? Maybe, it is set up by the Sultan's orders for the impaling of a horde of Turkish robbers, one by one. It is so, for cymbals clash, and the Sultan goes by to his palace in long procession. Ten thousand scimitars flash in the sunlight, and thrice ten thousand dancing-girls strew flowers. Then, follow white elephants caparisoned in countless gorgeous colours, and infinite in number and attendants. Still, the Cathedral tower rises in the background, where it cannot be, and still no writhing figure is on the grim spike. Stay! Is the spike so low a thing as the rusty spike on the top of a post of an old bedstead that has tumbled all awry? Some vague period of drowsy laughter must be devoted to the consideration of this possibility.

Shaking from head to foot, the man whose scattered consciousness has thus fantastically pieced itself together, at length rises, supports his trembling frame upon his arms, and looks around. He is in the meanest and closest of small rooms. Through the ragged window-curtain, the light of early day steals in from a miserable court. He lies, dressed, across a large unseemly bed, upon a bedstead that has indeed given way under the weight upon it. Lying, also dressed and also across the bed, not long-wise, are a Chinaman, a Lascar, and a haggard woman. The two first are in a sleep or stupor; the last is blowing at a kind of pipe, to kindle it. And as she blows, and shading it with her lean hand, concentrates its red spark of light, it serves in the dim morning as a lamp to show him what he sees of her.

'Another?' says this woman, in a querulous, rattling whisper. 'Have another?'

He looks about him, with his hand to his forehead.

'Ye've smoked as many as five since ye come in at midnight,' the woman goes on, as she chronically complains. 'Poor me, poor me, my head is so bad! Them two come in after ye. Ah, poor me, the business is slack, is slack! Few Chinamen about the Docks, and fewer Lascars, and no ships coming in, these say! Here's another ready for ye, deary. Ye'll remember like a good soul, won't ye, that the market price is dreffle high just now? More than three shillings and sixpence for a thimbleful! And ye'll remember, too, that nobody but me (and Jack Chinaman t'other side the court; but he can't do it as well as me) has the true secret of mixing it? Ye'll pay up according, deary, won't ye?'

She blows at the pipe as she speaks, and, occasionally bubbling at it, inhales much of its contents.

'Oh me, oh me, my lungs is weak, my lungs is bad! It's nearly ready for ye, deary. Ah, poor me, poor me, my poor hand shakes like to drop off! I see ye coming-to, and I ses to my poor self, "I'll have another ready for him, and he'll bear in mind the market price of opium, and pay according." Oh my poor head! I makes my pipes of old penny ink-bottles, ye see, deary – this is one – and I fits in a mouthpiece, this way, and I takes my mixter out of this thimble with this little horn spoon; and so I fills, deary. Ah, my poor nerves! I got Heavens-hard drunk for sixteen year afore I took to this; but this don't hurt me, not to speak of. And it takes away the hunger as well as wittles, deary.'

She hands him the nearly-emptied pipe, and sinks back, turning over on her face.

He rises unsteadily from the bed, lays the pipe upon the hearth-stone, draws back the ragged curtain, and looks with repugnance at his three companions. He notices that the woman has opium-smoked herself into a strange likeness of the Chinaman. His form of cheek, eye, and temple, and his colour, are repeated in her. As he lies on his back, the said Chinaman convulsively wrestles with one of his many Gods, or Devils, perhaps, and snarls horribly. The Lascar laughs and dribbles at the mouth. The hostess is still.

'What visions can *she* have?' the waking man muses, as he turns her face towards him, and stands looking down at it. 'Visions of many butchers' shops, and public houses, and much credit? Of an increase of hideous customers, and this horrible bedstead set upright again, and this horrible court swept clean? What can she rise to, under any quantity of opium, higher than that! – Eh?'

He bends down his ear, to listen to her mutterings.

'Unintelligible!'

As he watches the spasmodic shoots and darts that break out of her face and limbs, like fitful lightning out of a dark sky, some contagion in them seizes upon him: insomuch that he has to withdraw himself to a lean arm-chair by the hearth – placed there, perhaps, for such emergencies – and to sit in it, holding tight, until he has got the better of this unclean spirit of imitation.

Then he comes back, pounces on the Chinaman, and, seizing him with both hands by the throat, turns him violently on the bed. The Chinaman clutches the aggressive hands, resists, gasps, and protests.

'What do you say?'

A watchful pause.

'Unintelligible!'

Slowly loosening his grasp as he listens to the incoherent jargon with an attentive frown, he turns to the Lascar and fairly drags him forth upon the floor. As he falls, the Lascar starts into a half-risen attitude, glares with his eyes, lashes about him fiercely with his arms, and draws a phantom knife. It then becomes apparent that the woman has taken possession of his knife, for safety's sake; for, she too starting up, and restraining and expostulating with him, the knife is visible in her dress, not in his, when they drowsily drop back, side by side.

There has been wild chattering and clattering enough between them, but to no purpose. When any distinct word has been flung into the air, it has had no sense or sequence. Wherefore 'unintelligible!' is again the comment of the watcher, made with some reassured nodding of his head, and a gloomy smile. He then lays certain silver money on the table, finds his hat, gropes his way down the broken stairs, gives a good-morning to some rat-ridden doorkeeper, a-bed in a black hutch beneath the stairs, and passes out.

That same afternoon, the massive grey square tower of an old Cathedral rises before the sight of a jaded traveller. The bells are going for daily vesper service, and he must needs attend it, one would say, from his haste to reach the open Cathedral door. The choir are getting on their sullied white robes, in a hurry, when he arrives among them, gets on his own robe, and falls into the procession filing in to service. Then, the Sacristan locks the iron-barred gates that divide the sanctuary from the chancel, and all of the procession having scuttled into their places, hide their faces; and then the intoned words, 'WHEN THE WICKED MAN—' rise among groins of arches and beams of roof, awakening muttered thunder.

In the Court

CHAPTER II

A Dean, and a Chapter also

WHOSOEVER has observed that sedate and clerical bird, the rook, may perhaps have noticed that when he wings his way homeward towards nightfall, in a sedate and clerical company, two rooks will suddenly detach themselves from the rest, will retrace their flight for some distance, and will there poise and linger; conveying to mere men the fancy that it is of some occult importance to the body politic, that this artful couple should pretend to have renounced connexion with it.

Similarly, service being over in the old Cathedral with the square tower, and the choir scuffling out again, and divers venerable persons of rook-like aspect dispersing, two of these latter retrace their steps, and walk together in the echoing Close.

Not only is the day waning, but the year. The low sun is fiery and yet cold behind the monastery ruin, and the Virginia creeper on the Cathedral wall has showered half its deep-red leaves down on the pavement. There has been rain this afternoon, and a wintry shudder goes among the little pools on the cracked uneven flagstones, and through the giant elm trees as they shed a gust of tears. Their fallen leaves lie strewn thickly about. Some of these leaves, in a timid rush, seek sanctuary within the low arched Cathedral door; but two men coming out, resist them, and cast them forth again with their feet; this done, one of the two locks the door with a goodly key, and the other flits away with a folio music-book.

'Mr. Jasper was that, Tope?'

'Yes, Mr. Dean.'

'He has stayed late.'

'Yes, Mr. Dean. I have stayed for him, your Reverence. He has been took a little poorly.'

'Say "taken," Tope – to the Dean,' the younger rook interposes in a low tone with this touch of correction, as who should say: 'You may offer bad grammar to the laity, or the humbler clergy; not to the Dean.'

Mr. Tope, Chief Verger and Showman, and accustomed to be high with excursion parties, declines with a silent loftiness to perceive that any suggestion has been tendered to him.

'And when and how has Mr. Jasper been taken – for, as Mr. Crisparkle has remarked, it is better to say taken – taken –' repeats the Dean; 'when and how has Mr. Jasper been Taken—'

'Taken, sir,' Tope deferentially murmurs.

'—Poorly, Tope?'

'Why, sir, Mr. Jasper was that breathed—'

'I wouldn't say "That breathed," Tope,' Mr. Crisparkle interposes, with the same touch as before. 'Not English – to the Dean.'

'Breathed to that extent would be preferable,' the Dean (not unflattered by this indirect homage), condescendingly remarks; 'would be preferable.'

'Mr. Jasper's breathing was so remarkably short;' thus discreetly does Mr. Tope work his way round the sunken rock, 'when he came in, that it distressed him mightily to get his notes out: which was perhaps the cause of his having a kind of fit on him after a little. His memory grew DAZED.' Mr. Tope, with his eyes on the Reverend Mr. Crisparkle, shoots this word out, as defying him to improve upon it: 'and a dimness and giddiness crept over him as strange as ever I saw: though he didn't seem to mind it particularly, himself. However, a little time and a little water brought him out of his DAZE.' Mr. Tope repeats the word and its emphasis, with the air of saying: 'As I *have* made a success, I'll make it again.'

'And Mr. Jasper has gone home quite himself, has he?' asks the Dean.

'Your Reverence, he has gone home quite himself. And I'm glad to see he's having his fire kindled up, for it's chilly after the wet, and the Cathedral had both a damp feel and a damp touch this afternoon, and he was very shivery.'

They all three look towards an old stone Gate House crossing the Close, with an arched thoroughfare passing beneath it. Through its latticed window, a fire shines out upon the fast darkening scene, involving in shadow the pendent masses of ivy and creeper covering the building's front. As the deep Cathedral bell strikes the hour, a ripple of wind goes through these at their distance, like a ripple of the solemn sound that hums through tomb and tower, broken niche and defaced statue, in the pile close at hand.

'Is Mr. Jasper's nephew with him?' the Dean asks.

'No, sir,' replies the Verger, 'but expected. There's his own solitary shadow betwixt his two windows – the one looking this way, and the one looking down into the High Street – drawing his own curtains now.'

'Well, well,' says the Dean, with a sprightly air of breaking up the little conference, 'I hope Mr. Jasper's heart may not be too much set upon his nephew. Our affections, however laudable, in this transitory world, should never master us; we should guide them, guide them. I find I am not disagreeably reminded of my dinner, by hearing my dinner-bell. Perhaps Mr. Crisparkle you will, before going home, look in on Jasper?'

'Certainly, Mr. Dean. And tell him that you had the kindness to desire to know how he was?'

'Ay; do so, do so. Certainly. Wished to know how he was. By all means. Wished to know how he was.'

With a pleasant air of patronage, the Dean as nearly cocks his quaint hat as a Dean in good spirits may, and directs his comely gaiters towards the ruddy dining-room of the snug old red-brick house where he is at present 'in residence' with Mrs. Dean and Miss Dean.

Mr. Crisparkle, Minor Canon, fair and rosy, and perpetually pitching himself head-foremost into all the deep running water in the surrounding country; Mr. Crisparkle, Minor Canon, early riser, musical, classical, cheerful, kind, good-natured, social, contented, and boy-like; Mr. Crisparkle, Minor Canon and good man, lately 'Coach' upon the chief Pagan high roads, but since promoted by a patron (grateful for a well-taught son) to his present Christian beat;

betakes himself to the Gate House, on his way home to his early tea.

'Sorry to hear from Tope that you have not been well, Jasper.'

'Oh, it was nothing, nothing!'

'You look a little worn.'

'Do I? Oh, I don't think so. What is better, I don't feel so. Tope has made too much of it I suspect. It's his trade to make the most of everything appertaining to the Cathedral, you know.'

'I may tell the Dean – I call expressly from the Dean – that you are all right again?'

The reply, with a slight smile, is: 'Certainly; with my respects and thanks to the Dean.'

'I'm glad to hear that you expect young Drood.'

'I expect the dear fellow every moment.'

'Ah! He will do you more good than a doctor, Jasper.'

'More good than a dozen doctors. For I love him dearly, and I don't love doctors, or doctors' stuff.'

Mr. Jasper is a dark man of some six-and-twenty, with thick, lustrous, well-arranged black hair and whisker. He looks older than he is, as dark men often do. His voice is deep and good, his face and figure are good, his manner is a little sombre. His room is a little sombre, and may have had its influence in forming his manner. It is mostly in shadow. Even when the sun shines brilliantly, it seldom touches the grand piano in the recess, or the folio music-books on the stand, or the bookshelves on the wall, or the unfinished picture of a blooming schoolgirl hanging over the chimney-piece; her flowing brown hair tied with a blue riband, and her beauty remarkable for a quite childish, almost babyish, touch of saucy discontent, comically conscious of itself. (There is not the least artistic merit in this picture, which is a mere daub; but it is clear that the painter has made it humorously – one might almost say, revengefully – like the original.)

'We shall miss you, Jasper, at the "Alternate Musical Wednesdays" to-night; but no doubt you are best at home. Good-night. God bless you! "Tell me, shep-herds te-e-ell me;

tell me-e-e, have you seen (have you seen, have you seen, have you seen) my-y-y Flo-o-ora-a pass this way!"'
Melodiously good Minor Canon the Reverend Septimus Crisparkle thus delivers himself, in musical rhythm, as he withdraws his amiable face from the doorway and conveys it down stairs.

Sounds of recognition and greeting pass between the Reverend Septimus and somebody else, at the stair-foot. Mr. Jasper listens, starts from his chair, and catches a young fellow in his arms, exclaiming:

'My dear Edwin!'

'My dear Jack! So glad to see you!'

'Get off your greatcoat, bright boy, and sit down here in your own corner. Your feet are not wet? Pull your boots off. Do pull your boots off.'

'My dear Jack, I am as dry as a bone. Don't moddley-coddley, there's a good fellow. I like anything better than being moddley-coddleyed.'

With the check upon him of being unsympathetically restrained in a genial outburst of enthusiasm, Mr. Jasper stands still, and looks on intently at the young fellow, divesting himself of his outer coat, hat, gloves, and so forth. Once for all, a look of intentness and intensity – a look of hungry, exacting, watchful, and yet devoted affection – is always, now and ever afterwards, on the Jasper face whenever the Jasper face is addressed in this direction. And whenever it is so addressed, it is never, on this occasion or on any other, dividedly addressed; it is always concentrated.

'Now I am right, and now I'll take my corner, Jack. Any dinner, Jack?'

Mr. Jasper opens a door at the upper end of the room, and discloses a small inner room pleasantly lighted and prepared, wherein a comely dame is in the act of setting dishes on table.

'What a jolly old Jack it is!' cries the young fellow, with a clap of his hands. 'Look here, Jack; tell me; whose birthday is it?'

'Not yours, I know,' Mr. Jasper answers, pausing to consider.

'Not mine, you know? No; not mine, *I* know! Pussy's!'

Fixed as the look the young fellow meets, is, there is yet in it some strange power of suddenly including the sketch over the chimney-piece.

'Pussy's, Jack! We must drink Many happy returns to her. Come, uncle; take your dutiful and sharp-set nephew in to dinner.'

As the boy (for he is little more) lays a hand on Jasper's shoulder, Jasper cordially and gaily lays a hand on *his* shoulder, and so Marseillaise-wise they go in to dinner.

'And Lord! Here's Mrs. Tope!' cries the boy. 'Lovelier than ever!'

'Never you mind me, Master Edwin,' retorts the Verger's wife; 'I can take care of myself.'

'You can't. You're much too handsome. Give me a kiss, because it's Pussy's birthday.'

'I'd Pussy you, young man, if I was Pussy, as you call her,' Mrs. Tope blushingly retorts, after being saluted. 'Your uncle's too much wrapped up in you, that's where it is. He makes so much of you, that it's my opinion you think you've only to call your Pussys by the dozen, to make 'em come.'

'You forget, Mrs. Tope,' Mr. Jasper interposes, taking his place at table with a genial smile, 'and so do you, Ned, that Uncle and Nephew are words prohibited here by common consent and express agreement. For what we are going to receive His holy name be praised!'

'Done like the Dean! Witness, Edwin Drood! Please to carve, Jack, for I can't.'

This sally ushers in the dinner. Little to the present purpose, or to any purpose, is said, while it is in course of being disposed of. At length the cloth is drawn, and a dish of walnuts and a decanter of rich-coloured sherry are placed upon the table.

'I say! Tell me, Jack,' the young fellow then flows on: 'do you really and truly feel as if the mention of our relationship divided us at all? *I* don't.'

'Uncles as a rule, Ned, are so much older than their nephews,' is the reply, 'that I have that feeling instinctively.'

'As a rule? Ah, may-be! But what is a difference in age of half a dozen years or so? And some uncles, in large families, are even younger than their nephews. By George, I wish it was the case with us!'

'Why?'

'Because if it was, I'd take the lead with you, Jack, and be as wise as Begone dull care that turned a young man grey, and begone dull care that turned an old man to clay. – Halloa, Jack! Don't drink.'

'Why not?'

'Asks why not, on Pussy's birthday, and no Happy returns proposed! Pussy, Jack, and many of 'em! Happy returns, I mean.'

Laying an affectionate and laughing touch on the boy's extended hand, as if it were at once his giddy head and his light heart, Mr. Jasper drinks the toast in silence.

'Hip, hip, hip, and nine times nine, and one to finish with, and all that, understood. Hooray, hooray, hooray! And now, Jack, let's have a little talk about Pussy. Two pairs of nut-crackers? Pass me one, and take the other.' Crack. 'How's Pussy getting on, Jack?'

'With her music? Fairly.'

'What a dreadfully conscientious fellow you are, Jack. But *I* know Lord bless you! Inattentive, isn't she?'

'She can learn anything, if she will.'

'*If* she will? Egad that's it. But if she won't?'

Crack. On Mr. Jasper's part.

'How's she looking, Jack?'

Mr. Jasper's concentrated face again includes the portrait as he returns: 'Very like your sketch indeed.'

'I *am* a little proud of it,' says the young fellow, glancing up at the sketch with complacency, and then shutting one eye, and taking a corrected prospect of it over a level bridge of nut-cracker in the air: 'Not badly hit off from memory. But I ought to have caught that expression pretty well, for I have seen it often enough.'

Crack. On Edwin Drood's part.

Crack. On Mr. Jasper's part.

'In point of fact,' the former resumes, after some silent dipping among his fragments of walnut with an air of pique, 'I see it whenever I go to see Pussy. If I don't find it on her face, I leave it there. – You know I do, Miss Scornful Pert. Booh!' With a twirl of the nut-crackers at the portrait.

Crack. Crack. Crack. Slowly, on Mr. Jasper's part.

Crack. Sharply, on the part of Edwin Drood.

Silence on both sides.

'Have you lost your tongue, Jack?'

'Have you found yours, Ned?'

'No, but really; – isn't it, you know, after all?'

Mr. Jasper lifts his dark eyebrows inquiringly.

'Isn't it unsatisfactory to be cut off from choice in such a matter? There, Jack! I tell you! If I could choose, I would choose Pussy from all the pretty girls in the world.'

'But you have not got to choose.'

'That's what I complain of. My dead and gone father and Pussy's dead and gone father must needs marry us together by anticipation. Why the – Devil, I was going to say, if it had been respectful to their memory – couldn't they leave us alone?'

'Tut, tut, dear boy,' Mr. Jasper remonstrates, in a tone of gentle deprecation.

'Tut, tut? Yes, Jack, it's all very well for *you*. *You* can take it easily. *Your* life is not laid down to scale, and lined and dotted out for you, like a surveyor's plan. *You* have no uncomfortable suspicion that you are forced upon anybody, nor has anybody an uncomfortable suspicion that she is forced upon you, or that you are forced upon her. *You* can choose for yourself. Life, for *you*, is a plum with the natural bloom on; it hasn't been over-carefully wiped off for *you*—'

'Don't stop, dear fellow. Go on.'

'Can I anyhow have hurt your feelings, Jack?'

'How can you have hurt my feelings?'

'Good Heaven, Jack, you look frightfully ill! There's a strange film come over your eyes.'

Mr. Jasper, with a forced smile, stretches out his right hand, as if at once to disarm apprehension and gain time to get better. After a while he says faintly:

'I have been taking opium for a pain – an agony – that sometimes overcomes me. The effects of the medicine steal over me like a blight or a cloud, and pass. You see them in the act of passing; they will be gone directly. Look away from me. They will go all the sooner.'

With a scared face, the younger man complies, by casting his eyes downward at the ashes on the hearth. Not relaxing his own gaze at the fire, but rather strengthening it with a fierce, firm grip upon his elbow-chair, the elder sits for a few moments rigid, and then, with thick drops standing on his forehead, and a sharp catch of his breath, becomes as he was before. On his so subsiding in his chair, his nephew gently and assiduously tends him while he quite recovers. When Jasper is restored, he lays a tender hand upon his nephew's shoulder, and, in a tone of voice less troubled than the purport of his words – indeed with something of raillery or banter in it – thus addresses him:

'There is said to be a hidden skeleton in every house; but you thought there was none in mine, dear Ned.'

'Upon my life, Jack, I did think so. However, when I come to consider that even in Pussy's house – if she had one – and in mine – if I had one—'

'You were going to say (but that I interrupted you in spite of myself) what a quiet life mine is. No whirl and uproar around me, no distracting commerce or calculation, no risk, no change of place, myself devoted to the art I pursue, my business my pleasure.'

'I really was going to say something of the kind, Jack; but you see, you, speaking of yourself, almost necessarily leave out much that I should have put in. For instance: I should have put in the foreground, your being so much respected as Lay Precentor, or Lay Clerk, or whatever you call it, of this Cathedral; your enjoying the reputation of having done such wonders with the choir; your choosing your society, and holding such an independent position in this queer old place; your gift of teaching (why, even Pussy, who don't like being taught, says there never was such a Master as you are!) and your connexion.'

'Yes; I saw what you were tending to. I hate it.'

'Hate it, Jack?' (Much bewildered.)

'I hate it. The cramped monotony of my existence grinds me away by the grain. How does our service sound to you?'

'Beautiful! Quite celestial.'

'It often sounds to me quite devilish. I am so weary of it! The echoes of my own voice among the arches seem to mock me with my daily drudging round. No wretched monk who droned his life away in that gloomy place, before me, can have been more tired of it than I am. He could take for relief (and did take) to carving demons out of the stalls and seats and desks. What shall I do? Must I take to carving them out of my heart?'

'I thought you had so exactly found your niche in life, Jack,' Edwin Drood returns, astonished, bending forward in his chair to lay a sympathetic hand on Jasper's knee, and looking at him with an anxious face.

'I know you thought so. They all think so.'

'Well; I suppose they do,' says Edwin, meditating aloud. 'Pussy thinks so.'

'When did she tell you that?'

'The last time I was here. You remember when. Three months ago.'

'How did she phrase it?'

'Oh! She only said that she had become your pupil, and that you were made for your vocation.'

The younger man glances at the portrait. The elder sees it in him.

'Anyhow, my dear Ned,' Jasper resumes, as he shakes his head with a grave cheerfulness: 'I must subdue myself to my vocation: which is much the same thing outwardly. It's too late to find another now. This is a confidence between us.'

'It shall be sacredly preserved, Jack.'

'I have reposed it in you, because—'

'I feel it, I assure you. Because we are fast friends, and because you love and trust me, as I love and trust you. Both hands, Jack.'

As each stands looking into the other's eyes, and as the uncle holds the nephew's hands, the uncle thus proceeds:

'You know now, don't you, that even a poor monotonous chorister and grinder of music – in his niche – may be troubled with some stray sort of ambition, aspiration, restlessness, dissatisfaction, what shall we call it?'

'Yes, dear Jack.'

'And you will remember?'

'My dear Jack, I only ask you, am I likely to forget what you have said with so much feeling?'

'Take it as a warning, then.'

In the act of having his hands released, and of moving a step back, Edwin pauses for an instant to consider the application of these last words. The instant over, he says, sensibly touched:

'I am afraid I am but a shallow, surface kind of fellow, Jack, and that my headpiece is none of the best. But I needn't say I am young; and perhaps I shall not grow worse as I grow older. At all events, I hope I have something impressible within me, which feels – deeply feels – the disinterestedness of your painfully laying your inner self bare, as a warning to me.'

Mr. Jasper's steadiness of face and figure becomes so marvellous that his breathing seems to have stopped.

'I couldn't fail to notice, Jack, that it cost you a great effort, and that you were very much moved, and very unlike your usual self. Of course I knew that you were extremely fond of me, but I really was not prepared for your, as I may say, sacrificing yourself to me, in that way.'

Mr. Jasper, becoming a breathing man again without the smallest stage of transition between the two extreme states, lifts his shoulders, laughs, and waves his right arm.

'No; don't put the sentiment away, Jack; please don't; for I am very much in earnest. I have no doubt that that unhealthy state of mind which you have so powerfully described is attended with some real suffering, and is hard to bear. But let me reassure you, Jack, as to the chances of its overcoming Me. I don't think I am in the way of it. In some few months less than another year, you know, I shall carry Pussy off from school as Mrs. Edwin Drood. I shall then go engineering into the East, and Pussy with me. And although we have our little tiffs now, arising out of a certain unavoidable flatness that attends our love-making, owing to its end being all settled beforehand, still I have no doubt of our getting on capitally then, when it's done and can't be helped. In short, Jack, to go back to the old song I was freely quoting at dinner (and who knows old songs better than you!), my wife shall dance and I will sing, so merrily pass the day. Of Pussy's being beautiful there cannot be a doubt; – and when you are good besides, Little Miss Impudence,' once more apostrophizing the portrait, 'I'll burn your comic likeness and paint your music-master another.'

Mr. Jasper, with his hand to his chin, and with an expression of musing benevolence on his face, has attentively watched every animated look and gesture attending the delivery of these words. He remains in that attitude after they are spoken, as if in a kind of fascination attendant on his strong interest in the youthful spirit that he loves so well. Then, he says with a quiet smile:

'You won't be warned, then?'

'No, Jack.'

'You can't be warned, then?'

'No, Jack, not by you. Besides that I don't really consider myself in danger, I don't like your putting yourself in that position.'

'Shall we go and walk in the churchyard?'

'By all means. You won't mind my slipping out of it for half a moment to the Nuns' House, and leaving a parcel there? Only gloves for Pussy; as many pairs of gloves as she is years old to-day. Rather poetical, Jack?'

Mr. Jasper, still in the same attitude, murmurs: '"Nothing half so sweet in life," Ned!'

'Here's the parcel in my greatcoat pocket. They must be presented to-night, or the poetry is gone. It's against regulations for me to call at night, but not to leave a packet. I am ready, Jack!'

Mr. Jasper dissolves his attitude, and they go out together.

CHAPTER III

The Nuns' House

FOR sufficient reasons which this narrative will itself unfold as it advances, a fictitious name must be bestowed upon the old Cathedral town. Let it stand in these pages as Cloisterham. It was once possibly known to the Druids by another name, and certainly to the Romans by another, and to the Saxons by another, and to the Normans by another; and a name more or less in the course of many centuries can be of little moment to its dusty chronicles.

An ancient city, Cloisterham, and no meet dwelling-place for any one with hankerings after the noisy world. A monotonous, silent city, deriving an earthy flavour throughout, from its Cathedral crypt, and so abounding in vestiges of monastic graves, that the Cloisterham children grow small salad in the dust of abbots and abbesses, and make dirt-pies of nuns and friars; while every ploughman in its outlying fields renders to once puissant Lord Treasurers, Archbishops, Bishops, and such-like, the attention which the Ogre in the story-book desired to render to his unbidden visitor, and grinds their bones to make his bread.

A drowsy city, Cloisterham, whose inhabitants seem to suppose, with an inconsistency more strange than rare, that all its changes lie behind it, and that there are no more to come. A queer moral to derive from antiquity, yet older than any traceable antiquity. So silent are the streets of Cloisterham (though prone to echo on the smallest provocation), that of a summer day the sunblinds of its shops scarce dare to flap in the south wind; while the sun-browned tramps who pass along and stare, quicken their limp a little, that they may the sooner get beyond the confines of its oppressive respectability. This is a feat not difficult of achievement, seeing that the streets of Cloisterham city are little more than one narrow street by which you get into it and get out of it: the rest being mostly disappointing yards with pumps in them and no thoroughfare – exception made of the Cathedral Close, and a paved Quaker settlement, in colour and general conformation very like a Quakeress's bonnet, up in a shady corner.

In a word, a city of another and a bygone time is Cloisterham, with its hoarse Cathedral bell, its hoarse rooks hovering about the Cathedral tower, its hoarser and less distinct rooks in the stalls far beneath. Fragments of old wall, saint's chapel, chapter-house, convent, and monastery, have got incongruously or obstructively built into many of its houses and gardens, much as kindred jumbled notions have become incorporated into many of its citizens' minds. All things in it are of the past. Even its single pawnbroker takes in no pledges, nor has he for a long time, but offers vainly an unredeemed stock for sale, of which the costlier articles are dim and pale old watches apparently in a cold perspiration, tarnished sugar-tongs with ineffectual legs, and odd volumes of dismal books. The most abundant and the most agreeable evidences of progressing life in Cloisterham, are the evidences of vegetable life in its many gardens; even its drooping and despondent little theatre has its poor strip of garden, receiving the foul fiend, when he ducks from its stage into the infernal regions, among scarlet beans or oyster-shells, according to the season of the year.

In the midst of Cloisterham stands the Nuns' House; a venerable brick edifice whose present appellation is doubtless derived from the legend of its conventual uses. On the trim gate enclosing its old courtyard, is a resplendent brass plate flashing forth the legend: 'Seminary for Young Ladies. Miss Twinkleton.' The house-front is so old and worn, and the brass plate is so shining and staring, that the general result has reminded imaginative strangers of a battered old beau with a large modern eye-glass stuck in his blind eye.

Whether the nuns of yore, being of a submissive rather than a stiff-necked generation, habitually bent their contemplative heads to avoid collision with the beams in the low ceilings of the many chambers of their House; whether they sat in its long low windows, telling their beads for their mortification instead of making necklaces of them for their adornment; whether they were ever walled up alive in odd angles and jutting gables of the building for having some ineradicable leaven of busy mother Nature in them which has kept the fermenting world alive ever since; these may be matters of interest to its haunting ghosts (if any), but constitute no item in Miss Twinkleton's half-yearly accounts. They are neither of Miss Twinkleton's inclusive regulars, nor of her extras. The lady who undertakes the poetical department of the establishment at so much (or so little) a quarter, has no pieces in her list of recitals bearing on such unprofitable questions.

As, in some cases of drunkenness, and in others of animal magnetism, there are two states of consciousness which never clash, but each of which pursues its separate course as though it were continuous instead of broken (thus if I hide my watch when I am drunk, I must be drunk again before I can remember where), so Miss Twinkleton has two distinct and separate phases of being. Every night, the moment the young ladies have retired to rest, does Miss Twinkleton smarten up her curls a little, brighten up her eyes a little, and become a sprightly Miss Twinkleton whom the young ladies have never seen. Every night, at the same hour, does Miss Twinkleton resume the topics of the previous night, comprehending the tenderer scandal of Cloisterham, of which she has no knowledge whatever by day, and references to a certain season at Tunbridge Wells (airily called by Miss Twinkleton in this state of her existence 'The Wells'), notably the season wherein a certain finished gentleman (compassionately called by Miss Twinkleton in this state of her existence, 'Foolish Mr. Porters') revealed a homage of the heart, whereof Miss Twinkleton, in her scholastic state of existence, is as ignorant as a granite pillar. Miss Twinkleton's companion in both states of existence, and equally adaptable to either, is one Mrs. Tisher: a deferential widow with a weak back, a chronic sigh, and a suppressed voice, who looks after the young ladies' wardrobes, and leads them to infer that she has seen better days. Perhaps this is the reason why it is an article of faith with the servants, handed down from race to race, that the departed Tisher was a hairdresser.

The pet pupil of the Nuns' House is Miss Rosa Bud, of course called Rosebud; wonderfully pretty, wonderfully childish, wonderfully whimsical. An awkward interest (awkward because romantic) attaches to Miss Bud in the minds of the young ladies, on account of its being known to them that a husband has been chosen for her by will and bequest, and that her guardian is bound down to bestow her on that husband when he comes of age. Miss Twinkleton, in her seminarial state of existence, has combated the romantic aspect of this destiny by affecting to shake her head over it behind Miss Bud's dimpled shoulders, and to brood on the unhappy lot of that doomed little victim. But with no better effect – possibly some unfelt touch of foolish Mr. Porters has undermined the endeavour – than to evoke from the young ladies an unanimous bedchamber cry of 'Oh! what a pretending old thing Miss Twinkleton is, my dear!'

The Nuns' House is never in such a state of flutter as when this allotted husband calls to see little Rosebud. (It is unanimously understood by the young ladies that he is lawfully entitled to this privilege, and that if Miss Twinkleton disputed it she would be instantly taken up and transported.) When his ring at the gate bell is expected, or takes place, every young lady who can, under any pretence, look out of window, looks out of window: while every young lady who is 'practising,' practises out of time; and the French class becomes so demoralized that the Mark goes round as briskly as the bottle at a convivial party in the last century.

On the afternoon of the day next after the dinner of two at the Gate House, the bell is rung with the usual fluttering results.

'Mr. Edwin Drood to see Miss Rosa.'

This is the announcement of the parlour-maid in chief. Miss Twinkleton, with an exemplary air of melancholy on her, turns to the sacrifice, and says: 'You may go down, my dear.' Miss Bud goes down, followed by all eyes.

Mr. Edwin Drood is waiting in Miss Twinkleton's own parlour: a dainty room, with nothing more directly scholastic in it than a terrestrial and a celestial globe. These expressive machines imply (to parents and guardians) that even when

Miss Twinkleton retires into the bosom of privacy, duty may at any moment compel her to become a sort of Wandering Jewess, scouring the earth and soaring through the skies in search of knowledge for her pupils.

The last new maid, who has never seen the young gentleman Miss Rosa is engaged to, and who is making his acquaintance between the hinges of the open door, left open for the purpose, stumbles guiltily down the kitchen stairs, as a charming little apparition with its face concealed by a little silk apron thrown over its head, glides into the parlour.

'Oh! It *is* so ridiculous!' says the apparition, stopping and shrinking. 'Don't, Eddy!'

'Don't what, Rosa?'

'Don't come any nearer, please. It *is* so absurd.'

'What is absurd, Rosa?'

'The whole thing is. It *is* so absurd to be an engaged orphan; and it *is* so absurd to have the girls and the servants scuttling about after one, like mice in the wainscot; and it *is* so absurd to be called upon!'

The apparition appears to have a thumb in the corner of its mouth while making this complaint.

'You give me an affectionate reception, Pussy, I must say.'

'Well, I will in a minute, Eddy, but I can't just yet. How are you?' (very shortly).

'I am unable to reply that I am much the better for seeing you, Pussy, inasmuch as I see nothing of you.'

This second remonstrance brings a dark bright pouting eye out from a corner of the apron; but it swiftly becomes invisible again, as the apparition exclaims: 'Oh! Good Gracious, you have had half your hair cut off!'

'I should have done better to have had my head cut off, I think,' says Edwin, rumpling the hair in question, with a fierce glance at the looking-glass, and giving an impatient stamp. 'Shall I go?'

'No; you needn't go just yet, Eddy. The girls would all be asking questions why you went.'

'Once for all, Rosa, will you uncover that ridiculous little head of yours and give me a welcome?'

The apron is pulled off the childish head, as its wearer replies: 'You're very welcome, Eddy. There! I'm sure that's nice. Shake hands. No, I can't kiss you, because I've got an acidulated drop in my mouth.'

'Are you at all glad to see me, Pussy?'

'Oh, yes, I'm dreadfully glad. – Go and sit down. – Miss Twinkleton.'

It is the custom of that excellent lady, when these visits occur, to appear every three minutes, either in her own person or in that of Mrs. Tisher, and lay an offering on the shrine of Propriety by affecting to look for some desiderated article. On the present occasion, Miss Twinkleton, gracefully gliding in and out, says, in passing: 'How do you do, Mr. Drood? Very glad indeed to have the pleasure. Pray excuse me. Tweezers. Thank you!'

'I got the gloves last evening, Eddy, and I like them very much. They are beauties.'

'Well, that's something,' the affianced replies, half grumbling. 'The smallest encouragement thankfully received. And how did you pass your birthday, Pussy?'

'Delightfully! Everybody gave me a present. And we had a feast. And we had a ball at night.'

'A feast and a ball, eh? These occasions seem to go off tolerably well without me, Pussy.'

'De-lightfully!' cries Rosa, in a quite spontaneous manner, and without the least pretence of reserve.

'Hah! And what was the feast?'

'Tarts, oranges, jellies, and shrimps.'

'Any partners at the ball?'

'We danced with one another, of course, sir. But some of the girls made game to be their brothers. It *was* so droll!'

'Did anybody make game to be—'

'To be you? Oh dear yes!' cries Rosa, laughing with great enjoyment. 'That was the first thing done.'

'I hope she did it pretty well,' says Edwin, rather doubtfully.

'Oh! It was excellent! – I wouldn't dance with you, you know.'

Edwin scarcely seems to see the force of this; begs to know if he may take the liberty to ask why?

'Because I was so tired of you,' returns Rosa. But she quickly adds, and pleadingly too, seeing displeasure in his face: 'Dear Eddy, you were just as tired of me, you know.'

'Did I say so, Rosa?'

'Say so! Do you ever say so? No, you only showed it. Oh, she did it so well!' cries Rosa, in a sudden ecstasy with her counterfeit betrothed.

'It strikes me that she must be a devilish impudent girl,' says Edwin Drood. 'And so, Pussy, you have passed your last birthday in this old house.'

'Ah, yes!' Rosa clasps her hands, looks down with a sigh, and shakes her head.

'You seem to be sorry, Rosa.'

'I am sorry for the poor old place. Somehow, I feel as if it would miss me, when I am gone so far away, so young.'

'Perhaps we had better stop short, Rosa?'

She looks up at him with a swift bright look; next moment shakes her head, sighs, and looks down again.

'That is to say, is it Pussy, that we are both resigned?'

She nods her head again, and after a short silence, quaintly bursts out with: 'You know we must be married, and married from here, Eddy, or the poor girls will be so dreadfully disappointed!'

For the moment there is more of compassion, both for her and for himself, in her affianced husband's face, than there is of love. He checks the look, and asks: 'Shall I take you out for a walk, Rosa dear?'

Rosa dear does not seem at all clear on this point, until her face, which has been comically reflective, brightens. 'Oh, yes, Eddy; let us go for a walk! And I tell you what we'll do. You shall pretend that you are engaged to somebody else, and I'll pretend that I am not engaged to anybody, and then we shan't quarrel.'

'Do you think that will prevent our falling out, Rosa?'

'I know it will. Hush! Pretend to look out of window. – Mrs. Tisher!'

Through a fortuitous concourse of accidents, the matronly Tisher heaves in sight, says, in rustling through the room like the legendary ghost of a Dowager in silken skirts: 'I hope I see Mr. Drood well; though I needn't ask, if I may judge from his complexion? I trust I disturb no one; but there *was* a paper-knife – Oh, thank you, I am sure!' and disappears with her prize.

'One other thing you must do, Eddy, to oblige me,' says Rosebud. 'The moment we get into the street, you must put me outside, and keep close to the house yourself – squeeze and graze yourself against it.'

'By all means, Rosa, if you wish it. Might I ask why?'

'Oh! because I don't want the girls to see you.'

'It's a fine day; but would you like me to carry an umbrella up?'

'Don't be foolish, sir. You haven't got polished leather boots on,' pouting, with one shoulder raised.

'Perhaps that might escape the notice of the girls, even if they did see me,' remarks Edwin, looking down at his boots with a sudden distaste for them.

'Nothing escapes their notice, sir. And then I know what would happen. Some of them would begin reflecting on me by saying (for *they* are free) that they never will on any account engage themselves to lovers without polished leather boots. Hark! Miss Twinkleton. I'll ask for leave.'

That discreet lady being indeed heard without, inquiring of nobody in a blandly conversational tone as she advances: 'Eh? Indeed! Are you quite sure you saw my mother-of-pearl button-holder on the work-table in my room?' is at once solicited for walking leave, and graciously accords it. And soon the young couple go out of the Nuns' House, taking all precautions against the discovery of the so vitally defective boots of Mr. Edwin Drood: precautions, let us hope, effective for the peace of Mrs. Edwin Drood that is to be.

'Which way shall we take, Rosa?'

Rosa replies: 'I want to go to the Lumps-of-Delight shop.'

'To the—?'

'A Turkish sweetmeat, sir. My gracious me, don't you understand anything? Call yourself an Engineer, and not know *that*?'

'Why, how should I know it, Rosa?'

'Because I am very fond of them. But oh! I forgot what we are to pretend. No, you needn't know anything about them; never mind.'

So, he is gloomily borne off to the Lumps-of-Delight shop, where Rosa makes her purchase, and, after offering some to him (which he rather indignantly declines), begins to partake of it with great zest: previously taking off and rolling up a pair of little pink gloves, like rose-leaves, and occasionally putting her little pink fingers to her rosy lips, to cleanse them from the Dust of Delight that comes off the Lumps.

'Now, be a good-tempered Eddy, and pretend. And so you are engaged?'

'And so I am engaged.'

'Is she nice?'

'Charming.'

'Tall?'

'Immensely tall!' Rosa being short.

'Must be gawky, I should think,' is Rosa's quiet commentary.

'I beg your pardon; not at all,' contradiction rising in him. 'What is termed a fine woman; a splendid woman.'

'Big nose, no doubt,' is the quiet commentary again.

'Not a little one, certainly,' is the quick reply. (Rosa's being a little one.)

'Long pale nose, with a red knob in the middle. *I* know the sort of nose,' says Rosa, with a satisfied nod, and tranquilly enjoying the Lumps.

'You *don't* know the sort of nose, Rosa,' with some warmth; 'because it's nothing of the kind.'

'Not a pale nose, Eddy?'

'No.' Determined not to assent.

'A red nose? Oh! I don't like red noses. However; to be sure she can always powder it.'

'She would scorn to powder it,' says Edwin, becoming heated.

'Would she? What a stupid thing she must be! Is she stupid in everything?'

'No. In nothing.'

After a pause, in which the whimsically wicked face has not been unobservant of him, Rosa says:

'And this most sensible of creatures likes the idea of being carried off to Egypt; does she, Eddy?'

'Yes. She takes a sensible interest in triumphs of engineering skill: especially when they are to change the whole condition of an undeveloped country.'

'Lor!' says Rosa, shrugging her shoulders, with a little laugh of wonder.

'Do you object,' Edwin inquires, with a majestic turn of his eyes downward upon the fairy figure: 'do you object, Rosa, to her feeling that interest?'

'Object? My dear Eddy! But really. Doesn't she hate boilers and things?'

'I can answer for her not being so idiotic as to hate Boilers,' he returns with angry emphasis; 'though I cannot answer for her views about Things; really not understanding what Things are meant.'

'But don't she hate Arabs, and Turks, and Fellahs, and people?'

'Certainly not.' Very firmly.

'At least, she *must* hate the Pyramids? Come, Eddy?'

'Why should she be such a little – tall, I mean – Goose, as to hate the Pyramids, Rosa?'

'Ah! you should hear Miss Twinkleton,' often nodding her head, and much enjoying the Lumps, 'bore about them, and then you wouldn't ask. Tiresome old burying-grounds! Isises, and Ibises, and Cheopses, and Pharaohses; who cares about them? And then there was Belzoni or somebody, dragged out by the legs, half choked with bats and dust. All the girls say serve him right, and hope it hurt him, and wish he had been quite choked.'

The two youthful figures, side by side, but not now arm-in-arm, wander discontentedly about the old Close; and each sometimes stops and slowly imprints a deeper footstep in the fallen leaves.

'Well!' says Edwin, after a lengthy silence. 'According to custom. We can't get on, Rosa.'

Rosa tosses her head, and says she don't want to get on.

'That's a pretty sentiment, Rosa, considering.'

'Considering what?'

'If I say what, you'll go wrong again.'

'*You*'ll go wrong, you mean, Eddy. Don't be ungenerous.'

'Ungenerous! I like that!'

'Then I *don't* like that, and so I tell you plainly,' Rosa pouts.

'Now, Rosa, I put it to you. Who disparaged my profession, my destination—'

'You are not going to be buried in the Pyramids, I hope?' she interrupts, arching her delicate eyebrows. 'You never said you were. If you are, why haven't you mentioned it to me? I can't find out your plans by instinct.'

'Now, Rosa; you know very well what I mean, my dear.'

'Well then, why did you begin with your detestable red-nosed Giantesses? And she would, she would, she would, she would, she WOULD powder it!' cries Rosa, in a little burst of comical contradictory spleen.

'Somehow or other, I never can come right in these discussions,' says Edwin, sighing and becoming resigned.

'How is it possible, sir, that you ever can come right when you're always wrong? And as to Belzoni, I suppose he's dead; – I'm sure I hope he is – and how can his legs, or his chokes concern you?'

'It is nearly time for your return, Rosa. We have not had a very happy walk, have we?'

'A happy walk? A detestably unhappy walk, sir. If I go up stairs the moment I get in and cry till I can't take my dancing-lesson, you are responsible, mind!'

'Let us be friends, Rosa.'

'Ah!' cries Rosa, shaking her head and bursting into real tears. 'I wish we *could* be friends! It's because we can't be friends, that we try one another so. I am a young little thing, Eddy, to have an old heartache; but I really, really have, sometimes. Don't be angry. I know you have one yourself, too often. We should both of us have done better, if What is to be had been left, What might have been. I am quite a serious little thing now, and not teasing you. Let each of us forbear, this one time, on our own account, and on the other's!'

Disarmed by this glimpse of a woman's nature in the spoilt child, though for an instant disposed to resent it as seeming to involve the enforced infliction of himself upon her, Edwin Drood stands watching her as she childishly cries and sobs, with both hands to the handkerchief at her eyes, and then – she becoming more composed, and indeed beginning in her young inconstancy to laugh at herself for having been so moved – leads her to a seat hard by, under the elm trees.

'One clear word of understanding, Pussy dear. I am not clever out of my own line – now I come to think of it I don't know that I am particularly clever in it – but I want to do right. There is not – there may be – I really don't see my way to what I want to say, but I must say it before we part – there is not any other young—?'

'Oh no, Eddy! It's generous of you to ask me; but no, no, no!'

They have come very near to the Cathedral windows, and at this moment the organ and the choir sound out sublimely. As they sit listening to the solemn swell, the confidence of last night rises in young Edwin Drood's mind, and he thinks how unlike this music is, to that discordance.

'I fancy I can distinguish Jack's voice,' is his remark in a low tone in connexion with the train of thought.

'Take me back at once, please,' urges his Affianced, quickly laying her light hand upon his wrist. 'They will all be coming out directly; let us get away. Oh, what a resounding chord! But don't let us stop to listen to it; let us get away!'

Her hurry is over, as soon as they have passed out of the Close. They go, arm-in-arm now, gravely and deliberately enough, along the old High Street, to the Nuns' House. At the gate, the street being within sight empty, Edwin bends down his face to Rosebud's.

She remonstrates, laughing, and is a childish schoolgirl again.

Under the Trees

'Eddy, no! I'm too sticky to be kissed. But give me your hand, and I'll blow a kiss into that.'

He does so. She breathes a light breath into it, and asks, retaining it and looking into it:

'Now say, what do you see?'

'See, Rosa?'

'Why, I thought you Egyptian boys could look into a hand and see all sorts of phantoms? Can't you see a happy Future?'

For certain, neither of them sees a happy Present, as the gate opens and closes, and one goes in and the other goes away.

CHAPTER IV

Mr. Sapsea

ACCEPTING the Jackass as the type of self-sufficient stupidity and conceit – a custom, perhaps, like some few other customs, more conventional than fair – then the purest Jackass in Cloisterham is Mr. Thomas Sapsea, Auctioneer.

Mr. Sapsea 'dresses at' the Dean; has been bowed to for the Dean, in mistake; has even been spoken to in the street as My Lord, under the impression that he was the Bishop come down unexpectedly, without his chaplain. Mr. Sapsea is very proud of this, and of his voice, and of his style. He has even (in selling landed property), tried the experiment of slightly intoning in his pulpit, to make himself more like what he takes to be the genuine ecclesiastical article. So, in ending a Sale by Public Auction, Mr. Sapsea finishes off with an air of bestowing a benediction on the assembled brokers, which leaves the real Dean – a modest and worthy gentleman – far behind.

Mr. Sapsea has many admirers; indeed, the proposition is carried by a large local majority, even including non-believers in his wisdom, that he is a credit to Cloisterham. He possesses the great qualities of being portentous and dull, and of having a roll in his speech, and another roll in his gait; not to mention a certain gravely flowing action with his hands, as if he were presently going to Confirm the individual with whom he holds discourse. Much nearer sixty years of age than fifty, with a flowing outline of stomach, and horizontal creases in his waistcoat; reputed to be rich; voting at elections in the strictly respectable interest; morally satisfied that nothing but he himself has grown since he was a baby; how can dunder-headed Mr. Sapsea be otherwise than a credit to Cloisterham, and society?

Mr. Sapsea's premises are in the High Street, over against the Nuns' House. They are of about the period of the Nuns'

House, irregularly modernized here and there, as steadily deteriorating generations found, more and more, that they preferred air and light to Fever and the Plague. Over the doorway, is a wooden effigy, about half life-size, representing Mr. Sapsea's father, in a curly wig and toga, in the act of selling. The chastity of the idea, and the natural appearance of the little finger, hammer, and pulpit, have been much admired.

Mr. Sapsea sits in his dull ground-floor sitting-room, giving first on his paved back yard, and then on his railed-off garden. Mr. Sapsea has a bottle of port wine on a table before the fire – the fire is an early luxury, but pleasant on the cool, chill autumn evening – and is characteristically attended by his portrait, his eight-day clock, and his weather-glass. Characteristically, because he would uphold himself against mankind, his weather-glass against weather, and his clock against time.

By Mr. Sapsea's side on the table are a writing-desk and writing materials. Glancing at a scrap of manuscript, Mr. Sapsea reads it to himself with a lofty air, and then, slowly pacing the room with his thumbs in the arm-holes of his waistcoat, repeats it from memory: so internally, though with much dignity, that the word 'Ethelinda' is alone audible.

There are three clean wineglasses in a tray on the table. His serving-maid entering, and announcing 'Mr. Jasper is come, sir,' Mr. Sapsea waves 'Admit him' and draws two wineglasses from the rank, as being claimed.

'Glad to see you, sir. I congratulate myself on having the honour of receiving you here for the first time.' Mr. Sapsea does the honours of his house in this wise.

'You are very good. The honour is mine and the self-congratulation is mine.'

'You are pleased to say so, sir. But I do assure you that it is a satisfaction to me to receive you in my humble home. And that is what I would not say to everybody.' Ineffable loftiness on Mr. Sapsea's part accompanies these words, as leaving the sentence to be understood: 'You will not easily believe that your society can be a satisfaction to a man like myself; nevertheless, it is.'

'I have for some time desired to know you, Mr. Sapsea.'

'And I, sir, have long known you by reputation as a man of taste. Let me fill your glass. I will give you, sir,' says Mr. Sapsea, filling his own:

> 'When the French come over,
> May we meet them at Dover!'

This was a patriotic toast in Mr. Sapsea's infancy, and he is therefore fully convinced of its being appropriate to any subsequent era.

'You can scarcely be ignorant, Mr. Sapsea,' observes Jasper, watching the auctioneer with a smile as the latter stretches out his legs before the fire, 'that you know the world.'

'Well, sir,' is the chuckling reply, 'I think I know something of it; something of it.'

'Your reputation for that knowledge has always interested and surprised me, and made me wish to know you. For, Cloisterham is a little place. Cooped up in it myself, I know nothing beyond it, and feel it to be a very little place.'

'If I have not gone to foreign countries, young man,' Mr. Sapsea begins, and then stops: – 'You will excuse my calling you young man, Mr. Jasper? You are much my junior.'

'By all means.'

'If I have not gone to foreign countries, young man, foreign countries have come to me. They have come to me in the way of business, and I have improved upon my opportunities. Put it that I take an inventory, or make a catalogue. I see a French clock. I never saw him before, in my life, but I instantly lay my finger on him and say "Paris!" I see some cups and saucers of Chinese make, equally strangers to me personally: I put my finger on them, then and there, and I say "Pekin, Nankin, and Canton." It is the same with Japan, with Egypt, and with bamboo and sandal-wood from the East Indies; I put my finger on them all. I have put my finger on the North Pole before now, and said, "Spear of Esquimaux make, for half a pint of pale sherry!"'

'Really? A very remarkable way, Mr. Sapsea, of acquiring a knowledge of men and things.'

'I mention it, sir,' Mr. Sapsea rejoins, with unspeakable complacency, 'because, as I say, it don't do to boast of what you are; but show how you came to be it, and then you prove it.'

'Most interesting. We were to speak of the late Mrs. Sapsea.'

'We were, sir.' Mr. Sapsea fills both glasses, and takes the decanter into safe keeping again. 'Before I consult your opinion as a man of taste on this little trifle' – holding it up – 'which is *but* a trifle, and still has required some thought, sir, some little fever of the brow, I ought perhaps to describe the character of the late Mrs. Sapsea, now dead three quarters of a year.'

Mr. Jasper, in the act of yawning behind his wineglass, puts down that screen and calls up a look of interest. It is a little impaired in its expressiveness by his having a shut-up gape still to dispose of, with watering eyes.

'Half a dozen years ago, or so,' Mr. Sapsea proceeds, 'when I had enlarged my mind up to – I will not say to what it now is, for that might seem to aim at too much, but up to the pitch of wanting another mind to be absorbed in it – I cast my eye about me for a nuptial partner. Because, as I say, it is not good for man to be alone.'

Mr. Jasper appears to commit this original idea to memory.

'Miss Brobity at that time kept, I will not call it the rival establishment to the establishment at the Nuns' House opposite, but I will call it the other parallel establishment down town. The world did have it that she showed a passion for attending my sales, when they took place on half-holidays, or in vacation time. The world did put it about, that she admired my style. The world did notice that as time flowed by, my style became traceable in the dictation-exercises of Miss Brobity's pupils. Young man, a whisper even sprang up in obscure malignity, that one ignorant and besotted Churl (a parent) so committed himself as to object to it by name. But I do not believe this. For is it likely that any human creature in his right senses would so lay himself open to be pointed at, by what I call the finger of scorn?'

Mr. Jasper shakes his head. Not in the least likely. Mr. Sapsea, in a grandiloquent state of absence of mind, seems to refill his visitor's glass, which is full already; and does really refill his own, which is empty.

'Miss Brobity's Being, young man, was deeply imbued with homage to Mind. She revered Mind, when launched, or, as I say, precipitated, on an extensive knowledge of the world. When I made my proposal, she did me the honour to be so overshadowed with a species of Awe, as to be able to articulate only the two words, "Oh Thou!" – meaning myself. Her limpid blue eyes were fixed upon me, her semi-transparent hands were clasped together, pallor overspread her aquiline features, and, though encouraged to proceed, she never did proceed a word further. I disposed of the parallel establishment, by private contract, and we became as nearly one as could be expected under the circumstances. But she never could, and she never did, find a phrase satisfactory to her perhaps-too-favourable estimate of my intellect. To the very last (feeble action of liver), she addressed me in the same unfinished terms.'

Mr. Jasper has closed his eyes as the auctioneer has deepened his voice. He now abruptly opens them, and says, in unison with the deepened voice, 'Ah!' – rather as if stopping himself on the extreme verge of adding – 'men!'

'I have been since,' says Mr. Sapsea, with his legs stretched out, and solemnly enjoying himself with the wine and the fire, 'what you behold me; I have been since a solitary mourner; I have been since, as I say, wasting my evening conversation on the desert air. I will not say that I have reproached myself; but there have been times when I have asked myself the question: What if her husband had been nearer on a level with her? If she had not had to look up quite so high, what might the stimulating action have been upon the liver?'

Mr. Jasper says, with an appearance of having fallen into dreadfully low spirits, that he supposes 'it was to be.'

'We can only suppose so, sir,' Mr. Sapsea coincides. 'As I say, Man proposes, Heaven disposes. It may or may not

be putting the same thought in another form; but that is the
way I put it.'

Mr. Jasper murmurs assent.

'And now, Mr. Jasper,' resumes the auctioneer, producing
his scrap of manuscript, 'Mrs. Sapsea's monument having
had full time to settle and dry, let me take your opinion, as
a man of taste, on the inscription I have (as I before
remarked, not without some little fever of the brow), drawn
out for it. Take it in your own hand. The setting out of the
lines requires to be followed with the eye, as well as the
contents with the mind.'

Mr. Jasper complying, sees and reads as follows:

ETHELINDA,
Reverential Wife of
Mr. THOMAS SAPSEA,
AUCTIONEER, VALUER, ESTATE AGENT, &c.,
OF THIS CITY.
Whose Knowledge of the World,
Though somewhat extensive,
Never brought him acquainted with
A SPIRIT
More capable of
LOOKING UP TO HIM.
STRANGER PAUSE
And ask thyself the Question,
CANST THOU DO LIKEWISE?
If Not,
WITH A BLUSH RETIRE.

Mr. Sapsea having risen and stationed himself with his
back to the fire, for the purpose of observing the effect of
these lines on the countenance of a man of taste, consequently has his face towards the door, when his serving-
maid, again appearing, announces, 'Durdles is come, sir!'
He promptly draws forth and fills the third wineglass, as
being now claimed, and replies, 'Show Durdles in.'

'Admirable!' quoth Mr. Jasper, handing back the paper.

'You approve, sir?'

'Impossible not to approve. Striking, characteristic, and complete.'

The auctioneer inclines his head, as one accepting his due and giving a receipt; and invites the entering Durdles to take off that glass of wine (handing the same), for it will warm him.

Durdles is a stonemason; chiefly in the gravestone, tomb, and monument way, and wholly of their colour from head to foot. No man is better known in Cloisterham. He is the chartered libertine of the place. Fame trumpets him a wonderful workman – which, for aught that anybody knows, he may be (as he never works); and a wonderful sot – which everybody knows he is. With the Cathedral crypt he is better acquainted than any living authority; it may even be than any dead one. It is said that the intimacy of this acquaintance began in his habitually resorting to that secret place, to lock out the Cloisterham boy-populace, and sleep off the fumes of liquor: he having ready access to the Cathedral, as contractor for rough repairs. Be this as it may, he does know much about it, and, in the demolition of impedimental fragments of wall, buttress, and pavement, has seen strange sights. He often speaks of himself in the third person; perhaps being a little misty as to his own identity when he narrates; perhaps impartially adopting the Cloisterham nomenclature in reference to a character of acknowledged distinction. Thus he will say, touching his strange sights: 'Durdles come upon the old chap,' in reference to a buried magnate of ancient time and high degree, 'by striking right into the coffin with his pick. The old chap gave Durdles a look with his open eyes, as much as to say "Is your name Durdles? Why, my man, I've been waiting for you a Devil of a time!" And then he turned to powder.' With a two-foot rule always in his pocket, and a mason's hammer all but always in his hand, Durdles goes continually sounding and tapping all about and about the Cathedral; and whenever he says to Tope: 'Tope, here's another old 'un in here!' Tope announces it to the Dean as an established discovery.

In a suit of coarse flannel with horn buttons, a yellow neckerchief with draggled ends, an old hat more russet-

coloured than black, and laced boots of the hue of his stony
calling, Durdles leads a hazy, gipsy sort of life, carrying his
dinner about with him in a small bundle, and sitting on all
manner of tombstones to dine. This dinner of Durdles's has
become quite a Cloisterham institution: not only because of
his never appearing in public without it, but because of its
having been, on certain renowned occasions, taken into cus-
tody along with Durdles (as drunk and incapable), and ex-
hibited before the Bench of Justices at the Town Hall. These
occasions, however, have been few and far apart: Durdles
being as seldom drunk as sober. For the rest, he is an old
bachelor, and he lives in a little antiquated hole of a house
that was never finished: supposed to be built, so far, of stones
stolen from the city wall. To this abode there is an approach,
ankle-deep in stone chips, resembling a petrified grove of
tombstones, urns, draperies, and broken columns, in all
stages of sculpture. Herein, two journeymen incessantly
chip, while other two journeymen, who face each other,
incessantly saw stone; dipping as regularly in and out of
their sheltering sentry-boxes, as if they were mechanical
figures emblematical of Time and Death.

To Durdles, when he has consumed his glass of port,
Mr. Sapsea entrusts that precious effort of his Muse. Durdles
unfeelingly takes out his two-foot rule, and measures the
lines calmly, alloying them with stone-grit.

'This is for the monument, is it, Mr. Sapsea?'

'The Inscription. Yes.' Mr. Sapsea waits for its effect on a
common mind.

'It'll come in to a eighth of an inch,' says Durdles. 'Your
servant, Mr. Jasper. Hope I see you well.'

'How are you, Durdles?'

'I've got a touch of the Tombatism on me, Mr. Jasper, but
that I must expect.'

'You mean the Rheumatism,' says Sapsea, in a sharp tone.
(He is nettled by having his composition so mechanically
received.)

'No, I don't. I mean, Mr. Sapsea, the Tombatism. It's
another sort from Rheumatism. Mr. Jasper knows what Durdles means. You get among them Tombs afore it's well light

on a winter morning, and keep on, as the Catechism says, a walking in the same all the days of your life, and *you*'ll know what Durdles means.'

'It is a bitter cold place,' Mr. Jasper assents, with an anti-pathetic shiver.

'And if it's bitter cold for you, up in the chancel, with a lot of live breath smoking out about you, what the bitterness is to Durdles, down in the crypt among the earthy damps there, and the dead breath of the old 'uns,' returns that individual, 'Durdles leaves you to judge. – Is this to be put in hand at once, Mr. Sapsea?'

Mr. Sapsea, with an Author's anxiety to rush into publica-tion, replies that it cannot be out of hand too soon.

'You had better let me have the key, then,' says Durdles.

'Why, man, it is not to be put inside the monument!'

'Durdles knows where it's to be put, Mr. Sapsea; no man better. Ask e'er a man in Cloisterham whether Durdles knows his work.'

Mr. Sapsea rises, takes a key from a drawer, unlocks an iron safe let into the wall, and takes from it another key.

'When Durdles puts a touch or a finish upon his work, no matter where, inside or outside, Durdles likes to look at his work all round, and see that his work is a doing him credit,' Durdles explains, doggedly.

The key proffered him by the bereaved widower being a large one, he slips his two-foot rule into a side pocket of his flannel trousers made for it, and deliberately opens his flan-nel coat, and opens the mouth of a large breast pocket within it before taking the key to place in that repository.

'Why, Durdles!' exclaims Jasper, looking on amused. 'You are undermined with pockets!'

'And I carries weight in 'em too, Mr. Jasper. Feel those;' producing two other large keys.

'Hand me Mr. Sapsea's likewise. Surely this is the heaviest of the three.'

'You'll find 'em much of a muchness, I expect,' says Durdles. 'They all belong to monuments. They all open Durdles's work. Durdles keeps the keys of his work mostly. Not that they're much used.'

'By-the-bye,' it comes into Jasper's mind to say, as he idly examines the keys; 'I have been going to ask you, many a day, and have always forgotten. You know they sometimes call you Stony Durdles, don't you?'

'Cloisterham knows me as Durdles, Mr. Jasper.'

'I am aware of that, of course. But the boys sometimes—'

'Oh! If you mind them young Imps of boys—' Durdles gruffly interrupts.

'I don't mind them, any more than you do. But there was a discussion the other day among the choir, whether Stony stood for Tony;' clinking one key against another.

('Take care of the wards, Mr. Jasper.')

'Or whether Stony stood for Stephen;' clinking with a change of keys.

('You can't make a pitch-pipe of 'em, Mr. Jasper.')

'Or whether the name comes from your trade. How stands the fact?'

Mr. Jasper weighs the three keys in his hand, lifts his head from his idly stooping attitude over the fire, and delivers the keys to Durdles with an ingenuous and friendly face.

But the stony one is a gruff one likewise, and that hazy state of his is always an uncertain state, highly conscious of its dignity, and prone to take offence. He drops his two keys back into his pocket one by one, and buttons them up; he takes his dinner-bundle from the chair-back on which he hung it when he came in; he distributes the weight he carries, by tying the third key up in it, as though he were an Ostrich, and liked to dine off cold iron; and he gets out of the room, deigning no word of answer.

Mr. Sapsea then proposes a hit at backgammon, which, seasoned with his own improving conversation, and terminating in a supper of cold roast beef and salad, beguiles the golden evening until pretty late. Mr. Sapsea's wisdom being, in its delivery to mortals, rather of the diffuse than the epigrammatic order, is by no means expended even then; but his visitor intimates that he will come back for more of the precious commodity on future occasions, and Mr. Sapsea lets him off for the present, to ponder on the instalment he carries away.

CHAPTER V

Mr. Durdles and Friend

JOHN JASPER, on his way home through the Close, is
brought to a standstill by the spectacle of Stony Durdles,
dinner-bundle and all, leaning his back against the iron
railing of the burial-ground enclosing it from the old clois-
ter-arches; and a hideous small boy in rags flinging stones at
him as a well-defined mark in the moonlight. Sometimes the
stones hit him, and sometimes they miss him, but Durdles
seems indifferent to either fortune. The hideous small boy,
on the contrary, whenever he hits Durdles, blows a whistle of
triumph through a jagged gap convenient for the purpose, in
the front of his mouth, where half his teeth are wanting; and
whenever he misses him, yelps out 'Mulled agin!' and tries to
atone for the failure by taking a more correct and vicious aim.

'What are you doing to the man?' demands Jasper, stepping out into the moonlight from the shade.

'Making a cock-shy of him,' replies the hideous small boy.

'Give me those stones in your hand.'

'Yes, I'll give 'em you down your throat, if you come a
ketching hold of me,' says the small boy, shaking himself
loose, and backing. 'I'll smash your eye, if you don't look out!'

'Baby-devil that you are, what has the man done to you?'

'He won't go home.'

'What is that to you?'

'He gives me a 'apenny to pelt him home if I ketches him
out too late,' says the boy. And then chants, like a little savage,
half stumbling and half dancing among the rags and laces of
his dilapidated boots:

> 'Widdy widdy wen!
> I – ket – ches – Im – out – ar – ter – ten.
> Widdy widdy wy!
> Then – E – don't – go – then – I – shy –
> Widdy Widdy Waked-cock warning!'

– with a comprehensive sweep on the last word, and one more delivery at Durdles.

This would seem to be a poetical note of preparation, agreed upon, as caution to Durdles to stand clear if he can, or to betake himself homeward.

John Jasper invites the boy with a beck of his head to follow him (feeling it hopeless to drag him, or coax him) and crosses to the iron railing where the Stony (and stoned) One is profoundly meditating.

'Do you know this thing, this child?' asks Jasper, at a loss for a word that will define this thing.

'Deputy,' says Durdles, with a nod.

'Is that its – his – name?'

'Deputy,' assents Durdles.

'I'm man-servant up at the Travellers' Twopenny in Gas Works Garding,' this thing explains. 'All us man-servants at Travellers' Lodgings is named Deputy. When we're chock full and the Travellers is all a-bed I come out for my 'elth.' Then withdrawing into the road, and taking aim, he resumes:

> 'Widdy widdy wen!
> I – ket – ches – Im – out – ar – ter –'

'Hold your hand,' cries Jasper, 'and don't throw while I stand so near him, or I'll kill you! Come, Durdles; let me walk home with you to-night. Shall I carry your bundle?'

'Not on any account,' replies Durdles, adjusting it. 'Durdles was making his reflections here when you come up, sir, surrounded by his works, like a poplar Author. – Your own brother-in-law;' introducing a sarcophagus within the railing, white and cold in the moonlight. 'Mrs. Sapsea;' introducing the monument of that devoted wife. 'Late Incumbent;' introducing the Reverend Gentleman's broken column. 'Departed Assessed Taxes;' introducing a vase and towel, standing on what might represent the cake of soap. 'Former pastrycook and muffin-maker, much respected;' introducing gravestone with extinguished torch. 'All safe and sound here, sir, and all Durdles's work! Of the common folk that is merely bundled up in turf and brambles, the less said, the better. A poor lot, soon forgot.'

'This creature, Deputy, is behind us,' says Jasper, looking back. 'Is he to follow us?'

The relations between Durdles and Deputy are of a capricious kind; for, on Durdles's turning himself about with the slow gravity of beery soddenness, Deputy makes a pretty wide circuit into the road and stands on the defensive.

'You never cried Widdy Warning before you begun to-night,' says Durdles, unexpectedly reminded of, or imagining, an injury.

'Yer lie, I did,' says Deputy, in his only form of polite contradiction.

'Own brother, sir,' observes Durdles, turning himself about again, and as unexpectedly forgetting his offence as he had recalled or conceived it; 'own brother to Peter the Wild Boy! But I gave him an object in life.'

'At which he takes aim?' Mr. Jasper suggests.

'That's it, sir,' returns Durdles, quite satisfied; 'at which he takes aim. I took him in hand and gave him an object. What was he before? A destroyer. What work did he do? Nothing but destruction. What did he earn by it? Short terms in Cloisterham Jail. Not a person, not a piece of property, not a winder, not a horse, nor a dog, nor a cat, nor a bird, nor a fowl, nor a pig, but what he stoned, for want of an enlightened object. I put that enlightened object before him, and now he can turn his honest halfpenny by the three penn'orth a week.'

'I wonder he has no competitors.'

'He has plenty, Mr. Jasper, but he stones 'em all away. Now, I don't know what this scheme of mine comes to,' pursues Durdles, considering about it with the same sodden gravity; 'I don't know what you may precisely call it. It ain't a sort of a – scheme of a – National Education?'

'I should say not,' replies Jasper.

'*I* should say not,' assents Durdles; 'then we won't try to give it a name.'

'He still keeps behind us,' repeats Jasper, looking over his shoulder; 'is he to follow us?'

'We can't help going round by the Travellers' Twopenny, if we go the short way, which is the back way,' Durdles answers, 'and we'll drop him there.'

So they go on; Deputy, as a rear rank of one, taking open order, and invading the silence of the hour and place by stoning every wall, post, pillar, and other inanimate object, by the deserted way.

'Is there anything new down in the crypt, Durdles?' asks John Jasper.

'Anything old, I think you mean,' growls Durdles. 'It ain't a spot for novelty.'

'Any new discovery on your part, I meant.'

'There's a old 'un under the seventh pillar on the left as you go down the broken steps of the little under-ground chapel as formerly was; I make him out (so fur as I've made him out yet) to be one of them old 'uns with a crook. To judge from the size of the passages in the walls, and of the steps and doors, by which they come and went, them crooks must have been a good deal in the way of the old 'uns! Two on 'em meeting promiscuous must have hitched one another by the mitre, pretty often, I should say.'

Without any endeavour to correct the literality of this opinion, Jasper surveys his companion – covered from head to foot with old mortar, lime, and stone grit – as though he, Jasper, were getting imbued with a romantic interest in his weird life.

'Yours is a curious existence.'

Without furnishing the least clue to the question, whether he receives this as a compliment or as quite the reverse, Durdles gruffly answers: 'Yours is another.'

'Well! Inasmuch as my lot is cast in the same old earthy, chilly, never-changing place, Yes. But there is much more mystery and interest in your connexion with the Cathedral than in mine. Indeed, I am beginning to have some idea of asking you to take me on as a sort of student, or free 'prentice, under you, and to let me go about with you some-times, and see some of these odd nooks in which you pass your days.'

The Stony One replies, in a general way, All right. Everybody knows where to find Durdles, when he's wanted. Which, if not strictly true, is approximately so, if taken to express that Durdles may always be found in a state of vagabondage somewhere.

'What I dwell upon most,' says Jasper, pursuing his subject of romantic interest, 'is the remarkable accuracy with which you would seem to find out where people are buried. – What is the matter? That bundle is in your way; let me hold it.'

Durdles has stopped and backed a little (Deputy, attentive to all his movements, immediately skirmishing into the road) and was looking about for some ledge or corner to place his bundle on, when thus relieved of it.

'Just you give me my hammer out of that,' says Durdles, 'and I'll show you.'

Clink, clink. And his hammer is handed him.

'Now, look'ee here. You pitch your note, don't you, Mr. Jasper?'

'Yes.'

'So I sound for mine. I take my hammer, and I tap.' (Here he strikes the pavement, and the attentive Deputy skirmishes at a rather wider range, as supposing that his head may be in requisition.) 'I tap, tap, tap. Solid! I go on tapping. Solid still! Tap again. Halloa! Hollow! Tap again, persevering. Solid in hollow! Tap, tap, tap, to try it better. Solid in hollow; and inside solid, hollow again! There you are! Old 'un crumbled away in stone coffin, in vault!'

'Astonishing!'

'I have even done this,' says Durdles, drawing out his two-foot rule (Deputy meanwhile skirmishing nearer, as suspecting that Treasure may be about to be discovered, which may somehow lead to his own enrichment, and the delicious treat of the discoverers being hanged by the neck, on his evidence, until they are dead). 'Say that hammer of mine's a wall – my work. Two; four; and two is six,' measuring on the pavement. 'Six foot inside that wall is Mrs. Sapsea.'

'Not really Mrs. Sapsea?'

'Say Mrs. Sapsea. Her wall's thicker, but say Mrs. Sapsea. Durdles taps that wall represented by that hammer, and says, after good sounding: "Something betwixt us!" Sure enough, some rubbish has been left in that same six-foot space by Durdles's men!'

Jasper opines that such accuracy 'is a gift.'

'I wouldn't have it at a gift,' returns Durdles, by no means receiving the observation in good part. 'I worked it out for myself. Durdles comes by *his* knowledge through grubbing deep for it, and having it up by the roots when it don't want to come. – Halloa you Deputy!'

'Widdy!' is Deputy's shrill response, standing off again.

'Catch that ha'penny. And don't let me see any more of you to-night, after we come to the Travellers' Twopenny.'

'Warning!' returns Deputy, having caught the halfpenny, and appearing by this mystic word to express his assent to the arrangement.

They have but to cross what was once the vineyard, belonging to what was once the Monastery, to come into the narrow back lane wherein stands the crazy wooden house of two low stories currently known as the Travellers' Twopenny: – a house all warped and distorted, like the morals of the travellers, with scant remains of a lattice-work porch over the door, and also of a rustic fence before its stamped-out garden; by reason of the travellers being so bound to the premises by a tender sentiment (or so fond of having a fire by the roadside in the course of the day), that they can never be persuaded or threatened into departure, without violently possessing themselves of some wooden forget-me-not, and bearing it off.

The semblance of an inn is attempted to be given to this wretched place by fragments of conventional red curtaining in the windows, which rags are made muddily transparent in the night-season by feeble lights of rush or cotton dip burning dully in the close air of the inside. As Durdles and Jasper come near, they are addressed by an inscribed paper lantern over the door, setting forth the purport of the house. They are also addressed by some half-dozen other hideous small boys – whether twopenny lodgers or followers or hangers-on of such, who knows! – who, as if attracted by some carrion-scent of Deputy in the air, start into the moonlight, as vultures might gather in the desert, and instantly fall to stoning him and one another.

'Stop, you young brutes,' cries Jasper, angrily, 'and let us go by!'

This remonstrance being received with yells and flying stones, according to a custom of late years comfortably established among the police regulations of our English communities, where Christians are stoned on all sides, as if the days of Saint Stephen were revived, Durdles remarks of the young savages, with some point, that 'they haven't got an object,' and leads the way down the lane.

At the corner of the lane, Jasper, hotly enraged, checks his companion and looks back. All is silent. Next moment, a stone coming rattling at his hat, and a distant yell of 'Wake-Cock! Warning!' followed by a crow, as from some infernally-hatched Chanticleer, apprising him under whose victorious fire he stands, he turns the corner into safety, and takes Durdles home: Durdles stumbling among the litter of his stony yard as if he were going to turn head-foremost into one of the unfinished tombs.

John Jasper returns by another way to his Gate House, and entering softly with his key, finds his fire still burning. He takes from a locked press, a peculiar-looking pipe which he fills – but not with tobacco – and, having adjusted the contents of the bowl, very carefully, with a little instrument, ascends an inner staircase of only a few steps, leading to two rooms. One of these is his own sleeping-chamber: the other, is his nephew's. There is a light in each.

His nephew lies asleep, calm and untroubled. John Jasper stands looking down upon him, his unlighted pipe in his hand, for some time, with a fixed and deep attention. Then, hushing his footsteps, he passes to his own room, lights his pipe, and delivers himself to the Spectres it invokes at midnight.

CHAPTER VI

Philanthropy in Minor Canon Corner

THE Reverend Septimus Crisparkle (Septimus, because six little brother Crisparkles before him went out, one by one, as they were born, like six weak little rushlights, as they were lighted), having broken the thin morning ice near Cloisterham Weir with his amiable head, much to the invigoration of his frame, was now assisting his circulation by boxing at a looking-glass with great science and prowess. A fresh and healthy portrait the looking-glass presented of the Reverend Septimus, feinting and dodging with the utmost artfulness, and hitting out from the shoulder with the utmost straightness, while his radiant features teemed with innocence, and soft-hearted benevolence beamed from his boxing-gloves.

It was scarcely breakfast-time yet, for Mrs. Crisparkle – mother, not wife, of the Reverend Septimus – was only just down, and waiting for the urn. Indeed, the Reverend Septimus left off at this very moment to take the pretty old lady's entering face between his boxing-gloves and kiss it. Having done so with tenderness, the Reverend Septimus turned to again, countering with his left, and putting in his right, in a tremendous manner.

'I say, every morning of my life, that you'll do it at last, Sept,' remarked the old lady, looking on; 'and so you will.'

'Do what, Ma dear?'

'Break the pier-glass, or burst a blood-vessel.'

'Neither, please God, Ma dear. Here's wind, Ma. Look at this!'

In a concluding round of great severity, the Reverend Septimus administered and escaped all sorts of punishment, and wound up by getting the old lady's cap into Chancery – such is the technical term used in scientific circles by the learned in the Noble Art – with a lightness of touch that hardly stirred the lightest lavender or cherry riband on it.

Magnanimously releasing the defeated, just in time to get his gloves into a drawer and feign to be looking out of window in a contemplative state of mind when a servant entered, the Reverend Septimus then gave place to the urn and other preparations for breakfast. These completed, and the two alone again, it was pleasant to see (or would have been, if there had been any one to see it, which there never was), the old lady standing to say the Lord's Prayer aloud, and her son, Minor Canon nevertheless, standing with bent head to hear it, he being within five years of forty: much as he had stood to hear the same words from the same lips when he was within five months of four.

What is prettier than an old lady – except a young lady – when her eyes are bright, when her figure is trim and compact, when her face is cheerful and calm, when her dress is as the dress of a china shepherdess: so dainty in its colours, so individually assorted to herself, so neatly moulded on her? Nothing is prettier, thought the good Minor Canon frequently, when taking his seat at table opposite his long-widowed mother. Her thought at such times may be condensed into the two words that oftenest did duty together in all her conversations: 'My Sept!'

They were a good pair to sit breakfasting together in Minor Canon Corner, Cloisterham. For, Minor Canon Corner was a quiet place in the shadow of the Cathedral, which the cawing of the rooks, the echoing footsteps of rare passers, the sound of the Cathedral bell, or the roll of the Cathedral organ, seemed to render more quiet than absolute silence. Swaggering fighting men had had their centuries of ramping and raving about Minor Canon Corner, and beaten serfs had had their centuries of drudging and dying there, and powerful monks had had their centuries of being sometimes useful and sometimes harmful there, and behold they were all gone out of Minor Canon Corner, and so much the better. Perhaps one of the highest uses of their ever having been there, was, that there might be left behind, that blessed air of tranquillity which pervaded Minor Canon Corner, and that serenely romantic state of the mind – productive for the most part of pity and forbearance – which is engendered by a sorrowful story that is all told, or a pathetic play that is played out.

Red-brick walls harmoniously toned down in colour by time, strong-rooted ivy, latticed windows, panelled rooms, big oaken beams in little places, and stone-walled gardens where annual fruit yet ripened upon monkish trees, were the principal surroundings of pretty old Mrs. Crisparkle and the Reverend Septimus as they sat at breakfast.

'And what, Ma dear,' inquired the Minor Canon, giving proof of a wholesome and vigorous appetite, 'does the letter say?'

The pretty old lady, after reading it, had just laid it down upon the breakfast-cloth. She handed it over to her son.

Now, the old lady was exceedingly proud of her bright eyes being so clear that she could read writing without spectacles. Her son was also so proud of the circumstance, and so dutifully bent on her deriving the utmost possible gratification from it, that he had invented the pretence that he himself could *not* read writing without spectacles. Therefore he now assumed a pair, of grave and prodigious proportions, which not only seriously inconvenienced his nose and his breakfast, but seriously impeded his perusal of the letter. For, he had the eyes of a microscope and a telescope combined, when they were unassisted.

'It's from Mr. Honeythunder, of course,' said the old lady, folding her arms.

'Of course,' assented her son. He then lamely read on:

'Haven of Philanthropy,
'Chief Offices, London, Wednesday.

' "DEAR MADAM,

' "I write in the—;" In the what's this? What does he write in?'

'In the chair,' said the old lady.

The Reverend Septimus took off his spectacles, that he might see her face, as he exclaimed:

'Why, what should he write in?'

'Bless me, bless me, Sept,' returned the old lady, 'you don't see the context! Give it back to me, my dear.'

Glad to get his spectacles off (for they always made his eyes water) her son obeyed: murmuring that his sight for reading manuscript got worse and worse daily.

'"I write,"' his mother went on, reading very perspicuously and precisely, '"from the chair, to which I shall probably be confined for some hours."'

Septimus looked at the row of chairs against the wall, with a half-protesting and half-appealing countenance.

'"We have,"' the old lady read on with a little extra emphasis, '"a meeting of our Convened Chief Composite Committee of Central and District Philanthropists, at our Head Haven as above; and it is their unanimous pleasure that I take the chair."'

Septimus breathed more freely, and muttered: 'Oh! If he comes to *that*, let him.'

'"Not to lose a day's post, I take the opportunity of a long report being read, denouncing a public miscreant—"'

'It is a most extraordinary thing,' interposed the gentle Minor Canon, laying down his knife and fork to rub his ear in a vexed manner, 'that these Philanthropists are always denouncing somebody. And it is another most extraordinary thing that they are always so violently flush of miscreants!'

'"Denouncing a public miscreant!"' – the old lady resumed, '"to get our little affair of business off my mind. I have spoken with my two wards, Neville and Helena Landless, on the subject of their defective education, and they give in to the plan proposed; as I should have taken good care they did, whether they liked it or not."'

'And it is another most extraordinary thing,' remarked the Minor Canon in the same tone as before, 'that these Philanthropists are so given to seizing their fellow-creatures by the scruff of the neck, and (as one may say) bumping them into the paths of peace. – I beg your pardon, Ma dear, for interrupting.'

'"Therefore, dear Madam, you will please prepare your son, the Rev. Mr. Septimus, to expect Neville as an inmate to be read with, on Monday next. On the same day Helena will accompany him to Cloisterham, to take up her quarters at the Nuns' House, the establishment recommended by yourself and son jointly. Please likewise to prepare for her reception and tuition there. The terms in both cases are understood to be exactly as stated to me in writing by yourself, when I opened a correspondence with you on this subject, after the honour of being introduced to you at your sister's house in town here. With compliments to the Rev. Mr. Septimus, I am, Dear Madam, Your affectionate brother (In Philanthropy), LUKE HONEYTHUNDER."'

'Well, Ma,' said Septimus, after a little more rubbing of his ear, 'we must try it. There can be no doubt that we have room for an inmate, and that I have time to bestow upon him, and inclination too. I must confess to feeling rather glad that he is not to be Mr. Honeythunder himself. Though that seems wretchedly prejudiced – does it not? – for I never saw him. Is he a large man, Ma?'

'I should call him a large man, my dear,' the old lady replied after some hesitation, 'but that his voice is so much larger.'

'Than himself?'

'Than anybody.'

'Hah!' said Septimus. And finished his breakfast as if the flavour of the Superior Family Souchong, and also of the ham and toast and eggs, were a little on the wane.

Mrs. Crisparkle's sister, another piece of Dresden china, and matching her so neatly that they would have made a delightful pair of ornaments for the two ends of any capacious old-fashioned chimneypiece, and by right should never have been seen apart, was the childless wife of a clergyman holding Corporation preferment in London City. Mr. Honeythunder in his public character of Professor of Philanthropy had come to know Mrs. Crisparkle during the last re-matching of the china ornaments (in other words during her last annual visit to her sister), after a public occasion of a philanthropic nature, when certain devoted orphans of tender years had been glutted with plum buns, and plump bumptiousness. These were all the antecedents known in Minor Canon Corner of the coming pupils.

'I am sure you will agree with me, Ma,' said Mr. Crisparkle, after thinking the matter over, 'that the first thing to be done, is, to put these young people as much at their ease as possible. There is nothing disinterested in the notion, because we cannot be at our ease with them unless they are at their ease with us. Now, Jasper's nephew is down here at present; and like takes to like, and youth to youth. He is a cordial young fellow, and we will have him to meet the brother and sister at dinner. That's three. We can't think of asking him, without asking Jasper. That's four. Add Miss Twinkleton and the fairy bride that is to be, and that's six. Add our two selves, and that's eight. Would eight at a friendly dinner at all put you out, Ma?'

'Nine would, Sept,' returned the old lady, visibly nervous.

'My dear Ma, I particularize eight.'

'The exact size of the table and the room, my dear.'

So it was settled that way; and when Mr. Crisparkle called with his mother upon Miss Twinkleton, to arrange for the reception of Miss Helena Landless at the Nuns' House, the two other invitations having reference to that establishment were proffered and accepted. Miss Twinkleton did, indeed, glance at the globes, as regretting that they were not formed to be taken out into society; but became reconciled to leaving them behind. Plain instructions were then despatched to the Philanthropist for the departure and arrival, in good time for dinner, of Mr. Neville and Miss Helena; and stock for soup became fragrant in the air of Minor Canon Corner.

In those days there was no railway to Cloisterham, and Mr. Sapsea said there never would be. Mr. Sapsea said more; he said there never should be. And yet, marvellous to consider, it has come to pass, in these days, that Express Trains don't think Cloisterham worth stopping at, but yell and whirl through it on their larger errands, casting the dust off their wheels as a testimony against its insignificance. Some remote fragment of Main Line to somewhere else, there was, which was going to ruin the Money Market if it failed, and Church and State if it succeeded, and (of course), the Constitution, whether or no; but even that had already so unsettled Cloisterham traffic, that the traffic, deserting the high road, came sneaking

in from an unprecedented part of the country by a back
stable-way, for many years labelled at the corner: 'Beware
of the Dog.'

To this ignominious avenue of approach, Mr. Crisparkle
repaired, awaiting the arrival of a short squat omnibus, with a
disproportionate heap of luggage on the roof – like a little
Elephant with infinitely too much Castle – which was then the
daily service between Cloisterham and external mankind. As
this vehicle lumbered up, Mr. Crisparkle could hardly see
anything else of it for a large outside passenger seated on the
box, with his elbows squared, and his hands on his knees,
compressing the driver into a most uncomfortably small
compass, and glowering about him with a strongly marked
face.

'Is this Cloisterham?' demanded the passenger, in a
tremendous voice.

'It is,' replied the driver, rubbing himself as if he ached,
after throwing the reins to the ostler. 'And I never was so glad
to see it.'

'Tell your master to make his box seat wider then,'
returned the passenger. 'Your master is morally bound –
and ought to be legally, under ruinous penalties – to provide
for the comfort of his fellow-man.'

The driver instituted, with the palms of his hands, a
superficial perquisition into the state of his skeleton; which
seemed to make him anxious.

'Have I sat upon you?' asked the passenger.

'You have,' said the driver, as if he didn't like it at all.

'Take that card, my friend.'

'I think I won't deprive you on it,' returned the driver,
casting his eyes over it with no great favour, without taking it.
'What's the good of it to me?'

'Be a Member of that Society,' said the passenger.

'What shall I get by it?' asked the driver.

'Brotherhood,' returned the passenger, in a ferocious
voice.

'Thank'ee,' said the driver, very deliberately, as he got
down; 'my mother was contented with myself, and so am I.
I don't want no brothers.'

'But you must have them,' replied the passenger, also descending, 'whether you like it or not. I am your brother.'

'I say!' expostulated the driver, becoming more chafed in temper; 'not too fur! The worm *will*, when—'

But here Mr. Crisparkle interposed, remonstrating aside, in a friendly voice: 'Joe, Joe, Joe! Don't forget yourself, Joe, my good fellow!' and then, when Joe peaceably touched his hat, accosting the passenger with: 'Mr. Honeythunder?'

'That is my name, sir.'

'My name is Crisparkle.'

'Reverend Mr. Septimus? Glad to see you, sir. Neville and Helena are inside. Having a little succumbed of late, under the pressure of my public labours, I thought I would take a mouthful of fresh air, and come down with them, and return at night. So you are the Reverend Mr. Septimus, are you?' surveying him on the whole with disappointment, and twisting a double eye-glass by its riband, as if he were roasting it; but not otherwise using it. 'Hah! I expected to see you older, sir.'

'I hope you will,' was the good-humoured reply.

'Eh?' demanded Mr. Honeythunder.

'Only a poor little joke. Not worth repeating.'

'Joke? Ay; I never see a joke,' Mr. Honeythunder frowningly retorted. 'A joke is wasted upon me, sir. Where are they! Helena and Neville, come here! Mr. Crisparkle has come down to meet you.'

An unusually handsome lithe young fellow, and an unusually handsome lithe girl; much alike; both very dark, and very rich in colour; she, of almost the gipsy type; something untamed about them both; a certain air upon them of hunter and huntress; yet withal a certain air of being the objects of the chase, rather than the followers. Slender, supple, quick of eye and limb; half shy, half defiant; fierce of look; an indefinable kind of pause coming and going on their whole expression, both of face and form, which might be equally likened to the pause before a crouch, or a bound. The rough mental notes made in the first five minutes by Mr. Crisparkle, would have read thus, *verbatim*.

He invited Mr. Honeythunder to dinner, with a troubled mind (for the discomfiture of the dear old china shepherdess lay heavy on it), and gave his arm to Helena Landless. Both she and her brother, as they walked all together through the ancient streets, took great delight in what he pointed out of the Cathedral and the monastery ruin, and wondered – so his notes ran on – much as if they were beautiful barbaric captives brought from some wild tropical dominion. Mr. Honeythunder walked in the middle of the road, shouldering the natives out of his way, and loudly developing a scheme he had, for making a raid on all the unemployed persons in the United Kingdom, laying them every one by the heels in jail, and forcing them on pain of prompt extermination to become Philanthropists.

Mrs. Crisparkle had need of her own share of philanthropy when she beheld this very large and very loud excrescence on the little party. Always something in the nature of a Boil upon the face of society, Mr. Honeythunder expanded into an inflammatory Wen in Minor Canon Corner. Though it was not literally true, as was facetiously charged against him by public unbelievers, that he called aloud to his fellow-creatures: 'Curse your souls and bodies, come here and be blessed!' still his philanthropy was of that gunpowderous sort that the difference between it and animosity was hard to determine. You were to abolish military force, but you were first to bring all commanding officers who had done their duty, to trial by court martial for that offence, and shoot them. You were to abolish war, but were to make converts by making war upon them, and charging them with loving war as the apple of their eye. You were to have no capital punishment, but were first to sweep off the face of the earth all legislators, jurists, and judges, who were of the contrary opinion. You were to have universal concord, and were to get it by eliminating all the people who wouldn't, or conscientiously couldn't, be concordant. You were to love your brother as yourself, but after an indefinite interval of maligning him (very much as if you hated him), and calling him all manner of names. Above all things, you were to do nothing in private, or on your own account. You were to go to the offices of the Haven of Philanthropy, and put your name down as a Member and a Professing Philanthropist. Then, you were to pay up your subscription, get your card of membership and your riband and medal, and were evermore to live upon a platform, and evermore to say what Mr. Honeythunder said, and what the Treasurer said, and what the Vice Treasurer said, and what the Committee said, and what the sub-Committee said, and what the Secretary said, and what the Vice Secretary said. And this was usually said in the unanimously carried resolution under hand and seal, to the effect: 'That this assembled Body of Professing Philanthropists views, with indignant scorn and contempt, not unmixed with utter detestation and loathing abhorrence,' – in short, the baseness of all those who do not belong to it, and pledges itself to make as many obnoxious statements as possible about them, without being at all particular as to facts.

The dinner was a most doleful breakdown. The Philanthropist deranged the symmetry of the table, sat himself in the way of the waiting, blocked up the thoroughfare, and drove Mr. Tope (who assisted the parlour-maid), to the verge of distraction by passing plates and dishes on, over his own head. Nobody could talk to anybody, because he held forth to everybody at once, as if the company had no individual existence, but were a Meeting. He impounded the Reverend Mr. Septimus, as an official personage to be addressed, or kind of human peg to hang his oratorical hat on, and fell into the exasperating habit, common among such orators, of impersonating him as a wicked and weak opponent. Thus, he would ask: 'And will you, sir, now stultify yourself by telling me' – and so forth, when the innocent man had not opened his lips, nor meant to open them. Or he would say: 'Now see, sir, to what a position you are reduced. I will leave you no escape. After exhausting all the resources of fraud and falsehood, during years upon years; after exhibiting a combination of dastardly meanness with ensanguined daring, such as the world has not often witnessed; you have now the hypocrisy to bend the knee before the most degraded of mankind, and to sue and whine and howl for mercy!' Whereat the unfortunate Minor Canon would look,

in part indignant and in part perplexed: while his worthy
mother sat bridling, with tears in her eyes, and the remainder of the party lapsed into a sort of gelatinous state, in which
there was no flavour or solidity, and very little resistance.

But the gush of philanthropy that burst forth when the
departure of Mr. Honeythunder began to impend, must
have been highly gratifying to the feelings of that distinguished man. His coffee was produced, by the special activity
of Mr. Tope, a full hour before he wanted it. Mr. Crisparkle
sat with his watch in his hand, for about the same period, lest
he should overstay his time. The four young people were
unanimous in believing that the Cathedral clock struck three
quarters, when it actually struck but one. Miss Twinkleton
estimated the distance to the omnibus at five-and-twenty
minutes' walk, when it was really five. The affectionate kindness of the whole circle hustled him into his greatcoat, and
shoved him out into the moonlight, as if he were a fugitive
traitor with whom they sympathized, and a troop of horse
were at the back door. Mr. Crisparkle and his new charge,
who took him to the omnibus, were so fervent in their apprehensions of his catching cold, that they shut him up in it
instantly and left him, with still half an hour to spare.

CHAPTER VII

More Confidences than One

'I KNOW very little of that gentleman, sir,' said Neville to the Minor Canon as they turned back.

'You know very little of your guardian?' the Minor Canon repeated.

'Almost nothing.'

'How came he—'

'To *be* my guardian? I'll tell you, sir. I suppose you know that we come (my sister and I) from Ceylon?'

'Indeed, no.'

'I wonder at that. We lived with a stepfather there. Our mother died there, when we were little children. We have had a wretched existence. She made him our guardian, and he was a miserly wretch who grudged us food to eat, and clothes to wear. At his death, he passed us over to this man; for no better reason that I know of, than his being a friend or connexion of his, whose name was always in print and catching his attention.'

'That was lately, I suppose?'

'Quite lately, sir. This stepfather of ours was a cruel brute as well as a grinding one. It was well he died when he did, or I might have killed him.'

Mr. Crisparkle stopped short in the moonlight and looked at his hopeful pupil in consternation.

'I surprise you, sir?' he said, with a quick change to a submissive manner.

'You shock me; unspeakably shock me.'

The pupil hung his head for a little while, as they walked on, and then said: 'You never saw him beat your sister. I have seen him beat mine, more than once or twice, and I never forgot it.'

'Nothing,' said Mr. Crisparkle, 'not even a beloved and beautiful sister's tears under dastardly ill-usage;' he became less severe, in spite of himself, as his indignation rose; 'could justify those horrible expressions that you used.'

'I am sorry I used them, and especially to you, sir. I beg to recall them. But permit me to set you right on one point. You spoke of my sister's tears. My sister would have let him tear her to pieces, before she would have let him believe that he could make her shed a tear.'

Mr. Crisparkle reviewed those mental notes of his, and was neither at all surprised to hear it, nor at all disposed to question it.

'Perhaps you will think it strange, sir' – this was said in a hesitating voice – 'that I should so soon ask you to allow me to confide in you, and to have the kindness to hear a word or two from me in my defence?'

'Defence?' Mr. Crisparkle repeated. 'You are not on your defence, Mr. Neville.'

'I think I am, sir. At least I know I should be, if you were better acquainted with my character.'

'Well, Mr. Neville,' was the rejoinder. 'What if you leave me to find it out?'

'Since it is your pleasure, sir,' answered the young man, with a quick change in his manner to sullen disappointment: 'since it is your pleasure to check me in my impulse, I must submit.'

There was that in the tone of this short speech which made the conscientious man to whom it was addressed, uneasy. It hinted to him that he might, without meaning it, turn aside a trustfulness beneficial to a mis-shapen young mind and perhaps to his own power of directing and improving it. They were within sight of the lights in his windows, and he stopped.

'Let us turn back and take a turn or two up and down, Mr. Neville, or you may not have time to finish what you wish to say to me. You are hasty in thinking that I mean to check you. Quite the contrary. I invite your confidence.'

'You have invited it, sir, without knowing it, ever since I came here. I say "ever since," as if I had been here a week! The truth is, we came here (my sister and I) to quarrel with you, and affront you, and break away again.'

'Really?' said Mr. Crisparkle, at a dead loss for anything else to say.

'You see, we could not know what you were beforehand, sir; could we?'

'Clearly not,' said Mr. Crisparkle.

'And having liked no one else with whom we have ever been brought into contact, we had made up our minds not to like you.'

'Really?' said Mr. Crisparkle again.

'But we do like you, sir, and we see an immeasurable difference between your house and your reception of us, and anything else we have ever known. This – and my happening to be alone with you – and everything around us seeming so quiet and peaceful after Mr. Honeythunder's departure – and Cloisterham being so old and grave and beautiful, with the moon shining on it – these things inclined me to open my heart.'

'I quite understand, Mr. Neville. And it is salutary to listen to such influences.'

'In describing my own imperfections, sir, I must ask you not to suppose that I am describing my sister's. She has come out of the disadvantages of our miserable life, as much better than I am, as that Cathedral tower is higher than those chimneys.'

Mr. Crisparkle in his own breast was not so sure of this.

'I have had, sir, from my earliest remembrance, to suppress a deadly and bitter hatred. This has made me secret and revengeful. I have been always tyrannically held down by the strong hand. This has driven me, in my weakness, to the resource of being false and mean. I have been stinted of education, liberty, money, dress, the very necessaries of life, the commonest pleasures of childhood, the commonest possessions of youth. This has caused me to be utterly wanting in I don't know what emotions, or remembrances, or good instincts – I have not even a name for the thing, you see! – that you have had to work upon in other young men to whom you have been accustomed.'

'This is evidently true. But this is not encouraging,' thought Mr. Crisparkle as they turned again.

'And to finish with, sir: I have been brought up among abject and servile dependants, of an inferior race, and I may easily have contracted some affinity with them. Sometimes, I don't know but that it may be a drop of what is tigerish in their blood.'

'As in the case of that remark just now,' thought Mr. Crisparkle.

'In a last word of reference to my sister, sir (we are twin children), you ought to know, to her honour, that nothing in our misery ever subdued her, though it often cowed me. When we ran away from it (we ran away four times in six years, to be soon brought back and cruelly punished), the flight was always of her planning and leading. Each time she dressed as a boy, and showed the daring of a man. I take it we were seven years old when we first decamped; but I remember, when I lost the pocket-knife with which she was to have cut her hair short, how desperately she tried to tear it out, or bite it off. I have nothing further to say, sir, except that I hope you will bear with me and make allowance for me.'

'Of that, Mr. Neville, you may be sure,' returned the Minor Canon. 'I don't preach more than I can help, and I will not repay your confidence with a sermon. But I entreat you to bear in mind, very seriously and steadily, that if I am to do you any good, it can only be with your own assistance; and that you can only render that, efficiently, by seeking aid from Heaven.'

'I will try to do my part, sir.'

'And, Mr. Neville, I will try to do mine. Here is my hand on it. May God bless our endeavours!'

They were now standing at his house door, and a cheerful sound of voices and laughter was heard within.

'We will take one more turn before going in,' said Mr. Crisparkle, 'for I want to ask you a question. When you said you were in a changed mind concerning me, you spoke, not only for yourself, but for your sister too.'

'Undoubtedly I did, sir.'

'Excuse me, Mr. Neville, but I think you have had no opportunity of communicating with your sister, since I met you. Mr. Honeythunder was very eloquent; but perhaps I may venture to say, without ill-nature, that he rather monopolized the occasion. May you not have answered for your sister without sufficient warrant?'

Neville shook his head with a proud smile.

'You don't know, sir, yet, what a complete understanding can exist between my sister and me, though no spoken word – perhaps hardly as much as a look – may have passed between us. She not only feels as I have described, but she very well knows that I am taking this opportunity of speaking to you, both for her and for myself.'

Mr. Crisparkle looked in his face, with some incredulity; but his face expressed such absolute and firm conviction of the truth of what he said, that Mr. Crisparkle looked at the pavement, and mused, until they came to his door again.

'I will ask for one more turn, sir, this time,' said the young man with a rather heightened colour rising in his face. 'But for Mr. Honeythunder's – I think you called it eloquence, sir?' (somewhat slyly).

'I – yes, I called it eloquence,' said Mr. Crisparkle.

'But for Mr. Honeythunder's eloquence, I might have had no need to ask you what I am going to ask you. This Mr. Edwin Drood, sir: I think that's the name?'

'Quite correct,' said Mr. Crisparkle. 'D-r-double o-d.'

'Does he – or did he – read with you, sir?'

'Never, Mr. Neville. He comes here visiting his relation, Mr. Jasper.'

'Is Miss Bud his relation too, sir?'

('Now, why should he ask that, with sudden superciliousness!' thought Mr. Crisparkle.) Then he explained, aloud, what he knew of the little story of their betrothal.

'Oh! *That*'s it, is it?' said the young man. 'I understand his air of proprietorship now!'

This was said so evidently to himself, or to anybody rather than Mr. Crisparkle, that the latter instinctively felt as if to notice it would be almost tantamount to noticing a passage in a letter which he had read by chance over the writer's shoulder. A moment afterwards they re-entered the house.

At the Piano

Mr. Jasper was seated at the piano as they came into his drawing-room, and was accompanying Miss Rosebud while she sang. It was a consequence of his playing the accompaniment without notes, and of her being a heedless little creature very apt to go wrong, that he followed her lips most attentively, with his eyes as well as hands; carefully and softly hinting the key-note from time to time. Standing with an arm drawn round her, but with a face far more intent on Mr. Jasper than on her singing, stood Helena, between whom and her brother an instantaneous recognition passed, in which Mr. Crisparkle saw, or thought he saw, the understanding that had been spoken of, flash out. Mr. Neville then took his admiring station, leaning against the piano, opposite the singer; Mr. Crisparkle sat down by the china shepherdess; Edwin Drood gallantly furled and unfurled Miss Twinkleton's fan; and that lady passively claimed that sort of exhibitor's proprietorship in the accomplishment on view, which Mr. Tope, the Verger, daily claimed in the Cathedral service.

The song went on. It was a sorrowful strain of parting, and the fresh young voice was very plaintive and tender. As Jasper watched the pretty lips, and ever and again hinted the one note, as though it were a low whisper from himself, the voice became a little less steady, until all at once the singer broke into a burst of tears, and shrieked out, with her hands over her eyes: 'I can't bear this! I am frightened! Take me away!'

With one swift turn of her lithe figure, Helena laid the little beauty on a sofa, as if she had never caught her up. Then, on one knee beside her, and with one hand upon her rosy mouth, while with the other she appealed to all the rest, Helena said to them: 'It's nothing; it's all over; don't speak to her for one minute, and she is well!'

Jasper's hands had, in the same instant, lifted themselves from the keys, and were now poised above them, as though he waited to resume. In that attitude he yet sat quiet: not even looking round, when all the rest had changed their places and were reassuring one another.

'Pussy's not used to an audience; that's the fact,' said Edwin Drood. 'She got nervous, and couldn't hold out.

Besides, Jack, you are such a conscientious master, and require so much, that I believe you make her afraid of you. No wonder.'

'No wonder,' repeated Helena.

'There, Jack, you hear! You would be afraid of him, under similar circumstances, wouldn't you, Miss Landless?'

'Not under any circumstances,' returned Helena.

Jasper brought down his hands, looked over his shoulder, and begged to thank Miss Landless for her vindication of his character. Then he fell to dumbly playing, without striking the notes, while his little pupil was taken to an open window for air, and was otherwise petted and restored. When she was brought back, his place was empty. 'Jack's gone, Pussy,' Edwin told her. 'I am more than half afraid he didn't like to be charged with being the Monster who had frightened you.' But she answered never a word, and shivered, as if they had made her a little too cold.

Miss Twinkleton now opining that indeed these were late hours, Mrs. Crisparkle, for finding ourselves outside the walls of the Nuns' House, and that we who undertook the formation of the future wives and mothers of England (the last words in a lower voice, as requiring to be communicated in confidence) were really bound (voice coming up again) to set a better example than one of rakish habits, wrappers were put in requisition, and the two young cavaliers volunteered to see the ladies home. It was soon done, and the gate of the Nuns' House closed upon them.

The boarders had retired, and only Mrs. Tisher in solitary vigil awaited the new pupil. Her bedroom being within Rosa's, very little introduction or explanation was necessary, before she was placed in charge of her new friend, and left for the night.

'This is a blessed relief, my dear,' said Helena. 'I have been dreading all day, that I should be brought to bay at this time.'

'There are not many of us,' returned Rosa, 'and we are good-natured girls; at least the others are; I can answer for them.'

'I can answer for you,' laughed Helena, searching the lovely little face with her dark fiery eyes, and tenderly caressing the small figure. 'You will be a friend to me, won't you?'

'I hope so. But the idea of my being a friend to you seems too absurd, though.'

'Why?'

'Oh! I am such a mite of a thing, and you are so womanly and handsome. You seem to have resolution and power enough to crush me. I shrink into nothing by the side of your presence even.'

'I am a neglected creature, my dear, unacquainted with all accomplishments, sensitively conscious that I have everything to learn, and deeply ashamed to own my ignorance.'

'And yet you acknowledge everything to me!' said Rosa.

'My pretty one, can I help it? There is a fascination in you.'

'Oh! Is there though?' pouted Rosa, half in jest and half in earnest. 'What a pity Master Eddy doesn't feel it more!'

Of course her relations towards that young gentleman had been already imparted, in Minor Canon Corner.

'Why, surely he must love you with all his heart!' cried Helena, with an earnestness that threatened to blaze into ferocity if he didn't.

'Eh? Oh, well, I suppose he does,' said Rosa, pouting again; 'I am sure I have no right to say he doesn't. Perhaps it's my fault. Perhaps I am not as nice to him as I ought to be. I don't think I am. But it *is* so ridiculous!'

Helena's eyes demanded what was.

'*We* are,' said Rosa, answering as if she had spoken. 'We are such a ridiculous couple. And we are always quarrelling.'

'Why?'

'Because we both know we are ridiculous, my dear!' Rosa gave that answer as if it were the most conclusive answer in the world.

Helena's masterful look was intent upon her face for a few moments, and then she impulsively put out both her hands and said:

'You will be my friend and help me?'

'Indeed, my dear, I will,' replied Rosa, in a tone of affectionate childishness that went straight and true to her heart;

'I will be as good a friend as such a mite of a thing can be to such a noble creature as you. And be a friend to me, please; for I don't understand myself; and I want a friend who can understand me, very much indeed.'

Helena Landless kissed her, and retaining both her hands, said:

'Who is Mr. Jasper?'

Rosa turned aside her head in answering: 'Eddy's uncle, and my music-master.'

'You do not love him?'

'Ugh!' She put her hands up to her face, and shook with fear or horror.

'You know that he loves you?'

'Oh, don't, don't, don't!' cried Rosa, dropping on her knees, and clinging to her new resource. 'Don't tell me of it! He terrifies me. He haunts my thoughts, like a dreadful ghost. I feel that I am never safe from him. I feel as if he could pass in through the wall when he is spoken of.' She actually did look round, as if she dreaded to see him standing in the shadow behind her.

'Try to tell me more about it, darling.'

'Yes, I will, I will. Because you are so strong. But hold me the while, and stay with me afterwards.'

'My child! You speak as if he had threatened you in some dark way.'

'He has never spoken to me about – that. Never.'

'What has he done?'

'He has made a slave of me with his looks. He has forced me to understand him, without his saying a word; and he has forced me to keep silence, without his uttering a threat. When I play, he never moves his eyes from my hands. When I sing, he never moves his eyes from my lips. When he corrects me, and strikes a note, or a chord, or plays a passage, he himself is in the sounds, whispering that he pursues me as a lover, and commanding me to keep his secret. I avoid his eyes, but he forces me to see them without looking at them. Even when a glaze comes over them (which is sometimes the case), and he seems to wander away into a frightful sort of dream in which he threatens most, he obliges me to know it, and to know that he is sitting close at my side, more terrible to me then than ever.'

'What is this imagined threatening, pretty one? What is threatened?'

'I don't know. I have never even dared to think or wonder what it is.'

'And was this all, to-night?'

'This was all; except that to-night when he watched my lips so closely as I was singing, besides feeling terrified I felt ashamed and passionately hurt. It was as if he kissed me, and I couldn't bear it, but cried out. You must never breathe this to any one. Eddy is devoted to him. But you said to-night that you would not be afraid of him, under any circumstances, and that gives me – who am so much afraid of him – courage to tell only you. Hold me! Stay with me! I am too frightened to be left by myself.'

The lustrous gipsy-face drooped over the clinging arms and bosom, and the wild black hair fell down protectingly over the childish form. There was a slumbering gleam of fire in the intense dark eyes, though they were then softened with compassion and admiration. Let whomsoever it most concerned, look well to it!

CHAPTER VIII

Daggers Drawn

THE two young men, having seen the damsels, their charges, enter the courtyard of the Nuns' House, and finding themselves coldly stared at by the brazen door-plate, as if the battered old beau with the glass in his eye were insolent, look at one another, look along the perspective of the moonlit street, and slowly walk away together.

'Do you stay here long, Mr. Drood?' says Neville.

'Not this time,' is the careless answer. 'I leave for London again, to-morrow. But I shall be here, off and on, until next Midsummer; then I shall take my leave of Cloisterham, and England too; for many a long day, I expect.'

'Are you going abroad?'

'Going to wake up Egypt a little,' is the condescending answer.

'Are you reading?'

'Reading!' repeats Edwin Drood, with a touch of contempt. 'No. Doing, working, engineering. My small patrimony was left a part of the capital of the Firm I am with, by my father, a former partner; and I am a charge upon the Firm until I come of age; and then I step into my modest share in the concern. Jack – you met him at dinner – is, until then, my guardian and trustee.'

'I heard from Mr. Crisparkle of your other good fortune.'

'What do you mean by my other good fortune?'

Neville has made his remark in a watchfully advancing, and yet furtive and shy manner, very expressive of that peculiar air already noticed, of being at once hunter and hunted. Edwin has made his retort with an abruptness not at all polite. They stop and interchange a rather heated look.

'I hope,' says Neville, 'there is no offence, Mr. Drood, in my innocently referring to your betrothal?'

'By George!' cries Edwin, leading on again at a somewhat quicker pace. 'Everybody in this chattering old Cloisterham refers to it. I wonder no Public House has been set up, with my portrait for the sign of The Betrothed's Head. Or Pussy's portrait. One or the other.'

'I am not accountable for Mr. Crisparkle's mentioning the matter to me, quite openly,' Neville begins.

'No; that's true; you are not,' Edwin Drood assents.

'But,' resumes Neville, 'I am accountable for mentioning it to you. And I did so, on the supposition that you could not fail to be highly proud of it.'

Now, there are these two curious touches of human nature working the secret springs of this dialogue. Neville Landless is already enough impressed by Little Rosebud, to feel indignant that Edwin Drood (far below her) should hold his prize so lightly. Edwin Drood is already enough impressed by Helena, to feel indignant that Helena's brother (far below her) should dispose of him so coolly, and put him out of the way so entirely.

However, the last remark had better be answered. So, says Edwin:

'I don't know, Mr. Neville' (adopting that mode of address from Mr. Crisparkle), 'that what people are proudest of, they usually talk most about; I don't know either, that what they are proudest of, they most like other people to talk about. But I live a busy life, and I speak under correction by you readers, who ought to know everything, and I dare say do.'

By this time they have both become savage; Mr. Neville out in the open; Edwin Drood under the transparent cover of a popular tune, and a stop now and then to pretend to admire picturesque effects in the moonlight before him.

'It does not seem to me very civil in you,' remarks Neville, at length, 'to reflect upon a stranger who comes here, not having had your advantages, to try to make up for lost time. But, to be sure, *I* was not brought up in "busy life," and my ideas of civility were formed among Heathens.'

'Perhaps, the best civility, whatever kind of people we are brought up among,' retorts Edwin Drood, 'is to mind our own business. If you will set me that example, I promise to follow it.'

'Do you know that you take a great deal too much upon yourself,' is the angry rejoinder; 'and that in the part of the world I come from, you would be called to account for it?'

'By whom, for instance?' asks Edwin Drood, coming to a halt, and surveying the other with a look of disdain.

But, here a startling right hand is laid on Edwin's shoulder, and Jasper stands between them. For, it would seem that he, too, has strolled round by the Nuns' House, and has come up behind them on the shadowy side of the road.

'Ned, Ned, Ned!' he says. 'We must have no more of this. I don't like this. I have overheard high words between you two. Remember, my dear boy, you are almost in the position of host to-night. You belong, as it were, to the place, and in a manner represent it towards a stranger. Mr. Neville is a stranger, and you should respect the obligations of hospitality. And, Mr. Neville:' laying his left hand on the inner shoulder of that young gentleman, and thus walking on between them, hand to shoulder on either side: 'you will pardon me; but I appeal to you to govern your temper too. Now, what is amiss? But why ask! Let there be nothing amiss, and the question is superfluous. We are all three on a good understanding, are we not?'

After a silent struggle between the two young men who shall speak last, Edwin Drood strikes in with: 'So far as I am concerned, Jack, there is no anger in me.'

'Nor in me,' says Neville Landless, though not so freely; or perhaps so carelessly. 'But if Mr. Drood knew all that lies behind me, far away from here, he might know better how it is that sharp-edged words have sharp edges to wound me.'

'Perhaps,' says Jasper, in a smoothing manner, 'we had better not qualify our good understanding. We had better not say anything having the appearance of a remonstrance or condition; it might not seem generous. Frankly and freely, you see there is no anger in Ned. Frankly and freely, there is no anger in you, Mr. Neville?'

'None at all, Mr. Jasper.' Still, not quite so frankly or so freely; or, be it said once again, not quite so carelessly perhaps.

'All over then! Now, my bachelor Gate House is but a few yards from here, and the heater is on the fire, and the wine and glasses are on the table, and it is not a stone's throw from Minor Canon Corner. Ned, you are up and away to-morrow. We will carry Mr. Neville in with us, to take a stirrup-cup.'

'With all my heart, Jack.'

'And with all mine, Mr. Jasper.' Neville feels it impossible to say less, but would rather not go. He has an impression upon him that he has lost hold of his temper; feels that Edwin Drood's coolness, so far from being infectious, makes him red hot.

Mr. Jasper, still walking in the centre, hand to shoulder on either side, beautifully turns the refrain of a drinking-song, and they all go up to his rooms. There, the first object visible, when he adds the light of a lamp to that of the fire, is the portrait over the chimneypiece. It is not an object calculated to improve the understanding between the two young men, as rather awkwardly reviving the subject of their difference. Accordingly, they both glance at it consciously, but say nothing. Jasper, however (who would appear from his conduct to have gained but an imperfect clue to the cause of their late high words), directly calls attention to it.

'You recognize that picture, Mr. Neville?' shading the lamp to throw the light upon it.

'I recognize it, but it is far from flattering the original.'

'Oh, you are hard upon it! It was done by Ned, who made me a present of it.'

'I am sorry for that, Mr. Drood.' Neville apologizes, with a real intention to apologize; 'if I had known I was in the artist's presence—'

'Oh, a joke, sir, a mere joke,' Edwin cuts in, with a provoking yawn. 'A little humouring of Pussy's points! I'm going to paint her gravely, one of these days, if she's good.'

The air of leisurely patronage and indifference with which this is said, as the speaker throws himself back in a chair and clasps his hands at the back of his head, as a rest for it, is very exasperating to the excitable and excited Neville. Jasper looks observantly from the one to the other, slightly smiles, and turns his back to mix a jug of mulled wine at the fire. It seems to require much mixing and compounding.

'I suppose, Mr. Neville,' says Edwin, quick to resent the indignant protest against himself in the face of young Landless, which is fully as visible as the portrait, or the fire, or the lamp: 'I suppose that if you painted the picture of your lady love—'

'I can't paint,' is the hasty interruption.

'That's your misfortune, and not your fault. You would if you could. But if you could, I suppose you would make her (no matter what she was in reality), Juno, Minerva, Diana, and Venus, all in one. Eh?'

'I have no lady love, and I can't say.'

'If I were to try my hand,' says Edwin, with a boyish boastfulness getting up in him, 'on a portrait of Miss Landless – in earnest, mind you; in earnest – you should see what I could do!'

'My sister's consent to sit for it being first got, I suppose? As it never will be got, I am afraid I shall never see what you can do. I must bear the loss.'

Jasper turns round from the fire, fills a large goblet glass for Neville, fills a large goblet glass for Edwin, and hands each his own; then fills for himself, saying:

'Come, Mr. Neville, we are to drink to my Nephew, Ned. As it is his foot that is in the stirrup – metaphorically – our stirrup-cup is to be devoted to him. Ned, my dearest fellow, my love!'

Jasper sets the example of nearly emptying his glass, and Neville follows it. Edwin Drood says 'Thank you both very much,' and follows the double example.

'Look at him!' cries Jasper, stretching out his hand admiringly and tenderly, though rallyingly too. 'See where he lounges so easily, Mr. Neville! The world is all before him where to choose. A life of stirring work and interest, a life of change and excitement, a life of domestic ease and love! Look at him!'

Edwin Drood's face has become quickly and remarkably flushed by the wine; so has the face of Neville Landless.

Edwin still sits thrown back in his chair, making that rest of clasped hands for his head.

'See how little he heeds it all!' Jasper proceeds in a bantering vein. 'It is hardly worth his while to pluck the golden fruit that hangs ripe on the tree for him. And yet consider the contrast, Mr. Neville. You and I have no prospect of stirring work and interest, or of change and excitement, or of domestic ease and love. You and I have no prospect (unless you are more fortunate than I am, which may easily be), but the tedious, unchanging round of this dull place.'

'Upon my soul, Jack,' says Edwin, complacently, 'I feel quite apologetic for having my way smoothed as you describe. But you know what I know, Jack, and it may not be so very easy as it seems, after all. May it, Pussy?' To the portrait, with a snap of his thumb and finger. 'We have got to hit it off yet; haven't we, Pussy? You know what I mean, Jack.'

His speech has become thick and indistinct. Jasper, quiet and self-possessed, looks to Neville, as expecting his answer or comment. When Neville speaks, *his* speech is also thick and indistinct.

'It might have been better for Mr. Drood to have known some hardships,' he says, defiantly.

'Pray,' retorts Edwin, turning merely his eyes in that direction, 'pray why might it have been better for Mr. Drood to have known some hardships?'

'Ay,' Jasper assents with an air of interest; 'let us know why?'

'Because they might have made him more sensible,' says Neville, 'of good fortune that is not by any means necessarily the result of his own merits.'

Mr. Jasper quickly looks to his nephew for his rejoinder.

'Have *you* known hardships, may I ask?' says Edwin Drood, sitting upright.

Mr. Jasper quickly looks to the other for his retort.

'I have.'

'And what have they made *you* sensible of?'

Mr. Jasper's play of eyes between the two, holds good throughout the dialogue, to the end.

'I have told you once before to-night.'

'You have done nothing of the sort.'

'I tell you I have. That you take a great deal too much upon yourself.'

'You added something else to that, if I remember?'

'Yes, I did say something else.'

'Say it again.'

'I said that in the part of the world I come from, you would be called to account for it.'

'Only there?' cries Edwin Drood, with a contemptuous laugh. 'A long way off, I believe? Yes; I see! That part of the world is at a safe distance.'

'Say here, then,' rejoins the other, rising in a fury. 'Say anywhere! Your vanity is intolerable, your conceit is beyond endurance, you talk as if you were some rare and precious prize, instead of a common boaster. You are a common fellow, and a common boaster.'

'Pooh, pooh,' says Edwin Drood, equally furious, but more collected; 'how should you know? You may know a black common fellow, or a black common boaster, when you see him (and no doubt you have a large acquaintance that way); but you are no judge of white men.'

This insulting allusion to his dark skin infuriates Neville to that violent degree, that he flings the dregs of his wine at Edwin Drood, and is in the act of flinging the goblet after it, when his arm is caught in the nick of time by Jasper.

'Ned, my dear fellow!' he cries in a loud voice; 'I entreat you, I command you, to be still!' There has been a rush of all the three, and a clattering of glasses and overturning of chairs. 'Mr. Neville, for shame! Give this glass to me. Open your hand, sir. I WILL have it!'

But Neville throws him off, and pauses for an instant, in a raging passion, with the goblet yet in his uplifted hand. Then, he dashes it down under the grate, with such force that the broken splinters fly out again in a shower; and he leaves the house.

When he first emerges into the night air, nothing around him is still or steady; nothing around him shows like what it is; he only knows that he stands with a bare head in the midst

On Dangerous Ground

of a blood-red whirl, waiting to be struggled with, and to struggle to the death.

But, nothing happening, and the moon looking down upon him as if he were dead after a fit of wrath, he holds his steam-hammer beating head and heart, and staggers away. Then, he becomes half conscious of having heard himself bolted and barred out, like a dangerous animal; and thinks what shall he do?

Some wildly passionate ideas of the river dissolve under the spell of the moonlight on the Cathedral and the graves, and the remembrance of his sister, and the thought of what he owes to the good man who has but that very day won his confidence and given him his pledge. He repairs to Minor Canon Corner, and knocks softly at the door.

It is Mr. Crisparkle's custom to sit up last of the early household, very softly touching his piano and practising his favourite parts in concerted vocal music. The south wind that goes where it lists, by way of Minor Canon Corner on a still night, is not more subdued than Mr. Crisparkle at such times, regardful of the slumbers of the china shepherdess.

His knock is immediately answered by Mr. Crisparkle himself. When he opens the door, candle in hand, his cheerful face falls, and disappointed amazement is in it.

'Mr. Neville! In this disorder! Where have you been?'

'I have been to Mr. Jasper's, sir. With his nephew.'

'Come in.'

The Minor Canon props him by the elbow with a strong hand (in a strictly scientific manner, worthy of his morning trainings), and turns him into his own little book-room, and shuts the door.

'I have begun ill, sir. I have begun dreadfully ill.'

'Too true. You are not sober, Mr. Neville.'

'I am afraid I am not, sir, though I can satisfy you at another time that I have had very little indeed to drink, and that it overcame me in the strangest and most sudden manner.'

'Mr. Neville, Mr. Neville,' says the Minor Canon, shaking his head with a sorrowful smile; 'I have heard that said before.'

'I think – my mind is much confused, but I think – it is equally true of Mr. Jasper's nephew, sir.'

'Very likely,' is the dry rejoinder.

'We quarrelled, sir. He insulted me most grossly. He had heated that tigerish blood I told you of to-day, before then.'

'Mr. Neville,' rejoins the Minor Canon, mildly, but firmly: 'I request you not to speak to me with that clenched right hand. Unclench it, if you please.'

'He goaded me, sir,' pursues the young man, instantly obeying, 'beyond my power of endurance. I cannot say whether or no he meant it at first, but he did it. He certainly meant it at last. In short, sir,' with an irrepressible outburst, 'in the passion into which he lashed me, I would have cut him down if I could, and I tried to do it.'

'You have clenched that hand again,' is Mr. Crisparkle's quiet commentary.

'I beg your pardon, sir.'

'You know your room, for I showed it to you before dinner; but I will accompany you to it once more. Your arm, if you please. Softly, for the house is all a-bed.'

Scooping his hand into the same scientific elbow-rest as before, and backing it up with the inert strength of his arm, as skilfully as a Police Expert, and with an apparent repose quite unattainable by Novices, Mr. Crisparkle conducts his pupil to the pleasant and orderly old room prepared for him. Arrived there, the young man throws himself into a chair, and, flinging his arms upon his reading-table, rests his head upon them with an air of wretched self-reproach.

The gentle Minor Canon has had it in his thoughts to leave the room, without a word. But, looking round at the door, and seeing this dejected figure, he turns back to it, touches it with a mild hand, and says 'Good-night!' A sob is his only acknowledgement. He might have had many a worse; perhaps, could have had few better.

Another soft knock at the outer door, attracts his attention as he goes down stairs. He opens it to Mr. Jasper, holding in his hand the pupil's hat.

'We have had an awful scene with him,' says Jasper, in a low voice.

'Has it been so bad as that?'

'Murderous!'

Mr. Crisparkle remonstrates: 'No, no, no. Do not use such strong words.'

'He might have laid my dear boy dead at my feet. It is no fault of his, that he did not. But that I was, through the mercy of God, swift and strong with him, he would have cut him down on my hearth.'

The phrase smites home. 'Ah!' thinks Mr. Crisparkle. 'His own words!'

'Seeing what I have seen to-night, and hearing what I have heard,' adds Jasper, with great earnestness, 'I shall never know peace of mind when there is danger of those two coming together with no one else to interfere. It was horrible. There is something of the tiger in his dark blood.'

'Ah!' thinks Mr. Crisparkle. 'So he said!'

'You, my dear sir,' pursues Jasper, taking his hand, 'even you, have accepted a dangerous charge.'

'You need have no fear for me, Jasper,' returns Mr. Crisparkle, with a quiet smile. 'I have none for myself.'

'I have none for myself,' returns Jasper, with an emphasis on the last pronoun, 'because I am not, nor am I in the way of being, the object of his hostility. But you may be, and my dear boy has been. Good-night!'

Mr. Crisparkle goes in, with the hat that has so easily, so almost imperceptibly, acquired the right to be hung up in his hall; hangs it up; and goes thoughtfully to bed.

CHAPTER IX

Birds in the Bush

Rosa, having no relation that she knew of in the world, had, from the seventh year of her age, known no home but the Nuns' House, and no mother but Miss Twinkleton. Her remembrance of her own mother was of a pretty little creature like herself (not much older than herself it seemed to her), who had been brought home in her father's arms, drowned. The fatal accident had happened at a party of pleasure. Every fold and colour in the pretty summer dress, and even the long wet hair, with scattered petals of ruined flowers still clinging to it, as the beloved young figure, in its sad, sad beauty lay upon the bed, were fixed indelibly in Rosa's recollection. So were the wild despair and the subsequent bowed-down grief of her poor young father, who died broken-hearted on the first anniversary of that hard day.

The betrothal of Rosa grew out of the soothing of his year of mental distress by his fast friend and old college companion, Drood: who likewise had been left a widower in his youth. But he, too, went the silent road into which all earthly pilgrimages merge, some sooner, and some later; and thus the young couple had come to be as they were.

The atmosphere of pity surrounding the little orphan girl when she first came to Cloisterham, had never cleared away. It had taken brighter hues as she grew older, happier, prettier; now it had been golden, now roseate, and now azure; but it had always adorned her with some soft light of its own. The general desire to console and caress her, had caused her to be treated in the beginning as a child much younger than her years; the same desire had caused her to be still petted when she was a child no longer. Who should be her favourite, who should anticipate this or that small present, or do her this or that small service; who should take her home for the holidays; who should write to her the oftenest when they were separated, and whom she would most rejoice to see again when they were reunited; even these gentle rivalries were not without their slight dashes of bitterness in the Nuns' House. Well for the poor Nuns in their day, if they hid no harder strife under their veils and rosaries!

Thus Rosa had grown to be an amiable, giddy, wilful, winning little creature; spoilt, in the sense of counting upon kindness from all around her; but not in the sense of repaying it with indifference. Possessing an exhaustless well of affection in her nature, its sparkling waters had freshened and brightened the Nuns' House for years, and yet its depths had never yet been moved: what might betide when that came to pass; what developing changes might fall upon the heedless head, and light heart then; remained to be seen.

By what means the news that there had been a quarrel between the two young men over-night, involving even some kind of onslaught by Mr. Neville upon Edwin Drood, got into Miss Twinkleton's establishment before breakfast, it is impossible to say. Whether it was brought in by the birds of the air, or came blowing in with the very air itself, when the casement windows were set open; whether the baker brought it kneaded into the bread, or the milkman delivered it as part of the adulteration of his milk; or the housemaids, beating the dust out of their mats against the gateposts, received it in exchange deposited on the mats by the town atmosphere; certain it is that the news permeated every gable of the old building before Miss Twinkleton was down, and that Miss Twinkleton herself received it through Mrs. Tisher, while yet in the act of dressing; or (as she might have expressed the phrase to a parent or guardian of a mythological turn), of sacrificing to the Graces.

Miss Landless's brother had thrown a bottle at Mr. Edwin Drood.

Miss Landless's brother had thrown a knife at Mr. Edwin Drood.

A knife became suggestive of a fork, and Miss Landless's brother had thrown a fork at Mr. Edwin Drood.

As in the governing precedent of Peter Piper, alleged to have picked the peck of pickled pepper, it was held physically desirable to have evidence of the existence of the peck of

pickled pepper which Peter Piper was alleged to have picked:
so, in this case, it was held psychologically important to know
Why Miss Landless's brother threw a bottle, knife, or fork –
or bottle, knife, *and* fork – for the cook had been given to
understand it was all three – at Mr. Edwin Drood?

Well, then. Miss Landless's brother had said he admired
Miss Bud. Mr. Edwin Drood had said to Miss Landless's
brother that he had no business to admire Miss Bud. Miss
Landless's brother had then 'up'd' (this was the cook's exact
information), with the bottle, knife, fork, and decanter (the
decanter now coolly flying at everybody's head, without the
least introduction), and thrown them all at Mr. Edwin Drood.

Poor little Rosa put a forefinger into each of her ears when
these rumours began to circulate, and retired into a corner,
beseeching not to be told any more; but Miss Landless,
begging permission of Miss Twinkleton to go and speak
with her brother, and pretty plainly showing that she would
take it if it were not given, struck out the more definite course
of going to Mr. Crisparkle's for accurate intelligence.

When she came back (being first closeted with Miss Twinkleton, in order that anything objectionable in her tidings
might be retained by that discreet filter), she imparted to
Rosa only, what had really taken place; dwelling with a
flushed cheek on the provocation her brother had received,
but almost limiting it to that last gross affront as crowning
'some other words between them,' and, out of consideration
for her new friend, passing lightly over the fact that the other
words had originated in her lover's taking things in general
so very easily. To Rosa direct, she brought a petition from her
brother that she would forgive him; and, having delivered it
with sisterly earnestness, made an end of the subject.

It was reserved for Miss Twinkleton to tone down the
public mind of the Nuns' House. That lady, therefore,
entering in a stately manner what plebeians might have
called the school-room, but what, in the patrician language
of the head of the Nuns' House, was euphuistically, not to say
round-aboutedly, denominated 'the apartment allotted to
study,' and saying with a forensic air, 'Ladies!' all rose. Mrs.
Tisher at the same time grouped herself behind her chief, as

representing Queen Elizabeth's first historical female friend at Tilbury Fort. Miss Twinkleton then proceeded to remark that Rumour, Ladies, had been represented by the Bard of Avon – needless were it to mention the immortal SHAKE-SPEARE, also called the Swan of his native river, not improbably with some reference to the ancient superstition that that bird of graceful plumage (Miss Jennings will please stand upright) sang sweetly on the approach of death, for which we have no ornithological authority, – Rumour, Ladies, had been represented by that bard – hem! –

'who drew
The celebrated Jew,'

as painted full of tongues. Rumour in Cloisterham (Miss Ferdinand will honour me with her attention) was no exception to the great limner's portrait of Rumour elsewhere. A slight *fracas* between two young gentlemen occurring last night within a hundred miles of these peaceful walls (Miss Ferdinand, being apparently incorrigible, will have the kindness to write out this evening, in the original language, the first four fables of our vivacious neighbour, Monsieur La Fontaine) had been very grossly exaggerated by Rumour's voice. In the first alarm and anxiety arising from our sympathy with a sweet young friend, not wholly to be dissociated from one of the gladiators in the bloodless arena in question (the impropriety of Miss Reynolds's appearing to stab herself in the band with a pin, is far too obvious, and too glaringly unlady-like, to be pointed out), we descended from our maiden elevation to discuss this uncongenial and this unfit theme. Responsible inquiries having assured us that it was but one of those 'airy nothings' pointed at by the Poet (whose name and date of birth Miss Giggles will supply within half an hour), we would now discard the subject, and concentrate our minds upon the grateful labours of the day.

But the subject so survived all day, nevertheless, that Miss Ferdinand got into new trouble by surreptitiously clapping on a paper moustache at dinner-time, and going through the motions of aiming a water-bottle at Miss Giggles, who drew a table-spoon in defence.

Now, Rosa thought of this unlucky quarrel a great deal, and thought of it with an uncomfortable feeling that she was involved in it, as cause, or consequence, or what not, through being in a false position altogether as to her marriage engagement. Never free from such uneasiness when she was with her affianced husband, it was not likely that she would be free from it when they were apart. To-day, too, she was cast in upon herself, and deprived of the relief of talking freely with her new friend, because the quarrel had been with Helena's brother, and Helena undisguisedly avoided the subject as a delicate and difficult one to herself. At this critical time, of all times, Rosa's guardian was announced as having come to see her.

Mr. Grewgious had been well selected for his trust, as a man of incorruptible integrity, but certainly for no other appropriate quality discernible on the surface. He was an arid, sandy man, who, if he had been put into a grinding-mill, looked as if he would have ground immediately into high-dried snuff. He had a scanty flat crop of hair, in colour and consistency like some very mangy yellow fur tippet; it was so unlike hair, that it must have been a wig, but for the stupendous improbability of anybody's voluntarily sporting such a head. The little play of feature that his face presented, was cut deep into it, in a few hard curves that made it more like work; and he had certain notches in his forehead, which looked as though Nature had been about to touch them into sensibility or refinement, when she had impatiently thrown away the chisel, and said: 'I really cannot be worried to finish off this man; let him go as he is.'

With too great length of throat at his upper end, and too much ankle-bone and heel at his lower; with an awkward and hesitating manner; with a shambling walk, and with what is called a near sight – which perhaps prevented his observing how much white cotton stocking he displayed to the public eye, in contrast with his black suit – Mr. Grewgious still had some strange capacity in him of making on the whole an agreeable impression.

Mr. Grewgious was discovered by his ward, much discomfited by being in Miss Twinkleton's company in Miss

Twinkleton's own sacred room. Dim forebodings of being examined in something, and not coming well out of it, seemed to oppress the poor gentleman when found in these circumstances.

'My dear, how do you do? I am glad to see you. My dear, how much improved you are. Permit me to hand you a chair, my dear.'

Miss Twinkleton rose at her little writing-table, saying, with general sweetness, as to the polite Universe: 'Will you permit me to retire?'

'By no means, madam, on my account. I beg that you will not move.'

'I must entreat permission to *move*,' returned Miss Twinkleton, repeating the word with a charming grace; 'but I will not withdraw, since you are so obliging. If I wheel my desk to this corner window, shall I be in the way?'

'Madam! In the way!'

'You are very kind. Rosa, my dear, you will be under no restraint, I am sure.'

Here Mr. Grewgious, left by the fire with Rosa, said again: 'My dear, how do you do? I am glad to see you, my dear.' And having waited for her to sit down, sat down himself.

'My visits,' said Mr. Grewgious, 'are, like those of the angels – not that I compare myself to an angel.'

'No, sir,' said Rosa.

'Not by any means,' assented Mr. Grewgious. 'I merely refer to my visits, which are few and far between. The angels are, we know very well, up stairs.'

Miss Twinkleton looked round with a kind of stiff stare.

'I refer, my dear,' said Mr. Grewgious, laying his hand on Rosa's, as the possibility thrilled through his frame of his otherwise seeming to take the awful liberty of calling Miss Twinkleton my dear; 'I refer to the other young ladies.'

Miss Twinkleton resumed her writing.

Mr. Grewgious, with a sense of not having managed his opening point quite as neatly as he might have desired, smoothed his head from back to front as if he had just dived, and were pressing the water out – this smoothing action, however superfluous, was habitual with him – and took a pocket-book from his coat pocket, and a stump of black-lead pencil from his waistcoat pocket.

'I made,' he said, turning the leaves: 'I made a guiding memorandum or so – as I usually do, for I have no conversational powers whatever – to which I will, with your permission, my dear, refer. "Well and happy." Truly. You are well and happy, my dear? You look so.'

'Yes, indeed, sir,' answered Rosa.

'For which,' said Mr. Grewgious, with a bend of his head towards the corner window, 'our warmest acknowledgements are due, and I am sure are rendered, to the maternal kindness and the constant care and consideration of the lady whom I have now the honour to see before me.'

This point, again, made but a lame departure from Mr. Grewgious, and never got to its destination; for, Miss Twinkleton, feeling that the courtesies required her to be by this time quite outside the conversation, was biting the end of her pen, and looking upward, as waiting for the descent of an idea from any member of the Celestial Nine who might have one to spare.

Mr. Grewgious smoothed his smooth head again, and then made another reference to his pocket-book; lining out 'well and happy' as disposed of.

'"Pounds, shillings, and pence" is my next note. A dry subject for a young lady, but an important subject too. Life is pounds, shillings, and pence. Death is—' A sudden recollection of the death of her two parents seemed to stop him, and he said in a softer tone, and evidently inserting the negative as an after-thought: 'Death is *not* pounds, shillings, and pence.'

His voice was as hard and dry as himself, and Fancy might have ground it straight, like himself, into high-dried snuff. And yet, through the very limited means of expression that he possessed, he seemed to express kindness. If Nature had but finished him off, kindness might have been recognizable in his face at this moment. But if the notches in his forehead wouldn't fuse together, and if his face would work and couldn't play, what could he do, poor man!

' "Pounds, shillings, and pence." You find your allowance always sufficient for your wants, my dear?'

Rosa wanted for nothing, and therefore it was ample.

'And you are not in debt?'

Rosa laughed at the idea of being in debt. It seemed, to her inexperience, a comical vagary of the imagination. Mr. Grewgious stretched his near sight to be sure that this was her view of the case. 'Ah!' he said, as comment, with a furtive glance towards Miss Twinkleton, and lining out 'pounds, shillings, and pence': 'I spoke of having got among the angels! So I did!'

Rosa felt what his next memorandum would prove to be, and was blushing and folding a crease in her dress with one embarrassed hand, long before he found it.

' "Marriage." Hem!' Mr. Grewgious carried his smoothing hand down over his eyes and nose, and even chin, before drawing his chair a little nearer, and speaking a little more confidentially: 'I now touch, my dear, upon the point that is the direct cause of my troubling you with the present visit. Otherwise, being a particularly Angular man, I should not have intruded here. I am the last man to intrude into a sphere for which I am so entirely unfitted. I feel, on these premises, as if I was a bear – with the cramp – in a youthful Cotillon.'

His ungainliness gave him enough of the air of his simile to set Rosa off laughing heartily.

'It strikes you in the same light,' said Mr. Grewgious, with perfect calmness. 'Just so. To return to my memorandum. Mr. Edwin has been to and fro here, as was arranged. You have mentioned that, in your quarterly letters to me. And you like him, and he likes you.'

'I *like* him very much, sir,' rejoined Rosa.

'So I said, my dear,' returned her guardian, for whose ear the timid emphasis was much too fine. 'Good. And you correspond.'

'We write to one another,' said Rosa, pouting, as she recalled their epistolary differences.

'Such is the meaning that I attach to the word "correspond" in this application, my dear,' said Mr. Grewgious.

'Good. All goes well, time moves on, and at this next Christ-mas-time it will become necessary, as a matter of form, to give the exemplary lady in the corner window, to whom we are so much indebted, business notice of your departure in the ensuing half-year. Your relations with her are far more than business relations no doubt; but a residue of business remains in them, and business is business ever. I am a par-ticularly Angular man,' proceeded Mr. Grewgious, as if it suddenly occurred to him to mention it, 'and I am not used to give anything away. If, for these two reasons, some compe-tent Proxy would give *you* away, I should take it very kindly.'

Rosa intimated, with her eyes on the ground, that she thought a substitute might be found, if required.

'Surely, surely,' said Mr. Grewgious. 'For instance, the gentleman who teaches Dancing here – he would know how to do it with graceful propriety. He would advance and retire in a manner satisfactory to the feelings of the officiating clergyman, and of yourself, and the bridegroom, and all parties concerned. I am – I am a particularly Angular man,' said Mr. Grewgious, as if he had made up his mind to screw it out at last: 'and should only blunder.'

Rosa sat still and silent. Perhaps her mind had not got quite so far as the ceremony yet, but was lagging on the way there.

'Memorandum, "Will." Now, my dear,' said Mr. Grew-gious, referring to his notes, disposing of 'marriage' with his pencil, and taking a paper from his pocket: 'although I have before possessed you with the contents of your father's will, I think it right at this time to leave a certified copy of it in your hands. And although Mr. Edwin is also aware of its contents, I think it right at this time likewise to place a certified copy of it in Mr. Jasper's hands—'

'Not in his own?' asked Rosa, looking up quickly. 'Cannot the copy go to Eddy himself?'

'Why, yes, my dear, if you particularly wish it; but I spoke of Mr. Jasper as being his trustee.'

'I do particularly wish it, if you please,' said Rosa, hur-riedly and earnestly; 'I don't like Mr. Jasper to come between us, in any way.'

'It is natural, I suppose,' said Mr. Grewgious, 'that your young husband should be all in all. Yes. You observe that I say, I suppose. The fact is, I am a particularly Unnatural man, and I don't know from my own knowledge.'

Rosa looked at him with some wonder.

'I mean,' he explained, 'that young ways were never my ways. I was the only offspring of parents far advanced in life, and I half believe I was born advanced in life myself. No personality is intended towards the name you will so soon change, when I remark that while the general growth of people seem to have come into existence, buds, I seem to have come into existence a chip. I was a chip – and a very dry one – when I first became aware of myself. Respecting the other certified copy, your wish shall be complied with. Respecting your inheritance, I think you know all. It is an annuity of two hundred and fifty pounds. The savings upon that annuity, and some other items to your credit, all duly carried to account, with vouchers, will place you in possession of a lump-sum of money, rather exceeding Seventeen Hundred Pounds. I am empowered to advance the cost of your preparations for your marriage out of that fund. All is told.'

'Will you please tell me,' said Rosa, taking the paper with a prettily knitted brow, but not opening it: 'whether I am right in what I am going to say? I can understand what you tell me, so very much better than what I read in law-writings. My poor papa and Eddy's father made their agreement together, as very dear and firm and fast friends, in order that we, too, might be very dear and firm and fast friends after them?'

'Just so.'

'For the lasting good of both of us, and the lasting happiness of both of us?'

'Just so.'

'That we might be to one another even much more than they had been to one another?'

'Just so.'

'It was not bound upon Eddy, and it was not bound upon me, by any forfeit, in case—'

'Don't be agitated, my dear. In the case that it brings tears into your affectionate eyes even to picture to yourself – in the case of your not marrying one another – no, no forfeiture on either side. You would then have been my ward until you were of age. No worse would have befallen you. Bad enough perhaps!'

'And Eddy?'

'He would have come into his partnership derived from his father, and into its arrears to his credit (if any), on attaining his majority, just as now.'

Rosa with her perplexed face and knitted brow, bit the corner of her attested copy, as she sat with her head on one side, looking abstractedly on the floor, and smoothing it with her foot.

'In short,' said Mr. Grewgious, 'this betrothal is a wish, a sentiment, a friendly project, tenderly expressed on both sides. That it was strongly felt, and that there was a lively hope that it would prosper, there can be no doubt. When you were both children, you began to be accustomed to it, and it *has* prospered. But circumstances alter cases; and I made this visit to-day, partly, indeed principally, to discharge myself of the duty of telling you, my dear, that two young people can only be betrothed in marriage (except as a matter of convenience, and therefore mockery and misery), of their own free will, their own attachment, and their own assurance (it may or may not prove a mistaken one, but we must take our chance of that), that they are suited to each other and will make each other happy. Is it to be supposed, for example, that if either of your fathers were living now, and had any mistrust on that subject, his mind would not be changed by the change of circumstances involved in the change of your years? Untenable, unreasonable, inconclusive, and preposterous!'

Mr. Grewgious said all this, as if he were reading it aloud; or, still more, as if he were repeating a lesson. So expressionless of any approach to spontaneity were his face and manner.

'I have now, my dear,' he added, blurring out 'will' with his pencil, 'discharged myself of what is doubtless a formal duty in this case, but still a duty in such a case. Memorandum, "Wishes." Exactly. Is there any wish of yours that I can further?'

Rosa shook her head, with an almost plaintive air of hesitation in want of help.

'Is there any instruction that I can take from you with reference to your affairs?'

'I – I should like to settle them with Eddy first, if you please,' said Rosa, plaiting the crease in her dress.

'Surely, surely,' returned Mr. Grewgious. 'You two should be of one mind in all things. Is the young gentleman expected shortly?'

'He has gone away only this morning. He will be back at Christmas.'

'Nothing could happen better. You will, on his return at Christmas, arrange all matters of detail with him; you will then communicate with me; and I will discharge myself (as a mere business acquittance) of my business responsibilities towards the accomplished lady in the corner window. They will accrue at that season.' Blurring pencil once again. 'Memorandum, "Leave." Yes. I will now, my dear, take my leave.'

'Could I,' said Rosa, rising, as he jerked out of his chair in his ungainly way: 'could I ask you, most kindly to come to me at Christmas, if I had anything particular to say to you?'

'Why, certainly, certainly,' he rejoined; apparently – if such a word can be used of one who had no apparent lights or shadows about him – complimented by the question. 'As a particularly Angular man, I do not fit smoothly into the social circle, and consequently I have no other engagement at Christmas-time than to partake, on the twenty-fifth, of a boiled turkey and celery sauce with a – with a particularly Angular clerk I have the good fortune to possess, whose father, being a Norfolk farmer, sends him up (the turkey up), as a present to me, from the neighbourhood of Norwich. I should be quite proud of your wishing to see me, my dear. As a professional Receiver of rents, so very few people *do* wish to see me, that the novelty would be bracing.'

For his ready acquiescence, the grateful Rosa put her hands upon his shoulders, stood on tiptoe, and instantly kissed him.

'Lord bless me!' cried Mr. Grewgious. 'Thank you, my dear! The honour is almost equal to the pleasure. Miss Twinkleton, Madam, I have had a most satisfactory conversation with my ward, and I will now release you from the incumbrance of my presence.'

'Nay, sir,' rejoined Miss Twinkleton, rising with a gracious condescension: 'say not incumbrance. Not so, by any means. I cannot permit you to say so.'

'Thank you, Madam. I have read in the newspapers,' said Mr. Grewgious, stammering a little, 'that when a distinguished visitor (not that I am one: far from it), goes to a school (not that this is one: far from it), he asks for a holiday, or some sort of grace. It being now the afternoon in the – College – of which you are the eminent head, the young ladies might gain nothing, except in name, by having the rest of the day allowed them. But if there is any young lady at all under a cloud, might I solicit—?'

'Ah, Mr. Grewgious, Mr. Grewgious!' cried Miss Twinkleton, with a chastely-rallying forefinger. 'Oh, you gentlemen, you gentlemen! Fie for shame, that you are so hard upon us poor maligned disciplinarians of our sex, for your sakes! But as Miss Ferdinand is at present weighed down by an incubus' – Miss Twinkleton might have said a pen-and-ink-ubus of writing out Monsieur La Fontaine – 'go to her Rosa, my dear, and tell her the penalty is remitted, in deference to the intercession of your guardian, Mr. Grewgious.'

Miss Twinkleton here achieved a curtsey, suggestive of marvels happening to her respected legs, and which she came out of nobly, three yards behind her starting-point.

As he held it incumbent upon him to call on Mr. Jasper before leaving Cloisterham, Mr. Grewgious went to the Gate House, and climbed its postern stair. But Mr. Jasper's door being closed, and presenting on a slip of paper the word 'Cathedral,' the fact of its being service-time was borne into the mind of Mr. Grewgious. So, he descended the stair again, and, crossing the Close, paused at the great western folding-door of the Cathedral, which stood open on the fine and bright, though short-lived, afternoon, for the airing of the place.

'Dear me,' said Mr. Grewgious, peering in, 'it's like looking down the throat of Old Time.'

Old Time heaved a mouldy sigh from tomb and arch and vault; and gloomy shadows began to deepen in corners; and damps began to rise from green patches of stone; and jewels, cast upon the pavement of the nave from stained glass by the declining sun, began to perish. Within the grill-gate of the chancel, up the steps surmounted loomingly by the fast darkening organ, white robes could be dimly seen, and one feeble voice, rising and falling in a cracked monotonous mutter, could at intervals be faintly heard. In the free outer air, the river, the green pastures, and the brown arable lands, the teeming hills and dales, were reddened by the sunset: while the distant little windows in windmills and farm homesteads, shone, patches of bright beaten gold. In the Cathedral, all became grey, murky, and sepulchral, and the cracked monotonous mutter went on like a dying voice, until the organ and the choir burst forth, and drowned it in a sea of music. Then, the sea fell, and the dying voice made another feeble effort, and then the sea rose high, and beat its life out, and lashed the roof, and surged among the arches, and pierced the heights of the great tower; and then the sea was dry, and all was still.

Mr. Grewgious had by that time walked to the chancel-steps, where he met the living waters coming out.

'Nothing is the matter?' Thus Jasper accosted him, rather quickly. 'You have not been sent for?'

'Not at all, not at all. I came down of my own accord. I have been to my pretty ward's, and am now homeward bound again.'

'You found her thriving?'

'Blooming indeed. Most blooming. I merely came to tell her, seriously, what a betrothal by deceased parents is.'

'And what is it – according to your judgement?'

Mr. Grewgious noticed the whiteness of the lips that asked the question, and put it down to the chilling account of the Cathedral.

'I merely came to tell her that it could not be considered binding, against any such reason for its dissolution as a want of affection, or want of disposition to carry it into effect, on the side of either party.'

'May I ask, had you any especial reason for telling her that?'

Mr. Grewgious answered somewhat sharply: 'The especial reason of doing my duty, sir. Simply that.' Then he added: 'Come, Mr. Jasper; I know your affection for your nephew, and that you are quick to feel on his behalf. I assure you that this implies not the least doubt of, or disrespect to, your nephew.'

'You could not,' returned Jasper, with a friendly pressure of his arm, as they walked on side by side, 'speak more handsomely.'

Mr. Grewgious pulled off his hat to smooth his head, and, having smoothed it, nodded it contentedly, and put his hat on again.

'I will wager,' said Jasper, smiling – his lips were still so white that he was conscious of it, and bit and moistened them while speaking: 'I will wager that she hinted no wish to be released from Ned.'

'And you will win your wager, if you do,' retorted Mr. Grewgious. 'We should allow some margin for little maidenly delicacies in a young motherless creature, under such circumstances, I suppose; it is not in my line; what do you think?'

'There can be no doubt of it.'

'I am glad you say so. Because,' proceeded Mr. Grewgious, who had all this time very knowingly felt his way round to action on his remembrance of what she had said of Jasper himself: 'because she seems to have some little delicate instinct that all preliminary arrangements had best be made between Mr. Edwin Drood and herself, don't you see? She don't want us, don't you know?'

Jasper touched himself on the breast, and said, somewhat indistinctly: 'You mean me.'

Mr. Grewgious touched himself on the breast, and said: 'I mean us. Therefore, let them have their little discussions and councils together, when Mr. Edwin Drood comes back here at Christmas, and then you and I will step in, and put the final touches to the business.'

'So, you settled with her that you would come back at Christmas?' observed Jasper. 'I see! Mr. Grewgious, as you quite fairly said just now, there is such an exceptional attachment between my nephew and me, that I am more sensitive for the dear, fortunate, happy, happy fellow than for myself. But it is only right that the young lady should be considered, as you have pointed out, and that I should accept my cue from you. I accept it. I understand that at Christmas they will complete their preparations for May, and that their marriage will be put in final train by themselves, and that nothing will remain for us but to put ourselves in train also, and have everything ready for our formal release from our trusts, on Edwin's birthday.'

'That is my understanding,' assented Mr. Grewgious, as they shook hands to part. 'God bless them both!'

'God save them both!' cried Jasper.

'I said, bless them,' remarked the former, looking back over his shoulder.

'I said, save them,' returned the latter. 'Is there any difference?'

CHAPTER X

Smoothing the Way

IT has been often enough remarked that women have a curious power of divining the characters of men, which would seem to be innate and instinctive; seeing that it is arrived at through no patient process of reasoning, that it can give no satisfactory or sufficient account of itself, and that it pronounces in the most confident manner even against accumulated observation on the part of the other sex. But it has not been quite so often remarked that this power (fallible, like every other human attribute), is for the most part absolutely incapable of self-revision; and that when it has delivered an adverse opinion which by all human lights is subsequently proved to have failed, it is undistinguishable from prejudice, in respect of its determination not to be corrected. Nay, the very possibility of contradiction or disproof, however remote, communicates to this feminine judgement from the first, in nine cases out of ten, the weakness attendant on the testimony of an interested witness: so personally and strongly does the fair diviner connect herself with her divination.

'Now, don't you think, Ma dear,' said the Minor Canon to his mother one day as she sat at her knitting in his little book-room, 'that you are rather hard on Mr. Neville?'

'No, I do *not*, Sept,' returned the old lady.

'Let us discuss it, Ma.'

'I have no objection to discuss it, Sept. I trust, my dear, I am always open to discussion.' There was a vibration in the old lady's cap, as though she internally added: 'and I should like to see the discussion that would change *my* mind!'

'Very good, Ma,' said her conciliatory son. 'There is nothing like being open to discussion.'

'I hope not, my dear,' returned the old lady, evidently shut to it.

'Well! Mr. Neville, on that unfortunate occasion, commits himself under provocation.'

'And under mulled wine,' added the old lady.

'I must admit the wine. Though I believe the two young men were much alike in that regard.'

'I don't!' said the old lady.

'Why not, Ma?'

'Because I *don't*,' said the old lady. 'Still, I am quite open to discussion.'

'But, my dear Ma, I cannot see how we are to discuss, if you take that line.'

'Blame Mr. Neville for it, Sept, and not me,' said the old lady, with stately severity.

'My dear Ma! Why Mr. Neville?'

'Because,' said Mrs. Crisparkle, retiring on first principles, 'he came home intoxicated, and did great discredit to this house, and showed great disrespect to this family.'

'That is not to be denied, Ma. He was then, and he is now, very sorry for it.'

'But for Mr. Jasper's well-bred consideration in coming up to me next day, after service, in the nave itself, with his gown still on, and expressing his hope that I had not been greatly alarmed or had my rest violently broken, I believe I might never have heard of that disgraceful transaction,' said the old lady.

'To be candid, Ma, I think I should have kept it from you if I could: though I had not decidedly made up my mind. I was following Jasper out, to confer with him on the subject, and to consider the expediency of his and my jointly hushing the thing up on all accounts, when I found him speaking to you. Then it was too late.'

'Too late, indeed, Sept. He was still as pale as gentlemanly ashes at what had taken place in his rooms over-night.'

'If I *had* kept it from you, Ma, you may be sure it would have been for your peace and quiet, and for the good of the young men, and in my best discharge of my duty according to my lights.'

The old lady immediately walked across the room and kissed him; saying, 'Of course, my dear Sept, I am sure of that.'

'However, it became the town-talk,' said Mr. Crisparkle, rubbing his ear, as his mother resumed her seat, and her knitting, 'and passed out of my power.'

'And I said then, Sept,' returned the old lady, 'that I thought ill of Mr. Neville. And I say now, that I think ill of Mr. Neville. And I said then, and I say now, that I hope Mr. Neville may come to good, but I don't believe he will.' Here the cap vibrated again, considerably.

'I am sorry to hear you say so, Ma—'

'I am sorry to say so, my dear,' interposed the old lady, knitting on firmly, 'but I can't help it.'

'– For,' pursued the Minor Canon, 'it is undeniable that Mr. Neville is exceedingly industrious and attentive, and that he improves apace, and that he has – I hope I may say – an attachment to me.'

'There is no merit in the last article, my dear,' said the old lady, quickly; 'and if he says there is, I think the worse of him for the boast.'

'But, my dear Ma, he never said there was.'

'Perhaps not,' returned the old lady; 'still, I don't see that it greatly signifies.'

There was no impatience in the pleasant look with which Mr. Crisparkle contemplated the pretty old piece of china as it knitted; but there was, certainly, a humorous sense of its not being a piece of china to argue with very closely.

'Besides, Sept. Ask yourself what he would be without his sister. You know what an influence she has over him; you know what a capacity she has; you know that whatever he reads with you, he reads with her. Give her her fair share of your praise, and how much do you leave for him?'

At these words Mr. Crisparkle fell into a little reverie, in which he thought of several things. He thought of the times he had seen the brother and sister together in deep converse over one of his own old college books; now, in the rimy mornings, when he made those sharpening pilgrimages to Cloisterham Weir; now, in the sombre evenings, when he

faced the wind at sunset, having climbed his favourite out-
look, a beetling fragment of monastery ruin; and the two
studious figures passed below him along the margin of the
river, in which the town fires and lights already shone,
making the landscape bleaker. He thought how the consciousness had stolen upon him that in teaching one, he was
teaching two; and how he had almost insensibly adapted his
explanations to both minds – that with which his own was
daily in contact, and that which he only approached through
it. He thought of the gossip that had reached him from the
Nuns' House, to the effect that Helena, whom he had mis-
trusted as so proud and fierce, submitted herself to the fairy
bride (as he called her), and learnt from her what she knew.
He thought of the picturesque alliance between those two,
externally so very different. He thought – perhaps most of all
– could it be that these things were yet but so many weeks old,
and had become an integral part of his life?

As, whenever the Reverend Septimus fell a musing, his
good mother took it to be an infallible sign that he 'wanted
support,' the blooming old lady made all haste to the dining-
room closet, to produce from it the support embodied in a
glass of Constantia and a home-made biscuit. It was a most
wonderful closet, worthy of Cloisterham and of Minor Canon
Corner. Above it, a portrait of Handel in a flowing wig
beamed down at the spectator, with a knowing air of being
up to the contents of the closet, and a musical air of intending
to combine all its harmonies in one delicious fugue. No
common closet with a vulgar door on hinges, openable all
at once, and leaving nothing to be disclosed by degrees, this
rare closet had a lock in mid-air, where two perpendicular
slides met: the one pulling down, and the other pushing up.
The upper slide, on being pulled down (leaving the lower a
double mystery), revealed deep shelves of pickle-jars, jam-
pots, tin canisters, spice-boxes, and agreeably outlandish
vessels of blue and white, the luscious lodgings of preserved
tamarinds and ginger. Every benevolent inhabitant of this
retreat had his name inscribed upon his stomach. The
pickles, in a uniform of rich brown double-breasted buttoned
coat, and yellow or sombre drab continuations, announced

their portly forms, in printed capitals, as Walnut, Gherkin, Onion, Cabbage, Cauliflower, Mixed, and other members of that noble family. The jams, as being of a less masculine temperament, and as wearing curlpapers, announced themselves in feminine calligraphy, like a soft whisper, to be Raspberry, Gooseberry, Apricot, Plum, Damson, Apple, and Peach. The scene closing on these charmers, and the lower slide ascending, oranges were revealed, attended by a mighty japanned sugar-box, to temper their acerbity if unripe. Home-made biscuits waited at the Court of these Powers, accompanied by a goodly fragment of plum-cake, and various slender ladies' fingers, to be dipped into sweet wine and kissed. Lowest of all, a compact leaden vault enshrined the sweet wine and a stock of cordials: whence issued whispers of Seville Orange, Lemon, Almond, and Caraway-seed. There was a crowning air upon this closet of closets, of having been for ages hummed through by the Cathedral bell and organ, until those venerable bees had made sublimated honey of everything in store; and it was always observed that every dipper among the shelves (deep, as has been noticed, and swallowing up head, shoulders, and elbows), came forth again mellow-faced, and seeming to have undergone a saccharine transfiguration.

The Reverend Septimus yielded himself up quite as willing a victim to a nauseous medicinal herb-closet, also presided over by the china shepherdess, as to this glorious cupboard. To what amazing infusions of gentian, peppermint, gilliflower, sage, parsley, thyme, rue, rosemary, and dandelion, did his courageous stomach submit itself! In what wonderful wrappers enclosing layers of dried leaves, would he swathe his rosy and contented face, if his mother suspected him of a toothache! What botanical blotches would he cheerfully stick upon his cheek, or forehead, if the dear old lady convicted him of an imperceptible pimple there! Into this herbaceous penitentiary, situated on an upper staircase-landing: a low and narrow whitewashed cell, where bunches of dried leaves hung from rusty hooks in the ceiling, and were spread out upon shelves, in company with portentous bottles: would the Reverend Septimus submissively be led, like the highly-popular lamb who has so long and unresistingly been led to the slaughter, and there would he, unlike that lamb, bore nobody but himself. Not even doing that much, so that the old lady were busy and pleased, he would quietly swallow what was given him, merely taking a corrective dip of hands and face into one great bowl of dried rose-leaves, and into the other great bowl of dried lavender, and then would go out, as confident in the sweetening powers of Cloisterham Weir and a wholesome mind, as Lady Macbeth was hopeless of those of all the seas that roll.

In the present instance the good Minor Canon took his glass of Constantia with an excellent grace, and, so supported to his mother's satisfaction, applied himself to the remaining duties of the day. In their orderly and punctual progress they brought round vesper service and twilight. The Cathedral being very cold, he set off for a brisk trot after service; the trot to end in a charge at his favourite fragment of ruin, which was to be carried by storm, without a pause for breath.

He carried it in a masterly manner, and, not breathed even then, stood looking down upon the river. The river at Cloisterham is sufficiently near the sea to throw up oftentimes a quantity of seaweed. An unusual quantity had come in with the last tide, and this, and the confusion of the water, and the restless dipping and flapping of the noisy gulls, and an angry light out seaward beyond the brown-sailed barges that were turning black, foreshadowed a stormy night. In his mind he was contrasting the wild and noisy sea with the quiet harbour of Minor Canon Corner, when Helena and Neville Landless passed below him. He had had the two together in his thoughts all day, and at once climbed down to speak to them together. The footing was rough in an uncertain light for any tread save that of a good climber; but the Minor Canon was as good a climber as most men, and stood beside them before many good climbers would have been half-way down.

'A wild evening, Miss Landless! Do you not find your usual walk with your brother too exposed and cold for the time of year? Or at all events, when the sun is down, and the weather is driving in from the sea?'

Helena thought not. It was their favourite walk. It was very retired.

'It is very retired,' assented Mr. Crisparkle, laying hold of his opportunity straightway, and walking on with them. 'It is a place of all others where one can speak without interruption, as I wish to do. Mr. Neville, I believe you tell your sister everything that passes between us?'

'Everything, sir.'

'Consequently,' said Mr. Crisparkle, 'your sister is aware that I have repeatedly urged you to make some kind of apology for that unfortunate occurrence which befell, on the night of your arrival here.'

In saying it he looked to her, and not to him; therefore it was she, and not he, who replied:

'Yes.'

'I call it unfortunate, Miss Helena,' resumed Mr. Crisparkle, 'forasmuch as it certainly has engendered a prejudice against Neville. There is a notion about, that he is a dangerously passionate fellow, of an uncontrollable and furious temper: he is really avoided as such.'

'I have no doubt he is, poor fellow,' said Helena, with a look of proud compassion at her brother, expressing a deep sense of his being ungenerously treated. 'I should be quite sure of it, from your saying so; but what you tell me is confirmed by suppressed hints and references that I meet with every day.'

'Now,' Mr. Crisparkle again resumed, in a tone of mild though firm persuasion, 'is not this to be regretted, and ought it not to be amended? These are early days of Neville's in Cloisterham, and I have no fear of his outliving such a prejudice, and proving himself to have been misunderstood. But how much wiser to take action at once, than to trust to uncertain time! Besides; apart from its being politic, it is right. For there can be no question that Neville was wrong.'

'He was provoked,' Helena submitted.

'He was the assailant,' Mr. Crisparkle submitted.

They walked on in silence, until Helena raised her eyes to the Minor Canon's face, and said, almost reproachfully: 'Oh, Mr. Crisparkle, would you have Neville throw himself at young Drood's feet, or at Mr. Jasper's, who maligns him every day! In your heart you cannot mean it. From your heart you could not do it, if his case were yours.'

'I have represented to Mr. Crisparkle, Helena,' said Neville, with a glance of deference towards his tutor, 'that if I could do it from my heart, I would. But I cannot, and I revolt from the pretence. You forget, however, that to put the case to Mr. Crisparkle as his own, is to suppose Mr. Crisparkle to have done what I did.'

'I ask his pardon,' said Helena.

'You see,' remarked Mr. Crisparkle, again laying hold of his opportunity, though with a moderate and delicate touch, 'you both instinctively acknowledge that Neville did wrong! Then why stop short, and not otherwise acknowledge it?'

'Is there no difference,' asked Helena, with a little faltering in her manner, 'between submission to a generous spirit, and submission to a base or trivial one?'

Before the worthy Minor Canon was quite ready with his argument in reference to this nice distinction, Neville struck in:

'Help me to clear myself with Mr. Crisparkle, Helena. Help me to convince him that I cannot be the first to make concessions without mockery and falsehood. My nature must be changed before I can do so, and it is not changed. I am sensible of inexpressible affront, and deliberate aggravation of inexpressible affront, and I am angry. The plain truth is, I am still as angry when I recall that night as I was that night.'

'Neville,' hinted the Minor Canon, with a steady countenance, 'you have repeated that former action of your hands, which I so much dislike.'

'I am sorry for it, sir, but it was involuntary. I confessed that I was still as angry.'

'And I confess,' said Mr. Crisparkle, 'that I hoped for better things.'

'I am sorry to disappoint you, sir, but it would be far worse to deceive you, and I should deceive you grossly if I pretended that you had softened me in this respect. The time may come when your powerful influence will do even that with the difficult pupil whose antecedents you know; but it has not come yet. Is this so, and in spite of my struggles against myself, Helena?'

She, whose dark eyes were watching the effect of what he said on Mr. Crisparkle's face, replied – to Mr. Crisparkle: not to him: 'It is so.' After a short pause, she answered the slightest look of inquiry conceivable, in her brother's eyes, with as slight an affirmative bend of her own head; and he went on:

'I have never yet had the courage to say to you, sir, what in full openness I ought to have said when you first talked with me on this subject. It is not easy to say, and I have been withheld by a fear of its seeming ridiculous, which is very strong upon me down to this last moment, and might, but for my sister, prevent my being quite open with you even now. – I admire Miss Bud, sir, so very much, that I cannot bear her being treated with conceit or indifference; and even if I did not feel that I had an injury against young Drood on my own account, I should feel that I had an injury against him on hers.'

Mr. Crisparkle, in utter amazement, looked at Helena for corroboration, and met in her expressive face full corroboration, and a plea for advice.

'The young lady of whom you speak is, as you know, Mr. Neville, shortly to be married,' said Mr. Crisparkle, gravely; 'therefore your admiration, if it be of that special nature which you seem to indicate, is outrageously misplaced. Moreover, it is monstrous that you should take upon yourself to be the young lady's champion against her chosen husband. Besides, you have seen them only once. The young lady has become your sister's friend; and I wonder that your sister, even on her behalf, has not checked you in this irrational and culpable fancy.'

'She has tried, sir, but uselessly. Husband or no husband, that fellow is incapable of the feeling with which I am inspired towards the beautiful young creature whom he treats like a doll. I say he is as incapable of it, as he is unworthy of her. I say she is sacrificed in being bestowed upon him. I say that I love her, and despise and hate him!' This with a face so flushed, and a gesture so violent, that his sister crossed to his side, and caught his arm, remonstrating, 'Neville, Neville!'

Thus recalled to himself, he quickly became sensible of having lost the guard he had set upon his passionate tendency, and covered his face with his hand, as one repentant, and wretched.

Mr. Crisparkle, watching him attentively, and at the same time meditating how to proceed, walked on for some paces in silence. Then he spoke:

'Mr. Neville, Mr. Neville, I am sorely grieved to see in you more traces of a character as sullen, angry, and wild, as the night now closing in. They are of too serious an aspect to leave me the resource of treating the infatuation you have disclosed, as undeserving serious consideration. I give it very serious consideration, and I speak to you accordingly. This feud between you and young Drood must not go on. I cannot permit it to go on, any longer, knowing what I now know from you, and you living under my roof. Whatever prejudiced and unauthorized constructions your blind and envious wrath may put upon his character, it is a frank, good-natured character. I know I can trust to it for that. Now, pray observe what I am about to say. On reflection, and on your sister's representation, I am willing to admit that, in making peace with young Drood, you have a right to be met half-way. I will engage that you shall be, and even that young Drood shall make the first advance. This condition fulfilled, you will pledge me the honour of a Christian gentleman that the quarrel is for ever at an end on your side. What may be in your heart when you give him your hand, can only be known to the Searcher of all hearts; but it will never go well with you, if there be any treachery there. So far, as to that; next as to what I must again speak of as your infatuation. I understand it to have been confided to me, and to be known to no other person save your sister and yourself. Do I understand aright?'

Helena answered in a low voice: 'It is only known to us three who are here together.'

'It is not at all known to the young lady, your friend?'

'On my soul, no!'

'I require you, then, to give me your similar and solemn pledge, Mr. Neville, that it shall remain the secret it is, and that you will take no other action whatsoever upon it than endeavouring (and that most earnestly) to erase it from your mind. I will not tell you that it will soon pass; I will not tell you that it is the fancy of the moment; I will not tell you that such caprices have their rise and fall among the young and ardent every hour; I will leave you undisturbed in the belief that it has few parallels or none, that it will abide with you a long time, and that it will be very difficult to conquer. So much the more weight shall I attach to the pledge I require from you, when it is unreservedly given.'

The young man twice or thrice essayed to speak, but failed.

'Let me leave you with your sister, whom it is time you took home,' said Mr. Crisparkle. 'You will find me alone in my room by-and-bye.'

'Pray do not leave us yet,' Helena implored him. 'Another minute.'

'I should not,' said Neville, pressing his hand upon his face, 'have needed so much as another minute, if you had been less patient with me, Mr. Crisparkle, less considerate of me, and less unpretendingly good and true. Oh, if in my childhood I had known such a guide!'

'Follow your guide now, Neville,' murmured Helena, 'and follow him to Heaven!'

There was that in her tone which broke the good Minor Canon's voice, or it would have repudiated her exaltation of him. As it was, he laid a finger on his lips, and looked towards her brother.

'To say that I give both pledges, Mr. Crisparkle, out of my innermost heart, and to say that there is no treachery in it, is to say nothing!' Thus Neville, greatly moved. 'I beg your forgiveness for my miserable lapse into a burst of passion.'

'Not mine, Neville, not mine. You know with whom for-giveness lies, as the highest attribute conceivable. Miss Helena, you and your brother are twin children. You came into this world with the same dispositions, and you passed your younger days together surrounded by the same adverse

Mr. Crisparkle is overpaid

circumstances. What you have overcome in yourself, can you not overcome in him? You see the rock that lies in his course. Who but you can keep him clear of it?'

'Who but you, sir?' replied Helena. 'What is my influence, or my weak wisdom, compared with yours!'

'You have the wisdom of Love,' returned the Minor Canon, 'and it was the highest wisdom ever known upon this earth, remember. As to mine – but the less said of that commonplace commodity the better. Good-night!'

She took the hand he offered her, and gratefully and almost reverently raised it to her lips.

'Tut!' said the Minor Canon, softly, 'I am much overpaid!' And turned away.

Retracing his steps towards the Cathedral Close, he tried, as he went along in the dark, to think out the best means of bringing to pass what he had promised to effect, and what must somehow be done. 'I shall probably be asked to marry them,' he reflected, 'and I would they were married and gone! But this presses first.' He debated principally, whether he should write to young Drood, or whether he should speak to Jasper. The consciousness of being popular with the whole Cathedral establishment inclined him to the latter course, and the well-timed sight of the lighted Gate House decided him to take it. 'I will strike while the iron is hot,' he said, 'and see him now.'

Jasper was lying asleep on a couch before the fire, when, having ascended the postern stair, and received no answer to his knock at the door, Mr. Crisparkle gently turned the handle and looked in. Long afterwards he had cause to remember how Jasper sprang from the couch in a delirious state between sleeping and waking, crying out: 'What is the matter? Who did it?'

'It is only I, Jasper. I am sorry to have disturbed you.'

The glare of his eyes settled down into a look of recognition, and he moved a chair or two, to make a way to the fireside.

'I was dreaming at a great rate, and am glad to be disturbed from an indigestive after-dinner sleep. Not to mention that you are always welcome.'

'Thank you. I am not confident,' returned Mr. Crisparkle as he sat himself down in the easy chair placed for him, 'that my subject will at first sight be quite as welcome as myself; but I am a minister of peace, and I pursue my subject in the interests of peace. In a word, Jasper, I want to establish peace between these two young fellows.'

A very perplexed expression took hold of Mr. Jasper's face; a very perplexing expression too, for Mr. Crisparkle could make nothing of it.

'How?' was Jasper's inquiry, in a low and slow voice, after a silence.

'For the "How" I come to you. I want to ask you to do me the great favour and service of interposing with your nephew (I have already interposed with Mr. Neville), and getting him to write you a short note, in his lively way, saying that he is willing to shake hands. I know what a good-natured fellow he is, and what influence you have with him. And without in the least defending Mr. Neville, we must all admit that he was bitterly stung.'

Jasper turned that perplexed face towards the fire. Mr. Crisparkle continuing to observe it, found it even more perplexing than before, inasmuch as it seemed to denote (which could hardly be) some close internal calculation.

'I know that you are not prepossessed in Mr. Neville's favour,' the Minor Canon was going on, when Jasper stopped him:

'You have cause to say so. I am not, indeed.'

'Undoubtedly, and I admit his lamentable violence of temper, though I hope he and I will get the better of it between us. But I have exacted a very solemn promise from him as to his future demeanour towards your nephew, if you do kindly interpose; and I am sure he will keep it.'

'You are always responsible and trustworthy, Mr. Crisparkle. Do you really feel sure that you can answer for him so confidently?'

'I do.'

The perplexed and perplexing look vanished.

'Then you relieve my mind of a great dread, and a heavy weight,' said Jasper; 'I will do it.'

Mr. Crisparkle, delighted by the swiftness and completeness of his success, acknowledged it in the handsomest terms.

'I will do it,' repeated Jasper, 'for the comfort of having your guarantee against my vague and unformed fears. You will laugh – but do you keep a Diary?'

'A line for a day; not more.'

'A line for a day would be quite as much as my uneventful life would need, Heaven knows,' said Jasper, taking a book from a desk; 'but that my Diary is, in fact, a Diary of Ned's life too. You will laugh at this entry; you will guess when it was made:

'Past midnight. – After what I have just now seen, I have a morbid dread upon me of some horrible consequences resulting to my dear boy, that I cannot reason with or in any way contend against. All my efforts are vain. The demoniacal passion of this Neville Landless, his strength in his fury, and his savage rage for the destruction of its object, appal me. So profound is the impression, that twice since have I gone into my dear boy's room, to assure myself of his sleeping safely, and not lying dead in his blood.

'Here is another entry next morning:

'Ned up and away. Light-hearted and unsuspicious as ever. He laughed when I cautioned him, and said he was as good a man as Neville Landless any day. I told him that might be, but he was not as bad a man. He continued to make light of it, but I travelled with him as far as I could, and left him most unwillingly. I am unable to shake off these dark intangible presentiments of evil – if feelings founded upon staring facts are to be so called.

'Again and again,' said Jasper, in conclusion, twirling the leaves of the book before putting it by, 'I have relapsed into these moods, as other entries show. But I have now your assurance at my back, and shall put it in my book, and make it an antidote to my black humours.'

'Such an antidote, I hope,' returned Mr. Crisparkle, 'as will induce you before long to consign the black humours to the flames. I ought to be the last to find any fault with you this evening, when you have met my wishes so freely; but I must say, Jasper, that your devotion to your nephew has made you exaggerative here.'

'You are my witness,' said Jasper, shrugging his shoulders, 'what my state of mind honestly was, that night, before I sat down to write, and in what words I expressed it. You remember objecting to a word I used, as being too strong? It was a stronger word than any in my Diary.'

'Well, well. Try the antidote,' rejoined Mr. Crisparkle, 'and may it give you a brighter and better view of the case! We will discuss it no more, now. I have to thank you for myself, and I thank you sincerely.'

'You shall find,' said Jasper, as they shook hands, 'that I will not do the thing you wish me to do, by halves. I will take care that Ned, giving way at all, shall give way thoroughly.'

On the third day after this conversation, he called on Mr. Crisparkle with the following letter:

'MY DEAR JACK,

'I am touched by your account of your interview with Mr. Crisparkle, whom I much respect and esteem. At once I openly say that I forgot myself on that occasion quite as much as Mr. Landless did, and that I wish that bygone to be a bygone, and all to be right again.

'Look here, dear old boy. Ask Mr. Landless to dinner on Christmas Eve (the better the day the better the deed), and let there be only we three, and let us shake hands all round there and then, and say no more about it.

'My Dear Jack,

'Ever your most affectionate,

'EDWIN DROOD.

'P.S. – Love to Miss Pussy at the next music-lesson.'

'You expect Mr. Neville, then?' said Mr. Crisparkle. 'I count upon his coming,' said Mr. Jasper.

CHAPTER XI

A Picture and a Ring

BEHIND the most ancient part of Holborn, London, where certain gabled houses some centuries of age still stand looking on the public way, as if disconsolately looking for the Old Bourne that has long run dry, is a little nook composed of two irregular quadrangles, called Staple Inn. It is one of those nooks, the turning into which out of the clashing street, imparts to the relieved pedestrian the sensation of having put cotton in his ears, and velvet soles on his boots. It is one of those nooks where a few smoky sparrows twitter in smoky trees, as though they called to one another, 'Let us play at country,' and where a few feet of garden mould and a few yards of gravel enable them to do that refreshing violence to their tiny understandings. Moreover, it is one of those nooks which are legal nooks; and it contains a little Hall, with a little lantern in its roof: to what obstructive purposes devoted, and at whose expense, this history knoweth not.

In the days when Cloisterham took offence at the existence of a railroad afar off, as menacing that sensitive Constitution, the property of us Britons, the odd fortune of which sacred institution it is to be in exactly equal degrees croaked about, trembled for, and boasted of, whatever happens to anything, anywhere in the world: in those days no neighbouring architecture of lofty proportions had arisen to overshadow Staple Inn. The westering sun bestowed bright glances on it, and the south-west wind blew into it unimpeded.

Neither wind nor sun, however, favoured Staple Inn, one December afternoon towards six o'clock, when it was filled with fog, and candles shed murky and blurred rays through the windows of all its then-occupied sets of chambers; notably, from a set of chambers in a corner house in the little

inner quadrangle, presenting in black and white over its ugly
portal the mysterious inscription:

P

J   T

1747.

In which set of chambers, never having troubled his head
about the inscription, unless to bethink himself at odd times
on glancing up at it, that haply it might mean Perhaps John
Thomas, or Perhaps Joe Tyler, sat Mr. Grewgious writing by
his fire.

Who could have told, by looking at Mr. Grewgious,
whether he had ever known ambition or disappointment?
He had been bred to the Bar, and had laid himself out for
chamber practice; to draw deeds; 'convey the wise it call,' as
Pistol says. But Conveyancing and he had made such a very
indifferent marriage of it that they had separated by consent
– if there can be said to be separation where there has never
been coming together.

No. Coy Conveyancing would not come to Mr. Grewgious.
She was wooed, not won, and they went their several ways.
But an Arbitration being blown towards him by some unaccountable wind, and he gaining great credit in it as one
indefatigable in seeking out right and doing right, a pretty fat
Receivership was next blown into his pocket by a wind more
traceable to its source. So, by chance, he had found his niche.
Receiver and Agent now, to two rich estates, and deputing
their legal business, in an amount worth having, to a firm of
solicitors on the floor below, he had snuffed out his ambition
(supposing him to have ever lighted it) and had settled down
with his snuffers for the rest of his life under the dry vine and
fig-tree of P. J. T., who planted in seventeen-forty-seven.

Many accounts and account-books, many files of
correspondence, and several strong boxes, garnished Mr.
Grewgious's room. They can scarcely be represented as
having lumbered it, so conscientious and precise was their
orderly arrangement. The apprehension of dying suddenly,
and leaving one fact or one figure with any incomplete-
ness or obscurity attaching to it, would have stretched
Mr. Grewgious stone dead any day. The largest fidelity to a

trust was the life-blood of the man. There are sorts of life-blood that course more quickly, more gaily, more attractively; but there is no better sort in circulation.

There was no luxury in his room. Even its comforts were limited to its being dry and warm, and having a snug though faded fireside. What may be called its private life was confined to the hearth, and an easy chair, and an old-fashioned occasional round table that was brought out upon the rug after business hours, from a corner where it elsewise remained turned up like a shining mahogany shield. Behind it, when standing thus on the defensive, was a closet, usually containing something good to drink. An outer room was the clerk's room; Mr. Grewgious's sleeping-room was across the common stair; and he held some not empty cellarage at the bottom of the common stair. Three hundred days in the year, at least, he crossed over to the hotel in Furnival's Inn for his dinner, and after dinner crossed back again, to make the most of these simplicities until it should become broad business day once more, with P. J. T., date seventeen-forty-seven.

As Mr. Grewgious sat and wrote by his fire that afternoon, so did the clerk of Mr. Grewgious sit and write by *his* fire. A pale, puffy-faced, dark-haired person of thirty, with big dark eyes that wholly wanted lustre, and a dissatisfied doughy complexion, that seemed to ask to be sent to the baker's, this attendant was a mysterious being, possessed of some strange power over Mr. Grewgious. As though he had been called into existence, like a fabulous Familiar, by a magic spell which had failed when required to dismiss him, he stuck tight to Mr.3 Grewgious's stool, although Mr. Grewgious's comfort and convenience would manifestly have been advanced by dispossessing him. A gloomy person with tangled locks, and a general air of having been reared under the shadow of that baleful tree of Java which has given shelter to more lies than the whole botanical kingdom, Mr. Grewgious, nevertheless, treated him with unaccountable consideration.

'Now, Bazzard,' said Mr. Grewgious, on the entrance of his clerk: looking up from his papers as he arranged them for the night: 'what is in the wind besides fog?'

'Mr. Drood,' said Bazzard.

'What of him?'

'Has called,' said Bazzard.

'You might have shown him in.'

'I am doing it,' said Bazzard.

The visitor came in accordingly.

'Dear me!' said Mr. Grewgious, looking round his pair of office candles. 'I thought you had called and merely left your name, and gone. How do you do, Mr. Edwin? Dear me, you're choking!'

'It's this fog,' returned Edwin; 'and it makes my eyes smart, like cayenne pepper.'

'Is it really so bad as that? Pray undo your wrappers. It is fortunate I have so good a fire; but Mr. Bazzard has taken care of me.'

'No I haven't,' said Mr. Bazzard at the door.

'Ah! Then it follows that I must have taken care of myself without observing it,' said Mr. Grewgious. 'Pray be seated in my chair. No. I beg! Coming out of such an atmosphere, in *my* chair.'

Edwin took the easy chair in the corner; and the fog he had brought in with him, and the fog he took off with his greatcoat and neck-shawl, was speedily licked up by the eager fire.

'I look,' said Edwin, smiling, 'as if I had come to stop.'

'— By-the-bye,' cried Mr. Grewgious; 'excuse my interrupting you; do stop. The fog may clear in an hour or two. We can have dinner in from just across Holborn. You had better take your cayenne pepper here than outside; pray stop and dine.'

'You are very kind,' said Edwin, glancing about him, as though attracted by the notion of a new and relishing sort of gipsy-party.

'Not at all,' said Mr. Grewgious; '*you* are very kind to join issue with a bachelor in chambers, and take pot-luck. And I'll ask,' said Mr. Grewgious, dropping his voice, and speaking with a twinkling eye, as if inspired with a bright thought: 'I'll ask Bazzard. He mightn't like it else. Bazzard!'

Bazzard reappeared.

'Dine presently with Mr. Drood and me.'

'If I am ordered to dine, of course I will, sir,' was the gloomy answer.

'Save the man!' cried Mr. Grewgious. 'You're not ordered; you're invited.'

'Thank you, sir,' said Bazzard; 'in that case I don't care if I do.'

'That's arranged. And perhaps you wouldn't mind,' said Mr. Grewgious, 'stepping over to the hotel in Furnival's, and asking them to send in materials for laying the cloth. For dinner we'll have a tureen of the hottest and strongest soup available, and we'll have the best made-dish that can be recommended, and we'll have a joint (such as a haunch of mutton), and we'll have a goose, or a turkey, or any little stuffed thing of that sort that may happen to be in the bill of fare – in short, we'll have whatever there is on hand.'

These liberal directions Mr. Grewgious issued with his usual air of reading an inventory, or repeating a lesson, or doing anything else by rote. Bazzard, after drawing out the round table, withdrew to execute them.

'I was a little delicate, you see,' said Mr. Grewgious, in a lower tone, after his clerk's departure, 'about employing him in the foraging or commissariat department. Because he mightn't like it.'

'He seems to have his own way, sir,' remarked Edwin.

'His own way?' returned Mr. Grewgious. 'Oh dear no! Poor fellow, you quite mistake him. If he had his own way, he wouldn't be here.'

'I wonder where he would be!' Edwin thought. But he only thought it, because Mr. Grewgious came and stood himself with his back to the other corner of the fire, and his shoulder-blades against the chimneypiece, and collected his skirts for easy conversation.

'I take it, without having the gift of prophecy, that you have done me the favour of looking in to mention that you are going down yonder – where I can tell you, you are expected – and to offer to execute any little commission from me to my charming ward, and perhaps to sharpen me up a bit in my proceedings? Eh, Mr. Edwin?'

'I called, sir, before going down, as an act of attention.'

'Of attention!' said Mr. Grewgious. 'Ah! of course, not of impatience?'

'Impatience, sir?'

Mr. Grewgious had meant to be arch – not that he in the remotest degree expressed that meaning – and had brought himself into scarcely supportable proximity with the fire, as if to burn the fullest effect of his archness into himself, as other subtle impressions are burnt into hard metals. But his archness suddenly flying before the composed face and manner of his visitor, and only the fire remaining, he started and rubbed himself.

'I have lately been down yonder,' said Mr. Grewgious, rearranging his skirts; 'and that was what I referred to, when I said I could tell you you are expected.'

'Indeed, sir! Yes; I knew that Pussy was looking out for me.'

'Do you keep a cat down there?' asked Mr. Grewgious.

Edwin coloured a little, as he explained: 'I call Rosa Pussy.'

'Oh, really,' said Mr. Grewgious, smoothing down his head; 'that's very affable.'

Edwin glanced at his face, uncertain whether or no he seriously objected to the appellation. But Edwin might as well have glanced at the face of a clock.

'A pet name, sir,' he explained again.

'Umps,' said Mr. Grewgious, with a nod. But with such an extraordinary compromise between an unqualified assent and a qualified dissent, that his visitor was much disconcerted.

'Did PRosa—' Edwin began, by way of recovering himself.

'PRosa?' repeated Mr. Grewgious.

'I was going to say Pussy, and changed my mind; – did she tell you anything about the Landlesses?'

'No,' said Mr. Grewgious. 'What is the Landlesses? An estate? A villa? A farm?'

'A brother and sister. The sister is at the Nuns' House, and has become a great friend of P—'

'PRosa's,' Mr. Grewgious struck in, with a fixed face.

'She is a strikingly handsome girl, sir, and I thought she might have been described to you, or presented to you, perhaps?'

'Neither,' said Mr. Grewgious. 'But here is Bazzard.'

Bazzard returned, accompanied by two waiters – an immoveable waiter, and a flying waiter; and the three brought in with them as much fog as gave a new roar to the fire. The flying waiter, who had brought everything on his shoulders, laid the cloth with amazing rapidity and dexterity; while the immoveable waiter, who had brought nothing, found fault with him. The flying waiter then highly polished all the glasses he had brought, and the immoveable waiter looked through them. The flying waiter then flew across Holborn for the soup, and flew back again, and then took another flight for the made-dish, and flew back again, and then took another flight for the joint and poultry, and flew back again, and between whiles took supplementary flights for a great variety of articles, as it was discovered from time to time that the immoveable waiter had forgotten them all. But let the flying waiter cleave the air as he might, he was always reproached on his return by the immoveable waiter for bringing fog with him, and being out of breath. At the conclusion of the repast, by which time the flying waiter was severely blown, the immoveable waiter gathered up the tablecloth under his arm with a grand air, and having sternly (not to say with indignation) looked on at the flying waiter while he set clean glasses round, directed a valedictory glance towards Mr. Grewgious, conveying: 'Let it be clearly understood between us that the reward is mine, and that Nil is the claim of this slave,' and pushed the flying waiter before him out of the room.

It was like a highly finished miniature painting representing My Lords of the Circumlocutional Department, Commandership-in-Chief of any sort, Government. It was quite an edifying little picture to be hung on the line in the National Gallery.

As the fog had been the proximate cause of this sumptuous repast, so the fog served for its general sauce. To hear the outdoor clerks, sneezing, wheezing, and beating their feet on the gravel was a zest far surpassing Doctor Kitchener's. To bid, with a shiver, the unfortunate flying waiter shut the door before he had opened it, was a condiment of a profounder flavour than Harvey. And here let it be noticed, parenthetically, that the leg of this young man in its application to the door, evinced the finest sense of touch: always preceding himself and tray (with something of an angling air about it), by some seconds: and always lingering after he and the tray had disappeared, like Macbeth's leg when accompanying him off the stage with reluctance to the assassination of Duncan.

The host had gone below to the cellar, and had brought up bottles of ruby, straw-coloured, and golden, drinks, which had ripened long ago in lands where no fogs are, and had since lain slumbering in the shade. Sparkling and tingling after so long a nap, they pushed at their corks to help the corkscrew (like prisoners helping rioters to force their gates), and danced out gaily. If P. J. T. in seventeen-forty-seven, or in any other year of his period, drank such wines – then, for a certainty, P. J. T. was Pretty Jolly Too.

Externally, Mr. Grewgious showed no signs of being mellowed by these glowing vintages. Instead of his drinking them, they might have been poured over him in his high-dried snuff form, and run to waste, for any lights and shades they caused to flicker over his face. Neither was his manner influenced. But, in his wooden way, he had observant eyes for Edwin; and when, at the end of dinner, he motioned Edwin back to his own easy chair in the fireside corner, and Edwin luxuriously sank into it after very brief remonstrance, Mr. Grewgious, as he turned his seat round towards the fire too, and smoothed his head and face, might have been seen looking at his visitor between his smoothing fingers.

'Bazzard!' said Mr. Grewgious, suddenly turning to him.

'I follow you, sir,' returned Bazzard; who had done his work of consuming meat and drink, in a workmanlike manner, though mostly in speechlessness.

'I drink to you, Bazzard; Mr. Edwin, success to Mr. Bazzard!'

'Success to Mr. Bazzard!' echoed Edwin, with a totally unfounded appearance of enthusiasm, and with the unspoken addition: – 'What in, I wonder!'

'And May!' pursued Mr. Grewgious – 'I am not at liberty to be definite – May! – my conversational powers are so very limited that I know I shall not come well out of this – May! – it ought to be put imaginatively, but I have no imagination – May! – the thorn of anxiety is as near the mark as I am likely to get – May it come out at last!'

Mr. Bazzard, with a frowning smile at the fire, put a hand into his tangled locks, as if the thorn of anxiety were there; then into his waistcoat, as if it were there; then into his pockets, as if it were there. In all these movements he was closely followed by the eyes of Edwin, as if that young gentleman expected to see the thorn in action. It was not produced, however, and Mr. Bazzard merely said: 'I follow you, sir, and I thank you.'

'I am going,' said Mr. Grewgious, jingling his glass on the table, with one hand, and bending aside under cover of the other, to whisper to Edwin, 'to drink to my ward. But I put Bazzard first. He mightn't like it else.'

This was said with a mysterious wink; or what would have been a wink if, in Mr. Grewgious's hands, it could have been quick enough. So Edwin winked responsively, without the least idea what he meant by doing so.

'And now,' said Mr. Grewgious, 'I devote a bumper to the fair and fascinating Miss Rosa. Bazzard, the fair and fascinating Miss Rosa!'

'I follow you, sir,' said Bazzard, 'and I pledge you!'

'And so do I!' said Edwin.

'Lord bless me!' cried Mr. Grewgious, breaking the blank silence which of course ensued: though why these pauses *should* come upon us when we have performed any small social rite, not directly inducive of self-examination or mental despondency, who can tell! 'I am a particularly Angular man, and yet I fancy (if I may use the word, not having a morsel of fancy), that I could draw a picture of a true lover's state of mind, to-night.'

'Let us follow you, sir,' said Bazzard, 'and have the picture.'

'Mr. Edwin will correct it where it's wrong,' resumed Mr. Grewgious, 'and will throw in a few touches from the life. I dare say it is wrong in many particulars, and wants many touches from the life, for I was born a Chip, and have neither soft sympathies nor soft experiences. Well! I hazard the guess that the true lover's mind is completely permeated by the beloved object of his affections. I hazard the guess that her dear name is precious to him, cannot be heard or repeated without emotion, and is preserved sacred. If he has any distinguishing appellation of fondness for her, it is reserved for her, and is not for common ears. A name that it would be a privilege to call her by, being alone with her own bright self, it would be a liberty, a coldness, an insensibility, almost a breach of good faith, to flaunt elsewhere.'

It was wonderful to see Mr. Grewgious sitting bolt upright, with his hands on his knees, continuously chopping this discourse out of himself: much as a charity boy with a very good memory might get his catechism said: and evincing no correspondent emotion whatever, unless in a certain occasional little tingling perceptible at the end of his nose.

'My picture,' Mr. Grewgious proceeded, 'goes on to represent (under correction from you, Mr. Edwin), the true lover as ever impatient to be in the presence or vicinity of the beloved object of his affections; as caring very little for his ease in any other society; and as constantly seeking that. If I was to say seeking that, as a bird seeks its nest, I should make an ass of myself, because that would trench upon what I understand to be poetry; and I am so far from trenching upon poetry at any time, that I never, to my knowledge, got within ten thousand miles of it. And I am besides totally unacquainted with the habits of birds, except the birds of Staple Inn, who seek their nests on ledges, and in gutter-pipes and chimneypots, not constructed for them by the beneficent hand of Nature. I beg, therefore, to be understood as forgoing the bird's-nest. But my picture does represent the true lover as having no existence separable from that of the beloved object of his affections, and as living at once a doubled life and a halved life. And if I do not clearly express what I mean by that, it is either for the reason that having no conversational powers, I cannot express what I mean, or that having no meaning, I do not mean what I fail to express. Which, to the best of my belief, is not the case.'

Edwin had turned red and turned white, as certain points of this picture came into the light. He now sat looking at the fire, and bit his lip.

'The speculations of an Angular man,' resumed Mr. Grewgious, still sitting and speaking exactly as before, 'are probably erroneous on so globular a topic. But I figure to myself (subject, as before, to Mr. Edwin's correction), that there can be no coolness, no lassitude, no doubt, no indifference, no half fire and half smoke state of mind, in a real lover. Pray am I at all near the mark in my picture?'

As abrupt in his conclusion as in his commencement and progress, he jerked this inquiry at Edwin, and stopped when one might have supposed him in the middle of his oration.

'I should say, sir,' stammered Edwin, 'as you refer the question to me—'

'Yes,' said Mr. Grewgious, 'I refer it to you, as an authority.'

'I should say then, sir,' Edwin went on, embarrassed, 'that the picture you have drawn, is generally correct; but I submit that perhaps you may be rather hard upon the unlucky lover.'

'Likely so,' assented Mr. Grewgious, 'likely so. I am a hard man in the grain.'

'He may not show,' said Edwin, 'all he feels; or he may not—'

There he stopped so long, to find the rest of his sentence, that Mr. Grewgious rendered his difficulty a thousand times the greater, by unexpectedly striking in with:

'No to be sure; he *may* not!'

After that, they all sat silent; the silence of Mr. Bazzard being occasioned by slumber.

'His responsibility is very great though,' said Mr. Grewgious, at length, with his eyes on the fire.

Edwin nodded assent, with *his* eyes on the fire.

'And let him be sure that he trifles with no one,' said Mr. Grewgious; 'neither with himself, nor with any other.'

Edwin bit his lip again, and still sat looking at the fire.

'He must not make a plaything of a treasure. Woe betide him if he does! Let him take that well to heart,' said Mr. Grewgious.

Though he said these things in short dry sentences, much as the supposititious charity boy just now referred to, might have repeated a verse or two from the Book of Proverbs, there was something dreamy (for so literal a man) in the way in which he now shook his right forefinger at the live coals in the grate, and again fell silent.

But not for long. As he sat upright and stiff in his chair, he suddenly rapped his knees, like the carved image of some queer Joss or other coming out of its reverie, and said: 'We must finish this bottle, Mr. Edwin. Let me help you. I'll help Bazzard, too, though he *is* asleep. He mightn't like it else.'

He helped them both, and helped himself, and drained his glass, and stood it bottom upward on the table, as though he had just caught a blue-bottle in it.

'And now, Mr. Edwin,' he proceeded, wiping his mouth and hands upon his handkerchief: 'to a little piece of business. You received from me, the other day, a certified copy of Miss Rosa's father's will. You knew its contents before, but you received it from me as a matter of business. I should have sent it to Mr. Jasper, but for Miss Rosa's wishing it to come straight to you, in preference. You received it?'

'Quite safely, sir.'

'You should have acknowledged its receipt,' said Mr. Grewgious, 'business being business all the world over. However, you did not.'

'I meant to have acknowledged it when I first came in this evening, sir.'

'Not a business-like acknowledgement,' returned Mr. Grewgious; 'however, let that pass. Now, in that document you have observed a few words of kindly allusion to its being left to me to discharge a little trust, confided to me in conversation, at such time as I in my discretion may think best.'

'Yes, sir.'

'Mr. Edwin, it came into my mind just now, when I was looking at the fire, that I could, in my discretion, acquit myself of that trust at no better time than the present. Favour me with your attention, half a minute.'

He took a bunch of keys from his pocket, singled out by the candle-light the key he wanted, and then, with a candle in his hand, went to a bureau or escritoire, unlocked it, touched the spring of a little secret drawer, and took from it an ordinary ring-case made for a single ring. With this in his hand, he returned to his chair. As he held it up for the young man to see, his hand trembled.

'Mr. Edwin, this rose of diamonds and rubies delicately set in gold, was a ring belonging to Miss Rosa's mother. It was removed from her dead hand, in my presence, with such distracted grief as I hope it may never be my lot to contemplate again. Hard man as I am, I am not hard enough for that. See how bright these stones shine!' opening the case. 'And yet the eyes that were so much brighter, and that so often looked upon them with a light and a proud heart, have been ashes among ashes, and dust among dust, some years! If I had any imagination (which it is needless to say I have not), I might imagine that the lasting beauty of these stones was almost cruel.'

He closed the case again as he spoke.

'This ring was given to the young lady who was drowned so early in her beautiful and happy career, by her husband, when they first plighted their faith to one another. It was he who removed it from her unconscious hand, and it was he who, when his death drew very near, placed it in mine. The trust in which I received it, was, that, you and Miss Rosa growing to manhood and womanhood, and your betrothal prospering and coming to maturity, I should give it to you to place upon her finger. Failing those desired results, it was to remain in my possession.'

Some trouble was in the young man's face, and some indecision was in the action of his hand, as Mr. Grewgious, looking steadfastly at him, gave him the ring.

'Your placing it on her finger,' said Mr. Grewgious, 'will be the solemn seal upon your strict fidelity to the living and the dead. You are going to her, to make the last irrevocable preparations for your marriage. Take it with you.'

The young man took the little case, and placed it in his breast.

'If anything should be amiss, if anything should be even slightly wrong, between you; if you should have any secret consciousness that you are committing yourself to this step for no higher reason than because you have long been accustomed to look forward to it; then,' said Mr. Grewgious, 'I charge you once more, by the living and by the dead, to bring that ring back to me!'

Here Bazzard awoke himself by his own snoring; and, as is usual in such cases, sat apoplectically staring at vacancy, as defying vacancy to accuse him of having been asleep.

'Bazzard!' said Mr. Grewgious, harder than ever.

'I follow you, sir,' said Bazzard, 'and I have been following you.'

'In discharge of a trust, I have handed Mr. Edwin Drood a ring of diamonds and rubies. You see?'

Edwin reproduced the little case, and opened it; and Bazzard looked into it.

'I follow you both, sir,' returned Bazzard, 'and I witness the transaction.'

Evidently anxious to get away and be alone, Edwin Drood now resumed his outer clothing, muttering something about time and appointments. The fog was reported no clearer (by the flying waiter, who alighted from a speculative flight in the coffee interest), but he went out into it; and Bazzard, after his manner, 'followed' him.

Mr. Grewgious, left alone, walked softly and slowly to and fro, for an hour and more. He was restless to-night, and seemed dispirited.

'I hope I have done right,' he said. 'The appeal to him seemed necessary. It was hard to lose the ring, and yet it must have gone from me very soon.'

He closed the empty little drawer with a sigh, and shut and locked the escritoire, and came back to the solitary fireside.

'Her ring,' he went on. 'Will it come back to me? My mind hangs about her ring very uneasily to-night. But that is explainable. I have had it so long, and I have prized it so much! I wonder—'

He was in a wondering mood as well as a restless; for, though he checked himself at that point, and took another walk, he resumed his wondering when he sat down again.

'I wonder (for the ten thousandth time, and what a weak fool I, for what can it signify now!) whether he confided the charge of their orphan child to me, because he knew— Good God, how like her mother she has become!

'I wonder whether he ever so much as suspected that some one doted on her, at a hopeless, speechless distance, when he struck in and won her. I wonder whether it ever crept into his mind who that unfortunate some one was!

'I wonder whether I shall sleep to-night! At all events, I will shut out the world with the bedclothes, and try.'

Mr. Grewgious crossed the staircase to his raw and foggy bedroom, and was soon ready for bed. Dimly catching sight of his face in the misty looking-glass, he held his candle to it for a moment.

'A likely some one, *you*, to come into anybody's thoughts in such an aspect!' he exclaimed. 'There, there, there! Get to bed, poor man, and cease to jabber!'

With that, he extinguished his light, pulled up the bed-clothes around him, and with another sigh shut out the world. And yet there are such unexplored romantic nooks in the unlikeliest men, that even old tinderous and touch-woody P. J. T. Possibly Jabbered Thus, at some odd times, in or about seventeen-forty-seven.

CHAPTER XII

A Night with Durdles

WHEN Mr. Sapsea has nothing better to do, towards evening, and finds the contemplation of his own profundity becoming a little monotonous in spite of the vastness of the subject, he often takes an airing in the Cathedral Close and thereabout. He likes to pass the churchyard with a swelling air of proprietorship, and to encourage in his breast a sort of benignant-landlord feeling, in that he has been bountiful towards that meritorious tenant, Mrs. Sapsea, and has publicly given her a prize. He likes to see a stray face or two looking in through the railings, and perhaps reading his inscription. Should he meet a stranger coming from the churchyard with a quick step, he is morally convinced that the stranger is 'with a blush retiring,' as monumentally directed.

Mr. Sapsea's importance has received enhancement, for he has become Mayor of Cloisterham. Without mayors and many of them, it cannot be disputed that the whole framework of society – Mr. Sapsea is confident that he invented that forcible figure – would fall to pieces. Mayors have been knighted for 'going up' with addresses: explosive machines intrepidly discharging shot and shell into the English Grammar. Mr. Sapsea may 'go up' with an address. Rise, Sir Thomas Sapsea! Of such is the salt of the earth.

Mr. Sapsea has improved the acquaintance of Mr. Jasper, since their first meeting to partake of port, epitaph, backgammon, beef, and salad. Mr. Sapsea has been received at the Gate House with kindred hospitality; and on that occasion Mr. Jasper seated himself at the piano, and sang to him, tickling his ears: – figuratively long enough to present a considerable area for tickling. What Mr. Sapsea likes in that young man, is, that he is always ready to profit by the wisdom of his elders, and that he is sound, sir, at the core. In proof of which, he sang to Mr. Sapsea that evening, no kickshaw

ditties, favourites with national enemies, but gave him the
genuine George the Third home-brewed; exhorting him (as
'my brave boys') to reduce to a smashed condition all other
islands but this island, and all continents, peninsulas, isth-
muses, promontories, and other geographical forms of land
soever, besides sweeping the seas in all directions. In short,
he rendered it pretty clear that Providence made a distinct
mistake in originating so small a nation of hearts of oak, and
so many other verminous peoples.

Mr. Sapsea, walking slowly this moist evening near the
churchyard with his hands behind him, on the look out for
a blushing and retiring stranger, turns a corner, and comes
instead into the goodly presence of the Dean, conversing
with the Verger and Mr. Jasper. Mr. Sapsea makes his obei-
sance, and is instantly stricken far more ecclesiastical than
any Archbishop of York, or Canterbury.

'You are evidently going to write a book about us, Mr.
Jasper,' quoth the Dean; 'to write a book about us. Well! We
are very ancient, and we ought to make a good book. We are
not so richly endowed in possessions as in age; but perhaps
you will put *that* in your book, among other things, and call
attention to our wrongs.'

Mr. Tope, as in duty bound, is greatly entertained by this.

'I really have no intention at all, sir,' replies Jasper, 'of
turning author, or archæologist. It is but a whim of mine.
And even for my whim, Mr. Sapsea here is more accountable
than I am.'

'How so, Mr. Mayor?' says the Dean, with a nod of good-
natured recognition of his Fetch. 'How is that, Mr. Mayor?'

'I am not aware,' Mr. Sapsea remarks, looking about him
for information, 'to what the Very Reverend the Dean does
me the honour of referring.' And then falls to studying his
original in minute points of detail.

'Durdles,' Mr. Tope hints.

'Ay!' the Dean echoes; 'Durdles, Durdles!'

'The truth is, sir,' explains Jasper, 'that my curiosity in the
man was first really stimulated by Mr. Sapsea. Mr. Sapsea's
knowledge of mankind, and power of drawing out whatever
is recluse or odd around him, first led to my bestowing a

second thought upon the man: though of course I had met him constantly about. You would not be surprised by this, Mr. Dean, if you had seen Mr. Sapsea deal with him in his own parlour, as I did.'

'Oh!' cries Sapsea, picking up the ball thrown to him with ineffable complacency and pomposity; 'yes, yes. The Very Reverend the Dean refers to that? Yes. I happened to bring Durdles and Mr. Jasper together. I regard Durdles as a Character.'

'A character, Mr. Sapsea, that with a few skilful touches you turn inside out,' says Jasper.

'Nay, not quite that,' returns the lumbering auctioneer. 'I may have a little influence over him, perhaps; and a little insight into his character, perhaps. The Very Reverend the Dean will please to bear in mind that I have seen the world.' Here Mr. Sapsea gets a little behind the Dean, to inspect his coat-buttons.

'Well!' says the Dean, looking about him to see what has become of his copyist: 'I hope, Mr. Mayor, you will use your study and knowledge of Durdles to the good purpose of exhorting him not to break our worthy and respected Choir Master's neck; we cannot afford it; his head and voice are much too valuable to us.'

Mr. Tope is again highly entertained, and, having fallen into respectful convulsions of laughter, subsides into a deferential murmur, importing that surely any gentleman would deem it a pleasure and an honour to have his neck broken, in return for such a compliment from such a source.

'I will take it upon myself, sir,' observes Sapsea, loftily, 'to answer for Mr. Jasper's neck. I will tell Durdles to be careful of it. He will mind what *I* say. How is it at present endangered?' he inquires, looking about him with magnificent patronage.

'Only by my making a moonlight expedition with Durdles among the tombs, vaults, towers, and ruins,' returns Jasper. 'You remember suggesting when you brought us together, that, as a lover of the picturesque, it might be worth my while?'

Durdles cautions Mr. Sapsea against boasting

'*I* remember!' replies the auctioneer. And the solemn idiot really believes that he does remember.

'Profiting by your hint,' pursues Jasper, 'I have had some day-rambles with the extraordinary old fellow, and we are to make a moonlight hole-and-corner exploration to-night.'

'And here he is,' says the Dean.

Durdles, with his dinner-bundle in his hand, is indeed beheld slouching towards them. Slouching nearer, and perceiving the Dean, he pulls off his hat, and is slouching away with it under his arm, when Mr. Sapsea stops him.

'Mind you take care of my friend,' is the injunction Mr. Sapsea lays upon him.

'What friend o' yourn is dead?' asks Durdles. 'No orders has come in for any friend o' yourn.'

'I mean my live friend, there.'

'Oh! Him?' says Durdles. 'He can take care of himself, can Mister Jarsper.'

'But do you take care of him too,' says Sapsea.

Whom Durdles (there being command in his tone) surlily surveys from head to foot.

'With submission to his Reverence the Dean, if you'll mind what concerns you, Mr. Sapsea, Durdles he'll mind what concerns him.'

'You're out of temper,' says Mr. Sapsea, winking to the company to observe how smoothly he will manage him. 'My friend concerns me, and Mr. Jasper is my friend. And you are my friend.'

'Don't you get into a bad habit of boasting,' retorts Durdles, with a grave cautionary nod. 'It'll grow upon you.'

'You are out of temper,' says Sapsea again; reddening, but again winking to the company.

'I own to it,' returns Durdles; 'I don't like liberties.'

Mr. Sapsea winks a third wink to the company, as who should say: 'I think you will agree with me that I have settled *his* business;' and stalks out of the controversy.

Durdles then gives the Dean a good-evening, and adding, as he puts his hat on, 'You'll find me at home, Mister Jarsper, as agreed, when you want me; I'm a going home to clean myself,' soon slouches out of sight. This going home to

clean himself is one of the man's incomprehensible compromises with inexorable facts; he, and his hat, and his
boots, and his clothes, never showing any trace of cleaning,
but being uniformly in one condition of dust and grit.

The lamplighter now dotting the quiet Close with specks
of light, and running at a great rate up and down his little
ladder with that object – his little ladder under the sacred
shadow of whose inconvenience generations had grown up,
and which all Cloisterham would have stood aghast at the
idea of abolishing – the Dean withdraws to his dinner, Mr.
Tope to his tea, and Mr. Jasper to his piano. There, with no
light but that of the fire, he sits chanting choir-music in a low
and beautiful voice, for two or three hours; in short, until it
has been for some time dark, and the moon is about to rise.

Then, he closes his piano softly, softly changes his coat for
a pea-jacket with a goodly wicker-cased bottle in its largest
pocket, and, putting on a low-crowned flap-brimmed hat,
goes softly out. Why does he move so softly to-night? No
outward reason is apparent for it. Can there be any sympathetic reason crouching darkly within him?

Repairing to Durdles's unfinished house, or hole in the
city wall, and seeing a light within it, he softly picks his course
among the gravestones, monuments, and stony lumber of
the yard, already touched here and there, sidewise, by the
rising moon. The two journeymen have left their two great
saws sticking in their blocks of stone; and two skeleton journeymen out of the Dance of Death might be grinning in the
shadow of their sheltering sentry-boxes, about to slash away
at cutting out the gravestones of the next two people destined
to die in Cloisterham. Likely enough, the two think little of
that now, being alive, and perhaps merry. Curious, to make a
guess at the two; – or say at one of the two!

'Ho! Durdles!'

The light moves, and he appears with it at the door. He
would seem to have been 'cleaning himself' with the aid of a
bottle, jug, and tumbler; for no other cleansing instruments
are visible in the bare brick room with rafters overhead and
no plastered ceiling, into which he shows his visitor.

'Are you ready?'

'I am ready, Mister Jarsper. Let the old 'uns come out if they dare, when we go among their tombs. My spirits is ready for 'em.'

'Do you mean animal spirits, or ardent?'

'The one's the t'other,' answers Durdles, 'and I mean 'em both.'

He takes a lantern from a hook, puts a match or two in his pocket wherewith to light it, should there be need, and they go out together, dinner-bundle and all.

Surely an unaccountable sort of expedition! That Durdles himself, who is always prowling among old graves and ruins, like a Ghoule – that he should be stealing forth to climb, and dive, and wander without an object, is nothing extraordinary; but that the Choir Master or any one else should hold it worth his while to be with him, and to study moonlight effects in such company, is another affair. Surely an unaccountable sort of expedition therefore!

''Ware that there mound by the yard gate, Mister Jarsper.'

'I see it. What is it?'

'Lime.'

Mr. Jasper stops, and waits for him to come up, for he lags behind. 'What you call quick-lime?'

'Ay!' says Durdles; 'quick enough to eat your boots. With a little handy stirring, quick enough to eat your bones.'

They go on, presently passing the red windows of the Travellers' Twopenny, and emerging into the clear moonlight of the Monks' Vineyard. This crossed, they come to Minor Canon Corner: of which the greater part lies in shadow until the moon shall rise higher in the sky.

The sound of a closing house door strikes their ears, and two men come out. These are Mr. Crisparkle and Neville. Jasper, with a strange and sudden smile upon his face, lays the palm of his hand upon the breast of Durdles, stopping him where he stands.

At that end of Minor Canon Corner the shadow is profound in the existing state of the light: at that end, too, is a piece of old dwarf wall, breast high, the only remaining boundary of what was once a garden, but is now the thoroughfare. Jasper and Durdles would have turned this wall in another instant; but, stopping so short, stand behind it.

'Those two are only sauntering,' Jasper whispers; 'they will go out into the moonlight soon. Let us keep quiet here, or they will detain us, or want to join us, or what not.'

Durdles nods assent, and falls to munching some fragments from his bundle. Jasper folds his arms upon the top of the wall, and, with his chin resting on them, watches. He takes no note whatever of the Minor Canon, but watches Neville, as though his eye were at the trigger of a loaded rifle, and he had covered him, and were going to fire. A sense of destructive power is so expressed in his face, that even Durdles pauses in his munching, and looks at him, with an unmunched something in his cheek.

Meanwhile Mr. Crisparkle and Neville walk to and fro, quietly talking together. What they say cannot be heard consecutively; but Mr. Jasper has already distinguished his own name more than once.

'This is the first day of the week,' Mr. Crisparkle can be distinctly heard to observe, as they turn back; 'and the last day of the week is Christmas Eve.'

'You may be certain of me, sir.'

The echoes were favourable at those points, but as the two approach, the sound of their talking becomes confused again. The word 'confidence,' shattered by the echoes, but still capable of being pieced together, is uttered by Mr. Crisparkle. As they draw still nearer, this fragment of a reply is heard: 'Not deserved yet, but shall be, sir.' As they turn away again, Jasper again hears his own name, in connexion with the words from Mr. Crisparkle: 'Remember that I said I answered for you confidently.' Then the sound of their talk becomes confused again; they halting for a little while, and some earnest action on the part of Neville succeeding. When they move once more, Mr. Crisparkle is seen to look up at the sky, and to point before him. They then slowly disappear; passing out into the moonlight at the opposite end of the Corner.

It is not until they are gone, that Mr. Jasper moves. But then he turns to Durdles, and bursts into a fit of laughter.

Durdles, who still has that suspended something in his cheek, and who sees nothing to laugh at, stares at him until Mr. Jasper lays his face down on his arms to have his laugh out. Then Durdles bolts the something, as if desperately resigning himself to indigestion.

Among those secluded nooks there is very little stir or movement after dark. There is little enough in the high-tide of the day, but there is next to none at night. Besides that the cheerfully frequented High Street lies nearly parallel to the spot (the old Cathedral rising between the two), and is the natural channel in which the Cloisterham traffic flows, a certain awful hush pervades the ancient pile, the cloisters, and the churchyard, after dark, which not many people care to encounter. Ask the first hundred citizens of Cloisterham, met at random in the streets at noon, if they believed in ghosts, they would tell you no; but put them to choose at night between these eerie Precincts and the thoroughfare of shops, and you would find that ninety-nine declared for the longer round and the more frequented way. The cause of this is not to be found in any local superstition that attaches to the Precincts – albeit a mysterious lady, with a child in her arms and a rope dangling from her neck, has been seen flitting about there by sundry witnesses as intangible as herself – but it is to be sought in the innate shrinking of dust with the breath of life in it, from dust out of which the breath of life has passed; also, in the widely diffused, and almost as widely unacknowledged, reflection: 'If the dead do, under any circumstances, become visible to the living, these are such likely surroundings for the purpose that I, the living, will get out of them as soon as I can.'

Hence, when Mr. Jasper and Durdles pause to glance around them, before descending into the crypt by a small side door of which the latter has a key, the whole expanse of moonlight in their view is utterly deserted. One might fancy that the tide of life was stemmed by Mr. Jasper's own Gate House. The murmur of the tide is heard beyond; but no wave passes the archway, over which his lamp burns red behind his curtain, as if the building were a Lighthouse.

They enter, locking themselves in, descend the rugged steps, and are down in the crypt. The lantern is not wanted, for the moonlight strikes in at the groined windows, bare of glass, the broken frames for which cast patterns on the ground. The heavy pillars which support the roof engender masses of black shade, but between them there are lanes of light. Up and down these lanes, they walk, Durdles discoursing of the 'old 'uns' he yet counts on disinterring, and slapping a wall, in which he considers 'a whole family on 'em' to be stoned and earthed up, just as if he were a familiar friend of the family. The taciturnity of Durdles is for the time overcome by Mr. Jasper's wicker bottle, which circulates freely; – in the sense, that is to say, that its contents enter freely into Mr. Durdles's circulation, while Mr. Jasper only rinses his mouth once, and casts forth the rinsing.

They are to ascend the great Tower. On the steps by which they rise to the Cathedral, Durdles pauses for new store of breath. The steps are very dark, but out of the darkness they can see the lanes of light they have traversed. Durdles seats himself upon a step. Mr. Jasper seats himself upon another. The odour from the wicker bottle (which has somehow passed into Durdles's keeping), soon intimates that the cork has been taken out; but this is not ascertainable through the sense of sight, since neither can descry the other. And yet, in talking, they turn to one another, as though their faces could commune together.

'This is good stuff, Mister Jarsper!'

'It is very good stuff, I hope. I bought it on purpose.'

'They don't show, you see, the old 'uns don't, Mister Jarsper!'

'It would be a more confused world than it is, if they could.'

'Well, it *would* lead towards a mixing of things,' Durdles acquiesces: pausing on the remark, as if the idea of ghosts had not previously presented itself to him in a merely inconvenient light, domestically, or chronologically. 'But do you think there may be ghosts of other things, though not of men and women?'

'What things? Flower-beds and watering-pots? Horses and harness?'

'No. Sounds.'

'What sounds?'

'Cries.'

'What cries do you mean? Chairs to mend?'

'No. I mean screeches. Now, I'll tell you, Mister Jarsper. Wait a bit till I put the bottle right.' Here the cork is evidently taken out again, and replaced again. 'There! *Now* it's right! This time last year, only a few days later, I happened to have been doing what was correct by the season, in the way of giving it the welcome it had a right to expect, when them town-boys set on me at their worst. At length I gave 'em the slip, and turned in here. And here I fell asleep. And what woke me? The ghost of a cry. The ghost of one terrific shriek, which shriek was followed by the ghost of the howl of a dog: a long dismal woeful howl, such as a dog gives when a person's dead. That was *my* last Christmas Eve.'

'What do you mean?' is the very abrupt, and, one might say, fierce retort.

'I mean that I made inquiries everywheres about, and that no living ears but mine heard either that cry or that howl. So I say they was both ghosts; though why they came to me, I've never made out.'

'I thought you were another kind of man,' says Jasper, scornfully.

'So I thought, myself,' answers Durdles with his usual composure; 'and yet I was picked out for it.'

Jasper had risen suddenly, when he asked him what he meant, and he now says, 'Come; we shall freeze here; lead the way.'

Durdles complies, not over-steadily; opens the door at the top of the steps with the key he has already used; and so emerges on the Cathedral level, in a passage at the side of the chancel. Here, the moonlight is so very bright again that the colours of the nearest stained-glass window are thrown upon their faces. The appearance of the unconscious Durdles, holding the door open for his companion to follow, as if from the grave, is ghastly enough, with a purple band across his face, and a yellow splash upon his brow; but he bears the close scrutiny of his companion in an insensible way, although it is prolonged while the latter fumbles among his pockets for a key confided to him that will open an iron gate and enable them to pass to the staircase of the great tower.

'That and the bottle are enough for you to carry,' he says, giving it to Durdles; 'hand your bundle to me; I am younger and longer-winded than you.' Durdles hesitates for a moment between bundle and bottle; but gives the preference to the bottle as being by far the better company, and consigns the dry weight to his fellow-explorer.

Then they go up the winding staircase of the great tower, toilsomely, turning and turning, and lowering their heads to avoid the stairs above, or the rough stone pivot around which they twist. Durdles has lighted his lantern, by drawing from the cold hard wall a spark of that mysterious fire which lurks in everything, and, guided by this speck, they clamber up among the cobwebs and the dust. Their way lies through strange places. Twice or thrice they emerge into level low-arched galleries, whence they can look down into the moonlit nave; and where Durdles, waving his lantern, shows the dim angels' heads upon the corbels of the roof, seeming to watch their progress. Anon, they turn into narrower and steeper staircases, and the night air begins to blow upon them, and the chirp of some startled jackdaw or frightened rook pre-cedes the heavy beating of wings in a confined space, and the beating down of dust and straws upon their heads. At last, leaving their light behind a stair – for it blows fresh up here – they look down on Cloisterham, fair to see in the moonlight: its ruined habitations and sanctuaries of the dead, at the tower's base: its moss-softened red-tiled roofs and red-brick houses of the living, clustered beyond: its river winding down from the mist on the horizon, as though that were its source, and already heaving with a restless knowledge of its approach towards the sea.

Once again, an unaccountable expedition this! Jasper (always moving softly with no visible reason) contemplates the scene, and especially that stillest part of it which the

Cathedral overshadows. But he contemplates Durdles quite as curiously, and Durdles is by times conscious of his watchful eyes.

Only by times, because Durdles is growing drowsy. As aëronauts lighten the load they carry, when they wish to rise, similarly Durdles has lightened the wicker bottle in coming up. Snatches of sleep surprise him on his legs, and stop him in his talk. A mild fit of calenture seizes him, in which he deems that the ground, so far below, is on a level with the tower, and would as lief walk off the tower into the air as not. Such is his state when they begin to come down. And as aëronauts make themselves heavier when they wish to descend, similarly Durdles charges himself with more liquid from the wicker bottle, that he may come down the better.

The iron gate attained and locked – but not before Durdles has tumbled twice, and cut an eyebrow open once – they descend into the crypt again, with the intent of issuing forth as they entered. But, while returning among those lanes of light, Durdles becomes so very uncertain, both of foot and speech, that he half drops, half throws himself down, by one of the heavy pillars, scarcely less heavy than itself, and indistinctly appeals to his companion for forty winks of a second each.

'If you will have it so, or must have it so,' replies Jasper, 'I'll not leave you here. Take them, while I walk to and fro.'

Durdles is asleep at once; and in his sleep he dreams a dream.

It is not much of a dream, considering the vast extent of the domains of dreamland, and their wonderful productions; it is only remarkable for being unusually restless, and unusually real. He dreams of lying there, asleep, and yet counting his companion's footsteps as he walks to and fro. He dreams that the footsteps die away into distance of time and of space, and that something touches him, and that something falls from his hand. Then something clinks and gropes about, and he dreams that he is alone for so long a time, that the lanes of light take new directions as the moon advances in her course. From succeeding unconsciousness, he passes into a dream of slow uneasiness from cold; and painfully awakes to a perception of the lanes of light – really changed, much as he had dreamed – and Jasper walking among them, beating his hands and feet.

'Halloa!' Durdles cries out, unmeaningly alarmed.

'Awake at last?' says Jasper, coming up to him. 'Do you know that your forties have stretched into thousands?'

'No.'

'They have though.'

'What's the time?'

'Hark! The bells are going in the tower!'

They strike four quarters, and then the great bell strikes.

'Two!' cries Durdles, scrambling up; 'why didn't you try to wake me, Mister Jarsper?'

'I did. I might as well have tried to wake the dead: – your own family of dead, up in the corner there.'

'Did you touch me?'

'Touch you? Yes. Shook you.'

As Durdles recalls that touching something in his dream, he looks down on the pavement, and sees the key of the crypt door lying close to where he himself lay.

'I dropped you, did I?' he says, picking it up, and recalling that part of his dream. As he gathers himself again into an upright position, or into a position as nearly upright as he ever maintains, he is again conscious of being watched by his companion.

'Well?' says Jasper, smiling. 'Are you quite ready? Pray don't hurry.'

'Let me get my bundle right, Mister Jarsper, and I'm with you.'

As he ties it afresh, he is once more conscious that he is very narrowly observed.

'What do you suspect me of, Mister Jarsper?' he asks, with drunken displeasure. 'Let them as has any suspicions of Durdles, name 'em.'

'I've no suspicions of you, my good Mr. Durdles; but I have suspicions that my bottle was filled with something stiffer than either of us supposed. And I also have suspicions,' Jasper adds, taking it from the pavement and turning it bottom upward, 'that it's empty.'

Durdles condescends to laugh at this. Continuing to chuckle when his laugh is over, as though remonstrant with himself on his drinking powers, he rolls to the door and unlocks it. They both pass out, and Durdles relocks it, and pockets his key.

'A thousand thanks for a curious and interesting night,' says Jasper, giving him his hand; 'you can make your own way home?'

'I should think so!' answers Durdles. 'If you was to offer Durdles the affront to show him his way home, he wouldn't go home.

> Durdles wouldn't go home till morning,
> And *then* Durdles wouldn't go home,

Durdles wouldn't.' This, with the utmost defiance.

'Good-night, then.'

'Good-night, Mister Jarsper.'

Each is turning his own way, when a sharp whistle rends the silence, and the jargon is yelped out:

> 'Widdy widdy wen!
> I – ket – ches – Im – out – ar – ter – ten.
> Widdy widdy wy!
> Then – E – don't – go – then – I – shy –
> Widdy Widdy Wake-cock warning!'

Instantly afterwards, a rapid fire of stones rattles at the Cathedral wall, and the hideous small boy is beheld opposite, dancing in the moonlight.

'What! Is that baby-devil on the watch there!' cries Jasper in a fury: so quickly roused, and so violent, that he seems an older devil himself. 'I shall shed the blood of that Impish wretch! I know I shall do it!' Regardless of the fire, though it hits him more than once, he rushes at Deputy, collars him, and tries to bring him across. But Deputy is not to be so easily brought across. With a diabolical insight into the strongest part of his position, he is no sooner taken by the throat than he curls up his legs, forces his assailant to hang him, as it were, and gurgles in his throat, and screws his body, and twists, as already undergoing the first agonies of strangulation. There is nothing for it but to drop him. He instantly gets himself together, backs over to Durdles, and cries to his assailant, gnashing the great gap in front of his mouth with rage and malice:

'I'll blind yer, s'elp me! I'll stone yer eyes out, s'elp me! If I don't have yer eyesight, bellows me!' At the same time dodging behind Durdles, and snarling at Jasper, now from this side of him, and now from that: prepared, if pounced upon, to dart away in all manner of curvilinear directions, and, if run down after all, to grovel in the dust, and cry: 'Now, hit me when I'm down! Do it!'

'Don't hurt the boy, Mister Jarsper,' urges Durdles, shielding him. 'Recollect yourself.'

'He followed us to-night, when we first came here!'

'Yer lie, I didn't!' replies Deputy, in his one form of polite contradiction.

'He has been prowling near us ever since!'

'Yer lie, I haven't,' returns Deputy. 'I'd only jist come out for my 'elth when I see you two a coming out of the Kinfree-derel. If –

'I – ket – ches – Im – out – ar – ter – ten,'

(with the usual rhythm and dance, though dodging behind Durdles), 'it ain't *my* fault, is it?'

'Take him home, then,' retorts Jasper, ferociously, though with a strong check upon himself, 'and let my eyes be rid of the sight of you!'

Deputy, with another sharp whistle, at once expressing his relief, and his commencement of a milder stoning of Mr. Durdles, begins stoning that respectable gentleman home, as if he were a reluctant ox. Mr. Jasper goes to his Gate House, brooding. And thus, as everything comes to an end, the unaccountable expedition comes to an end – for the time.

CHAPTER XIII

Both at their Best

MISS TWINKLETON'S establishment was about to undergo a serene hush. The Christmas recess was at hand. What had once, and at no remote period, been called, even by the erudite Miss Twinkleton herself, 'the half;' but what was now called, as being more elegant, and more strictly collegiate, 'the term;' would expire to-morrow. A noticeable relaxation of discipline had for some few days pervaded the Nuns' House. Club suppers had occurred in the bed-rooms, and a dressed tongue had been carved with a pair of scissors, and handed round with the curling-tongs. Portions of marmalade had likewise been distributed on a service of plates constructed of curlpaper; and cowslip wine had been quaffed from the small squat measuring glass in which little Rickitts (a junior of weakly constitution), took her steel drops daily. The housemaids had been bribed with various fragments of riband, and sundry pairs of shoes, more or less down at heel, to make no mention of crumbs in the beds; the airiest costumes had been worn on these festive occasions; and the daring Miss Ferdinand had even surprised the company with a sprightly solo on the comb-and-curlpaper, until suffocated in her own pillow by two flowing-haired executioners.

Nor were these the only tokens of dispersal. Boxes appeared in the bedrooms (where they were capital at other times), and a surprising amount of packing took place, out of all proportion to the amount packed. Largesse, in the form of odds and ends of cold cream and pomatum, and also of hairpins, was freely distributed among the attendants. On charges of inviolable secrecy, confidences were interchanged respecting golden youth of England expected to call, 'at home,' on the first opportunity. Miss Giggles (deficient in sentiment) did indeed profess that she, for her part, acknowledged such homage by making faces at the golden youth; but this young lady was outvoted by an immense majority.

On the last night before a recess, it was always expressly made a point of honour that nobody should go to sleep, and that ghosts should be encouraged by all possible means. This compact invariably broke down, and all the young ladies went to sleep very soon, and got up very early.

The concluding ceremony came off at twelve o'clock on the day of departure; when Miss Twinkleton, supported by Mrs. Tisher, held a Drawing-Room in her own apartment (the globes already covered with brown holland), where glasses of white wine, and plates of cut pound-cake were discovered on the table. Miss Twinkleton then said, Ladies, another revolving year had brought us round to that festive period at which the finest feelings of our nature bounded in our— Miss Twinkleton was annually going to add 'bosoms,' but annually stopped on the brink of that expression, and substituted 'hearts.' Hearts; our hearts. Hem! Again a revolving year, ladies, had brought us to a pause in our studies – let us hope our greatly advanced studies – and, like the mariner in his bark, the warrior in his tent, the captive in his dungeon, and the traveller in his various conveyances, we yearned for home. Did we say, on such an occasion, in the opening words of Mr. Addison's impressive tragedy:

> 'The dawn is overcast, the morning lowers,
> And heavily in clouds brings on the day,
> The great, th' important day—'?

Not so. From horizon to zenith all was *couleur de rose*, for all was redolent of our relations and friends. Might *we* find *them* prospering as *we* expected; might *they* find *us* prospering as *they* expected! Ladies, we would now, with our love to one another, wish one another good-bye, and happiness, until we met again. And when the time should come for our resumption of those pursuits which (here, general depression set in all round), pursuits which, pursuits which; – then let us ever remember what was said by the Spartan General, in words too trite for repetition, at the battle it were superfluous to specify.

The handmaidens of the establishment, in their best caps, then handed the trays, and the young ladies sipped and crumbled, and the bespoken coaches began to choke the street. Then, leave-taking was not long about, and Miss Twinkleton, in saluting each young lady's cheek, confided to her an exceedingly neat letter, addressed to her next friend at law, 'with Miss Twinkleton's best compliments' in the corner. This missive she handed with an air as if it had not the least connexion with the bill, but were something in the nature of a delicate and joyful surprise.

So many times had Rosa seen such dispersals, and so very little did she know of any other Home, that she was contented to remain where she was, and was even better contented than ever before, having her latest friend with her. And yet her latest friendship had a blank place in it of which she could not fail to be sensible. Helena Landless, having been a party to her brother's revelation about Rosa, and having entered into that compact of silence with Mr. Crisparkle, shrank from any allusion to Edwin Drood's name. Why she so avoided it, was mysterious to Rosa, but she perfectly perceived the fact. But for the fact, she might have relieved her own little perplexed heart of some of its doubts and hesitations, by taking Helena into her confidence. As it was, she had no such vent: she could only ponder on her own difficulties, and wonder more and more why this avoidance of Edwin's name should last, now that she knew – for so much Helena had told her – that a good understanding was to be re-established between the two young men, when Edwin came down.

It would have made a pretty picture, so many pretty girls kissing Rosa in the cold porch of the Nuns' House, and that sunny little creature peeping out of it (unconscious of sly faces carved on spout and gable peeping at her), and waving farewells to the departing coaches, as if she represented the spirit of rosy youth abiding in the place to keep it bright and warm in its desertion. The hoarse High Street became musical with the cry, in various silvery voices, 'Good-bye, Rosebud, Darling!' and the effigy of Mr. Sapsea's father over the opposite doorway, seemed to say to mankind: 'Gentlemen, favour me with your attention to this charming little last lot left behind, and bid with a spirit worthy of the occasion!' Then the staid street, so unwontedly sparkling, youthful, and fresh for a few rippling moments, ran dry, and Cloisterham was itself again.

If Rosebud in her bower now waited Edwin Drood's coming with an uneasy heart, Edwin for his part was uneasy too. With far less force of purpose in his composition than the childish beauty, crowned by acclamation fairy queen of Miss Twinkleton's establishment, he had a conscience, and Mr. Grewgious had pricked it. That gentleman's steady convictions of what was right and what was wrong in such a case as his, were neither to be frowned aside, nor laughed aside. They would not be moved. But for the dinner in Staple Inn, and but for the ring he carried in the breast pocket of his coat, he would have drifted into their wedding-day without another pause for real thought, loosely trusting that all would go well, left alone. But that serious putting him on his truth to the living and the dead had brought him to a check. He must either give the ring to Rosa, or he must take it back. Once put into this narrowed way of action, it was curious that he began to consider Rosa's claims upon him more unselfishly than he had ever considered them before, and began to be less sure of himself than he had ever been in all his easy-going days.

'I will be guided by what she says, and by how we get on,' was his decision, walking from the Gate House to the Nuns' House. 'Whatever comes of it, I will bear his words in mind, and try to be true to the living and the dead.'

Rosa was dressed for walking. She expected him. It was a bright frosty day, and Miss Twinkleton had already graciously sanctioned fresh air. Thus they got out together before it became necessary for either Miss Twinkleton, or the Deputy High Priest, Mrs. Tisher, to lay even so much as one of those usual offerings on the shrine of Propriety.

'My dear Eddy,' said Rosa, when they had turned out of the High Street, and had got among the quiet walks in the neighbourhood of the Cathedral and the river: 'I want to say something very serious to you. I have been thinking about it for a long, long time.'

'Good-bye, Rosebud, darling!'

'I want to be serious with you too, Rosa dear. I mean to be serious and earnest.'

'Thank you, Eddy. And you will not think me unkind because I begin, will you? You will not think I speak for myself only, because I speak first? That would not be generous, would it? And I know you are generous!'

He said, 'I hope I am not ungenerous to you, Rosa.' He called her Pussy no more. Never again.

'And there is no fear,' pursued Rosa, 'of our quarrelling, is there? Because, Eddy,' clasping her hand on his arm, 'we have so much reason to be very lenient to each other!'

'We will be, Rosa.'

'That's a dear good boy! Eddy, let us be courageous. Let us change to brother and sister from this day forth.'

'Never be husband and wife?'

'Never!'

Neither spoke again for a little while. But after that pause he said, with some effort:

'Of course I know that this has been in both our minds, Rosa, and of course I am in honour bound to confess freely that it does not originate with you.'

'No, nor with you, dear,' she returned, with pathetic earnestness. 'It has sprung up between us. You are not truly happy in our engagement; I am not truly happy in it. Oh, I am so sorry, so sorry!' And there she broke into tears.

'I am deeply sorry too, Rosa. Deeply sorry for you.'

'And I for you, poor boy! And I for you!'

This pure young feeling, this gentle and forbearing feeling of each towards the other, brought with it its reward in a softening light that seemed to shine on their position. The relations between them did not look wilful, or capricious, or a failure, in such a light; they became elevated into something more self-denying, honourable, affectionate, and true.

'If we knew yesterday,' said Rosa, as she dried her eyes, 'and we did know yesterday, and on many, many yesterdays, that we were far from right together in those relations which were not of our own choosing, what better could we do to-day than change them? It is natural that we should be sorry, and you see how sorry we both are; but how much better to be sorry now than then!'

'When, Rosa?'

'When it would be too late. And then we should be angry, besides.'

Another silence fell upon them.

'And you know,' said Rosa, innocently, 'you couldn't like me then; and you can always like me now, for I shall not be a drag upon you, or a worry to you. And I can always like you now, and your sister will not tease or trifle with you. I often did when I was not your sister, and I beg your pardon for it.'

'Don't let us come to that, Rosa; or I shall want more pardoning than I like to think of.'

'No, indeed, Eddy; you are too hard, my generous boy, upon yourself. Let us sit down, brother, on these ruins, and let me tell you how it was with us. I think I know, for I have considered about it very much since you were here, last time. You liked me, didn't you? You thought I was a nice little thing?'

'Everybody thinks that, Rosa.'

'Do they?' She knitted her brow musingly for a moment, and then flashed out with the bright little induction: 'Well; but say they do. Surely it was not enough that you should think of me, only as other people did; now, was it?'

The point was not to be got over. It was not enough.

'And that is just what I mean; that is just how it was with us,' said Rosa. 'You liked me very well, and you had grown used to me, and had grown used to the idea of our being married. You accepted the situation as an inevitable kind of thing, didn't you? It was to be, you thought, and why discuss or dispute it.'

It was new and strange to him to have himself presented to himself so clearly, in a glass of her holding up. He had always patronized her, in his superiority to her share of woman's wit. Was that but another instance of something radically amiss in the terms on which they had been gliding towards a life-long bondage?

'All this that I say of you, is true of me as well, Eddy. Unless it was, I might not be bold enough to say it. Only, the difference between us was, that by little and little there crept into my mind a habit of thinking about it, instead of dismissing it. My life is not so busy as yours, you see, and I have not so many things to think of. So I thought about it very much, and I cried about it very much too (though that was not your fault, poor boy); when all at once my guardian came down, to prepare for my leaving the Nuns' House. I tried to hint to him that I was not quite settled in my mind, but I hesitated and failed, and he didn't understand me. But he is a good, good man. And he put before me so kindly, and yet so strongly, how seriously we ought to consider, in our circumstances, that I resolved to speak to you the next moment we were alone and grave. And if I seemed to come to it easily just now, because I came to it all at once, don't think it was so really, Eddy, for Oh, it was very, very hard, and Oh, I am very, very sorry!'

Her full heart broke into tears again. He put his arm about her waist, and they walked by the river side together.

'Your guardian has spoken to me too, Rosa dear. I saw him before I left London.' His right hand was in his breast, seeking the ring; but he checked it as he thought: 'If I am to take it back, why should I tell her of it?'

'And that made you more serious about it, didn't it, Eddy? And if I had not spoken to you, as I have, you would have spoken to me? I hope you can tell me so? I don't like it to be *all* my doing, though it *is* so much better for us.'

'Yes, I should have spoken; I should have put everything before you; I came intending to do it. But I never could have spoken to you as you have spoken to me, Rosa.'

'Don't say you mean so coldly or unkindly, Eddy, please, if you can help it.'

'I mean so sensibly and delicately, so wisely and affectionately.'

'That's my dear brother!' She kissed his hand in a little rapture. 'The dear girls will be dreadfully disappointed,' added Rosa, laughing, with the dew-drops glistening in her bright eyes. 'They have looked forward to it so, poor pets!'

'Ah! But I fear it will be a worse disappointment to Jack,' said Edwin Drood, with a start. 'I never thought of Jack!'

Her swift and intent look at him as he said the words, could no more be recalled than a flash of lightning can. But it appeared as though she would have instantly recalled it, if she could; for she looked down, confused, and breathed quickly.

'You don't doubt its being a blow to Jack, Rosa?'

She merely replied, and that, evasively and hurriedly: Why should she? She had not thought about it. He seemed, to her, to have so little to do with it.

'My dear child! Can you suppose that any one so wrapped up in another – Mrs. Tope's expression: not mine – as Jack is in me, could fail to be struck all of a heap by such a sudden and complete change in my life? I say sudden, because it will be sudden to *him*, you know.'

She nodded twice or thrice, and her lips parted as if she would have assented. But she uttered no sound, and her breathing was no slower.

'How shall I tell Jack!' said Edwin, ruminating. If he had been less occupied with the thought, he must have seen her singular emotion. 'I never thought of Jack. It must be broken to him, before the town crier knows it. I dine with the dear fellow to-morrow and next day – Christmas Eve and Christmas Day – but it would never do to spoil his feast days. He always worries about me, and moddley-coddleys in the merest trifles. The news is sure to overset him. How on earth shall this be broken to Jack!'

'He must be told, I suppose?' said Rosa.

'My dear Rosa! Who ought to be in our confidence, if not Jack?'

'My guardian promised to come down, if I should write and ask him. I am going to do so. Would you like to leave it to him?'

'A bright idea!' cried Edwin. 'The other trustee. Nothing more natural. He comes down, he goes to Jack, he relates what we have agreed upon, and he states our case better than we could. He has already spoken feelingly to you, he has already spoken feelingly to me, and he'll put the whole thing feelingly to Jack. That's it! I am not a coward, Rosa, but to tell you a secret, I am a little afraid of Jack.'

'No, no! You are not afraid of him?' cried Rosa, turning white and clasping her hands.

'Why, sister Rosa, sister Rosa, what do you see from the turret?' said Edwin, rallying her. 'My dear girl!'

'You frightened me.'

'Most unintentionally, but I am as sorry as if I had meant to do it. Could you possibly suppose for a moment, from any loose way of speaking of mine, that I was literally afraid of the dear fond fellow? What I mean is, that he is subject to a kind of paroxysm, or fit – I saw him in it once – and I don't know but that so great a surprise, coming upon him direct from me whom he is so wrapped up in, might bring it on perhaps. Which – and this is the secret I was going to tell you – is another reason for your guardian's making the communication. He is so steady, precise, and exact, that he will talk Jack's thoughts into shape, in no time: whereas with me Jack is always impulsive and hurried, and, I may say, almost womanish.'

Rosa seemed convinced. Perhaps from her own very different point of view of 'Jack,' she felt comforted and protected by the interposition of Mr. Grewgious between herself and him.

And now, Edwin Drood's right hand closed again upon the ring in its little case, and again was checked by the consideration: 'It is certain, now, that I am to give it back to him; then why should I tell her of it?' That pretty sympathetic nature which could be so sorry for him in the blight of their childish hopes of happiness together, and could so quietly find itself alone in a new world to weave fresh wreaths of such flowers as it might prove to bear, the old world's flowers being withered, would be grieved by those sorrowful jewels; and to what purpose? Why should it be? They were but a sign of broken joys and baseless projects; in their very beauty, they were (as the unlikeliest of men had said), almost a cruel satire on the loves, hopes, plans, of humanity, which are able to forecast nothing, and are so much brittle dust. Let them be. He would restore them to her guardian when he came down; he in his turn would restore them to the cabinet from which he had unwillingly taken them; and there, like old letters or old vows, or other records of old aspirations come to nothing, they would be disregarded, until, being valuable, they were sold into circulation again, to repeat their former round.

Let them be. Let them lie unspoken of, in his breast. However distinctly or indistinctly he entertained these thoughts, he arrived at the conclusion, Let them be. Among the mighty store of wonderful chains that are for ever forging, day and night, in the vast iron-works of time and circumstance, there was one chain forged in the moment of that small conclusion, riveted to the foundations of heaven and earth, and gifted with invincible force to hold and drag.

They walked on by the river. They began to speak of their separate plans. He would quicken his departure from England, and she would remain where she was, at least as long as Helena remained. The poor dear girls should have their disappointment broken to them gently, and, as the first preliminary, Miss Twinkleton should be confided in by Rosa, even in advance of the reappearance of Mr. Grewgious. It should be made clear in all quarters that she and Edwin were the best of friends. There had never been so serene an understanding between them since they were first affianced. And yet there was one reservation on each side; on hers, that she intended through her guardian to withdraw herself immediately from the tuition of her music-master; on his, that he did already entertain some wandering speculations whether it might ever come to pass that he would know more of Miss Landless.

The bright frosty day declined as they walked and spoke together. The sun dipped in the river far behind them, and the old city lay red before them, as their walk drew to a close. The moaning water cast its seaweed duskily at their feet, when they turned to leave its margin; and the rooks hovered above them with hoarse cries, darker splashes in the darkening air.

'I will prepare Jack for my flitting soon,' said Edwin, in a low voice, 'and I will but see your guardian when he comes, and then go before they speak together. It will be better done without my being by. Don't you think so?'

'Yes.'

'We know we have done right, Rosa?'

'Yes.'

'We know we are better so, even now?'

'And shall be far, far, better so, by-and-bye.'

Still, there was that lingering tenderness in their hearts towards the old positions they were relinquishing, that they prolonged their parting. When they came among the elm trees by the Cathedral, where they had last sat together, they stopped, as by consent, and Rosa raised her face to his, as she had never raised it in the old days; – for they were old already.

'God bless you, dear! Good-bye!'

'God bless you, dear! Good-bye!'

They kissed each other, fervently.

'Now, please take me home, Eddy, and let me be by myself.'

'Don't look round, Rosa,' he cautioned her, as he drew her arm through his, and led her away. 'Didn't you see Jack?'

'No! Where?'

'Under the trees. He saw us, as we took leave of each other. Poor fellow! he little thinks we have parted. This will be a blow to him, I am much afraid!'

She hurried on, without resting, and hurried on until they had passed under the Gate House into the street; once there, she asked:

'Has he followed us? You can look without seeming to. Is he behind?'

'No. Yes! he is! He has just passed out under the gateway. The dear sympathetic old fellow likes to keep us in sight. I am afraid he will be bitterly disappointed!'

She pulled hurriedly at the handle of the hoarse old bell, and the gate soon opened. Before going in, she gave him one last wide wondering look, as if she would have asked him with imploring emphasis: 'Oh! don't you understand?' And out of that look he vanished from her view.

CHAPTER XIV

When shall these Three meet again?

CHRISTMAS EVE in Cloisterham. A few strange faces in the streets; a few other faces, half strange and half familiar, once the faces of Cloisterham children, now the faces of men and women who come back from the outer world at long intervals to find the city wonderfully shrunken in size, as if it had not washed by any means well in the meanwhile. To these, the striking of the Cathedral clock, and the cawing of the rooks from the Cathedral tower, are like voices of their nursery time. To such as these, it has happened in their dying hours afar off, that they have imagined their chamber floor to be strewn with the autumnal leaves fallen from the elm trees in the Close: so have the rustling sounds and fresh scents of their earliest impressions, revived, when the circle of their lives was very nearly traced, and the beginning and the end were drawing close together.

Seasonable tokens are about. Red berries shine here and there in the lattices of Minor Canon Corner; Mr. and Mrs. Tope are daintily sticking sprigs of holly into the carvings and sconces of the Cathedral stalls, as if they were sticking them into the coat-buttonholes of the Dean and Chapter. Lavish profusion is in the shops: particularly in the articles of currants, raisins, spices, candied peel, and moist sugar. An unusual air of gallantry and dissipation is abroad; evinced in an immense bunch of mistletoe hanging in the greengrocer's shop doorway, and a poor little Twelfth Cake, culminating in the figure of a Harlequin – such a very poor little Twelfth Cake, that one would rather call it a Twenty Fourth Cake, or a Forty Eighth Cake – to be raffled for at the pastrycook's, terms one shilling per member. Public amusements are not wanting. The Wax-Work which made so deep an impression on the reflective mind of the Emperor of China is to be seen by particular desire during Christmas Week only, on the premises of the bankrupt livery-stable keeper up the lane;

and a new grand comic Christmas pantomime is to be produced at the Theatre: the latter heralded by the portrait of Signor Jacksonini the clown, saying 'How do you do tomorrow?' quite as large as life, and almost as miserably. In short, Cloisterham is up and doing: though from this description the High School and Miss Twinkleton's are to be excluded. From the former establishment, the scholars have gone home, every one of them in love with one of Miss Twinkleton's young ladies (who knows nothing about it); and only the handmaidens flutter occasionally in the windows of the latter. It is noticed, by-the-bye, that these damsels become, within the limits of decorum, more skittish when thus entrusted with the concrete representation of their sex, than when dividing the representation with Miss Twinkleton's young ladies.

Three are to meet at the Gate House to-night. How does each one of the three get through the day?

Neville Landless, though absolved from his books for the time by Mr. Crisparkle – whose fresh nature is by no means insensible to the charms of a holiday – reads and writes in his quiet room, with a concentrated air, until it is two hours past noon. He then sets himself to clearing his table, to arranging his books, and to tearing up and burning his stray papers. He makes a clean sweep of all untidy accumulations, puts all his drawers in order, and leaves no note or scrap of paper undestroyed, save such memoranda as bear directly on his studies. This done, he turns to his wardrobe, selects a few articles of ordinary wear – among them, change of stout shoes and socks for walking – and packs these in a knapsack. This knapsack is new, and he bought it in the High Street yesterday. He also purchased, at the same time and at the same place, a heavy walking-stick: strong in the handle for the grip of the hand, and iron-shod. He tries this, swings it, poises it, and lays it by, with the knapsack, on a window-seat. By this time his arrangements are complete.

He dresses for going out, and is in the act of going – indeed has left his room, and has met the Minor Canon on the staircase, coming out of his bedroom upon the same story

– when he turns back again for his walking-stick, thinking he will carry it now. Mr. Crisparkle, who has paused on the staircase, sees it in his hand on his immediately reappearing, takes it from him, and asks him with a smile how he chooses a stick?

'Really I don't know that I understand the subject,' he answers. 'I chose it for its weight.'

'Much too heavy, Neville; *much* too heavy.'

'To rest upon in a long walk, sir?'

'Rest upon?' repeats Mr. Crisparkle, throwing himself into pedestrian form. 'You don't rest upon it; you merely balance with it.'

'I shall know better, with practice, sir. I have not lived in a walking country, you know.'

'True,' says Mr. Crisparkle. 'Get into a little training, and we will have a few score miles together. I should leave you nowhere now. Do you come back before dinner?'

'I think not, as we dine early.'

Mr. Crisparkle gives him a bright nod and a cheerful good-bye: expressing (not without intention), absolute confidence and ease.

Neville repairs to the Nuns' House, and requests that Miss Landless may be informed that her brother is there, by appointment. He waits at the gate, not even crossing the threshold; for he is on his parole not to put himself in Rosa's way.

His sister is at least as mindful of the obligation they have taken on themselves, as he can be, and loses not a moment in joining him. They meet affectionately, avoid lingering there, and walk towards the upper inland country.

'I am not going to tread upon forbidden ground, Helena,' says Neville, when they have walked some distance and are turning; 'you will understand in another moment that I cannot help referring to – what shall I say – my infatuation.'

'Had you not better avoid it, Neville? You know that I can hear nothing.'

'You can hear, my dear, what Mr. Crisparkle has heard, and heard with approval.'

'Yes; I can hear so much.'

'Well, it is this. I am not only unsettled and unhappy myself, but I am conscious of unsettling and interfering with other people. How do I know that, but for my unfortunate presence, you, and – and – the rest of that former party, our engaging guardian excepted, might be dining cheerfully in Minor Canon Corner to-morrow? Indeed it probably would be so. I can see too well that I am not high in the old lady's opinion, and it is easy to understand what an irksome clog I must be upon the hospitalities of her orderly house – especially at this time of year – when I must be kept asunder from this person, and there is such a reason for my not being brought into contact with that person, and an unfavourable reputation has preceded me with such another person, and so on. I have put this very gently to Mr. Crisparkle, for you know his self-denying ways; but still I have put it. What I have laid much greater stress upon at the same time, is, that I am engaged in a miserable struggle with myself, and that a little change and absence may enable me to come through it the better. So, the weather being bright and hard, I am going on a walking expedition, and intend taking myself out of everybody's way (my own included, I hope), to-morrow morning.'

'When to come back?'

'In a fortnight.'

'And going quite alone?'

'I am much better without company, even if there were any one but you to bear me company, my dear Helena.'

'Mr. Crisparkle entirely agrees, you say?'

'Entirely. I am not sure but that at first he was inclined to think it rather a moody scheme, and one that might do a brooding mind harm. But we took a moonlight walk, last Monday night, to talk it over at leisure, and I represented the case to him as it really is. I showed him that I do want to conquer myself, and that, this evening well got over, it is surely better that I should be away from here just now, than here. I could hardly help meeting certain people walking together here, and that could do no good, and is certainly not the way to forget. A fortnight hence, that chance will probably be over, for the time; and when it again arises for the last time, why, I can again go away. Further, I really do feel hopeful of bracing exercise and wholesome fatigue. You know that Mr. Crisparkle allows such things their full weight in the preservation of his own sound mind in his own sound body, and that his just spirit is not likely to maintain one set of natural laws for himself and another for me. He yielded to my view of the matter, when convinced that I was honestly in earnest, and so, with his full consent, I start to-morrow morning. Early enough to be not only out of the streets, but out of hearing of the bells, when the good people go to church.'

Helena thinks it over, and thinks well of it. Mr. Crisparkle doing so, she would do so; but she does originally, out of her own mind, think well of it, as a healthy project, denoting a sincere endeavour, and an active attempt at self-correction. She is inclined to pity him, poor fellow, for going away solitary on the great Christmas festival; but she feels it much more to the purpose to encourage him. And she does encourage him.

He will write to her?

He will write to her every alternate day, and tell her all his adventures.

Does he send clothes on, in advance of him?

'My dear Helena, no. Travel like a pilgrim, with wallet and staff. My wallet – or my knapsack – is packed, and ready for strapping on; and here is my staff!'

He hands it to her; she makes the same remark as Mr. Crisparkle, that it is very heavy; and gives it back to him, asking what wood it is? Iron-wood.

Up to this point, he has been extremely cheerful. Perhaps, the having to carry his case with her, and therefore to present it in its brightest aspect, has roused his spirits. Perhaps, the having done so with success, is followed by a revulsion. As the day closes in, and the city lights begin to spring up before them, he grows depressed.

'I wish I were not going to this dinner, Helena.'

'Dear Neville, is it worth while to care much about it? Think how soon it will be over.'

'How soon it will be over,' he repeats, gloomily. 'Yes. But I don't like it.'

There may be a moment's awkwardness, she cheeringly represents to him, but it can only last a moment. He is quite sure of himself.

'I wish I felt as sure of everything else, as I feel of myself,' he answers her.

'How strangely you speak, dear! What do you mean?'

'Helena, I don't know. I only know that I don't like it. What a strange dead weight there is in the air!'

She calls his attention to those copperous clouds beyond the river, and says that the wind is rising. He scarcely speaks again, until he takes leave of her, at the gate of the Nuns' House. She does not immediately enter, when they have parted, but remains looking after him along the street. Twice, he passes the Gate House, reluctant to enter. At length, the Cathedral clock chiming one quarter, with a rapid turn he hurries in.

And so *he* goes up the postern stair.

Edwin Drood passes a solitary day. Something of deeper moment than he had thought, has gone out of his life; and in the silence of his own chamber he wept for it last night. Though the image of Miss Landless still hovers in the background of his mind, the pretty little affectionate creature, so much firmer and wiser than he had supposed, occupies its stronghold. It is with some misgiving of his own unworthiness that he thinks of her, and of what they might have been to one another, if he had been more in earnest some time ago; if he had set a higher value on her; if, instead of accepting his lot in life as an inheritance of course, he had studied the right way to its appreciation and enhancement. And still, for all this, and though there is a sharp heartache in all this, the vanity and caprice of youth sustain that handsome figure of Miss Landless in the background of his mind.

That was a curious look of Rosa's when they parted at the gate. Did it mean that she saw below the surface of his thoughts, and down into their twilight depths? Scarcely that, for it was a look of astonished and keen inquiry. He decides that he cannot understand it, though it was remarkably expressive.

As he only waits for Mr. Grewgious now, and will depart immediately after having seen him, he takes a sauntering leave of the ancient city and its neighbourhood. He recalls the time when Rosa and he walked here or there, mere children, full of the dignity of being engaged. Poor children! he thinks, with a pitying sadness.

Finding that his watch has stopped, he turns into the jeweller's shop, to have it wound and set. The jeweller is knowing on the subject of a bracelet, which he begs leave to submit, in a general and quite aimless way. It would suit (he considers) a young bride, to perfection; especially if of a rather diminutive style of beauty. Finding the bracelet but coldly looked at, the jeweller invites attention to a tray of rings for gentlemen; here is a style of ring, now, he remarks – a very chaste signet – which gentlemen are much given to purchasing, when changing their condition. A ring of a very responsible appearance. With the date of their wedding-day engraved inside, several gentlemen have preferred it to any other kind of memento.

The rings are as coldly viewed as the bracelet. Edwin tells the tempter that he wears no jewellery but his watch and chain, which were his father's; and his shirt-pin.

'That I was aware of,' is the jeweller's reply, 'for Mr. Jasper dropped in for a watch-glass the other day, and, in fact, I showed these articles to him, remarking that if he *should* wish to make a present to a gentleman relative, on any particular occasion – But he said with a smile that he had an inventory in his mind of all the jewellery his gentleman relative ever wore; namely, his watch and chain, and his shirt-pin.' Still (the jeweller considers) that might not apply to all times, though applying to the present time. 'Twenty minutes past two, Mr. Drood, I set your watch at. Let me recommend you not to let it run down, sir.'

Edwin takes his watch, puts it on, and goes out, thinking: 'Dear old Jack! If I were to make an extra crease in my neckcloth, he would think it worth noticing!'

He strolls about and about, to pass the time until the dinner hour. It somehow happens that Cloisterham seems reproachful to him to-day; has fault to find with him, as if he had not used it well; but is far more pensive with him than angry. His wonted carelessness is replaced by a wistful looking at, and dwelling upon, all the old landmarks. He will soon be far away, and may never see them again, he thinks. Poor youth! Poor youth!

As dusk draws on, he paces the Monks' Vineyard. He has walked to and fro, full half an hour by the Cathedral chimes, and it has closed in dark, before he becomes quite aware of a woman crouching on the ground near a wicket gate in a corner. The gate commands a cross bye-path, little used in the gloaming; and the figure must have been there all the time, though he has but gradually and lately made it out.

He strikes into that path, and walks up to the wicket. By the light of a lamp near it, he sees that the woman is of a haggard appearance, and that her weazen chin is resting on her hands, and that her eyes are staring – with an unwinking, blind sort of steadfastness – before her.

Always kindly, but moved to be unusually kind this evening, and having bestowed kind words on most of the children and aged people he has met, he at once bends down, and speaks to this woman.

'Are you ill?'

'No, deary,' she answers, without looking at him, and with no departure from her strange blind stare.

'Are you blind?'

'No, deary.'

'Are you lost, homeless, faint? What is the matter, that you stay here in the cold so long, without moving?'

By slow and stiff efforts, she appears to contract her vision until it can rest upon him; and then a curious film passes over her, and she begins to shake.

He straightens himself, recoils a step, and looks down at her in a dread amazement; for he seems to know her.

'Good Heaven!' he thinks, next moment. 'Like Jack that night!'

As he looks down at her, she looks up at him, and whimpers: 'My lungs is weak; my lungs is dreffle bad. Poor me, poor me, my cough is rattling dry!' And coughs in confirmation, horribly.

'Where do you come from?'

'Come from London, deary.' (Her cough still rending her.)

'Where are you going to?'

'Back to London, deary. I came here, looking for a needle in a haystack, and I ain't found it. Look'ee, deary; give me three and sixpence, and don't you be afeard for me. I'll get back to London then, and trouble no one. I'm in a business. – Ah, me! It's slack, it's slack, and times is very bad! – but I can make a shift to live by it.'

'Do you eat opium?'

'Smokes it,' she replies with difficulty, still racked by her cough. 'Give me three and sixpence, and I'll lay it out well, and get back. If you don't give me three and sixpence, don't give me a brass farden. And if you do give me three and sixpence, deary, I'll tell you something.'

He counts the money from his pocket, and puts it in her hand. She instantly clutches it tight, and rises to her feet with a croaking laugh of satisfaction.

'Bless ye! Hark'ee, dear gen'lm'n. What's your Chris'en name?'

'Edwin.'

'Edwin, Edwin, Edwin,' she repeats, trailing off into a drowsy repetition of the word; and then asks suddenly: 'Is the short of that name, Eddy?'

'It is sometimes called so,' he replies, with the colour starting to his face.

'Don't sweethearts call it so?' she asks, pondering.

'How should I know!'

'Haven't you a sweetheart, upon my soul?'

'None.'

She is moving away with another 'Bless ye, and thank'ee, deary!' when he adds: 'You were to tell me something; you may as well do so.'

'So I was, so I was. Well, then. Whisper. You be thankful that your name ain't Ned.'

He looks at her, quite steadily, as he asks: 'Why?'

'Because it's a bad name to have just now.'

'How a bad name?'

'A threatened name. A dangerous name.'

'The proverb says that threatened men live long,' he tells her, lightly.

'Then Ned – so threatened is he, wherever he may be while I am a talking to you, deary – should live to all eternity!' replies the woman.

She has leaned forward, to say it in his ear, with her forefinger shaking before his eyes, and now huddles herself together, and with another 'Bless ye, and thank'ee!' goes away in the direction of the Travellers' Lodging House.

This is not an inspiriting close to a dull day. Alone, in a sequestered place, surrounded by vestiges of old time and decay, it rather has a tendency to call a shudder into being. He makes for the better lighted streets, and resolves as he walks on to say nothing of this to-night, but to mention it to Jack (who alone calls him Ned), as an odd coincidence, to-morrow; of course only as a coincidence, and not as anything better worth remembering.

Still, it holds to him, as many things much better worth remembering never did. He has another mile or so, to linger out before the dinner-hour; and, when he walks over the bridge and by the river, the woman's words are in the rising wind, in the angry sky, in the troubled water, in the flickering lights. There is some solemn echo of them, even in the Cathedral chime, which strikes a sudden surprise to his heart as he turns in under the archway of the Gate House.

And so *he* goes up the postern stair.

John Jasper passes a more agreeable and cheerful day than either of his guests. Having no music-lessons to give in the holiday season, his time is his own, but for the Cathedral services. He is early among the shopkeepers, ordering little table luxuries that his nephew likes. His nephew will not be with him long, he tells his provision-dealers, and so must be petted and made much of. While out on his hospitable prep-arations, he looks in on Mr. Sapsea; and mentions that dear Ned, and that inflammable young spark of Mr. Crisparkle's, are to dine at the Gate House to-day, and make up their difference. Mr. Sapsea is by no means friendly towards the inflammable young spark. He says that his complexion is 'Un-English.' And when Mr. Sapsea has once declared anything to be Un-English, he considers that thing everlastingly sunk in the bottomless pit.

John Jasper is truly sorry to hear Mr. Sapsea speak thus, for he knows right well that Mr. Sapsea never speaks without a meaning, and that he has a subtle trick of being right. Mr. Sapsea (by a very remarkable coincidence) is of exactly that opinion.

Mr. Jasper is in beautiful voice this day. In the pathetic supplication to have his heart inclined to keep this law, he quite astonishes his fellows by his melodious power. He has never sung difficult music with such skill and harmony, as in this day's Anthem. His nervous temperament is occasionally prone to take difficult music a little too quickly; to-day, his time is perfect.

These results are probably attained through a grand composure of the spirits. The mere mechanism of his throat is a little tender, for he wears, both with his singing-robe and with his ordinary dress, a large black scarf of strong close-woven silk, slung loosely round his neck. But his composure is so noticeable, that Mr. Crisparkle speaks of it as they come out from Vespers.

'I must thank you, Jasper, for the pleasure with which I have heard you to-day. Beautiful! Delightful! You could not have so outdone yourself, I hope, without being wonderfully well.'

'I *am* wonderfully well.'

'Nothing unequal,' says the Minor Canon, with a smooth motion of his hand: 'nothing unsteady, nothing forced, nothing avoided; all thoroughly done in a masterly manner, with perfect self-command.'

'Thank you. I hope so, if it is not too much to say.'

'One would think, Jasper, you had been trying a new medicine for that occasional indisposition of yours.'

'No, really? That's well observed; for I have.'

'Then stick to it, my good fellow,' says Mr. Crisparkle, clapping him on the shoulder with friendly encouragement, 'stick to it.'

'I will.'

'I congratulate you,' Mr. Crisparkle pursues, as they come out of the Cathedral, 'on all accounts.'

'Thank you again. I will walk round to the Corner with you, if you don't object; I have plenty of time before my company come; and I want to say a word to you, which I think you will not be displeased to hear.'

'What is it?'

'Well. We were speaking, the other evening, of my black humours.'

Mr. Crisparkle's face falls, and he shakes his head deploringly.

'I said, you know, that I should make you an antidote to those black humours; and you said you hoped I would consign them to the flames.'

'And I still hope so, Jasper.'

'With the best reason in the world! I mean to burn this year's Diary at the year's end.'

'Because you—?' Mr. Crisparkle brightens greatly as he thus begins.

'You anticipate me. Because I feel that I have been out of sorts, gloomy, bilious, brain-oppressed, whatever it may be. You said I had been exaggerative. So I have.'

Mr. Crisparkle's brightened face brightens still more.

'I couldn't see it then, because I *was* out of sorts; but I am in a healthier state now, and I acknowledge it with genuine pleasure. I made a great deal of a very little; that's the fact.'

'It does me good,' cries Mr. Crisparkle, 'to hear you say it!'

'A man leading a monotonous life,' Jasper proceeds, 'and getting his nerves, or his stomach, out of order, dwells upon an idea until it loses its proportions. That was my case with the idea in question. So I shall burn the evidence of my case, when the book is full, and begin the next volume with a clearer vision.'

'This is better,' says Mr. Crisparkle, stopping at the steps of his own door to shake hands, 'than I could have hoped!'

'Why, naturally,' returns Jasper. 'You had but little reason to hope that I should become more like yourself. You are always training yourself to be, mind and body, as clear as crystal, and you always are, and never change; whereas, I am a muddy, solitary, moping weed. However, I have got over that mope. Shall I wait, while you ask if Mr. Neville has left for my place? If not, he and I may walk round together.'

'I think,' says Mr. Crisparkle, opening the entrance door with his key, 'that he left some time ago; at least I know he left, and I think he has not come back. But I'll inquire. You won't come in?'

'My company wait,' says Jasper, with a smile.

The Minor Canon disappears, and in a few moments returns. As he thought, Mr. Neville has not come back; indeed, as he remembers now, Mr. Neville said he would probably go straight to the Gate House.

'Bad manners in a host!' says Jasper. 'My company will be there before me! What will you bet that I don't find my company embracing?'

'I will bet – or I would, if I ever did bet,' returns Mr. Crisparkle, 'that your company will have a gay entertainer this evening.'

Jasper nods, and laughs Good-night!

He retraces his steps to the Cathedral door, and turns down past it to the Gate House. He sings, in a low voice and with delicate expression, as he walks along. It still seems as if a false note were not within his power to-night, and as if nothing could hurry or retard him. Arriving thus, under the arched entrance of his dwelling, he pauses for an instant in the shelter to pull off that great black scarf, and hang it in a loop upon his arm. For that brief time, his face is knitted and stern. But it immediately clears, as he resumes his singing, and his way.

And so *he* goes up the postern stair.

The red light burns steadily all the evening in the Lighthouse on the margin of the tide of busy life. Softened sounds and hum of traffic pass it and flow on irregularly into the lonely Precincts; but very little else goes by, save violent rushes of wind. It comes on to blow a boisterous gale.

The Precincts are never particularly well lighted; but the strong blasts of wind blowing out many of the lamps (in some instances shattering the frames too, and bringing the glass rattling to the ground), they are unusually dark to-night. The darkness is augmented and confused, by flying dust from the earth, dry twigs from the trees, and great ragged fragments from the rooks' nests up in the tower. The trees themselves so toss and creak, as this tangible part of the darkness madly whirls about, that they seem in peril of being torn out of the earth: while ever and again a crack, and a rushing fall, denote that some large branch has yielded to the storm.

No such power of wind has blown for many a winter night. Chimneys topple in the streets, and people hold to posts and corners, and to one another, to keep themselves upon their feet. The violent rushes abate not, but increase in frequency and fury until at midnight, when the streets are empty, the storm goes thundering along them, rattling at all the latches, and tearing at all the shutters, as if warning the people to get up and fly with it, rather than have the roofs brought down upon their brains.

Still, the red light burns steadily. Nothing is steady but the red light.

All through the night, the wind blows, and abates not. But early in the morning when there is barely enough light in the east to dim the stars, it begins to lull. From that time, with occasional wild charges, like a wounded monster dying, it drops and sinks; and at full daylight it is dead.

It is then seen that the hands of the Cathedral clock are torn off; that lead from the roof has been stripped away, rolled up, and blown into the Close; and that some stones have been displaced upon the summit of the great tower. Christmas morning though it be, it is necessary to send up workmen, to ascertain the extent of the damage done. These, led by Durdles, go aloft; while Mr. Tope and a crowd of early idlers gather down in Minor Canon Corner, shading their eyes and watching for their appearance up there.

This cluster is suddenly broken and put aside by the hands of Mr. Jasper; all the gazing eyes are brought down to the earth by his loudly inquiring of Mr. Crisparkle, at an open window:

'Where is my nephew?'

'He has not been here. Is he not with you?'

'No. He went down to the river last night, with Mr. Neville, to look at the storm, and has not been back. Call Mr. Neville!'

'He left this morning, early.'

'Left this morning, early? Let me in, let me in!'

There is no more looking up at the tower, now. All the assembled eyes are turned on Mr. Jasper, white, half dressed, panting, and clinging to the rail before the Minor Canon's house.

CHAPTER XV

Impeached

NEVILLE LANDLESS had started so early and walked at so good a pace, that when the church bells began to ring in Cloisterham for morning service, he was eight miles away. As he wanted his breakfast by that time, having set forth on a crust of bread, he stopped at the next roadside tavern to refresh.

Visitors in want of breakfast – unless they were horses or cattle, for which class of guests there was preparation enough in the way of water-trough and hay – were so unusual at the sign of The Tilted Wagon, that it took a long time to get the wagon into the track of tea and toast and bacon. Neville, in the interval, sitting in a sanded parlour, wondering in how long a time after he had gone, the sneezy fire of damp faggots would begin to make somebody else warm.

Indeed, The Tilted Wagon, as a cool establishment on the top of a hill, where the ground before the door was puddled with damp hoofs and trodden straw; where a scolding land-lady slapped a moist baby (with one red sock on and one wanting), in the bar; where the cheese was cast aground upon a shelf, in company with a mouldy tablecloth and a green-handled knife, in a sort of cast-iron canoe; where the pale-faced bread shed tears of crumb over its shipwreck in another canoe; where the family linen, half washed and half dried, led a public life of lying about; where everything to drink was drunk out of mugs, and everything else was sug-gestive of a rhyme to mugs; The Tilted Wagon, all these things considered, hardly kept its painted promise of provid-ing good entertainment for Man and Beast. However, Man, in the present case, was not critical, but took what entertain-ment he could get, and went on again after a longer rest than he needed.

He stopped at some quarter of a mile from the house, hesitating whether to pursue the road, or to follow a cart-track between two high hedgerows, which led across the slope of a breezy heath, and evidently struck into the road again by-and-bye. He decided in favour of this latter track, and pursued it with some toil; the rise being steep, and the way worn into deep ruts.

He was labouring along, when he became aware of some other pedestrians behind him. As they were coming up at a faster pace than his, he stood aside, against one of the high banks, to let them pass. But their manner was very curious. Only four of them passed. Other four slackened speed, and loitered as intending to follow him when he should go on. The remainder of the party (half a dozen perhaps) turned, and went back at a great rate.

He looked at the four behind him, and he looked at the four before him. They all returned his look. He resumed his way. The four in advance went on, constantly looking back; the four in the rear came closing up.

When they all ranged out from the narrow track upon the open slope of the heath, and this order was maintained, let him diverge as he would to either side, there was no longer room to doubt that he was beset by these fellows. He stopped, as a last test; and they all stopped.

'Why do you attend upon me in this way?' he asked the whole body. 'Are you a pack of thieves?'

'Don't answer him,' said one of the number; he did not see which. 'Better be quiet.'

'Better be quiet?' repeated Neville. 'Who said so?'

Nobody replied.

'It's good advice, whichever of you skulkers gave it,' he went on angrily. 'I will not submit to be penned in between four men there, and four men there. I wish to pass, and I mean to pass, those four in front.'

They were all standing still: himself included.

'If eight men, or four men, or two men, set upon one,' he proceeded, growing more enraged, 'the one has no chance but to set his mark upon some of them. And by the Lord I'll do it, if I am interrupted any further!'

Shouldering his heavy stick, and quickening his pace, he shot on to pass the four ahead. The largest and strongest man of the number changed swiftly to the side on which he came up, and dexterously closed with him and went down with him; but not before the heavy stick had descended smartly.

'Let him be!' said this man in a suppressed voice, as they struggled together on the grass. 'Fair play! His is the build of a girl to mine, and he's got a weight strapped to his back besides. Let him alone. I'll manage him.'

After a little rolling about, in a close scuffle which caused the faces of both to be besmeared with blood, the man took his knee from Neville's chest, and rose, saying: 'There! Now take him arm-in-arm, any two of you!'

It was immediately done.

'As to our being a pack of thieves, Mr. Landless,' said the man, as he spat out some blood, and wiped more from his face: 'you know better than that, at midday. We wouldn't have touched you, if you hadn't forced us. We're going to take you round to the high road, anyhow, and you'll find help enough against thieves there, if you want it. Wipe his face somebody; see how it's a trickling down him!'

When his face was cleansed, Neville recognized in the speaker, Joe, driver of the Cloisterham omnibus, whom he had seen but once, and that on the day of his arrival.

'And what I recommend you for the present, is, don't talk, Mr. Landless. You'll find a friend waiting for you, at the high road – gone ahead by the other way when we split into two parties – and you had much better say nothing till you come up with him. Bring that stick along, somebody else, and let's be moving!'

Utterly bewildered, Neville stared around him and said not a word. Walking between his two conductors, who held his arms in theirs, he went on, as in a dream, until they came again into the high road, and into the midst of a little group of people. The men who had turned back were among the group; and its central figures were Mr. Jasper and Mr. Crisparkle. Neville's conductors took him up to the Minor Canon, and there released him, as an act of deference to that gentleman.

'What is all this, sir? What is the matter? I feel as if I had lost my senses!' cried Neville, the group closing in around him.

'Where is my nephew?' asked Mr. Jasper, wildly.

'Where is your nephew?' repeated Neville. 'Why do you ask me?'

'I ask you,' retorted Jasper, 'because you were the last person in his company, and he is not to be found.'

'Not to be found!' cried Neville, aghast.

'Stay, stay,' said Mr. Crisparkle. 'Permit me, Jasper. Mr. Neville, you are confounded; collect your thoughts; it is of great importance that you should collect your thoughts; attend to me.'

'I will try, sir, but I seem mad.'

'You left Mr. Jasper's last night, with Edwin Drood?'

'Yes.'

'At what hour?'

'Was it at twelve o'clock?' asked Neville, with his hand to his confused head, and appealing to Jasper.

'Quite right,' said Mr. Crisparkle; 'the hour Mr. Jasper has already named to me. You went down to the river together?'

'Undoubtedly. To see the action of the wind there.'

'What followed? How long did you stay there?'

'About ten minutes; I should say not more. We then walked together to your house, and he took leave of me at the door.'

'Did he say that he was going down to the river again?'

'No. He said that he was going straight back.'

The bystanders looked at one another, and at Mr. Crisparkle. To whom, Mr. Jasper, who had been intently watching Neville, said in a low distinct suspicious voice: 'What are those stains upon his dress?'

All eyes were turned towards the blood upon his clothes.

'And here are the same stains upon this stick!' said Jasper, taking it from the hand of the man who held it. 'I know the stick to be his, and he carried it last night. What does this mean?'

'In the name of God, say what it means, Neville!' urged Mr. Crisparkle.

'That man and I,' said Neville, pointing out his late adversary, 'had a struggle for the stick just now, and you may see the same marks on him, sir. What was I to suppose, when

I found myself molested by eight people? Could I dream of the true reason when they would give me none at all?'

They admitted that they had thought it discreet to be silent, and that the struggle had taken place. And yet the very men who had seen it, looked darkly at the smears which the bright cold air had already dried.

'We must return, Neville,' said Mr. Crisparkle; 'of course you will be glad to come back to clear yourself?'

'Of course, sir.'

'Mr. Landless will walk at my side,' the Minor Canon continued, looking around him. 'Come, Neville!'

They set forth on the walk back; and the others, with one exception, straggled after them at various distances. Jasper walked on the other side of Neville, and never quitted that position. He was silent, while Mr. Crisparkle more than once repeated his former questions, and while Neville repeated his former answers; also, while they both hazarded some explanatory conjectures. He was obstinately silent, because Mr. Crisparkle's manner directly appealed to him to take some part in the discussion, and no appeal would move his fixed face. When they drew near to the city, and it was suggested by the Minor Canon that they might do well in calling on the Mayor at once, he assented with a stern nod; but he spake no word until they stood in Mr. Sapsea's parlour.

Mr. Sapsea being informed by Mr. Crisparkle of the circumstances under which they desired to make a voluntary statement before him, Mr. Jasper broke silence by declaring that he placed his whole reliance, humanly speaking, on Mr. Sapsea's penetration. There was no conceivable reason why his nephew should have suddenly absconded, unless Mr. Sapsea could suggest one, and then he would defer. There was no intelligible likelihood of his having returned to the river, and been accidentally drowned in the dark, unless it should appear likely to Mr. Sapsea, and then again he would defer. He washed his hands as clean as he could, of all horrible suspicions, unless it should appear to Mr. Sapsea that some such were inseparable from his last companion before his disappearance (not on good terms with previously), and then, once more, he would defer. His own state of mind, he being distracted with doubts, and labouring under dismal apprehensions, was not to be safely trusted; but Mr. Sapsea's was.

Mr. Sapsea expressed his opinion that the case had a dark look; in short (and here his eyes rested full on Neville's countenance), an Un-English complexion. Having made this grand point, he wandered into a denser haze and maze of nonsense than even a mayor might have been expected to disport himself in, and came out of it with the brilliant discovery that to take the life of a fellow-creature was to take something that didn't belong to you. He wavered whether or no he should at once issue his warrant for the committal of Neville Landless to jail, under circumstances of grave suspicion; and he might have gone so far as to do it but for the indignant protest of the Minor Canon: who undertook for the young man's remaining in his own house, and being produced by his own hands, whenever demanded. Mr. Jasper then understood Mr. Sapsea to suggest that the river should be dragged, that its banks should be rigidly examined, that particulars of the disappearance should be sent to all outlying places and to London, and that placards and advertisements should be widely circulated imploring Edwin Drood, if for any unknown reason he had withdrawn himself from his uncle's home and society, to take pity on that loving kinsman's sore bereavement and distress, and somehow inform him that he was yet alive. Mr. Sapsea was perfectly understood, for this was exactly his meaning (though he had said nothing about it); and measures were taken towards all these ends immediately.

It would be difficult to determine which was the more oppressed with horror and amazement: Neville Landless, or John Jasper. But that Jasper's position forced him to be active, while Neville's forced him to be passive, there would have been nothing to choose between them. Each was bowed down and broken.

With the earliest light of the next morning, men were at work upon the river, and other men – most of whom volunteered for the service – were examining the banks. All the

livelong day, the search went on; upon the river, with barge
and pole, and drag and net; upon the muddy and rushy
shore, with jack-boot, hatchet, spade, rope, dogs, and all
imaginable appliances. Even at night, the river was specked
with lanterns, and lurid with fires; far-off creeks, into which
the tide washed as it changed, had their knots of watchers,
listening to the lapping of the stream, and looking out for any
burden it might bear; remote shingly causeways near the sea,
and lonely points off which there was a race of water, had
their unwonted flaring cressets and rough-coated figures
when the next day dawned; but no trace of Edwin Drood
revisited the light of the sun.

All that day, again, the search went on. Now, in barge and
boat; and now ashore among the osiers, or tramping amidst
mud and stakes and jagged stones in low-lying places, where
solitary watermarks and signals of strange shapes showed
like spectres, John Jasper worked and toiled. But to no
purpose; for still no trace of Edwin Drood revisited the
light of the sun.

Setting his watches for that night again, so that vigilant
eyes should be kept on every change of tide, he went home
exhausted. Unkempt and disordered, bedaubed with mud
that had dried upon him, and with much of his clothing torn
to rags, he had but just dropped into his easy chair, when Mr.
Grewgious stood before him.

'This is strange news,' said Mr. Grewgious.

'Strange and fearful news.'

Jasper had merely lifted up his heavy eyes to say it, and
now dropped them again as he drooped, worn out, over one
side of his easy chair.

Mr. Grewgious smoothed his head and face, and stood
looking at the fire.

'How is your ward?' asked Jasper, after a time, in a faint,
fatigued voice.

'Poor little thing! You may imagine her condition.'

'Have you seen his sister?' inquired Jasper, as before.

'Whose?'

The curtness of the counter-question, and the cool slow
manner in which, as he put it, Mr. Grewgious moved his eyes

from the fire to his companion's face, might at any other time have been exasperating. In his depression and exhaustion, Jasper merely opened his eyes to say: 'The suspected young man's.'

'Do you suspect him?' asked Mr. Grewgious.

'I don't know what to think. I cannot make up my mind.'

'Nor I,' said Mr. Grewgious. 'But as you spoke of him as the suspected young man, I thought you *had* made up your mind. – I have just left Miss Landless.'

'What is her state?'

'Defiance of all suspicion, and unbounded faith in her brother.'

'Poor thing!'

'However,' pursued Mr. Grewgious, 'it is not of her that I came to speak. It is of my ward. I have a communication to make that will surprise you. At least, it has surprised me.'

Jasper, with a groaning sigh, turned wearily in his chair.

'Shall I put it off till to-morrow?' said Mr. Grewgious. 'Mind! I warn you, that I think it will surprise you!'

More attention and concentration came into John Jasper's eyes as they caught sight of Mr. Grewgious smoothing his head again, and again looking at the fire; but now, with a compressed and determined mouth.

'What is it?' demanded Jasper, becoming upright in his chair.

'To be sure,' said Mr. Grewgious, provokingly slowly and internally, as he kept his eyes on the fire: 'I might have known it sooner; she gave me the opening; but I am such an exceedingly Angular man, that it never occurred to me; I took all for granted.'

'What is it?' demanded Jasper, once more.

Mr. Grewgious, alternately opening and shutting the palms of his hands as he warmed them at the fire, and looking fixedly at him sideways, and never changing either his action or his look in all that followed, went on to reply.

'This young couple, the lost youth and Miss Rosa, my ward, though so long betrothed, and so long recognizing their betrothal, and so near being married—'

Mr. Grewgious has his Suspicions

Mr. Grewgious saw a staring white face, and two quivering white lips, in the easy chair, and saw two muddy hands gripping its sides. But for the hands, he might have thought he had never seen the face.

'– This young couple came gradually to the discovery (made on both sides pretty equally, I think), that they would be happier and better, both in their present and their future lives, as affectionate friends, or say rather as brother and sister, than as husband and wife.'

Mr. Grewgious saw a lead-coloured face in the easy chair, and on its surface dreadful starting drops or bubbles, as if of steel.

'This young couple formed at length the healthy resolution of interchanging their discoveries, openly, sensibly, and tenderly. They met for that purpose. After some innocent and generous talk, they agreed to dissolve their existing, and their intended, relations, for ever and ever.'

Mr. Grewgious saw a ghastly figure rise, open-mouthed, from the easy chair, and lift its outspread hands towards its head.

'One of this young couple, and that one your nephew, fearful, however, that in the tenderness of your affection for him you would be bitterly disappointed by so wide a departure from his projected life, forbore to tell you the secret, for a few days, and left it to be disclosed by me, when I should come down to speak to you, and he would be gone. I speak to you, and he is gone.'

Mr. Grewgious saw the ghastly figure throw back its head, clutch its hair with its hands, and turn with a writhing action from him.

'I have now said all I have to say: except that this young couple parted, firmly, though not without tears and sorrow, on the evening when you last saw them together.'

Mr. Grewgious heard a terrible shriek, and saw no ghastly figure, sitting or standing; saw nothing but a heap of torn and miry clothes upon the floor.

Not changing his action even then, he opened and shut the palms of his hands as he warmed them, and looked down at it.

CHAPTER XVI

Devoted

WHEN John Jasper recovered from his fit or swoon, he found himself being tended by Mr. and Mrs. Tope, whom his visitor had summoned for the purpose. His visitor, wooden of aspect, sat stiffly in a chair, with his hands upon his knees, watching his recovery.

'There! You've come to, nicely now, sir,' said the tearful Mrs. Tope; 'you were thoroughly worn out, and no wonder!'

'A man,' said Mr. Grewgious, with his usual air of repeating a lesson, 'cannot have his rest broken, and his mind cruelly tormented, and his body overtaxed by fatigue, without being thoroughly worn out.'

'I fear I have alarmed you?' Jasper apologized faintly, when he was helped into his easy chair.

'Not at all, I thank you,' answered Mr. Grewgious.

'You are too considerate.'

'Not at all, I thank you,' answered Mr. Grewgious again.

'You must take some wine, sir,' said Mrs. Tope, 'and the jelly that I had ready for you, and that you wouldn't put your lips to at noon, though I warned you what would come of it, you know, and you not breakfasted; and you must have a wing of the roast fowl that has been put back twenty times if it's been put back once. It shall all be on table in five minutes, and this good gentleman belike will stop and see you take it.'

This good gentleman replied with a snort, which might mean yes, or no, or anything, or nothing, and which Mrs. Tope would have found highly mystifying, but that her attention was divided by the service of the table.

'You will take something with me?' said Jasper, as the cloth was laid.

'I couldn't get a morsel down my throat, I thank you,' answered Mr. Grewgious.

Jasper both ate and drank almost voraciously. Combined with the hurry in his mode of doing it, was an evident indif-

ference to the taste of what he took, suggesting that he ate
and drank to fortify himself against any other failure of the
spirits, far more than to gratify his palate. Mr. Grewgious in
the meantime sat upright, with no expression in his face, and
a hard kind of imperturbably polite protest all over him: as
though he would have said, in reply to some invitation to
discourse: 'I couldn't originate the faintest approach to an
observation on any subject whatever, I thank you.'

'Do you know,' said Jasper, when he had pushed away his
plate and glass, and had sat meditating for a few minutes: 'do
you know that I find some crumbs of comfort in the communication with which you have so much amazed me?'

'*Do* you?' returned Mr. Grewgious; pretty plainly adding
the unspoken clause: 'I don't, I thank you!'

'After recovering from the shock of a piece of news of my
dear boy, so entirely unexpected, and so destructive of all the
castles I had built for him; and after having had time to think
of it; yes.'

'I shall be glad to pick up your crumbs,' said Mr. Grewgious, dryly.

'Is there not, or is there – if I deceive myself, tell me so,
and shorten my pain – is there not, or is there, hope that,
finding himself in this new position, and becoming sensitively
alive to the awkward burden of explanation, in this quarter,
and that, and the other, with which it would load him, he
avoided the awkwardness, and took to flight?'

'Such a thing might be,' said Mr. Grewgious, pondering.

'Such a thing has been. I have read of cases in which
people, rather than face a seven days' wonder, and have to
account for themselves to the idle and impertinent, have
taken themselves away, and been long unheard of.'

'I believe such things have happened,' said Mr. Grewgious, pondering still.

'When I had, and could have, no suspicion,' pursued
Jasper, eagerly following the new track, 'that the dear lost
boy had with-held anything from me – most of all, such a
leading matter as this – what gleam of light was there for me
in the whole black sky? When I supposed that his intended
wife was here, and his marriage close at hand, how could

I entertain the possibility of his voluntarily leaving this place, in a manner that would be so unaccountable, capricious, and cruel? But now that I know what you have told me, is there no little chink through which day pierces? Supposing him to have disappeared of his own act, is not his disappearance more accountable and less cruel? The fact of his having just parted from your ward, is in itself a sort of reason for his going away. It does not make his mysterious departure the less cruel to me, it is true; but it relieves it of cruelty to her.'

Mr. Grewgious could not but assent to this.

'And even as to me,' continued Jasper, still pursuing the new track, with ardour, and, as he did so, brightening with hope: 'he knew that you were coming to me; he knew that you were entrusted to tell me what you have told me; if your doing so has awakened a new train of thought in my perplexed mind, it reasonably follows that, from the same premises, he might have foreseen the inferences that I should draw. Grant that he did foresee them; and even the cruelty to me – and who am I! – John Jasper, Music-Master! – vanishes.'

Once more, Mr. Grewgious could not but assent to this.

'I have had my distrusts, and terrible distrusts they have been,' said Jasper; 'but your disclosure, overpowering as it was at first – showing me that my own dear boy had had a great disappointing reservation from me, who so fondly loved him – kindles hope within me. You do not extinguish it when I state it, but admit it to be a reasonable hope. I begin to believe it possible:' here he clasped his hands: 'that he may have disappeared from among us of his own accord, and that he may yet be alive and well!'

Mr. Crisparkle came in at the moment. To whom Mr. Jasper repeated:

'I begin to believe it possible that he may have disappeared of his own accord, and may yet be alive and well!'

Mr. Crisparkle taking a seat, and inquiring: 'Why so?' Mr. Jasper repeated the arguments he had just set forth. If they had been less plausible than they were, the good Minor Canon's mind would have been in a state of preparation to receive them, as exculpatory of his unfortunate pupil. But he, too, did really attach great importance to the lost young man's having been, so immediately before his disappearance, placed in a new and embarrassing relation towards every one acquainted with his projects and affairs; and the fact seemed to him to present the question in a new light.

'I stated to Mr. Sapsea, when we waited on him,' said Jasper: as he really had done: 'that there was no quarrel or difference between the two young men at their last meeting. We all know that their first meeting was, unfortunately, very far from amicable; but all went smoothly and quietly when they were last together at my house. My dear boy was not in his usual spirits; he was depressed – I noticed that – and I am bound henceforth to dwell upon the circumstance the more, now that I know there was a special reason for his being depressed: a reason, moreover, which may possibly have induced him to absent himself.'

'I pray to Heaven it may turn out so!' exclaimed Mr. Crisparkle.

'*I* pray to Heaven it may turn out so!' repeated Jasper. 'You know – and Mr. Grewgious should now know likewise – that I took a great prepossession against Mr. Neville Landless, arising out of his furious conduct on that first occasion. You know that I came to you, extremely apprehensive, on my dear boy's behalf, of his mad violence. You know that I even entered in my Diary, and showed the entry to you, that I had dark forebodings against him. Mr. Grewgious ought to be possessed of the whole case. He shall not, through any suppression of mine, be informed of a part of it, and kept in ignorance of another part of it. I wish him to be good enough to understand that the communication he has made to me has hopefully influenced my mind, in spite of its having been, before this mysterious occurrence took place, profoundly impressed against young Landless.'

This fairness troubled the Minor Canon much. He felt that he was not as open in his own dealing. He charged against himself reproachfully that he had suppressed, so far, the two points of a second strong outbreak of temper against Edwin Drood on the part of Neville, and of the passion of jealousy having, to his own certain knowledge, flamed up in Neville's breast against him. He was convinced of Neville's innocence of any part in the ugly disappearance, and yet so many little circumstances combined so woefully against him, that he dreaded to add two more to their cumulative weight. He was among the truest of men; but he had been balancing in his mind, much to its distress, whether his volunteering to tell these two fragments of truth, at this time, would not be tantamount to a piecing together of falsehood in the place of truth.

However, here was a model before him. He hesitated no longer. Addressing Mr. Grewgious, as one placed in authority by the revelation he had brought to bear on the mystery (and surpassingly Angular Mr. Grewgious became when he found himself in that unexpected position), Mr. Crisparkle bore his testimony to Mr. Jasper's strict sense of justice, and, expressing his absolute confidence in the complete clearance of his pupil from the least taint of suspicion, sooner or later, avowed that his confidence in that young gentleman had been formed, in spite of his confidential knowledge that his temper was of the hottest and fiercest, and that it was directly incensed against Mr. Jasper's nephew, by the circumstance of his romantically supposing himself to be enamoured of the same young lady. The sanguine reaction manifest in Mr. Jasper was proof even against this unlooked-for declaration. It turned him paler; but he repeated that he would cling to the hope he had derived from Mr. Grewgious; and that if no trace of his dear boy were found, leading to the dreadful inference that he had been made away with, he would cherish unto the last stretch of possibility, the idea, that he might have absconded of his own wild will.

Now, it fell out that Mr. Crisparkle, going away from this conference still very uneasy in his mind, and very much troubled on behalf of the young man whom he held as a kind of prisoner in his own house, took a memorable night walk.

He walked to Cloisterham Weir.

He often did so, and consequently there was nothing remarkable in his footsteps tending that way. But the preoccupation of his mind so hindered him from planning any

walk, or taking heed of the objects he passed, that his first
consciousness of being near the Weir was derived from the
sound of the falling water close at hand.

'How did I come here!' was his first thought, as he
stopped.

'Why did I come here!' was his second.

Then, he stood intently listening to the water. A familiar
passage in his reading, about airy tongues that syllable men's
names, rose so unbidden to his ear, that he put it from him
with his hand, as if it were tangible.

It was starlight. The Weir was full two miles above the spot
to which the young men had repaired to watch the storm. No
search had been made up here, for the tide had been running strongly down, at that time of the night of Christmas
Eve, and the likeliest places for the discovery of a body, if a
fatal accident had happened under such circumstances, all
lay – both when the tide ebbed, and when it flowed again –
between that spot and the sea. The water came over the Weir,
with its usual sound on a cold starlight night, and little could
be seen of it; yet Mr. Crisparkle had a strange idea that
something unusual hung about the place.

He reasoned with himself: What was it? Where was it? Put
it to the proof. Which sense did it address?

No sense reported anything unusual there. He listened
again, and his sense of hearing again checked the water
coming over the Weir, with its usual sound on a cold starlight
night.

Knowing very well that the mystery with which his mind
was occupied, might of itself give the place this haunted air,
he strained those hawk's eyes of his for the correction of his
sight. He got closer to the Weir, and peered at its well-known
posts and timbers. Nothing in the least unusual was remotely
shadowed forth. But he resolved that he would come back
early in the morning.

The Weir ran through his broken sleep, all night, and he
was back again at sunrise. It was a bright frosty morning. The
whole composition before him, when he stood where he had
stood last night, was clearly discernible in its minutest details.
He had surveyed it closely for some minutes, and was about

to withdraw his eyes, when they were attracted keenly to one spot.

He turned his back upon the Weir, and looked far away at the sky, and at the earth, and then looked again at that one spot. It caught his sight again immediately, and he concentrated his vision upon it. He could not lose it now, though it was but such a speck in the landscape. It fascinated his sight. His hands began plucking off his coat. For it struck him that at that spot – a corner of the Weir – something glistened, which did not move and come over with the glistening water-drops, but remained stationary.

He assured himself of this, he threw off his clothes, he plunged into the icy water, and swam for the spot. Climbing the timbers, he took from them, caught among their interstices by its chain, a gold watch, bearing engraved upon its back, E. D.

He brought the watch to the bank, swam to the Weir again, climbed it, and dived off. He knew every hole and corner of all the depths, and dived and dived and dived, until he could bear the cold no more. His notion was, that he would find the body; he only found a shirt-pin sticking in some mud and ooze.

With these discoveries he returned to Cloisterham, and, taking Neville Landless with him, went straight to the Mayor. Mr. Jasper was sent for, the watch and shirt-pin were identified, Neville was detained, and the wildest frenzy and fatuity of evil report arose against him. He was of that vindictive and violent nature, that but for his poor sister, who alone had influence over him, and out of whose sight he was never to be trusted, he would be in the daily commission of murder. Before coming to England he had caused to be whipped to death sundry 'Natives' – nomadic persons, encamping now in Asia, now in Africa, now in the West Indies, and now at the North Pole – vaguely supposed in Cloisterham to be always black, always of great virtue, always calling themselves Me, and everybody else Massa or Missie (according to sex), and always reading tracts of the obscurest meaning, in broken English, but always accurately understanding them in the purest mother tongue. He had nearly brought Mrs. Crisparkle's grey hairs with sorrow to the grave. (Those original expressions were Mr. Sapsea's.) He had repeatedly said he would have Mr. Crisparkle's life. He had repeatedly said he would have everybody's life, and become in effect the last man. He had been brought down to Cloisterham, from London, by an eminent Philanthropist, and why? Because that Philanthropist had expressly declared: 'I owe it to my fellow-creatures that he should be, in the words of BENTHAM, where he is the cause of the greatest danger to the smallest number.'

These dropping shots from the blunderbusses of blunderheadedness might not have hit him in a vital place. But he had to stand against a trained and well-directed fire of arms of precision too. He had notoriously threatened the lost young man, and had, according to the showing of his own faithful friend and tutor who strove so hard for him, a cause of bitter animosity (created by himself, and stated by himself), against that ill-starred fellow. He had armed himself with an offensive weapon for the fatal night, and he had gone off early in the morning, after making preparations for departure. He had been found with traces of blood on him; truly, they might have been wholly caused as he represented, but they might not, also. On a search-warrant being issued for the examination of his room, clothes, and so forth, it was discovered that he had destroyed all his papers, and rearranged all his possessions, on the very afternoon of the disappearance. The watch found at the Weir was challenged by the jeweller as one he had wound and set for Edwin Drood, at twenty minutes past two on that same afternoon; and it had run down, before being cast into the water; and it was the jeweller's positive opinion that it had never been rewound. This would justify the hypothesis that the watch was taken from him not long after he left Mr. Jasper's house at midnight, in company with the last person seen with him, and that it had been thrown away after being retained some hours. Why thrown away? If he had been murdered, and so artfully disfigured, or concealed, or both, as that the murderer hoped identification to be impossible, except from something that he wore, assuredly the murderer would seek to remove from the body the most lasting, the best known, and the most easily recognizable, things upon it. Those things would be the watch and shirt-pin. As to his opportunities of casting them into the river; if he were the object of these suspicions, they were easy. For, he had been seen by many persons, wandering about on that side of the city – indeed on all sides of it – in a miserable and seemingly half-distracted manner. As to the choice of the spot, obviously such criminating evidence had better take its chance of being found anywhere, rather than upon himself, or in his possession. Concerning the reconciliatory nature of the appointed meeting between the two young men, very little could be made of that, in young Landless's favour; for, it distinctly appeared that the meeting originated, not with him, but with Mr. Crisparkle, and that it had been urged on by Mr. Crisparkle; and who could say how unwillingly, or in what ill-conditioned mood, his enforced pupil had gone to it? The more his case was looked into, the weaker it became in every point. Even the broad suggestion that the lost young man had absconded, was rendered additionally improbable on the showing of the young lady from whom he had so lately parted; for, what did she say, with great earnestness and sorrow, when interrogated? That he had, expressly and enthusiastically, planned with her, that he would await the arrival of her guardian, Mr. Grewgious. And yet, be it observed, he disappeared before that gentleman appeared.

On the suspicions thus urged and supported, Neville was detained and re-detained, and the search was pressed on every hand, and Jasper laboured night and day. But nothing more was found. No discovery being made which proved the lost man to be dead, it at length became necessary to release the person suspected of having made away with him. Neville was set at large. Then, a consequence ensued which Mr. Crisparkle had too well foreseen. Neville must leave the place, for the place shunned him and cast him out. Even had it not been so, the dear old china shepherdess would have worried herself to death with fears for her son, and with general trepidation occasioned by their having such an inmate. Even had that not been so, the authority to which the

Minor Canon deferred officially, would have settled the point.

'Mr. Crisparkle,' quoth the Dean, 'human justice may err, but it must act according to its lights. The days of taking sanctuary are past. This young man must not take sanctuary with us.'

'You mean that he must leave my house, sir?'

'Mr. Crisparkle,' returned the prudent Dean, 'I claim no authority in your house. I merely confer with you, on the painful necessity you find yourself under, of depriving this young man of the great advantages of your counsel and instruction.'

'It is very lamentable, sir,' Mr. Crisparkle represented.

'Very much so,' the Dean assented.

'And if it be a necessity –' Mr. Crisparkle faltered.

'As you unfortunately find it to be,' returned the Dean.

Mr. Crisparkle bowed submissively. 'It is hard to prejudge his case, sir, but I am sensible that—'

'Just so. Perfectly. As you say, Mr. Crisparkle,' interposed the Dean, nodding his head smoothly, 'there is nothing else to be done. No doubt, no doubt. There is no alternative, as your good sense has discovered.'

'I am entirely satisfied of his perfect innocence, sir, nevertheless.'

'We-e-ell!' said the Dean, in a more confidential tone, and slightly glancing around him, 'I would not say so, generally. Not generally. Enough of suspicion attaches to him to – no, I think I would not say so, generally.'

Mr. Crisparkle bowed again.

'It does not become us, perhaps,' pursued the Dean, 'to be partizans. Not partizans. We clergy keep our hearts warm and our heads cool, and we hold a judicious middle course.'

'I hope you do not object, sir, to my having stated in public, emphatically, that he will reappear here, whenever any new suspicion may be awakened, or any new circumstance may come to light in this extraordinary matter?'

'Not at all,' returned the Dean. 'And yet, do you know, I don't think,' with a very nice and neat emphasis on those two words: 'I *don't think* I would state it, emphatically. State it?

Ye-e-es! But emphatically? No-o-o. I *think* not. In point of fact, Mr. Crisparkle, keeping our hearts warm and our heads cool, we clergy need do nothing emphatically.'

So, Minor Canon Row knew Neville Landless no more; and he went whithersoever he would, or could, with a blight upon his name and fame.

It was not until then that John Jasper silently resumed his place in the choir. Haggard and red-eyed, his hopes plainly had deserted him, his sanguine mood was gone, and all his worst misgivings had come back. A day or two afterwards, while unrobing, he took his Diary from a pocket of his coat, turned the leaves, and with an expressive look, and without one spoken word, handed this entry to Mr. Crisparkle to read:

'My dear boy is murdered. The discovery of the watch and shirt-pin convinces me that he was murdered that night, and that his jewellery was taken from him to prevent identification by its means. All the delusive hopes I had founded on his separation from his betrothed wife, I give to the winds. They perish before this fatal discovery. I now swear, and record the oath on this page, That I nevermore will discuss this mystery with any human creature, until I hold the clue to it in my hand. That I never will relax in my secrecy or in my search. That I will fasten the crime of the murder of my dear dead boy, upon the murderer. And That I devote myself to his destruction.'

CHAPTER XVII

Philanthropy, Professional and Unprofessional

Full half a year had come and gone, and Mr. Crisparkle sat in a waiting-room in the London chief offices of the Haven of Philanthropy, until he could have audience of Mr. Honeythunder.

In his college-days of athletic exercises, Mr. Crisparkle had known professors of the Noble Art of fisticuffs, and had attended two or three of their gloved gatherings. He had now an opportunity of observing that as to the phrenological formation of the backs of their heads, the Professing Philanthropists were uncommonly like the Pugilists. In the development of all those organs which constitute, or attend, a propensity to 'pitch into' your fellow-creatures, the Philanthropists were remarkably favoured. There were several Professors passing in and out, with exactly the aggressive air upon them of being ready for a turn-up with any Novice who might happen to be on hand, that Mr. Crisparkle well remembered in the circles of the Fancy. Preparations were in progress for a moral little Mill somewhere on the rural circuit, and other Professors were backing this or that Heavy-Weight as good for such or such speech-making hits, so very much after the manner of the sporting publicans that the intended Resolutions might have been Rounds. In an official manager of these displays much celebrated for his platform tactics, Mr. Crisparkle recognized (in a suit of black) the counterpart of a deceased benefactor of his species, an eminent public character, once known to fame as Frosty-faced Fogo, who in days of yore superintended the formation of the magic circle with the ropes and stakes. There were only three conditions of resemblance wanting between these Professors and those. Firstly, the Philanthropists were in very bad training: much too fleshy, and presenting, both in face and figure, a superabundance of what is known to Pugilistic Experts as

Suet Pudding. Secondly, the Philanthropists had not the good temper of the Pugilists, and used worse language. Thirdly, their fighting code stood in great need of revision, as empowering them not only to bore their man to the ropes, but to bore him to the confines of distraction; also to hit him when he was down, hit him anywhere and anyhow, kick him, stamp upon him, gouge him, and maul him behind his back without mercy. In these last particulars the Professors of the Noble Art were much nobler than the Professors of Philanthropy.

Mr. Crisparkle was so completely lost in musing on these similarities and dissimilarities, at the same time watching the crowd which came and went, always, as it seemed, on errands of antagonistically snatching something from somebody, and never giving anything to anybody: that his name was twice called before he heard it. On his at length responding, he was shown by a miserably shabby and underpaid stipendiary Philanthropist (who could hardly have done worse if he had taken service with a declared enemy of the human race) to Mr. Honeythunder's room.

'Sir,' said Mr. Honeythunder, in his tremendous voice, like a schoolmaster issuing orders to a boy of whom he had a bad opinion, 'sit down.'

Mr. Crisparkle seated himself.

Mr. Honeythunder, having signed the remaining few score of a few thousand circulars, calling upon a corresponding number of families without means to come forward, stump up instantly, and be Philanthropists, or go to the Devil, another shabby stipendiary Philanthropist (highly disinterested, if in earnest) gathered these into a basket and walked off with them.

'Now, Mr. Crisparkle,' said Mr. Honeythunder, turning his chair half round towards him when they were alone, and squaring his arms with his hands on his knees, and his brows knitted, as if he added, I am going to make short work of *you*: 'Now, Mr. Crisparkle, we entertain different views, you and I, sir, of the sanctity of human life.'

'Do we?' returned the Minor Canon.

'We do, sir.'

'Might I ask you,' said the Minor Canon: 'what are your views on that subject?'

'That human life is a thing to be held sacred, sir.'

'Might I ask you,' pursued the Minor Canon as before: 'what you suppose to be my views on that subject?'

'By George, sir!' returned the Philanthropist, squaring his arms still more, as he frowned on Mr. Crisparkle: 'they are best known to yourself.'

'Readily admitted. But you began by saying that we took different views, you know. Therefore (or you could not say so) you must have set up some views as mine. Pray, what views *have* you set up as mine?'

'Here is a man – and a young man,' said Mr. Honeythunder, as if that made the matter infinitely worse, and he could have easily borne the loss of an old one: 'swept off the face of the earth by a deed of violence. What do you call that?'

'Murder,' said the Minor Canon.

'What do you call the doer of that deed, sir?'

'A murderer,' said the Minor Canon.

'I am glad to hear you admit so much, sir,' retorted Mr. Honeythunder, in his most offensive manner; 'and I candidly tell you that I didn't expect it.' Here he lowered heavily at Mr. Crisparkle again.

'Be so good as to explain what you mean by those very unjustifiable expressions.'

'I don't sit here, sir,' returned the Philanthropist, raising his voice to a roar, 'to be browbeaten.'

'As the only other person present, no one can possibly know that better than I do,' returned the Minor Canon very quietly. 'But I interrupt your explanation.'

'Murder!' proceeded Mr. Honeythunder, in a kind of boisterous reverie, with his platform folding of his arms, and his platform nod of abhorrent reflection after each short sentence of a word. 'Bloodshed! Abel! Cain! I hold no terms with Cain. I repudiate with a shudder the red hand when it is offered me.'

Instead of instantly leaping into his chair and cheering himself hoarse, as the Brotherhood in public meeting assembled would infallibly have done on this cue, Mr. Crisparkle merely reversed the quiet crossing of his legs, and said mildly: 'Don't let me interrupt your explanation – when you begin it.'

'The Commandments say no murder. NO murder, sir!' proceeded Mr. Honeythunder, platformally pausing as if he took Mr. Crisparkle to task for having distinctly asserted that they said, You may do a little murder and then leave off.

'And they also say, you shall bear no false witness,' observed Mr. Crisparkle.

'Enough!' bellowed Mr. Honeythunder, with a solemnity and severity that would have brought the house down at a meeting, 'E – e – nough! My late wards being now of age, and I being released from a trust which I cannot contemplate without a thrill of horror, there are the accounts which you have undertaken to accept on their behalf, and there is a statement of the balance which you have undertaken to receive, and which you cannot receive too soon. And let me tell you, sir, I wish, that as a man and a Minor Canon, you were better employed,' with a nod. 'Better employed,' with another nod. 'Bet – ter em – ployed!' with another and the three nods added up.

Mr. Crisparkle rose; a little heated in the face, but with perfect command of himself.

'Mr. Honeythunder,' he said, taking up the papers referred to: 'my being better or worse employed than I am at present is a matter of taste and opinion. You might think me better employed in enrolling myself a member of your Society.'

'Ay, indeed, sir!' retorted Mr. Honeythunder, shaking his head in a threatening manner. 'It would have been better for you if you had done that long ago!'

'I think otherwise.'

'Or,' said Mr. Honeythunder, shaking his head again, 'I might think one of your profession better employed in devoting himself to the discovery and punishment of guilt than in leaving that duty to be undertaken by a layman.'

'I may regard my profession from a point of view which teaches me that its first duty is towards those who are in necessity and tribulation, who are desolate and oppressed,' said Mr. Crisparkle. 'However, as I have quite clearly satisfied myself that it is no part of my profession to make professions, I say no more of that. But I owe it to Mr. Neville, and to Mr. Neville's sister (and in a much lower degree to myself), to say to you that I *know* I was in the full possession and understanding of Mr. Neville's mind and heart at the time of this occurrence; and that, without in the least colouring or concealing what was to be deplored in him and required to be corrected, I feel certain that his tale is true. Feeling that certainty, I befriend him. As long as that certainty shall last I will befriend him. And if any consideration could shake me in this resolve, I should be so ashamed of myself for my meanness that no man's good opinion – no, nor no woman's – so gained, could compensate me for the loss of my own.'

Good fellow! Manly fellow! And he was so modest, too. There was no more self-assertion in the Minor Canon than in the schoolboy who had stood in the breezy playing-fields keeping a wicket. He was simply and staunchly true to his duty alike in the large case and in the small. So all true souls ever are. So every true soul ever was, ever is, and ever will be. There is nothing little to the really great in spirit.

'Then who do you make out did the deed?' asked Mr. Honeythunder, turning on him abruptly.

'Heaven forbid,' said Mr. Crisparkle, 'that in my desire to clear one man I should lightly criminate another! I accuse no one.'

'Tcha!' ejaculated Mr. Honeythunder with great disgust; for this was by no means the principle on which the Philanthropic Brotherhood usually proceeded. 'And, sir, you are not a disinterested witness, we must bear in mind.'

'How am I an interested one?' inquired Mr. Crisparkle, smiling innocently, at a loss to imagine.

'There was a certain stipend, sir, paid to you for your pupil, which may have warped your judgement a bit,' said Mr. Honeythunder, coarsely.

'Perhaps I expect to retain it still?' Mr. Crisparkle returned, enlightened; 'do you mean that too?'

'Well, sir,' returned the professional Philanthropist, getting up, and thrusting his hands down into his trousers pockets; 'I don't go about measuring people for caps. If people find I have any about me that fit 'em, they can put 'em on and wear 'em, if they like. That's their look out: not mine.'

Mr. Crisparkle eyed him with a just indignation, and took him to task thus:

'Mr. Honeythunder, I hoped when I came in here that I might be under no necessity of commenting on the introduction of platform manners or platform manœuvres among the decent forbearances of private life. But you have given me such a specimen of both, that I should be a fit subject for both if I remained silent respecting them. They are detestable.'

'They don't suit *you*, I dare say, sir.'

'They are,' repeated Mr. Crisparkle, without noticing the interruption, 'detestable. They violate equally the justice that should belong to Christians, and the restraints that should belong to gentlemen. You assume a great crime to have been committed by one whom I, acquainted with the attendant circumstances, and having numerous reasons on my side, devoutly believe to be innocent of it. Because I differ from you on that vital point, what is your platform resource? Instantly to turn upon me, charging that I have no sense of the enormity of the crime itself, but am its aider and abettor! So, another time – taking me as representing your opponent in other cases – you set up a platform credulity: a moved and seconded and carried unanimously profession of faith in some ridiculous delusion or mischievous imposition. I decline to believe it, and you fall back upon your platform resource of proclaiming that I believe nothing; that because I will not bow down to a false God of your making, I deny the true God! Another time, you make the platform discovery that War is a vast calamity, and you propose to abolish it by a string of twisted resolutions tossed into the air like the tail of a kite. I do not admit the discovery to be yours in the least, and I have not a grain of faith in your remedy. Again, your platform resource of representing me as revelling in the horrors of a battle-field like a fiend incarnate! Another time, in another of your undiscriminating platform rushes,

you would punish the sober for the drunken. I claim consideration for the comfort, convenience, and refreshment, of
the sober; and you presently make platform proclamation
that I have a depraved desire to turn Heaven's creatures into
swine and wild beasts! In all such cases your movers, and
your seconders, and your supporters – your regular Professors of all degrees – run amuck like so many mad Malays;
habitually attributing the lowest and basest motives with
the utmost recklessness (let me call your attention to a
recent instance in yourself for which you should blush), and
quoting figures which you know to be as wilfully one-sided
as a statement of any complicated account that should be
all Creditor side and no Debtor, or all Debtor side and no
Creditor. Therefore it is, Mr. Honeythunder, that I consider
the platform a sufficiently bad example and a sufficiently bad
school, even in public life; but hold that, carried into private
life, it becomes an unendurable nuisance.'

'These are strong words, sir!' exclaimed the Philanthropist.

'I hope so,' said Mr. Crisparkle. 'Good-morning.'

He walked out of the Haven at a great rate, but soon fell
into his regular brisk pace, and soon had a smile upon his
face as he went along, wondering what the china shepherdess
would have said if she had seen him pounding Mr. Honeythunder in the late little lively affair. For Mr. Crisparkle
had just enough of harmless vanity to hope that he had hit
hard, and to glow with the belief that he had trimmed the
Philanthropic jacket pretty handsomely.

He betook himself to Staple Inn, but not to P. J. T. and
Mr. Grewgious. Full many a creaking stair he climbed before
he reached some attic rooms in a corner, turned the latch of
their unbolted door, and stood beside the table of Neville
Landless.

An air of retreat and solitude hung about the rooms, and
about their inhabitant. He was much worn, and so were they.
Their sloping ceilings, cumbrous rusty locks and grates, and
heavy wooden bins and beams, slowly mouldering withal,
had a prisonous look, and he had the haggard face of a
prisoner. Yet the sunlight shone in at the ugly garret window
which had a penthouse to itself thrust out among the tiles;

and on the cracked and smoke-blackened parapet beyond, some of the deluded sparrows of the place rheumatically hopped, like little feathered cripples who had left their crutches in their nests; and there was a play of living leaves at hand that changed the air, and made an imperfect sort of music in it that would have been melody in the country.

The rooms were sparely furnished, but with good store of books. Everything expressed the abode of a poor student. That Mr. Crisparkle had been either chooser, lender, or donor of the books, or that he combined the three characters, might have been easily seen in the friendly beam of his eyes upon them as he entered.

'How goes it, Neville?'

'I am in good heart, Mr. Crisparkle, and working away.'

'I wish your eyes were not quite so large, and not quite so bright,' said the Minor Canon, slowly releasing the hand he had taken in his.

'They brighten at the sight of you,' returned Neville. 'If you were to fall away from me, they would soon be dull enough.'

'Rally, rally!' urged the other, in a stimulating tone. 'Fight for it, Neville!'

'If I were dying, I feel as if a word from you would rally me; if my pulse had stopped, I feel as if your touch would make it beat again,' said Neville. 'But I *have* rallied, and am doing famously.'

Mr. Crisparkle turned him with his face a little more towards the light.

'I want to see a ruddier touch here, Neville,' he said, indicating his own healthy cheek by way of pattern; 'I want more sun to shine upon you.'

Neville drooped suddenly as he replied in a lowered voice: 'I am not hardy enough for that, yet. I may become so, but I cannot bear it yet. If you had gone through those Cloisterham streets as I did; and if you had seen, as I did, those averted eyes, and the better sort of people silently giving me too much room to pass, that I might not touch them or come near them, you wouldn't think it quite unreasonable that I cannot go about in the daylight.'

'My poor fellow!' said the Minor Canon, in a tone so purely sympathetic that the young man caught his hand: 'I never said it was unreasonable: never thought so. But I should like you to do it.'

'And that would give me the strongest motive to do it. But I cannot yet. I cannot persuade myself that the eyes of even the stream of strangers I pass in this vast city look at me without suspicion. I feel marked and tainted, even when I go out – as I only do – at night. But the darkness covers me then, and I take courage from it.'

Mr. Crisparkle laid a hand upon his shoulder, and stood looking down at him.

'If I could have changed my name,' said Neville, 'I would have done so. But as you wisely pointed out to me, I can't do that, for it would look like guilt. If I could have gone to some distant place, I might have found relief in that, but the thing is not to be thought of, for the same reason. Hiding and escaping would be the construction in either case. It seems a little hard to be so tied to a stake, and innocent; but I don't complain.'

'And you must expect no miracle to help you, Neville,' said Mr. Crisparkle, compassionately.

'No, sir, I know that. The ordinary fulness of time and circumstance is all I have to trust to.'

'It will right you at last, Neville.'

'So I believe, and I hope I may live to know it.'

But perceiving that the despondent mood into which he was falling cast a shadow on the Minor Canon, and (it may be) feeling that the broad hand upon his shoulder was not then quite as steady as its own natural strength had rendered it when it first touched him just now, he brightened and said:

'Excellent circumstances for study, anyhow! and you know, Mr. Crisparkle, what need I have of study in all ways. Not to mention that you have advised me to study for the difficult profession of the law, specially, and that of course I am guiding myself by the advice of such a friend and helper. Such a good friend and helper!'

He took the fortifying hand from his shoulder, and kissed it. Mr. Crisparkle beamed at the books, but not so brightly as when he had entered.

'I gather from your silence on the subject that my late guardian is adverse, Mr. Crisparkle?'

The Minor Canon answered: 'Your late guardian is a – a most unreasonable person, and it signifies nothing to any reasonable person whether he is *ad*verse or *per*verse, or the *re*verse.'

'Well for me that I have enough with economy to live upon,' sighed Neville, half wearily and half cheerily, 'while I wait to be learned, and wait to be righted! Else I might have proved the proverb that while the grass grows, the steed starves!'

He opened some books as he said it, and was soon immersed in their interleaved and annotated passages, while Mr. Crisparkle sat beside him, expounding, correcting, and advising. The Minor Canon's Cathedral duties made these visits of his difficult to accomplish, and only to be compassed at intervals of many weeks. But they were as serviceable as they were precious to Neville Landless.

When they had got through such studies as they had in hand, they stood leaning on the window-sill, and looking down upon the patch of garden. 'Next week,' said Mr. Crisparkle, 'you will cease to be alone, and will have a devoted companion.'

'And yet,' returned Neville, 'this seems an uncongenial place to bring my sister to!'

'I don't think so,' said the Minor Canon. 'There is duty to be done here; and there are womanly feeling, sense, and courage wanted here.'

'I meant,' explained Neville, 'that the surroundings are so dull and unwomanly, and that Helena can have no suitable friend or society here.'

'You have only to remember,' said Mr. Crisparkle, 'that you are here yourself, and that she has to draw you into the sunlight.'

They were silent for a little while, and then Mr. Crisparkle began anew.

'When we first spoke together, Neville, you told me that your sister had risen out of the disadvantages of your past lives as superior to you as the tower of Cloisterham Cathedral is higher than the chimneys of Minor Canon Corner. Do you remember that?'

'Right well!'

'I was inclined to think it at the time an enthusiastic flight. No matter what I think it now. What I would emphasize is, that under the head of Pride your sister is a great and opportune example to you.'

'Under *all* heads that are included in the composition of a fine character, she is.'

'Say so; but take this one. Your sister has learnt how to govern what is proud in her nature. She can dominate it even when it is wounded through her sympathy with you. No doubt she has suffered deeply in those same streets where you suffered deeply. No doubt her life is darkened by the cloud that darkens yours. But bending her pride into a grand composure that is not haughty or aggressive, but is a sustained confidence in you and in the truth, she has won her way through those streets until she passes along them as high in the general respect as any one who treads them. Every day and hour of her life since Edwin Drood's disappearance, she has faced malignity and folly – for you – as only a brave nature well directed can. So it will be with her to the end. Another and weaker kind of pride might sink brokenhearted, but never such a pride as hers: which knows no shrinking, and can get no mastery of her.'

The pale cheek beside him flushed under the comparison and the hint implied in it. 'I will do all I can to imitate her,' said Neville.

'Do so, and be a truly brave man as she is a truly brave woman,' answered Mr. Crisparkle, stoutly. 'It is growing dark. Will you go my way with me, when it is quite dark? Mind! It is not I who wait for darkness.'

Neville replied that he would accompany him directly. But Mr. Crisparkle said he had a moment's call to make on Mr. Grewgious as an act of courtesy, and would run across to that gentleman's chambers, and rejoin Neville on his own doorstep if he would come down there to meet him.

Mr. Grewgious, bolt upright as usual, sat taking his wine in the dusk at his open window; his wineglass and decanter on the round table at his elbow; himself and his legs on the window-seat; only one hinge in his whole body, like a bootjack.

'How do you do, reverend sir?' said Mr. Grewgious, with abundant offers of hospitality which were as cordially declined as made. 'And how is your charge getting on over the way in the set that I had the pleasure of recommending to you as vacant and eligible?'

Mr. Crisparkle replied suitably.

'I am glad you approved of them,' said Mr. Grewgious, 'because I entertain a sort of fancy for having him under my eye.'

As Mr. Grewgious had to turn his eye up considerably, before he could see the chambers, the phrase was to be taken figuratively and not literally.

'And how did you leave Mr. Jasper, reverend sir?' said Mr. Grewgious.

Mr. Crisparkle had left him pretty well.

'And where did you leave Mr. Jasper, reverend sir?'

Mr. Crisparkle had left him at Cloisterham.

'And when did you leave Mr. Jasper, reverend sir?'

That morning.

'Umps!' said Mr. Grewgious. 'He didn't say he was coming, perhaps?'

'Coming where?'

'Anywhere, for instance?' said Mr. Grewgious.

'No.'

'Because here he is,' said Mr. Grewgious, who had asked all these questions, with his preoccupied glance directed out at window. 'And he don't look agreeable, does he?'

Mr. Crisparkle was craning towards the window, when Mr. Grewgious added:

'If you will kindly step round here behind me, in the gloom of the room, and will cast your eye at the second-floor landing window, in yonder house, I think you will hardly fail to see a slinking individual in whom I recognize our local friend.'

'You are right!' cried Mr. Crisparkle.

'Umps!' said Mr. Grewgious. Then he added, turning his face so abruptly that his head nearly came into collision with Mr. Crisparkle's: 'what should you say that our local friend was up to?'

The last passage he had been shown in the Diary returned on Mr. Crisparkle's mind with the force of a strong recoil, and he asked Mr. Grewgious if he thought it possible that Neville was to be harassed by the keeping of a watch upon him?

'A watch,' repeated Mr. Grewgious, musingly. 'Ay!'

'Which would not only of itself haunt and torture his life,' said Mr. Crisparkle, warmly, 'but would expose him to the torment of a perpetually reviving suspicion, whatever he might do, or wherever he might go?'

'Ay!' said Mr. Grewgious, musingly still. 'Do I see him waiting for you?'

'No doubt you do.'

'Then *would* you have the goodness to excuse my getting up to see you out, and to go out to join him, and to go the way that you were going, and to take no notice of our local friend?' said Mr. Grewgious. 'I entertain a sort of fancy for having *him* under my eye to-night, do you know?'

Mr. Crisparkle, with a significant nod, complied, and, rejoining Neville, went away with him. They dined together, and parted at the yet unfinished and undeveloped railway station: Mr. Crisparkle to get home; Neville to walk the streets, cross the bridges, make a wide round of the city in the friendly darkness, and tire himself out.

It was midnight when he returned from his solitary ex-pedition, and climbed his staircase. The night was hot, and the windows of the staircase were all wide open. Coming to the top, it gave him a passing chill of surprise (there being no rooms but his up there) to find a stranger sitting on the window-sill, more after the manner of a venturesome glazier than an amateur ordinarily careful of his neck; in fact, so much more outside the window than inside, as to suggest the thought that he must have come up by the water-spout instead of the stairs.

The stranger said nothing until Neville put his key in his door; then, seeming to make sure of his identity from the action, he spoke:

'I beg your pardon,' he said, coming from the window with a frank and smiling air, and a prepossessing address; 'the beans.'

Neville was quite at a loss.

'Runners,' said the visitor. 'Scarlet. Next door at the back.'

'Oh!' returned Neville. 'And the mignonette and wall-flower?'

'The same,' said the visitor.

'Pray walk in.'

'Thank you.'

Neville lighted his candles, and the visitor sat down. A handsome gentleman, with a young face, but an older figure in its robustness and its breadth of shoulder; say a man of eight-and-twenty, or at the utmost thirty: so extremely sunburnt that the contrast between his brown visage and the white forehead shaded out of doors by his hat, and the glimpses of white throat below his neckerchief, would have been almost ludicrous but for his broad temples, bright blue eyes, clustering brown hair, and laughing teeth.

'I have noticed,' said he; '– my name is Tartar.'

Neville inclined his head.

'I have noticed (excuse me) that you shut yourself up a good deal, and that you seem to like my garden aloft here. If you would like a little more of it, I could throw out a few lines and stays between my windows and yours, which the runners would take to directly. And I have some boxes, both of mignonette and wallflower, that I could shove on along the gutter (with a boat-hook I have by me) to your windows, and draw back again when they wanted watering or gardening, and shove on again when they were ship-shape, so that they would cause you no trouble. I couldn't take this liberty without asking permission, so I venture to ask it. Tartar, corresponding set, next door.'

'You are very kind.'

'Not at all. I beg you will not think so. I ought to apologize for looking in so late. But having noticed (excuse me) that you generally walk out at night, I thought I should inconvenience you least by awaiting your return. I am always afraid of inconveniencing busy men, being an idle man.'

'I should not have thought so, from your appearance.'

'No? I take it as a compliment. In fact, I was bred in the Royal Navy and was First Lieutenant when I quitted it. But, an uncle disappointed in the service leaving me his property on condition that I left the Navy, I accepted the fortune and resigned my commission.'

'Lately, I presume?'

'Well, I had had twelve or fifteen years of knocking about first. I came here some nine months before you; I had had one crop before you came. I chose this place, because, having served last in a little Corvette, I knew I should feel more at home where I had a constant opportunity of knocking my head against the ceiling. Besides: it would never do for a man who had been aboard ship from his boyhood to turn luxurious all at once. Besides, again: having been accustomed to a very short allowance of land all my life, I thought I'd feel my way to the command of a landed estate, by beginning in boxes.'

Whimsically as this was said, there was a touch of merry earnestness in it that made it doubly whimsical.

'However,' said the Lieutenant, 'I have talked quite enough about myself. It is not my way I hope; it has merely been to present myself to you naturally. If you will allow me to take the liberty I have described, it will be a charity, for it will give me something more to do. And you are not to suppose that it will entail any interruption or intrusion on you, for that is far from my intention.'

Neville replied that he was greatly obliged, and that he thankfully accepted the kind proposal.

'I am very glad to take your windows in tow,' said the Lieutenant. 'From what I have seen of you when I have been gardening at mine, and you have been looking on, I have thought you (excuse me) rather too studious and delicate! May I ask, is your health at all affected?'

'I have undergone some mental distress,' said Neville, confused, 'which has stood me in the stead of illness.'

'Pardon me,' said Mr. Tartar.

With the greatest delicacy he shifted his ground to the windows again, and asked if he could look at one of them. On Neville's opening it, he immediately sprang out, as if he were going aloft with a whole watch in an emergency, and were setting a bright example.

'For Heaven's sake!' cried Neville, 'don't do that! Where are you going, Mr. Tartar? You'll be dashed to pieces!'

'All well!' said the Lieutenant, coolly looking about him on the housetop. 'All taut and trim here. Those lines and stays shall be rigged before you turn out in the morning. May I take the short cut home and say, Good-night?'

'Mr. Tartar!' urged Neville. 'Pray! It makes me giddy to see you!'

But Mr. Tartar, with a wave of his hand and the deftness of a cat, had already dipped through his scuttle of scarlet runners without breaking a leaf, and 'gone below.'

Mr. Grewgious, his bedroom window-blind held aside with his hand, happened at that moment to have Neville's chambers under his eye for the last time that night. Fortunately his eye was on the front of the house and not the back, or this remarkable appearance and disappearance might have broken his rest as a phenomenon. But, Mr. Grewgious seeing nothing there, not even a light in the windows, his gaze wandered from the windows to the stars, as if he would have read in them something that was hidden from him. Many of us would if we could; but none of us so much as know our letters in the stars yet – or seem likely to, in this state of existence – and few languages can be read until their alphabets are mastered.

CHAPTER XVIII

A Settler in Cloisterham

A<small>T</small> about this time, a stranger appeared in Cloisterham; a white-haired personage with black eyebrows. Being buttoned up in a tightish blue surtout, with a buff waistcoat and grey trousers, he had something of a military air; but he announced himself at the Crozier (the orthodox hotel, where he put up with a portmanteau) as an idle dog who lived upon his means; and he further announced that he had a mind to take a lodging in the picturesque old city for a month or two, with the view of settling down there altogether. Both announcements were made in the coffee-room of the Crozier, to all whom it might, or might not, concern, by the stranger as he stood with his back to the empty fireplace, waiting for his fried sole, veal cutlet, and pint of sherry. And the waiter (business being chronically slack at the Crozier) represented all whom it might or might not concern, and absorbed the whole of the information.

This gentleman's white head was unusually large, and his shock of white hair was unusually thick and ample. 'I suppose, waiter,' he said, shaking his shock of hair, as a Newfoundland dog might shake his before sitting down to dinner, 'that a fair lodging for a single buffer might be found in these parts, eh?'

The waiter had no doubt of it.

'Something old,' said the gentleman. 'Take my hat down for a moment from that peg, will you? No, I don't want it; look into it. What do you see written there?'

The waiter read: 'Datchery.'

'Now you know my name,' said the gentleman; 'Dick Datchery. Hang it up again. I was saying something old is what I should prefer, something odd and out of the way; something venerable, architectural, and inconvenient.'

'We have a good choice of inconvenient lodgings in the town, sir, I think,' replied the waiter, with modest confidence in its resources that way; 'indeed, I have no doubts that we could suit you that far, however particular you might be. But a architectural lodging!' That seemed to trouble the waiter's head, and he shook it.

'Anything Cathedrally now,' Mr. Datchery suggested.

'Mr. Tope,' said the waiter, brightening, as he rubbed his chin with his hand, 'would be the likeliest party to inform in that line.'

'Who is Mr. Tope?' inquired Dick Datchery.

The waiter explained that he was the Verger, and that Mrs. Tope had indeed once upon a time let lodgings herself – or offered to let them; but that as nobody had ever taken them, Mrs. Tope's window-bill, long a Cloisterham Institution, had disappeared; probably had tumbled down one day, and never been put up again.

'I'll call on Mrs. Tope,' said Mr. Datchery, 'after dinner.'

So when he had done his dinner, he was duly directed to the spot, and sallied out for it. But the Crozier being an hotel of a most retiring disposition, and the waiter's directions being fatally precise, he soon became bewildered, and went boggling about and about the Cathedral tower, whenever he could catch a glimpse of it, with a general impression on his mind that Mrs. Tope's was somewhere very near it, and that, like the children in the game of hot boiled beans and very good butter, he was warm in his search when he saw the tower, and cold when he didn't see it.

He was getting very cold indeed when he came upon a fragment of burial-ground in which an unhappy sheep was grazing. Unhappy, because a hideous small boy was stoning it through the railings, and had already lamed it in one leg, and was much excited by the benevolent sportsmanlike purpose of breaking its other three legs, and bringing it down.

"It 'im agin!' cried the boy, as the poor creature leaped; 'and made a dint in 'is wool!'

'Let him be!' said Mr. Datchery. 'Don't you see you have lamed him?'

'Yer lie,' returned the sportsman. "E went and lamed 'isself. I see 'im do it, and I giv' 'im a shy as a Widdy-warning to 'im not to go a bruisin' 'is master's mutton any more.'

'Come here.'

'I won't; I'll come when yer can ketch me.'

'Stay there then, and show me which is Mr. Tope's.'

''Ow can I stay here and show you which is Topeseses, when Topeseses is t'other side the Kinfreederel, and over the crossings, and round ever so many corners? Stoo-pid! Ya-a-ah!'

'Show me where it is, and I'll give you something.'

'Come on, then!'

This brisk dialogue concluded, the boy led the way, and by-and-bye stopped at some distance from an arched passage, pointing.

'Look'ee yonder. You see that there winder and door?'

'That's Tope's?'

'Yer lie; it ain't. That's Jarsper's.'

'Indeed?' said Mr. Datchery, with a second look of some interest.

'Yes, and I ain't a goin' no nearer 'IM, I tell yer.'

'Why not?'

''Cos I ain't a going to be lifted off my legs and 'ave my braces bust and be choked; not if I knows it and not by 'Im. Wait till I set a jolly good flint a flyin' at the back o' 'is jolly old 'ed some day! Now look t'other side the harch; not the side where Jarsper's door is; t'other side.'

'I see.'

'A little way in, o' that side, there's a low door, down two steps. That's Topeseses with 'is name on a hoval plate.'

'Good. See here,' said Mr. Datchery, producing a shilling. 'You owe me half of this.'

'Yer lie; I don't owe yer nothing; I never seen yer.'

'I tell you you owe me half of this, because I have no sixpence in my pocket. So the next time you meet me you shall do something else for me, to pay me.'

'All right, give us 'old.'

'What is your name, and where do you live?'

'Deputy. Travellers' Twopenny, 'cross the green.'

The boy instantly darted off with the shilling, lest Mr. Datchery should repent, but stopped at a safe distance, on the happy chance of his being uneasy in his mind about

it, to goad him with a demon dance expressive of its irrevoc-
ability. Mr. Datchery, taking off his hat to give that shock of
white hair of his another shake, seemed quite resigned, and
betook himself whither he had been directed.

Mr. Tope's official dwelling, communicating by an upper
stair with Mr. Jasper's (hence Mrs. Tope's attendance on
that gentleman), was of very modest proportions, and par-
took of the character of a cool dungeon. Its ancient walls
were massive and its rooms rather seemed to have been
dug out of them, than to have been designed beforehand
with any reference to them. The main door opened at
once on a chamber of no describable shape, with a groined
roof, which in its turn opened on another chamber of
no describable shape, with another groined roof: their
windows small, and in the thickness of the walls. These two
chambers, close as to their atmosphere and swarthy as
to their illumination by natural light, were the apartments
which Mrs. Tope had so long offered to an unappreciative
city. Mr. Datchery, however, was more appreciative. He
found that if he sat with the main door open he would
enjoy the passing society of all comers to and fro by
the gateway, and would have light enough. He found that
if Mr. and Mrs. Tope, living overhead, used for their own
egress and ingress a little side stair that came plump into
the Precincts by a door opening outward, to the surprise
and inconvenience of a limited public of pedestrians in
a narrow way, he would be alone, as in a separate residence.
He found the rent moderate, and everything as quaintly
inconvenient as he could desire. He agreed therefore
to take the lodging then and there, and money down, possession to be had next evening on condition that reference
was permitted him to Mr. Jasper as occupying the
Gate House, of which, on the other side of the gateway
the Verger's hole in the wall was an appanage or subsidiary
part.

The poor dear gentleman was very solitary and very sad,
Mrs. Tope said, but she had no doubt he would 'speak for
her.' Perhaps Mr. Datchery had heard something of what had
occurred there last winter?

Mr. Datchery had as confused a knowledge of the event in question, on trying to recall it, as he well could have. He begged Mrs. Tope's pardon when she found it incumbent on her to correct him in every detail of his summary of the facts, but pleaded that he was merely a single buffer getting through life upon his means as idly as he could, and that so many people were so constantly making away with so many other people, as to render it difficult for a buffer of an easy temper to preserve the circumstances of the several cases unmixed in his mind.

Mr. Jasper proving willing to speak for Mrs. Tope, Mr. Datchery, who had sent up his card, was invited to ascend the postern staircase. The Mayor was there, Mrs. Tope said; but he was not to be regarded in the light of company, as he and Mr. Jasper were great friends.

'I beg pardon,' said Mr. Datchery, making a leg with his hat under his arm, as he addressed himself equally to both gentlemen; 'a selfish precaution on my part and not person-ally interesting to anybody but myself. But as a buffer living on his means, and having an idea of doing it in this lovely place in peace and quiet, for remaining span of life, beg to ask if the Tope family are quite respectable?'

Mr. Jasper could answer for that without the slightest hesitation.

'That is enough, sir,' said Mr. Datchery.

'My friend the Mayor,' added Mr. Jasper, presenting Mr. Datchery with a courtly motion of his hand towards that potentate; 'whose recommendation is naturally much more important to a stranger than that of an obscure person like myself, will testify in their behalf, I am sure.'

'The Worshipful the Mayor,' said Mr. Datchery, with a low bow, 'places me under an infinite obligation.'

'Very good people, sir, Mr. and Mrs. Tope,' said Mr. Sap-sea, with condescension. 'Very good opinions. Very well be-haved. Very respectful. Much approved by the Dean and Chapter.'

'The Worshipful the Mayor gives them a character,' said Mr. Datchery, 'of which they may indeed be proud. I would ask His Honour (if I might be permitted) whether there are not many objects of great interest in the city which is under his beneficent sway?'

'We are, sir,' returned Mr. Sapsea, 'an ancient city, and an ecclesiastical city. We are a constitutional city, as it becomes such a city to be, and we uphold and maintain our glorious privileges.'

'His Honour,' said Mr. Datchery, bowing, 'inspires me with a desire to know more of the city, and confirms me in my inclination to end my days in the city.'

'Retired from the Army, sir?' suggested Mr. Sapsea.

'His Honour the Mayor does me too much credit,' returned Mr. Datchery.

'Navy, sir?' suggested Mr. Sapsea.

'Again,' repeated Mr. Datchery, 'His Honour the Mayor does me too much credit.'

'Diplomacy is a fine profession,' said Mr. Sapsea, as a general remark.

'There, I confess, His Honour the Mayor is too many for me,' said Mr. Datchery, with an ingenuous smile and bow; 'even a diplomatic bird must fall to such a gun.'

Now, this was very soothing. Here was a gentleman of a great – not to say a grand – address, accustomed to rank and dignity, really setting a fine example how to behave to a Mayor. There was something in that third person style of being spoken to, that Mr. Sapsea found particularly recognizant of his merits and position.

'But I crave pardon,' said Mr. Datchery. 'His Honour the Mayor will bear with me, if for a moment I have been deluded into occupying his time, and have forgotten the humble claims upon my own, of my hotel, the Crozier.'

'Not at all, sir,' said Mr. Sapsea. 'I too am returning home, and if you would like to take the exterior of our Cathedral in your way, I shall be glad to point it out.'

'His Honour the Mayor,' said Mr. Datchery, 'is more than kind and gracious.'

As Mr. Datchery, when he had made his acknowledgements to Mr. Jasper, could not be induced to go out of the room before the Worshipful, the Worshipful led the way down stairs; Mr. Datchery following with his hat under his arm, and his shock of white hair streaming in the evening breeze.

'Might I ask His Honour,' said Mr. Datchery, 'whether that gentleman we have just left is the gentleman of whom I have heard in the neighbourhood as being much afflicted by the loss of a nephew, and concentrating his life on avenging the loss?'

'That is the gentleman. John Jasper, sir.'

'Would His Honour allow me to inquire whether there are strong suspicions of any one?'

'More than suspicions, sir,' returned Mr. Sapsea, 'all but certainties.'

'Only think now!' cried Mr. Datchery.

'But proof, sir, proof, must be built up stone by stone,' said the Mayor. 'As I say, the end crowns the work. It is not enough that Justice should be morally certain; she must be *im*morally certain – legally, that is.'

'His Honour,' said Mr. Datchery, 'reminds me of the nature of the law. Immoral. How true!'

'As I say, sir,' pompously went on the Mayor, 'the arm of the law is a strong arm, and a long arm. That is the way *I* put it. A strong arm and a long arm.'

'How forcible! – And yet, again, how true!' murmured Mr. Datchery.

'And without betraying what I call the secrets of the prison-house,' said Mr. Sapsea; 'the secrets of the prison-house is the term I used on the bench.'

'And what other term than His Honour's would express it?' said Mr. Datchery.

'Without, I say, betraying them, I predict to you, knowing the iron will of the gentleman we have just left (I take the bold step of calling it iron, on account of its strength), that in this case the long arm will reach, and the strong arm will strike. – This is our Cathedral, sir. The best judges are pleased to admire it, and the best among our townsmen own to being a little vain of it.'

All this time Mr. Datchery had walked with his hat under his arm, and his white hair streaming. He had an odd momentary appearance upon him of having forgotten his hat, when Mr. Sapsea now touched it; and he clapped his hand up to his head as if with some vague expectation of finding another hat upon it.

'Pray be covered, sir,' entreated Mr. Sapsea; magnificently implying: 'I shall not mind it, I assure you.'

'His Honour is very good, but I do it for coolness,' said Mr. Datchery.

Then Mr. Datchery admired the Cathedral, and Mr. Sapsea pointed it out as if he himself had invented and built it; there were a few details indeed of which he did not approve, but those he glossed over, as if the workmen had made mistakes in his absence. The Cathedral disposed of, he led the way by the churchyard, and stopped to extol the beauty of the evening – by chance – in the immediate vicinity of Mrs. Sapsea's epitaph.

'And by-the-bye,' said Mr. Sapsea, appearing to descend from an elevation to remember it all of a sudden; like Apollo shooting down from Olympus to pick up his forgotten lyre; '*that* is one of our small lions. The partiality of our people has made it so, and strangers have been seen taking a copy of it now and then. I am not a judge of it myself, for it is a little work of my own. But it was troublesome to turn, sir; I may say, difficult to turn with elegance.'

Mr. Datchery became so ecstatic over Mr. Sapsea's composition that, in spite of his intention to end his days in Cloisterham, and therefore his probably having in reserve many opportunities of copying it, he would have transcribed it into his pocket-book on the spot, but for the slouching towards them of its material producer and perpetuator, Durdles, whom Mr. Sapsea hailed, not sorry to show him a bright example of behaviour to superiors.

'Ah, Durdles! This is the mason, sir; one of our Cloister-ham worthies; everybody here knows Durdles. Mr. Datchery, Durdles; a gentleman who is going to settle here.'

'I wouldn't do it if I was him,' growled Durdles. 'We're a heavy lot.'

'You surely don't speak for yourself, Mr. Durdles,' returned Mr. Datchery, 'any more than for His Honour.'

A SETTLER IN CLOISTERHAM

'Who's His Honour?' demanded Durdles.

'His Honour the Mayor.'

'I never was brought afore him,' said Durdles, with any-thing but the look of a loyal subject of the mayoralty, 'and it'll be time enough for me to Honour him when I am. Until which, and when, and where:

> 'Mister Sapsea is his name,
> England is his nation,
> Cloist'rham's his dwelling-place,
> Aukshneer's his occupation.'

Here, Deputy (preceded by a flying oyster-shell) appeared upon the scene, and requested to have the sum of threepence instantly 'chucked' to him by Mr. Durdles, whom he had been vainly seeking up and down, as lawful wages overdue. While that gentleman, with his bundle under his arm, slowly found and counted out the money, Mr. Sapsea informed the new settler of Durdles's habits, pursuits, abode, and reputation. 'I suppose a curious stranger might come to see you, and your works, Mr. Durdles, at any odd time?' said Mr. Datchery upon that.

'Any gentleman is welcome to come and see me any evening if he brings liquor for two with him,' returned Dur-dles, with a penny between his teeth and certain halfpence in his hands. 'Or if he likes to make it twice two, he'll be double welcome.'

'I shall come. Master Deputy, what do you owe me?'

'A job.'

'Mind you pay me honestly with the job of showing me Mr. Durdles's house when I want to go there.'

Deputy, with a piercing broadside of whistle through the whole gap in his mouth, as a receipt in full for all arrears, vanished.

The Worshipful and the Worshipper then passed on together until they parted, with many ceremonies, at the Worshipful's door; even then, the Worshipper carried his hat under his arm, and gave his streaming white hair to the breeze.

Said Mr. Datchery to himself that night, as he looked at his white hair in the gas-lighted looking-glass over the coffee-room chimneypiece at the Crozier, and shook it out: 'For a single buffer, of an easy temper, living idly on his means, I have had a rather busy afternoon!'

CHAPTER XIX

Shadow on the Sun-dial

AGAIN Miss Twinkleton has delivered her valedictory address, with the accompaniments of white wine and pound-cake, and again the young ladies have departed to their several homes. Helena Landless has left the Nuns' House to attend her brother's fortunes, and pretty Rosa is alone.

Cloisterham is so bright and sunny in these summer days, that the Cathedral and the monastery ruin show as if their strong walls were transparent. A soft glow seems to shine from within them, rather than upon them from without, such is their mellowness as they look forth on the hot corn-fields and the smoking roads that distantly wind among them. The Cloisterham gardens blush with ripening fruit. Time was when travel-stained pilgrims rode in clattering parties through the city's welcome shades; time is when wayfarers, leading a gipsy life between hay-making time and harvest, and looking as if they were just made of the dust of the earth, so very dusty are they, lounge about on cool doorsteps, trying to mend their unmendable shoes, or giving them to the city kennels as a hopeless job, and seeking others in the bundles that they carry, along with their yet unused sickles swathed in bands of straw. At all the more public pumps there is much cooling of bare feet, together with much bubbling and gurgling of drinking with hand to spout on the part of these Bedouins; the Cloisterham police meanwhile looking askant from their beats with suspicion, and manifest impatience that the intruders should depart from within the civic bounds, and once more fry themselves on the simmering high roads.

On the afternoon of such a day, when the last Cathedral service is done, and when that side of the High Street on which the Nuns' House stands is in grateful shade, save where its quaint old garden opens to the west between the

boughs of trees, a servant informs Rosa, to her terror, that
Mr. Jasper desires to see her.

If he had chosen his time for finding her at a disadvantage, he could have done no better. Perhaps he has chosen it.
Helena Landless is gone, Mrs. Tisher is absent on leave, Miss
Twinkleton (in her amateur state of existence) has contrib-
uted herself and a veal pie to a picnic.

'Oh why, why, why, did you say I was at home!' cries Rosa,
helplessly.

The maid replies, that Mr. Jasper never asked the question. That he said he knew she was at home, and begged she
might be told that he asked to see her.

'What shall I do, what shall I do?' thinks Rosa, clasping her
hands.

Possessed by a kind of desperation, she adds in the next
breath that she will come to Mr. Jasper in the garden. She
shudders at the thought of being shut up with him in the
house; but many of its windows command the garden, and
she can be seen as well as heard, there, and can shriek in the
free air and run away. Such is the wild idea that flutters
through her mind.

She has never seen him since the fatal night, except when
she was questioned before the Mayor, and then he was present in gloomy watchfulness, as representing his lost nephew
and burning to avenge him. She hangs her garden-hat on
her arm, and goes out. The moment she sees him from the
porch, leaning on the sun-dial, the old horrible feeling of
being compelled by him, asserts its hold upon her. She feels
that she would even then go back, but that he draws her feet
towards him. She cannot resist, and sits down, with her head
bent, on the garden-seat beside the sun-dial. She cannot look
up at him for abhorrence, but she has perceived that he is
dressed in deep mourning. So is she. It was not so at first; but
the lost has long been given up, and mourned for, as the
dead.

He would begin by touching her hand. She feels the
intention, and draws her hand back. His eyes are then fixed
upon her, she knows, though her own see nothing but the
grass.

'I have been waiting,' he begins, 'for some time, to be summoned back to my duty near you.'

After several times forming her lips, which she knows he is closely watching, into the shape of some other hesitating reply, and then into none, by turns, she answers: 'Duty, sir?'

'The duty of teaching you, serving you as your faithful music-master.'

'I have left off that study.'

'Not left off, I think. Discontinued. I was told by your guardian that you discontinued it under the shock that we have all felt so acutely. When will you resume?'

'Never, sir.'

'Never? You could have done no more if you had loved my dear boy.'

'I did love him!' cries Rosa, with a flash of anger.

'Yes; but not quite – not quite in the right way, shall I say? Not in the intended and expected way. Much as my dear boy was, unhappily, too self-conscious and self-satisfied (but I draw no parallel between him and you in that respect) to love as he should have loved, or as any one in his place would have loved – must have loved!'

She sits in the same still attitude, but shrinking a little more.

'Then, to be told that you discontinued your study with me, was to be politely told that you abandoned it altogether?' he suggests.

'Yes,' says Rosa, with sudden spirit. 'The politeness was my guardian's, not mine. I told him that I was resolved to leave off, and that I was determined to stand by my resolution.'

'And you still are?'

'I still am, sir. And I beg not to be questioned any more about it. At all events, I will not answer any more; I have that in my power.'

She is so conscious of his looking at her with a gloating admiration of the touch of anger on her, and the fire and animation it brings with it, that even as her spirit rises, it falls again, and she struggles with a sense of shame, affront, and fear, much as she did that night at the piano.

'I will not question you any more, since you object to it so much; I will confess.'

'I do not wish to hear you, sir,' cries Rosa, rising.

This time he does touch her with his outstretched hand. In shrinking from it, she shrinks into her seat again.

'We must sometimes act in opposition to our wishes,' he tells her in a low voice. 'You must do so now, or do more harm to others than you can ever set right.'

'What harm?'

'Presently, presently. You question *me*, you see, and surely that is not fair when you forbid me to question you. Nevertheless, I will answer the question presently. Dearest Rosa! Charming Rosa!'

She starts up again.

This time he does not touch her. But his face looks so wicked and menacing, as he stands leaning against the sun-dial – setting, as it were, his black mark upon the very face of day – that her flight is arrested by horror as she looks at him.

'I do not forget how many windows command a view of us,' he says, glancing towards them. 'I will not touch you again, I will come no nearer to you than I am. Sit down, and there will be no mighty wonder in your music-master's leaning idly against a pedestal and speaking with you, remembering all that has happened and our shares in it. Sit down, my beloved.'

She would have gone once more – was all but gone – and once more his face, darkly threatening what would follow if she went, has stopped her. Looking at him with the expression of the instant frozen on her face, she sits down on the seat again.

'Rosa, even when my dear boy was affianced to you, I loved you madly; even when I thought his happiness in having you for his wife was certain, I loved you madly; even when I strove to make him more ardently devoted to you, I loved you madly; even when he gave me the picture of your lovely face so carelessly traduced by him, which I feigned to hang always in my sight for his sake, but worshipped in torment for yours, I loved you madly. In the distasteful work of the day, in the wakeful misery of the night, girded

Jasper's Sacrifices

by sordid realities, or wandering through Paradises and Hells of visions into which I rushed, carrying your image in my arms, I loved you madly.'

If anything could make his words more hideous to her than they are in themselves, it would be the contrast between the violence of his look and delivery, and the composure of his assumed attitude.

'I endured all in silence. So long as you were his, or so long as I supposed you to be his, I hid my secret loyally. Did I not?'

This lie, so gross, while the mere words in which it is told are so true, is more than Rosa can endure. She answers with kindling indignation: 'You were as false throughout, sir, as you are now. You were false to him, daily and hourly. You know that you made my life unhappy by your pursuit of me. You know that you made me afraid to open his generous eyes, and that you forced me, for his own trusting, good, good sake, to keep the truth from him, that you were a bad, bad, man!'

His preservation of his easy attitude rendering his working features and his convulsive hands absolutely diabolical, he returns, with a fierce extreme of admiration:

'How beautiful you are! You are more beautiful in anger than in repose. I don't ask you for your love; give me yourself and your hatred; give me yourself and that pretty rage; give me yourself and that enchanting scorn; it will be enough for me.'

Impatient tears rise to the eyes of the trembling little beauty, and her face flames; but as she again rises to leave him in indignation, and seek protection within the house, he stretches out his hand towards the porch, as though he invited her to enter it.

'I told you, you rare charmer, you sweet witch, that you must stay and hear me, or do more harm than can ever be undone. You asked me what harm. Stay, and I will tell you. Go, and I will do it!'

Again Rosa quails before his threatening face, though innocent of its meaning, and she remains. Her panting breathing comes and goes as if it would choke her; but with a repressive hand upon her bosom, she remains.

'I have made my confession that my love is mad. It is so mad that, had the ties between me and my dear lost boy been one silken thread less strong, I might have swept even him from your side when you favoured him.'

A film comes over the eyes she raises for an instant, as though he had turned her faint.

'Even him,' he repeats. 'Yes, even him! Rosa, you see me and you hear me. Judge for yourself whether any other admirer shall love you and live, whose life is in my hand.'

'What do you mean, sir?'

'I mean to show you how mad my love is. It was hawked through the late inquiries by Mr. Crisparkle, that young Landless had confessed to him that he was a rival of my lost boy. That is an inexpiable offence in my eyes. The same Mr. Crisparkle knows under my hand that I devoted myself to the murderer's discovery and destruction, be he who he might, and that I determined to discuss the mystery with no one until I should hold the clue in which to entangle the murderer as in a net. I have since worked patiently to wind and wind it round him; and it is slowly winding as I speak.'

'Your belief, if you believe in the criminality of Mr. Landless, is not Mr. Crisparkle's belief, and he is a good man,' Rosa retorts.

'My belief is my own; and I reserve it, worshipped of my soul! Circumstances may accumulate so strongly *even against an innocent man*, that, directed, sharpened, and pointed, they may slay him. One wanting link discovered by perseverance against a guilty man, proves his guilt, however slight its evidence before, and he dies. Young Landless stands in deadly peril either way.'

'If you really suppose,' Rosa pleads with him, turning paler, 'that I favour Mr. Landless, or that Mr. Landless has ever in any way addressed himself to me, you are wrong.'

He puts that from him with a slighting action of his hand and a curled lip.

'I was going to show you how madly I love you. More madly now than ever, for I am willing to renounce the second object that has arisen in my life to divide it with you; and henceforth to have no object in existence but you only.

Miss Landless has become your bosom friend. You care for her peace of mind?'

'I love her dearly.'

'You care for her good name?'

'I have said, sir, I love her dearly.'

'I am unconsciously,' he observes, with a smile, as he folds his hands upon the sun-dial and leans his chin upon them, so that his talk would seem from the windows (faces occasionally come and go there) to be of the airiest and playfullest: 'I am unconsciously giving offence by questioning again. I will simply make statements, therefore, and not put questions. You do care for your bosom friend's good name, and you do care for her peace of mind. Then remove the shadow of the gallows from her, dear one!'

'You dare propose to me to—'

'Darling, I dare propose to you. Stop there. If it be bad to idolize you, I am the worst of men; if it be good, I am the best. My love for you is above all other love, and my truth to you is above all other truth. Let me have hope and favour, and I am a forsworn man for your sake.'

Rosa puts her hands to her temples, and, pushing back her hair, looks wildly and abhorrently at him, as though she were trying to piece together what it is his deep purpose to present to her only in fragments.

'Reckon up nothing at this moment, angel, but the sacrifices that I lay at those dear feet, which I could fall down among the vilest ashes and kiss, and put upon my head as a poor savage might. There is my fidelity to my dear boy after death. Tread upon it!'

With an action of his hands, as though he cast down something precious.

'There is the inexpiable offence against my adoration of you. Spurn it!'

With a similar action.

'There are my labours in the cause of a just vengeance for six toiling months. Crush them!'

With another repetition of the action.

'There is my past and my present wasted life. There is the desolation of my heart and my soul. There is my peace; there is my despair. Stamp them into the dust, so that you take me, were it even mortally hating me!'

The frightful vehemence of the man, now reaching its full height, so additionally terrifies her as to break the spell that has held her to the spot. She swiftly moves towards the porch; but in an instant he is at her side, and speaking in her ear.

'Rosa, I am self-repressed again. I am walking calmly beside you to the house. I shall wait for some encouragement and hope. I shall not strike too soon. Give me a sign that you attend to me.'

She slightly and constrainedly moves her hand.

'Not a word of this to any one, or it will bring down the blow, as certainly as night follows day. Another sign that you attend to me.'

She moves her hand once more.

'I love you, love you, love you. If you were to cast me off now – but you will not – you would never be rid of me. No one should come between us. I would pursue you to the death.'

The handmaid coming out to open the gate for him, he quietly pulls off his hat as a parting salute, and goes away with no greater show of agitation than is visible in the effigy of Mr. Sapsea's father opposite. Rosa faints in going up stairs, and is carefully carried to her room, and laid down on her bed. A thunderstorm is coming on, the maids say, and the hot and stifling air has overset the pretty dear; no wonder; they have felt their own knees all of a tremble all day long.

CHAPTER XX

A Flight

ROSA no sooner came to herself than the whole of the late interview was before her. It even seemed as if it had pursued her into her insensibility, and she had not had a moment's unconsciousness of it. What to do, she was at a frightened loss to know: the only one clear thought in her mind, was, that she must fly from this terrible man.

But where could she take refuge, and how could she go? She had never breathed her dread of him to any one but Helena. If she went to Helena, and told her what had passed, that very act might bring down the irreparable mischief that he threatened he had the power, and that she knew he had the will, to do. The more fearful he appeared to her excited memory and imagination, the more alarming her responsibility appeared: seeing that a slight mistake on her part, either in action or delay, might let his malevolence loose on Helena's brother.

Rosa's mind throughout the last six months had been stormily confused. A half-formed, wholly unexpressed suspicion tossed in it, now heaving itself up, and now sinking into the deep; now gaining palpability, and now losing it. His self-absorption in his nephew when he was alive, and his unceasing pursuit of the inquiry how he came by his death, if he were dead, were themes so rife in the place, that no one appeared able to suspect the possibility of foul play at his hands. She had asked herself the question, 'Am I so wicked in my thoughts as to conceive a wickedness that others cannot imagine?' Then she had considered, Did the suspicion come of her previous recoiling from him before the fact? And if so, was not that a proof of its baselessness? Then she had reflected, 'What motive could he have, according to my accusation?' She was ashamed to answer in her mind, 'The motive of gaining *me!*' And covered her face, as if the lightest shadow of the idea of founding murder on such an idle vanity were a crime almost as great.

She ran over in her mind again, all that he had said by the sun-dial in the garden. He had persisted in treating the disappearance as murder, consistently with his whole public course since the finding of the watch and shirt-pin. If he were afraid of the crime being traced out, would he not rather encourage the idea of a voluntary disappearance? He had unnecessarily declared that if the ties between him and his nephew had been less strong, he might have swept 'even him' away from her side. Was that like his having really done so? He had spoken of laying his six months' labours in the cause of a just vengeance at her feet. Would he have done that, with that violence of passion, if they were a pretence? Would he have ranged them with his desolate heart and soul, his wasted life, his peace, and his despair? The very first sacrifice that he represented himself as making for her, was his fidelity to his dear boy after death. Surely these facts were strong against a fancy that scarcely dared to hint itself. And yet he was so terrible a man! In short, the poor girl (for what could she know of the criminal intellect, which its own professed students perpetually misread, because they persist in trying to reconcile it with the average intellect of average men, instead of identifying it as a horrible wonder apart) could get by no road to any other conclusion than that he *was* a terrible man, and must be fled from.

She had been Helena's stay and comfort during the whole time. She had constantly assured her of her full belief in her brother's innocence, and of her sympathy with him in his misery. But she had never seen him since the disappearance, nor had Helena ever spoken one word of his avowal to Mr. Crisparkle in regard of Rosa, though as a part of the interest of the case it was well known far and wide. He was Helena's unfortunate brother, to her, and nothing more. The assurance she had given her odious suitor was strictly true, though it would have been better (she considered now) if she could have restrained herself from giving it. Afraid of him as the bright and delicate little creature was, her spirit swelled at the thought of his knowing it from her own lips.

But where was she to go? Anywhere beyond his reach, was no reply to the question. Somewhere must be thought of. She determined to go to her guardian, and to go immediately. The feeling she had imparted to Helena on the night of their first confidence, was so strong upon her – the feeling of not being safe from him, and of the solid walls of the old convent being powerless to keep out his ghostly following of her – that no reasoning of her own could calm her terrors. The fascination of repulsion had been upon her so long, and now culminated so darkly, that she felt as if he had power to bind her by a spell. Glancing out at window, even now, as she rose to dress, the sight of the sun-dial on which he had leaned when he declared himself, turned her cold, and made her shrink from it, as though he had invested it with some awful quality from his own nature.

She wrote a hurried note to Miss Twinkleton, saying that she had sudden reason for wishing to see her guardian promptly, and had gone to him; also, entreating the good lady not to be uneasy, for all was well with her. She hurried a few quite useless articles into a very little bag, left the note in a conspicuous place, and went out, softly closing the gate after her.

It was the first time she had ever been even in Cloisterham High Street, alone. But knowing all its ways and windings very well, she hurried straight to the corner from which the omnibus departed. It was, at that very moment, going off.

'Stop and take me, if you please, Joe. I am obliged to go to London.'

In less than another minute she was on her road to the railway, under Joe's protection. Joe waited on her when she got there, put her safely into the railway carriage, and handed in the very little bag after her, as though it were some enormous trunk, hundredweights heavy, which she must on no account endeavour to lift.

'Can you go round when you get back, and tell Miss Twinkleton that you saw me safely off, Joe?'

'It shall be done, Miss.'

'With my love, please, Joe.'

'Yes, Miss – and I wouldn't mind having it myself!' But Joe did not articulate the last clause; only thought it.

Now that she was whirling away for London in real earnest, Rosa was at leisure to resume the thoughts which her personal hurry had checked. The indignant thought that his declaration of love soiled her; that she could only be cleansed from the stain of its impurity by appealing against it to the honest and true; supported her for a time against her fears, and confirmed her in her hasty resolution. But as the evening grew darker and darker, and the great city impended nearer and nearer, the doubts usual in such cases began to arise. Whether this was not a wild proceeding after all; how Mr. Grewgious might regard it; whether she would find him at the journey's end; how she would act if he were absent; what might become of her, alone, in a place so strange and crowded; how if she had but waited and taken counsel first; whether, if she could now go back, she would not do it thankfully: a multitude of such uneasy speculations disturbed her, more and more as they accumulated. At length the train came into London over the housetops; and down below lay the gritty streets with their yet un-needed lamps aglow, on a hot light summer night.

'Hiram Grewgious, Esquire, Staple Inn, London.' This was all Rosa knew of her destination; but it was enough to send her rattling away again in a cab, through deserts of gritty streets, where many people crowded at the corners of courts and bye-ways, to get some air, and where many other people walked with a miserably monotonous noise of shuffling feet on hot paving-stones, and where all the people and all their surroundings were so gritty and so shabby.

There was music playing here and there, but it did not enliven the case. No barrel-organ mended the matter, and no big drum beat dull care away. Like the chapel bells that were also going here and there, they only seemed to evoke echoes from brick surfaces, and dust from everything. As to the flat wind instruments, they seemed to have cracked their hearts and souls in pining for the country.

Her jingling conveyance stopped at last at a fast-closed gateway which appeared to belong to somebody who had gone to bed very early, and was much afraid of housebreakers; Rosa, discharging her conveyance, timidly knocked at this gateway, and was let in, very little bag and all, by a watchman.

'Does Mr. Grewgious live here?'

'Mr. Grewgious lives there, Miss,' said the watchman, pointing further in.

So Rosa went further in, and, when the clocks were striking ten, stood on P. J. T.'s doorsteps, wondering what P. J. T. had done with his street door.

Guided by the painted name of Mr. Grewgious, she went up stairs and softly tapped and tapped several times. But no one answering, and Mr. Grewgious's door-handle yielding to her touch, she went in, and saw her guardian sitting on a window-seat at an open window, with a shaded lamp placed far from him on a table in a corner.

Rosa drew nearer to him in the twilight of the room. He saw her, and he said in an under-tone: 'Good Heaven!'

Rosa fell upon his neck, with tears, and then he said, returning her embrace:

'My child, my child! I thought you were your mother!

'But what, what, what,' he added, soothingly, 'has happened? My dear, what has brought you here? Who has brought you here?'

'No one. I came alone.'

'Lord bless me!' ejaculated Mr. Grewgious. 'Came alone! Why didn't you write to me to come and fetch you?'

'I had no time. I took a sudden resolution. Poor, poor Eddy!'

'Ah, poor fellow, poor fellow!'

'His uncle has made love to me. I cannot bear it,' said Rosa, at once with a burst of tears, and a stamp of her little foot; 'I shudder with horror of him, and I have come to you to protect me and all of us from him. You will?'

'I will!' cried Mr. Grewgious, with a sudden rush of amazing energy. 'Damn him!

'Confound his politics,
Frustrate his knavish tricks!

> On Thee his hopes to fix?
> Damn him again!'

After this most extraordinary outburst, Mr. Grewgious, quite beside himself, plunged about the room, to all appearance undecided whether he was in a fit of loyal enthusiasm, or combative denunciation.

He stopped and said, wiping his face: 'I beg your pardon, my dear, but you will be glad to know I feel better. Tell me no more just now, or I might do it again. You must be refreshed and cheered. What did you take last? Was it breakfast, lunch, dinner, tea, or supper? And what will you take next? Shall it be breakfast, lunch, dinner, tea, or supper?'

The respectful tenderness with which, on one knee before her, he helped her to remove her hat, and disentangle her pretty hair from it, was quite a chivalrous sight. Yet who, knowing him only on the surface, would have expected chivalry – and of the true sort, too: not the spurious – from Mr. Grewgious?

'Your rest too must be provided for,' he went on; 'and you shall have the prettiest chamber in Furnival's. Your toilet must be provided for, and you shall have everything that an unlimited head chambermaid – by which expression I mean a head chambermaid not limited as to outlay – can procure. Is that a bag?' he looked hard at it; sooth to say, it required hard looking at to be seen at all in a dimly lighted room: 'and is it your property, my dear?'

'Yes, sir. I brought it with me.'

'It is not an extensive bag,' said Mr. Grewgious, candidly, 'though admirably calculated to contain a day's provision for a canary bird. Perhaps you brought a canary bird?'

Rosa smiled, and shook her head.

'If you had he should have been made welcome,' said Mr. Grewgious, 'and I think he would have been pleased to be hung upon a nail outside and pit himself against our Staple sparrows; whose execution must be admitted to be not quite equal to their intention. Which is the case with so many of us! You didn't say what meal, my dear. Have a nice jumble of all meals.'

Rosa thanked him, but said she could only take a cup of tea. Mr. Grewgious, after several times running out, and in again, to mention such supplementary items as marmalade, eggs, water-cresses, salted fish, and frizzled ham, ran across to Furnival's without his hat, to give his various directions. And soon afterwards they were realized in practice, and the board was spread.

'Lord bless my soul!' cried Mr. Grewgious, putting the lamp upon it, and taking his seat opposite Rosa; 'what a new sensation for a poor old Angular bachelor, to be sure!'

Rosa's expressive little eyebrows asked him what he meant?

'The sensation of having a sweet young presence in the place that whitewashes it, paints it, papers it, decorates it with gilding, and makes it Glorious!' said Mr. Grewgious. 'Ah me! Ah me!'

As there was something mournful in his sigh, Rosa, in touching him with his tea-cup, ventured to touch him with her small hand too.

'Thank you, my dear,' said Mr. Grewgious. 'Ahem! Let's talk.'

'Do you always live here, sir?' asked Rosa.

'Yes, my dear.'

'And always alone?'

'Always alone; except that I have daily company in a gentleman by the name of Bazzard; my clerk.'

'*He* doesn't live here?'

'No, he goes his ways after office hours. In fact, he is off duty here, altogether, just at present; and a Firm down stairs with which I have business relations, lend me a substitute. But it would be extremely difficult to replace Mr. Bazzard.'

'He must be very fond of you,' said Rosa.

'He bears up against it with commendable fortitude if he is,' returned Mr. Grewgious, after considering the matter. 'But I doubt if he is. Not particularly so. You see, he is discontented, poor fellow.'

'Why isn't he contented?' was the natural inquiry.

'Misplaced,' said Mr. Grewgious, with great mystery.

Rosa's eyebrows resumed their inquisitive and perplexed expression.

'So misplaced,' Mr. Grewgious went on, 'that I feel constantly apologetic towards him. And he feels (though he doesn't mention it) that I have reason to be.'

Mr. Grewgious had by this time grown so very mysterious, that Rosa did not know how to go on. While she was thinking about it Mr. Grewgious suddenly jerked out of himself for the second time:

'Let's talk. We were speaking of Mr. Bazzard. It's a secret, and moreover it is Mr. Bazzard's secret; but the sweet presence at my table makes me so unusually expansive, that I feel I must impart it in inviolable confidence. What do you think Mr. Bazzard has done?'

'Oh dear!' cried Rosa, drawing her chair a little nearer, and her mind reverting to Jasper, 'nothing dreadful, I hope?'

'He has written a play,' said Mr. Grewgious, in a solemn whisper. 'A tragedy.'

Rosa seemed much relieved.

'And nobody,' pursued Mr. Grewgious in the same tone, 'will hear, on any account whatever, of bringing it out.'

Rosa looked reflective, and nodded her head slowly; as who should say: 'Such things are, and why are they!'

'Now, you know,' said Mr. Grewgious, '*I* couldn't write a play.'

'Not a bad one, sir?' asked Rosa, innocently, with her eyebrows again in action.

'No. If I was under sentence of decapitation, and was about to be instantly decapitated, and an express arrived with a pardon for the condemned convict Grewgious if he wrote a play, I should be under the necessity of resuming the block and begging the executioner to proceed to extremities, – meaning,' said Mr. Grewgious, passing his hand under his chin, 'the singular number, and this extremity.'

Rosa appeared to consider what she would do if the awkward supposititious case were hers.

'Consequently,' said Mr. Grewgious, 'Mr. Bazzard would have a sense of my inferiority to himself under any

Mr. Grewgious experiences a New Sensation

circumstances; but when I am his master, you know, the case is greatly aggravated.'

Mr. Grewgious shook his head seriously, as if he felt the offence to be a little too much, though of his own committing.

'How came you to be his master, sir?' asked Rosa.

'A question that naturally follows,' said Mr. Grewgious. 'Let's talk. Mr. Bazzard's father, being a Norfolk farmer, would have furiously laid about him with a flail, a pitchfork, and every agricultural implement available for assaulting purposes, on the slightest hint of his son's having written a play. So the son, bringing to me the father's rent (which I receive), imparted his secret, and pointed out that he was determined to pursue his genius, and that it would put him in peril of starvation, and that he was not formed for it.'

'For pursuing his genius, sir?'

'No, my dear,' said Mr. Grewgious, 'for starvation. It was impossible to deny the position that Mr. Bazzard was not formed to be starved, and Mr. Bazzard then pointed out that it was desirable that I should stand between him and a fate so perfectly unsuited to his formation. In that way Mr. Bazzard became my clerk, and he feels it very much.'

'I am glad he is grateful,' said Rosa.

'I didn't quite mean that, my dear. I mean that he feels the degradation. There are some other geniuses that Mr. Bazzard has become acquainted with, who have also written tragedies, which likewise nobody will on any account whatever hear of bringing out, and these choice spirits dedicate their plays to one another in a highly panegyrical manner. Mr. Bazzard has been the subject of one of these dedications. Now, you know, *I* never had a play dedicated to *me!*'

Rosa looked at him as if she would have liked him to be the recipient of a thousand dedications.

'Which again, naturally, rubs against the grain of Mr. Bazzard,' said Mr. Grewgious. 'He is very short with me sometimes, and then I feel that he is meditating: "This blockhead my master! A fellow who couldn't write a tragedy on pain of death, and who will never have one dedicated to him with the most complimentary congratulations on the high position he has taken in the eyes of posterity!" Very trying, very trying. However, in giving him directions, I reflect beforehand: "Perhaps he may not like this," or "He might take it ill if I asked that," and so we get on very well. Indeed, better than I could have expected.'

'Is the tragedy named, sir?' asked Rosa.

'Strictly between ourselves,' answered Mr. Grewgious, 'it has a dreadfully appropriate name. It is called The Thorn of Anxiety. But Mr. Bazzard hopes – and I hope – that it will come out at last.'

It was not hard to divine that Mr. Grewgious had related the Bazzard history thus fully, at least quite as much for the recreation of his ward's mind from the subject that had driven her there, as for the gratification of his own tendency to be social and communicative. 'And now, my dear,' he said at this point, 'if you are not too tired to tell me more of what passed to-day – but only if you feel quite able – I should be glad to hear it. I may digest it the better, if I sleep on it to-night.'

Rosa, composed now, gave him a faithful account of the interview. Mr. Grewgious often smoothed his head while it was in progress, and begged to be told a second time those parts which bore on Helena and Neville. When Rosa had finished, he sat, grave, silent, and meditative, for a while.

'Clearly narrated,' was his only remark at last, 'and, I hope, clearly put away here,' smoothing his head again: 'See, my dear,' taking her to the open window, 'where they live! The dark windows over yonder.'

'I may go to Helena to-morrow?' asked Rosa.

'I should like to sleep on that question to-night,' he answered, doubtfully. 'But let me take you to your own rest, for you must need it.'

With that, Mr. Grewgious helped her to get her hat on again, and hung upon his arm the very little bag that was of no earthly use, and led her by the hand (with a certain stately awkwardness, as if he were going to walk a minuet) across Holborn, and into Furnival's Inn. At the hotel door, he confided her to the Unlimited head chambermaid, and said that while she went up to see her room, he would remain below, in case she should wish it exchanged for another, or should find that there was anything she wanted.

Rosa's room was airy, clean, comfortable, almost gay. The Unlimited had laid in everything omitted from the very little bag (that is to say, everything she could possibly need), and Rosa tripped down the great many stairs again, to thank her guardian for his thoughtful and affectionate care of her.

'Not at all, my dear,' said Mr. Grewgious, infinitely gratified; 'it is I who thank you for your charming confidence and for your charming company. Your breakfast will be provided for you in a neat, compact, and graceful little sitting-room (appropriate to your figure), and I will come to you at ten o'clock in the morning. I hope you don't feel very strange indeed, in this strange place.'

'Oh no, I feel so safe!'

'Yes, you may be sure that the stairs are fire-proof,' said Mr. Grewgious, 'and that any outbreak of the devouring element would be perceived and suppressed by the watchmen.'

'I did not mean that,' Rosa replied. 'I mean, I feel so safe from him.'

'There is a stout gate of iron bars to keep him out,' said Mr. Grewgious, smiling, 'and Furnival's is specially watched and lighted, and *I* live over the way!' In the stoutness of his knight-errantry, he seemed to think the last-named protection all-sufficient. In the same spirit, he said to the gate-porter as he went out, 'If some one staying in the hotel should wish to send across the road to me in the night, a crown will be ready for the messenger.' In the same spirit, he walked up and down outside the iron gate for the best part of an hour, with some solicitude: occasionally looking in between the bars, as if he had laid a dove in a high roost in a cage of lions, and had it on his mind that she might tumble out.

CHAPTER XXI

A Recognition

NOTHING occurred in the night to flutter the tired dove, and the dove arose refreshed. With Mr. Grewgious when the clocks struck ten in the morning, came Mr. Crisparkle, who had come at one plunge out of the river at Cloisterham.

'Miss Twinkleton was so uneasy, Miss Rosa,' he explained to her, 'and came round to Ma and me with your note, in such a state of wonder, that, to quiet her, I volunteered on this service by the very first train to be caught in the morning. I wished at the time that you had come to me; but now I think it best that you did *as* you did, and came to your guardian.'

'I did think of you,' Rosa told him; 'but Minor Canon Corner was so near him—'

'I understand. It was quite natural.'

'I have told Mr. Crisparkle,' said Mr. Grewgious, 'all that you told me last night, my dear. Of course I should have written it to him immediately; but his coming was most opportune. And it was particularly kind of him to come, for he had but just gone.'

'Have you settled,' asked Rosa, appealing to them both, 'what is to be done for Helena and her brother?'

'Why really,' said Mr. Crisparkle, 'I am in great perplexity. If even Mr. Grewgious, whose head is much longer than mine and who is a whole night's cogitation in advance of me, is undecided, what must I be!'

The Unlimited here put her head in at the door – after having tapped, and been authorized to present herself – announcing that a gentleman wished for a word with another gentleman named Crisparkle, if any such gentleman were there. If no such gentleman were there, he begged pardon for being mistaken.

'Such a gentleman is here,' said Mr. Crisparkle, 'but is engaged just now.'

'Oh, is it a dark gentleman?' interposed Rosa, retreating on her guardian.

'No, Miss, more of a brown gentleman.'

'You are sure not with black hair?' asked Rosa, taking courage.

'Quite sure of that, Miss. Brown hair and blue eyes.'

'Perhaps,' hinted Mr. Grewgious, with habitual caution, 'it might be well to see him, reverend sir, if you don't object. When one is in a difficulty, or at a loss, one never knows in what direction a way out may chance to open. It is a business principle of mine, in such a case, not to close up any direction, but to keep an eye on every direction that may present itself. I could relate an anecdote in point, but that it would be premature.'

'If Miss Rosa will allow me then? Let the gentleman come in,' said Mr. Crisparkle.

The gentleman came in; apologized, with a frank but modest grace, for not finding Mr. Crisparkle alone; turned to Mr. Crisparkle, and smilingly asked the unexpected question: 'Who am I?'

'You are the gentleman I saw smoking under the trees in Staple Inn a few minutes ago.'

'True. There I saw you. Who else am I?'

Mr. Crisparkle concentrated his attention on a handsome face, much sunburnt; and the ghost of some departed boy seemed to rise, gradually and dimly, in the room.

The gentleman saw a struggling recollection lighten up the Minor Canon's features, and smiling again, said: 'What will you have for breakfast this morning? You are out of jam.'

'Wait a moment!' cried Mr. Crisparkle, raising his right hand. 'Give me another instant! Tartar!'

The two shook hands with the greatest heartiness, and then went the wonderful length – for Englishmen – of laying their hands each on the other's shoulders, and looking joyfully each into the other's face.

'My old fag!' said Mr. Crisparkle.

'My old master!' said Mr. Tartar.

'You saved me from drowning!' said Mr. Crisparkle.

'After which you took to swimming, you know!' said Mr. Tartar.

'God bless my soul!' said Mr. Crisparkle.

'Amen!' said Mr. Tartar.

And then they fell to shaking hands most heartily again.

'Imagine,' exclaimed Mr. Crisparkle, with glistening eyes: 'Miss Rosa Bud and Mr. Grewgious: imagine Mr. Tartar, when he was the smallest of juniors, diving for me, catching me, a big heavy senior, by the hair of my head, and striking out for the shore with me like a water-giant!'

'Imagine my not letting him sink, as I was his fag!' said Mr. Tartar. 'But the truth being that he was my best protector and friend, and did me more good than all the masters put together, an irrational impulse seized me either to pick him up, or go down with him.'

'Hem! Permit me, sir, to have the honour,' said Mr. Grewgious, advancing with extended hand, 'for an honour I truly esteem it. I am proud to make your acquaintance. I hope you didn't take cold. I hope you were not inconvenienced by swallowing too much water. How have you been since?'

It was by no means apparent that Mr. Grewgious knew what he said, though it was very apparent that he meant to say something highly friendly and appreciative.

If Heaven, Rosa thought, had but sent such courage and skill to her poor mother's aid! And he to have been so slight and young then!

'I don't wish to be complimented upon it, I thank you, but I think I have an idea,' Mr. Grewgious announced, after taking a jog-trot or two across the room, so very unexpected and unaccountable that they had all stared at him, doubtful whether he was choking, or had the cramp. 'I *think* I have an idea. I believe I have had the pleasure of seeing Mr. Tartar's name as tenant of the top set in the house next the top set in the corner?'

'Yes, sir,' returned Mr. Tartar. 'You are right so far.'

'I am right so far,' said Mr. Grewgious. 'Tick that off,' which he did, with his right thumb on his left. 'Might you happen to know the name of your neighbour in the top set on the other side of the party-wall?' coming very close to Mr. Tartar, to lose nothing of his face, in his shortness of sight.

'Landless.'

'Tick that off,' said Mr. Grewgious, taking another trot, and then coming back. 'No personal knowledge, I suppose, sir?'

'Slight, but some.'

'Tick that off,' said Mr. Grewgious, taking another trot, and again coming back. 'Nature of knowledge, Mr. Tartar?'

'I thought he seemed to be a young fellow in a poor way, and I asked his leave – only within a day or so – to share my flowers up there with him; that is to say, to extend my flower-garden to his windows.'

'Would you have the kindness to take seats?' said Mr. Grewgious. 'I *have* an idea!'

They complied; Mr. Tartar none the less readily, for being all abroad; and Mr. Grewgious, seated in the centre, with his hands upon his knees, thus stated his idea, with his usual manner of having got the statement by heart.

'I cannot as yet make up my mind whether it is prudent to hold open communication under present circumstances, and on the part of the fair member of the present company, with Mr. Neville or Miss Helena. I have reason to know that a local friend of ours (on whom I beg to bestow a passing but a hearty malediction, with the kind permission of my reverend friend) sneaks to and fro, and dodges up and down. When not doing so himself, he may have some informant skulking about, in the person of any watchman, porter, or such-like hanger-on of Staple. On the other hand, Miss Rosa very naturally wishes to see her friend Miss Helena, and it would seem important that at least Miss Helena (if not her brother too, through her) should privately know from Miss Rosa's lips what has occurred, and what has been threatened. Am I agreed with generally in the views I take?'

'I entirely coincide with them,' said Mr. Crisparkle, who had been very attentive.

'As I have no doubt I should,' added Mr. Tartar, smiling, 'if I understood them.'

'Fair and softly, dear sir,' said Mr. Grewgious; 'we shall fully confide in you directly, if you will favour us with your permission. Now, if our local friend should have any informant on the spot, it is tolerably clear that such informant can only be set to watch the chambers in the occupation of Mr. Neville. He reporting, to our local friend, who comes and goes there, our local friend would supply for himself, from his own previous knowledge, the identity of the parties. Nobody can be set to watch all Staple, or to concern himself with comers and goers to other sets of chambers: unless, indeed, mine.'

'I begin to understand to what you tend,' said Mr. Crisparkle, 'and I highly approve of your caution.'

'I needn't repeat that I know nothing yet of the why and wherefore,' said Mr. Tartar; 'but I also understood to what you tend, so let me say at once that my chambers are freely at your disposal.'

'There!' cried Mr. Grewgious, smoothing his head triumphantly. 'Now we have all got the idea. You have it, my dear?'

'I think I have,' said Rosa, blushing a little as Mr. Tartar looked quickly towards her.

'You see, you go over to Staple with Mr. Crisparkle and Mr. Tartar,' said Mr. Grewgious; 'I going in and out and out and in, alone, in my usual way; you go up with those gentlemen to Mr. Tartar's rooms; you look into Mr. Tartar's flower-garden; you wait for Miss Helena's appearance there, or you signify to Miss Helena that you are close by; and you communicate with her freely, and no spy can be the wiser.'

'I am very much afraid I shall be—'

'Be what, my dear?' asked Mr. Grewgious, as she hesitated. 'Not frightened?'

'No, not that,' said Rosa, shyly; – 'in Mr. Tartar's way. We seem to be appropriating Mr. Tartar's residence so very coolly.'

'I protest to you,' returned that gentleman, 'that I shall think the better of it for evermore, if your voice sounds in it only once.'

Rosa, not quite knowing what to say about that, cast down her eyes, and turning to Mr. Grewgious, dutifully asked if she should put her hat on? Mr. Grewgious being of opinion that she could not do better, she withdrew for the purpose. Mr. Crisparkle took the opportunity of giving Mr. Tartar a summary of the distresses of Neville and his sister; the opportunity was quite long enough, as the hat happened to require a little extra fitting on.

Mr. Tartar gave his arm to Rosa, and Mr. Crisparkle walked, detached, in front.

'Poor, poor Eddy!' thought Rosa, as they went along.

Mr. Tartar waved his right hand as he bent his head down over Rosa, talking in an animated way.

'It was not so powerful or so sun-browned when it saved Mr. Crisparkle,' thought Rosa, glancing at it; 'but it must have been very steady and determined even then.'

Mr. Tartar told her he had been a sailor, roving everywhere for years and years.

'When are you going to sea again?' asked Rosa.

'Never!'

Rosa wondered what the girls would say if they could see her crossing the wide street on the sailor's arm. And she feared that the passers-by must think her very little and very helpless, contrasted with the strong figure that could have caught her up and carried her out of any danger, miles and miles, without resting.

She was thinking further, that his far-seeing blue eyes looked as if they had been used to watch danger afar off, and to watch it without flinching, drawing nearer and nearer: when, happening to raise her own eyes, she found that he seemed to be thinking something about *them*.

This a little confused Rosebud, and may account for her never afterwards quite knowing how she ascended (with his help) to his garden in the air, and seemed to get into a marvellous country that came into sudden bloom like the country on the summit of the magic beanstalk. May it flourish for ever!

CHAPTER XXII

A Gritty State of Things comes on

Mr. TARTAR's chambers were the neatest, the cleanest, and the best ordered chambers ever seen under the sun, moon, and stars. The floors were scrubbed to that extent, that you might have supposed the London blacks emancipated for ever, and gone out of the land for good. Every inch of brass-work in Mr. Tartar's possession was polished and burnished, till it shone like a brazen mirror. No speck, nor spot, nor spatter soiled the purity of any of Mr. Tartar's household gods, large, small, or middle-sized. His sitting-room was like the admiral's cabin, his bath-room was like a dairy, his sleeping-chamber, fitted all about with lockers and drawers, was like a seedsman's shop; and his nicely-balanced cot just stirred in the midst, as if it breathed. Everything belonging to Mr. Tartar had quarters of its own assigned to it: his maps and charts had their quarters; his books had theirs; his brushes had theirs; his boots had theirs; his clothes had theirs; his case-bottles had theirs; his telescopes and other instruments had theirs. Everything was readily accessible. Shelf, bracket, locker, hook, and drawer were equally within reach, and were equally contrived with a view to avoiding waste of room, and providing some snug inches of stowage for something that would have exactly fitted nowhere else. His gleaming little service of plate was so arranged upon his sideboard as that a slack salt-spoon would have instantly betrayed itself; his toilet implements were so arranged upon his dressing-table as that a toothpick of slovenly deportment could have been reported at a glance. So with the curiosities he had brought home from various voyages. Stuffed, dried, repolished, or otherwise preserved, according to their kind; birds, fishes, reptiles, arms, articles of dress, shells, seaweeds, grasses, or memorials of coral reef; each was displayed in its especial place, and each could have been displayed in no better place. Paint and varnish seemed to be kept somewhere out of sight, in constant readiness to obliterate stray finger-marks wherever any might become perceptible in Mr. Tartar's chambers. No man-of-war was ever kept more spick and span from careless touch. On this bright summer day, a neat awning was rigged over Mr. Tartar's flower-garden as only a sailor could rig it; and there was a sea-going air upon the whole effect, so delightfully complete, that the flower-garden might have appertained to stern-windows afloat, and the whole concern might have bowled away gallantly with all on board, if Mr. Tartar had only clapped to his lips the speaking-trumpet that was slung in a corner, and given hoarse orders to have the anchor up, look alive there, men, and get all sail upon her!

Mr. Tartar doing the honours of this gallant craft was of a piece with the rest. When a man rides an amiable hobby that shies at nothing and kicks nobody, it is always agreeable to find him riding it with a humorous sense of the droll side of the creature. When the man is a cordial and an earnest man by nature, and withal is perfectly fresh and genuine, it may be doubted whether he is ever seen to greater advantage than at such a time. So Rosa would have naturally thought (even if she *hadn't* been conducted over the ship with all the homage due to the First Lady of the Admiralty, or First Fairy of the Sea), that it was charming to see and hear Mr. Tartar half laughing at, and half rejoicing in, his various contrivances. So Rosa would have naturally thought, anyhow, that the sun-burnt sailor showed to great advantage when, the inspection finished, he delicately withdrew out of his admiral's cabin, beseeching her to consider herself its Queen, and waving her free of its flower-garden with the hand that had had Mr. Crisparkle's life in it.

'Helena! Helena Landless! Are you there?'

'Who speaks to me? Not Rosa?' Then a second handsome face appearing.

'Yes, my darling!'

'Why, how did you come here, dearest?'

'I – I don't quite know,' said Rosa with a blush; 'unless I am dreaming!'

Why with a blush? For their two faces were alone with the other flowers. Are blushes among the fruits of the country of the magic beanstalk?

'*I* am not dreaming,' said Helena, smiling. 'I should take more for granted if I were. How do we come together – or so near together – so very unexpectedly?'

Unexpectedly indeed, among the dingy gables and chimneypots of P. J. T.'s connexion, and the flowers that had sprung from the salt sea. But Rosa, waking, told in a hurry how they came to be together, and all the why and wherefore of that matter.

'And Mr. Crisparkle is here,' said Rosa, in rapid conclusion; 'and could you believe it? Long ago, he saved his life!'

'I could believe any such thing of Mr. Crisparkle,' returned Helena, with a mantling face.

(More blushes in the beanstalk country!)

'Yes, but it wasn't Mr. Crisparkle,' said Rosa, quickly putting in the correction.

'I don't understand, love.'

'It was very nice of Mr. Crisparkle to be saved,' said Rosa, 'and he couldn't have shown his high opinion of Mr. Tartar more expressively. But it was Mr. Tartar who saved him.'

Helena's dark eyes looked very earnestly at the bright face among the leaves, and she asked, in a slower and more thoughtful tone:

'Is Mr. Tartar with you now, dear?'

'No; because he has given up his rooms to me – to us, I mean. It *is* such a beautiful place!'

'Is it?'

'It is like the inside of the most exquisite ship that ever sailed. It is like – it is like—'

'Like a dream?' suggested Helena.

Rosa answered with a little nod, and smelled the flowers.

Helena resumed, after a short pause of silence, during which she seemed (or it was Rosa's fancy) to compassionate somebody: 'My poor Neville is reading in his own room, the sun being so very bright on this side just now. I think he had better not know that you are so near.'

'Oh, I think so too!' cried Rosa very readily.

'I suppose,' pursued Helena, doubtfully, 'that he must know by-and-bye all you have told me; but I am not sure. Ask Mr. Crisparkle's advice, my darling. Ask him whether I may tell Neville as much or as little of what you have told me as I think best,'

Rosa subsided into her state-cabin, and propounded the question. The Minor Canon was for the free exercise of Helena's judgement.

'I thank him very much,' said Helena, when Rosa emerged again with her report. 'Ask him whether it would be best to wait until any new maligning and pursuing of Neville on the part of this wretch shall disclose itself, or to try to anticipate it: I mean, so far as to find out whether any such goes on darkly about us?'

The Minor Canon found this point so difficult to give a confident opinion on, that, after two or three attempts and failures, he suggested a reference to Mr. Grewgious. Helena acquiescing, he betook himself (with a most unsuccessful assumption of lounging indifference) across the quadrangle to P. J. T.'s, and stated it. Mr. Grewgious held decidedly to the general principle, that if you could steal a march upon a brigand or a wild beast, you had better do it; he also held decidedly to the special case, that John Jasper was a brigand *and* a wild beast in combination.

Thus advised, Mr. Crisparkle came back again and reported to Rosa, who in her turn reported to Helena. She, now steadily pursuing her train of thought at her window, considered thereupon.

'We may count on Mr. Tartar's readiness to help us, Rosa?' she inquired.

Oh yes! Rosa shyly thought so. Oh yes, Rosa shyly believed she could almost answer for that. But should she ask Mr. Crisparkle? 'I think your authority on the point as good as his, my dear,' said Helena, sedately, 'and you needn't disappear again for that.' Odd of Helena!

'You see, Neville,' Helena pursued after more reflection, 'knows no one else here: he has not so much as exchanged a word with any one else here. If Mr. Tartar would call to see him openly and often; if he would spare a minute for the

purpose, frequently; if he would even do so, almost daily;
something might come of it.'

'Something might come of it, dear?' repeated Rosa,
surveying her friend's beauty with a highly perplexed face.
'Something might?'

'If Neville's movements are really watched, and if the
purpose really is to isolate him from all friends and acquaintance and wear his daily life out grain by grain (which would
seem to be in the threat to you), does it not appear likely,' said
Helena, 'that his enemy would in some way communicate
with Mr. Tartar to warn him off from Neville? In which case,
we might not only know the fact but might know from
Mr. Tartar what the terms of the communication were.'

'I see!' cried Rosa. And immediately darted into her state-
cabin again.

Presently her pretty face reappeared, with a heightened
colour, and she said that she had told Mr. Crisparkle, and that
Mr. Crisparkle had fetched in Mr. Tartar, and that Mr. Tartar
– 'who is waiting now in case you want him,' added Rosa, with
a half look back, and in not a little confusion between the
inside of the state-cabin and the out – had declared his
readiness to act as she had suggested, and to enter on his
task that very day.

'I thank him from my heart,' said Helena. 'Pray tell him
so.'

Again not a little confused between the flower-garden and
the cabin, Rosa dipped in with her message, and dipped out
again with more assurances from Mr. Tartar, and stood
wavering in a divided state between Helena and him, which
proved that confusion is not always necessarily awkward, but
may sometimes present a very pleasant appearance.

'And now, darling,' said Helena, 'we will be mindful of the
caution that has restricted us to this interview for the present,
and will part. I hear Neville moving too. Are you going back?'

'To Miss Twinkleton's?' asked Rosa.

'Yes.'

'Oh, I could never go there any more; I couldn't indeed,
after that dreadful interview!' said Rosa.

'Then where *are* you going, pretty one?'

'Now I come to think of it, I don't know,' said Rosa. 'I have settled nothing at all yet, but my guardian will take care of me. Don't be uneasy, dear. I shall be sure to be somewhere.'

(It did seem likely.)

'And I shall hear of my Rosebud from Mr. Tartar?' inquired Helena.

'Yes, I suppose so; from—' Rosa looked back again in a flutter, instead of supplying the name. 'But tell me one thing before we part, dearest Helena. Tell me that you are sure, sure, sure, I couldn't help it.'

'Help it, love?'

'Help making him malicious and revengeful. I couldn't hold any terms with him, could I?'

'You know how I love you, darling,' answered Helena, with indignation; 'but I would sooner see you dead at his wicked feet.'

'That's a great comfort to me! And you will tell your poor brother so, won't you? And you will give him my remembrance and my sympathy? And you will ask him not to hate me?'

With a mournful shake of the head, as if that would be quite a superfluous entreaty, Helena lovingly kissed her two hands to her friend, and her friend's two hands were kissed to her; and then she saw a third hand (a brown one) appear among the flowers and leaves, and help her friend out of sight.

The refection that Mr. Tartar produced in the admiral's cabin by merely touching the spring knob of a locker and the handle of a drawer, was a dazzling enchanted repast. Wonderful macaroons, glittering liqueurs, magically preserved tropical spices, and jellies of celestial tropical fruits, displayed themselves profusely at an instant's notice. But Mr. Tartar could not make time stand still; and time, with his hard-hearted fleetness, strode on so fast, that Rosa was obliged to come down from the beanstalk country to earth, and her guardian's chambers.

'And now, my dear,' said Mr. Grewgious, 'what is to be done next? To put the same thought in another form; what is to be done with you?'

Rosa could only look apologetically sensible of being very much in her own way, and in everybody else's. Some passing idea of living, fire-proof, up a good many stairs in Furnival's Inn for the rest of her life, was the only thing in the nature of a plan that occurred to her.

'It has come into my thoughts,' said Mr. Grewgious, 'that the respected lady, Miss Twinkleton, occasionally repairs to London in the recess, with the view of extending her connexion, and being available for interviews with metropolitan parents, if any. Whether, until we have time in which to turn ourselves round, we might invite Miss Twinkleton to come and stay with you for a month?'

'Stay where, sir?'

'Whether,' explained Mr. Grewgious, 'we might take a furnished lodging in town for a month, and invite Miss Twinkleton to assume the charge of you in it for that period?'

'And afterwards?' hinted Rosa.

'And afterwards,' said Mr. Grewgious, 'we should be no worse off than we are now.'

'I think that might smooth the way,' assented Rosa.

'Then let us,' said Mr. Grewgious, rising, 'go and look for a furnished lodging. Nothing could be more acceptable to me than the sweet presence of last evening, for all the remaining evenings of my existence; but these are not fit surroundings for a young lady. Let us set out in quest of adventures, and look for a furnished lodging. In the meantime, Mr. Crisparkle here, about to return home immediately, will no doubt kindly see Miss Twinkleton and invite that lady to co-operate in our plan.'

Mr. Crisparkle, willingly accepting the commission, took his departure; Mr. Grewgious and his ward set forth on their expedition.

As Mr. Grewgious's idea of looking at a furnished lodging was to get on the opposite side of the street to a house with a suitable bill in the window, and stare at it; and then work his way tortuously to the back of the house, and stare at that; and then not go in, but make similar trials of another house, with the same result; their progress was but slow. At length he bethought himself of a widowed cousin, divers times removed, of Mr. Bazzard's, who had once solicited his influence in the lodger world, and who lived in Southampton Street, Bloomsbury Square. This lady's name, stated in uncompromising capitals of considerable size on a brass door-plate, and yet not lucidly stated as to sex or condition, was BILLICKIN.

Personal faintness, and an overpowering personal candour, were the distinguishing features of Mrs. Billickin's organization. She came languishing out from her own exclusive back parlour, with the air of having been expressly brought-to for the purpose, from an accumulation of several swoons.

'I hope I see you well, sir,' said Mrs. Billickin, recognizing her visitor with a bend.

'Thank you, quite well. And you, ma'am?' returned Mr. Grewgious.

'I am as well,' said Mrs. Billickin, becoming aspirational with excess of faintness, 'as I hever ham.'

'My ward and an elder lady,' said Mr. Grewgious, 'wish to find a genteel lodging for a month or so. Have you any apartments available, ma'am?'

'Mr. Grewgious,' returned Mrs. Billickin, 'I will not deceive you; far from it. I *have* apartments available.'

This, with the air of adding: 'Convey me to the stake, if you will; but while I live, I will be candid.'

'And now, what apartments, ma'am?' asked Mr. Grewgious, cosily. To tame a certain severity apparent on the part of Mrs. Billickin.

'There is this sitting-room – which call it what you will, it is the front parlior, Miss,' said Mrs. Billickin, impressing Rosa into the conversation: 'the back parlior being what I cling to and never part with; and there is two bedrooms at the top of the 'ouse with gas laid on. I do not tell you that your bedroom floors is firm, for firm they are not. The gas-fitter himself allowed that to make a firm job, he must go right under your jistes, and it were not worth the outlay as a yearly tenant so to do. The piping is carried above your jistes, and it is best that it should be made known to you.'

Mr. Grewgious and Rosa exchanged looks of some dismay,
though they had not the least idea what latent horrors this
carriage of the piping might involve. Mrs. Billickin put her
hand to her heart, as having eased it of a load.

'Well! The roof is all right, no doubt,' said Mr. Grewgious,
plucking up a little.

'Mr. Grewgious,' returned Mrs. Billickin, 'if I was to tell
you, sir, that to have nothink above you is to have a floor
above you, I should put a deception upon you which I will
not do. No, sir. Your slates WILL rattle loose at that elewation
in windy weather, do your utmost, best or worst! I defy you,
sir, be you who you may, to keep your slates tight, try how you
can.' Here Mrs. Billickin, having been warm with Mr. Grewgious, cooled a little, not to abuse the moral power she held
over him. 'Consequent,' proceeded Mrs. Billickin, more
mildly, but still firmly in her incorruptible candour: 'consequent it would be worse than of no use for me to trapse and
travel up to the top of the 'ouse with you, and for you to
say, "Mrs. Billickin, what stain do I notice in the ceiling, for a
stain I do consider it?" and for me to answer, "I do not
understand you, sir." No sir; I will not be so underhand.
I *do* understand you before you pint it out. It is the wet, sir.
It do come in, and it do not come in. You may lay dry there,
half your lifetime; but the time will come, and it is best that
you should know it, when a dripping sop would be no name
for you.'

Mr. Grewgious looked much disgraced by being prefig-
ured in this pickle.

'Have you any other apartments, ma'am?' he asked.

'Mr. Grewgious,' returned Mrs. Billickin, with much solemnity, 'I have. You ask me have I, and my open and my
honest answer air, I have. The first and second floors is
wacant, and sweet rooms.'

'Come, come! There's nothing against *them*,' said Mr.
Grewgious, comforting himself.

'Mr. Grewgious,' replied Mrs. Billickin, 'pardon me, there
is the stairs. Unless your mind is prepared for the stairs, it will
lead to inevitable disapintmink. You cannot, Miss,' said
Mrs. Billickin, addressing Rosa, reproachfully, 'place a first

floor, and far less a second, on the level footing of a parlior. No, you can not do it, Miss, it is beyond your power, and wherefore try?'

Mrs. Billickin put it very feelingly, as if Rosa had shown a headstrong determination to hold the untenable position.

'Can we see these rooms, ma'am?' inquired her guardian.

'Mr. Grewgious,' returned Mrs. Billickin, 'you can. I will not disguise it from you, sir, you can.'

Mrs. Billickin then sent into her back parlour for her shawl (it being a state fiction, dating from immemorial antiquity, that she could never go anywhere without being wrapped up), and having been enrobed by her attendant, led the way. She made various genteel pauses on the stairs for breath, and clutched at her heart in the drawing-room as if it had very nearly got loose, and she had caught it in the act of taking wing.

'And the second floor?' said Mr. Grewgious, on finding the first satisfactory.

'Mr. Grewgious,' replied Mrs. Billickin, turning upon him with ceremony, as if the time had now come when a distinct understanding on a difficult point must be arrived at, and a solemn confidence established, 'the second floor is over this.'

'Can we see that too, ma'am?'

'Yes, sir,' returned Mrs. Billickin, 'it is open as the day.'

That also proving satisfactory, Mr. Grewgious retired into a window with Rosa for a few words of consultation, and then, asking for pen and ink, sketched out a line or two of agreement. In the meantime Mrs. Billickin took a seat, and delivered a kind of Index to, or Abstract of, the general question.

'Five-and-forty shillings per week by the month certain at the time of year,' said Mrs. Billickin, 'is only reasonable to both parties. It is not Bond Street nor yet St. James's Palace; but it is not pretended that it is. Neither is it attempted to be denied – for why should it? – that the Archway leads to a Mews. Mewses must exist. Respectin' attendance; two is kep', at liberal wages. Words *has* arisen as to tradesmen, but dirty shoes on fresh hearth-stoning was attributable, and no wish for a commission on your orders. Coals is either *by* the fire, or *per* the scuttle.' She emphasized the prepositions as marking a subtle but immense difference. 'Dogs is not viewed with favior. Besides litter, they gets stole, and sharing suspicions is apt to creep in, and unpleasantness takes place.'

By this time Mr. Grewgious had his agreement-lines, and his earnest-money, ready. 'I have signed it for the ladies, ma'am,' he said, 'and you'll have the goodness to sign it for yourself, Christian and Surname, there, if you please.'

'Mr. Grewgious,' said Mrs. Billickin in a new burst of candour, 'no, sir! You must excuse the Chris'en name.'

Mr. Grewgious stared at her.

'The door-plate is used as a protection,' said Mrs. Billickin, 'and acts as such, and go from it I will not.'

Mr. Grewgious stared at Rosa.

'No, Mr. Grewgious, you must excuse me. So long as this 'ouse is known indefinite as Billickin's, and so long as it is a doubt with the riff-raff where Billickin may be hidin', near the street door or down the airy, and what his weight and size, so long I feel safe. But commit myself to a solitary female statement, no, Miss! Nor would you for a moment wish,' said Mrs. Billickin, with a strong sense of injury, 'to take that advantage of your sex, if you was not brought to it by inconsiderate example.'

Rosa reddening as if she had made some most disgraceful attempt to overreach the good lady, besought Mr. Grewgious to rest content with any signature. And accordingly, in a baronial way, the sign-manual BILLICKIN got appended to the document.

Details were then settled for taking possession on the next day but one, when Miss Twinkleton might be reasonably expected; and Rosa went back to Furnival's Inn on her guardian's arm.

Behold Mr. Tartar walking up and down Furnival's Inn, checking himself when he saw them coming, and advancing towards them!

'It occurred to me,' hinted Mr. Tartar, 'that we might go up the river, the weather being so delicious and the tide serving. I have a boat of my own at the Temple Stairs.'

'I have not been up the river for this many a day,' said Mr. Grewgious, tempted.

'I was never up the river,' added Rosa.

Within half an hour they were setting this matter right by going up the river. The tide was running with them, the afternoon was charming. Mr. Tartar's boat was perfect. Mr. Tartar and Lobley (Mr. Tartar's man) pulled a pair of oars. Mr. Tartar had a yacht, it seemed, lying somewhere down by Greenhithe; and Mr. Tartar's man had charge of this yacht, and was detached upon his present service. He was a jolly favoured man, with tawny hair and whiskers, and a big red face. He was the dead image of the sun in old wood-cuts, his hair and whiskers answering for rays all round him. Resplendent in the bow of the boat, he was a shining sight, with a man-of-war's man's shirt on – or off, according to opinion – and his arms and breast tattoo'd all sorts of patterns. Lobley seemed to take it easily, and so did Mr. Tartar; yet their oars bent as they pulled, and the boat bounded under them. Mr. Tartar talked as if he were doing nothing, to Rosa who was really doing nothing, and to Mr. Grewgious who was doing this much that he steered all wrong; but what did that matter, when a turn of Mr. Tartar's skilful wrist, or a mere grin of Mr. Lobley's over the bow, put all to rights! The tide bore them on in the gayest and most sparkling manner, until they stopped to dine in some everlastingly green garden, needing no matter-of-fact identification here; and then the tide obligingly turned – being devoted to that party alone for that day; and as they floated idly among some osier beds, Rosa tried what she could do in the rowing way, and came off splendidly, being much assisted; and Mr. Grewgious tried what he could do, and came off on his back, doubled up with an oar under his chin, being not assisted at all. Then there was an interval of rest under boughs (such rest!) what time Mr. Lobley mopped, and, arranging cushions, stretchers, and the like, danced the tight rope the whole length of the boat like a man to whom shoes were a superstition and stockings slavery; and then came the sweet return among delicious odours of limes in bloom, and musical ripplings; and, all too soon, the great black city cast its shadow on the waters, and its dark bridges spanned them as death spans life, and the everlastingly green garden seemed to be left for everlasting, unregainable and far away.

'Cannot people get through life without gritty stages, I wonder!' Rosa thought next day, when the town was very gritty again, and everything had a strange and an uncomfortable appearance on it of seeming to wait for something that wouldn't come. No. She began to think, that, now the Cloisterham school-days had glided past and gone, the gritty stages would begin to set in at intervals and make themselves wearily known!

Yet what did Rosa expect? Did she expect Miss Twinkleton? Miss Twinkleton duly came. Forth from her back parlour issued the Billickin to receive Miss Twinkleton, and War was in the Billickin's eye from that fell moment.

Miss Twinkleton brought a quantity of luggage with her, having all Rosa's as well as her own. The Billickin took it ill that Miss Twinkleton's mind, being sorely disturbed by this luggage, failed to take in her personal identity with that clearness of perception which was due to its demands. Stateliness mounted her gloomy throne upon the Billickin's brow in consequence. And when Miss Twinkleton, in agitation taking stock of her trunks and packages, of which she had seventeen, particularly counted in the Billickin herself as number eleven, the B found it necessary to repudiate.

'Things cannot too soon be put upon the footing,' said she, with a candour so demonstrative as to be almost obtrusive, 'that the person of the 'ouse is not a box nor yet a bundle, nor a carpet bag. No, I am 'ily obleeged to you, Miss Twinkleton, nor yet a beggar.'

This last disclaimer had reference to Miss Twinkleton's distractedly pressing two and sixpence on her, instead of the cabman.

Thus cast off, Miss Twinkleton wildly inquired, 'which gentleman' was to be paid? There being two gentlemen in that position (Miss Twinkleton having arrived with two cabs), each gentleman on being paid held forth his two and sixpence on the flat of his open hand, and, with a speechless stare and a dropped jaw, displayed his wrong to heaven and

Up the River

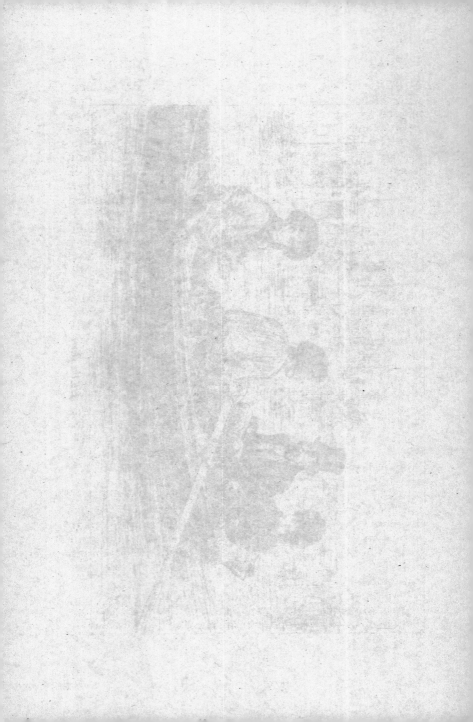

earth. Terrified by this alarming spectacle, Miss Twinkleton placed another shilling in each hand; at the same time appealing to the law in flurried accents, and re-counting her luggage this time with the two gentlemen in, who caused the total to come out complicated. Meanwhile the two gentlemen, each looking very hard at the last shilling, as if it might become eighteenpence if he kept his eyes on it, grumblingly descended the doorsteps, ascended their carriages, and drove away, leaving Miss Twinkleton bewildered on a bonnet-box in tears.

The Billickin beheld this manifestation of weakness without sympathy, and gave directions for 'a young man to be got in' to wrestle with the luggage. When that gladiator had disappeared from the arena, peace ensued, and the new lodgers dined.

But the Billickin had somehow come to the knowledge that Miss Twinkleton kept a school. The leap from that knowledge to the inference that Miss Twinkleton would set herself to teach *her* something, was easy. 'But you don't do it,' soliloquized the Billickin; '*I* am not your pupil, whatever she,' meaning Rosa, 'may be, poor thing!'

Miss Twinkleton on the other hand, having changed her dress and recovered her spirits, was animated by a bland desire to improve the occasion in all ways, and to be as serene a model as possible. In a happy compromise between her two states of existence, she had already become, with her work-basket before her, the equally vivacious companion with a slight judicious flavouring of information, when the Billickin announced herself.

'I will not hide from you, ladies,' said the B, enveloped in the shawl of state, 'for it is not my character to hide neither my motives nor my actions, that I take the liberty to look in upon you to express a 'ope that your dinner was to your liking. Though not Professed but Plain, still her wages should be a sufficient object to her to stimilate to soar above mere roast and biled.'

'We dined very well indeed,' said Rosa, 'thank you.'

'Accustomed,' said Miss Twinkleton, with a gracious air which to the jealous ears of the Billickin seemed to

add 'my good woman' – 'Accustomed to a liberal and nutri-
tious, yet plain and salutary diet, we have found no reason
to bemoan our absence from the ancient city, and the
methodical household, in which the quiet routine of our lot
has been hitherto cast.'

'I did think it well to mention to my cook,' observed
the Billickin with a gush of candour, 'which I 'ope you will
agree with me, Miss Twinkleton, was a right precaution,
that the young lady being used to what we should consider
here but poor diet, had better be brought forard by degrees.
For, a rush from scanty feeding to generous feeding, and
from what you may call messing to what you may call
method, do require a power of constitution, which is not
often found in youth, particular when undermined by
boarding-school!'

It will be seen that the Billickin now openly pitted herself
against Miss Twinkleton, as one whom she had fully ascertained to be her natural enemy.

'Your remarks,' returned Miss Twinkleton, from a remote
moral eminence, 'are well meant, I have no doubt; but you
will permit me to observe that they develop a mistaken view
of the subject, which can only be imputed to your extreme
want of accurate information.'

'My informiation,' retorted the Billickin, throwing in an
extra syllable for the sake of an emphasis at once polite and
powerful: 'My informiation, Miss Twinkleton, were my own
experience, which I believe is usually considered to be good
guidance. But whether so or not, I was put in youth to a very
genteel boarding-school, the mistress being no less a lady
than yourself, of about your own age or it may be some
years younger, and a poorness of blood flowed from the
table which has run through my life.'

'Very likely,' said Miss Twinkleton, still from her distant
eminence; 'and very much to be deplored. Rosa, my dear,
how are you getting on with your work?'

'Miss Twinkleton,' resumed the Billickin, in a courtly
manner, 'before retiring on the 'Int, as a lady should, I wish
to ask of yourself as a lady, whether I am to consider that my
words is doubted?'

'I am not aware on what ground you cherish such a supposition,' began Miss Twinkleton, when the Billickin neatly stopped her.

'Do not, if you please, put suppositions betwixt my lips, where none such have been imparted by myself. Your flow of words is great, Miss Twinkleton, and no doubt is expected from you by your pupils, and no doubt is considered worth the money. *No* doubt, I am sure. But not paying for flows of words, and not asking to be faviored with them here, I wish to repeat my question.'

'If you refer to the poverty of your circulation,' began Miss Twinkleton again, when again the Billickin neatly stopped her.

'I have used no such expressions.'

'If you refer then to the poorness of your blood.'

'Brought upon me,' stipulated the Billickin, expressly, 'at a boarding-school.'

'Then,' resumed Miss Twinkleton, 'all I can say, is, that I am bound to believe on your asseveration that it is very poor indeed. I cannot forbear adding, that if that unfortunate circumstance influences your conversation, it is much to be lamented, and it is eminently desirable that your blood were richer. Rosa, my dear, how are you getting on with your work?'

'Hem! Before retiring, Miss,' proclaimed the Billickin to Rosa, loftily cancelling Miss Twinkleton, 'I should wish it to be understood between yourself and me that my transactions in future is with you alone. I know no elderly lady here, Miss, none older than yourself.'

'A highly desirable arrangement, Rosa, my dear,' observed Miss Twinkleton.

'It is not, Miss,' said the Billickin, with a sarcastic smile, 'that I possess the Mill I have heard of, in which old single ladies could be ground up young (what a gift it would be to some of us!), but that I limit myself to you totally.'

'When I have any desire to communicate a request to the person of the house, Rosa, my dear,' observed Miss Twinkleton, with majestic cheerfulness, 'I will make it known to you, and you will kindly undertake, I am sure, that it is conveyed to the proper quarter.'

'Good-evening, Miss,' said the Billickin, at once affectionately and distantly. 'Being alone in my eyes, I wish you
good-evening with best wishes, and do not find myself
drove, I am truly 'appy to say, into expressing my contempt
for any indiwidual, unfortunately for yourself, belonging
to you.'

The Billickin gracefully withdrew with this parting
speech, and from that time Rosa occupied the restless position of shuttlecock between these two battledores. Nothing
could be done without a smart match being played out. Thus,
on the daily-arising question of dinner, Miss Twinkleton
would say, the three being present together:

'Perhaps, my love, you will consult with the person of the
house, whether she could procure us a lamb's fry; or, failing
that, a roast fowl.'

On which the Billickin would retort (Rosa not having
spoken a word), 'If you was better accustomed to butcher's
meat, Miss, you would not entertain the idea of a lamb's fry.
Firstly, because lambs has long been sheep, and secondly,
because there is such things as killing-days, and there is not.
As to roast fowls, Miss, why you must be quite surfeited with
roast fowls, letting alone your buying, when you market for
yourself, the agedest of poultry with the scaliest of legs, quite
as if you was accustomed to picking 'em out for cheapness.
Try a little inwention, Miss. Use yourself to 'ousekeeping a
bit. Come now, think of somethink else.'

To this encouragement, offered with the indulgent toler-
ation of a wise and liberal expert, Miss Twinkleton would
rejoin, reddening:

'Or, my dear, you might propose to the person of the
house a duck.'

'Well, Miss!' the Billickin would exclaim (still no word
being spoken by Rosa), 'you do surprise me when you speak
of ducks! Not to mention that they're getting out of season
and very dear, it really strikes to my heart to see you have a
duck; for the breast, which is the only delicate cuts in a duck,
always goes in a direction which I cannot imagine where, and
your own plate comes down so miserable skin-and-bony! Try
again, Miss. Think more of yourself and less of others. A dish

of sweetbreads now, or a bit of mutton. Somethink at which you can get your equal chance.'

Occasionally the game would wax very brisk indeed, and would be kept up with a smartness rendering such an encounter as this quite tame. But the Billickin almost invariably made by far the higher score; and would come in with side hits of the most unexpected and extraordinary description, when she seemed without a chance.

All this did not improve the gritty state of things in London, or the air that London had acquired in Rosa's eyes of waiting for something that never came. Tired of working and conversing with Miss Twinkleton, she suggested working and reading: to which Miss Twinkleton readily assented, as an admirable reader, of tried powers. But Rosa soon made the discovery that Miss Twinkleton didn't read fairly. She cut the love scenes, interpolated passages in praise of female celibacy, and was guilty of other glaring pious frauds. As an instance in point, take the glowing passage: ' "Ever dearest and best adored," said Edward, clasping the dear head to his breast, and drawing the silken hair through his caressing fingers, from which he suffered it to fall like golden rain; "ever dearest and best adored, let us fly from the unsympathetic world and the sterile coldness of the stony-hearted, to the rich warm Paradise of Trust and Love." ' Miss Twinkleton's fraudulent version tamely ran thus: ' "Ever engaged to me with the consent of our parents on both sides, and the approbation of the silver-haired rector of the district," said Edward, respectfully raising to his lips the taper fingers so skilful in embroidery, tambour, crochet, and other truly feminine arts; "let me call on thy papa ere to-morrow's dawn has sunk into the west, and propose a suburban establishment, lowly it may be, but within our means, where he will be always welcome as an evening guest, and where every arrangement shall invest economy, and the constant interchange of scholastic acquirements, with the attributes of the ministering angel to domestic bliss." '

As the days crept on and nothing happened, the neighbours began to say that the pretty girl at Billickin's, who looked so wistfully and so much out of the gritty windows of the drawing-room, seemed to be losing her spirits. The pretty girl might have lost them but for the accident of lighting on some books of voyages and sea-adventure. As a compensation against their romance, Miss Twinkleton, reading aloud, made the most of all the latitudes and longitudes, bearings, winds, currents, offsets, and other statistics (which she felt to be none the less improving because they expressed nothing whatever to her); while Rosa, listening intently, made the most of what was nearest to her heart. So they both did better than before.

CHAPTER XXIII

The Dawn again

ALTHOUGH Mr. Crisparkle and John Jasper met daily under the Cathedral roof, nothing at any time passed between them bearing reference to Edwin Drood after the time, more than half a year gone by, when Jasper mutely showed the Minor Canon the conclusion and the resolution entered in his Diary. It is not likely that they ever met, though so often, without the thoughts of each reverting to the subject. It is not likely that they ever met, though so often, without a sensation on the part of each that the other was a perplexing secret to him. Jasper as the denouncer and pursuer of Neville Landless, and Mr. Crisparkle as his consistent advocate and protector, must at least have stood sufficiently in opposition, to have speculated with keen interest each on the steadiness and next direction of the other's designs. But neither ever broached the theme.

False pretence not being in the Minor Canon's nature, he doubtless displayed openly that he would at any time have revived the subject, and even desired to discuss it. The determined reticence of Jasper, however, was not to be so approached. Impassive, moody, solitary, resolute, concentrated on one idea, and on its attendant fixed purpose that he would share it with no fellow-creature, he lived apart from human life. Constantly exercising an Art which brought him into mechanical harmony with others, and which could not have been pursued unless he and they had been in the nicest mechanical relations and unison, it is curious to consider that the spirit of the man was in moral accordance or interchange with nothing around him. This indeed he had confided to his lost nephew, before the occasion for his present inflexibility arose.

That he must know of Rosa's abrupt departure, and that he must divine its cause, was not to be doubted. Did he suppose that he had terrified her into silence, or did he suppose that she had imparted to any one – to Mr. Crisparkle himself for instance – the particulars of his last interview with her? Mr. Crisparkle could not determine this in his mind. He could not but admit, however, as a just man, that it was not, of itself, a crime to fall in love with Rosa, any more than it was a crime to offer to set love above revenge.

The dreadful suspicion of Jasper which Rosa was so shocked to have received into her imagination, appeared to have no harbour in Mr. Crisparkle's. If it ever haunted Helena's thoughts, or Neville's, neither gave it one spoken word of utterance. Mr. Grewgious took no pains to conceal his implacable dislike of Jasper, yet he never referred it, however distantly, to such a source. But he was a reticent as well as an eccentric man; and he made no mention of a certain evening when he warmed his hands at the Gate House fire, and looked steadily down upon a certain heap of torn and miry clothes upon the floor.

Drowsy Cloisterham, whenever it awoke to a passing re-consideration of a story above six months old and dismissed by the bench of magistrates, was pretty equally divided in opinion whether John Jasper's beloved nephew had been killed by his passionate rival, treacherously, or in an open struggle; or had, for his own purposes, spirited himself away. It then lifted up its head, to notice that the bereaved Jasper was still ever devoted to discovery and revenge; and then dozed off again. This was the condition of matters, all round, at the period to which the present history has now attained.

The Cathedral doors have closed for the night; and the Choir Master, on a short leave of absence for two or three services, sets his face towards London. He travels thither by the means by which Rosa travelled, and arrives, as Rosa arrived, on a hot, dusty evening.

His travelling baggage is easily carried in his hand, and he repairs with it, on foot, to a hybrid hotel in a little square behind Aldersgate Street, near the General Post Office. It is hotel, boarding-house, or lodging-house, at its visitor's option. It announces itself, in the new Railway Advertisers, as a novel enterprise, timidly beginning to spring up. It bashfully, almost apologetically, gives the traveller to under-

stand that it does not expect him, on the good old constitutional hotel plan, to order a pint of sweet blacking for his
drinking, and throw it away; but insinuates that he may have
his boots blacked instead of his stomach, and maybe also have
bed, breakfast, attendance, and a porter up all night, for a
certain fixed charge. From these and similar premises, many
true Britons in the lowest spirits deduce that the times are
levelling times, except in the article of high roads, of which
there will shortly be not one in England.

He eats without appetite, and soon goes forth again. Eastward and still eastward through the stale streets he takes his
way, until he reaches his destination: a miserable court, specially miserable among many such.

He ascends a broken staircase, opens a door, looks into a
dark stifling room, and says: 'Are you alone here?'

'Alone, deary; worse luck for me and better for you,'
replies a croaking voice. 'Come in, come in, whoever you
be: I can't see you till I light a match, yet I seem to know the
sound of your speaking. I am acquainted with you, ain't I?'

'Light your match, and try.'

'So I will, deary, so I will; but my hand that shakes, as
I can't lay it on a match all in a moment. And I cough so, that,
put my matches where I may, I never find 'em there. They
jump and start, as I cough and cough, like live things. Are
you off a voyage, deary?'

'No.'

'Not seafaring?'

'No.'

'Well, there's land customers, and there's water customers. I'm a mother to both. Different from Jack Chinaman
t'other side the court. He ain't a father to neither. It ain't in
him. And he ain't got the true secret of mixing, though he
charges as much as me that has, and more if he can get it.
Here's a match, and now where's the candle? If my cough
takes me, I shall cough out twenty matches afore I gets a
light.'

But she finds the candle, and lights it before the
cough comes on. It seizes her in the moment of success,
and she sits down rocking herself to and fro, and gasping at

intervals, 'Oh, my lungs is awful bad, my lungs is wore away to cabbage-nets!' until the fit is over. During its continuance she has had no power of sight, or any other power not absorbed in the struggle; but as it leaves her, she begins to strain her eyes, and as soon as she is able to articulate, she cries, staring:

'Why, it's you!'

'Are you so surprised to see me?'

'I thought I never should have seen you again, deary. I thought you was dead, and gone to Heaven.'

'Why?'

'I didn't suppose you could have kept away, alive, so long, from the poor old soul with the real receipt for mixing it. And you are in mourning too! Why didn't you come and have a pipe or two of comfort? Did they leave you money, perhaps, and so you didn't want comfort?'

'No!'

'Who was they as died, deary?'

'A relative.'

'Died of what, lovey?'

'Probably, Death.'

'We are short to-night!' cries the woman, with a propitiatory laugh. 'Short and snappish, we are! But we're out of sorts for want of a smoke. We've got the all-overs, haven't us, deary? But this is the place to cure 'em in; this is the place where the all-overs is smoked off!'

'You may make ready then,' replies the visitor, 'as soon as you like.'

He divests himself of his shoes, loosens his cravat, and lies across the foot of the squalid bed, with his head resting on his left hand.

'Now, you begin to look like yourself,' says the woman, approvingly. 'Now, I begin to know my old customer indeed! Been trying to mix for yourself this long time, poppet?'

'I have been taking it now and then in my own way.'

'Never take it your own way. It ain't good for trade, and it ain't good for you. Where's my ink-bottle, and where's my thimble, and where's my little spoon? He's going to take it in a artful form now, my deary dear!'

Entering on her process, and beginning to bubble and blow at the faint spark enclosed in the hollow of her hands, she speaks from time to time, in a tone of snuffling satisfaction, without breaking off. When he speaks, he does so without looking at her, and as if his thoughts were already roaming away by anticipation.

'I've got a pretty many smokes ready for you, first and last, haven't I, chuckey?'

'A good many.'

'When you first come, you was quite new to it; warn't ye?'

'Yes, I was easily disposed of, then.'

'But you got on in the world, and was able by-and-bye to take your pipe with the best of 'em, warn't ye?'

'Ay. And the worst.'

'It's just ready for you. What a sweet singer you was when you first come! Used to drop your head, and sing yourself off, like a bird! It's ready for you now, deary.'

He takes it from her with great care, and puts the mouth-piece to his lips. She seats herself beside him, ready to refill the pipe. After inhaling a few whiffs in silence, he doubtingly accosts her with:

'Is it as potent as it used to be?'

'What do you speak of, deary?'

'What should I speak of, but what I have in my mouth?'

'It's just the same. Always the identical same.'

'It doesn't taste so. And it's slower.'

'You've got more used to it, you see.'

'That may be the cause, certainly. Look here.' He stops, becomes dreamy, and seems to forget that he has invited her attention. She bends over him, and speaks in his ear.

'I'm attending to you. Says you just now, look here. Says I now, I am attending to ye. We was talking just before of your being used to it.'

'I know all that. I was only thinking. Look here. Suppose you had something in your mind; something you were going to do.'

'Yes, deary; something I was going to do?'

'But had not quite determined to do.'

'Yes, deary.'

'Might or might not do, you understand.'

'Yes.' With the point of a needle she stirs the contents of the bowl.

'Should you do it in your fancy, when you were lying here doing this?'

She nods her head. 'Over and over again.'

'Just like me! I did it over and over again. I have done it hundreds of thousands of times in this room.'

'It's to be hoped it was pleasant to do, deary.'

'It *was* pleasant to do!'

He says this with a savage air, and a spring or start at her. Quite unmoved, she retouches or replenishes the contents of the bowl with her little spatula. Seeing her intent upon the occupation, he sinks into his former attitude.

'It was a journey, a difficult and dangerous journey. That was the subject in my mind. A hazardous and perilous journey, over abysses where a slip would be destruction. Look down, look down! You see what lies at the bottom there?'

He has darted forward to say it, and to point at the ground, as though at some imaginary object far beneath. The woman looks at him, as his spasmodic face approaches close to hers, and not at his pointing. She seems to know what the influence of her perfect quietude will be; if so, she has not miscalculated it, for he subsides again.

'Well; I have told you, I did it, here, hundreds of thousands of times. What do I say? I did it millions and billions of times. I did it so often, and through such vast expanses of time, that when it was really done, it seemed not worth the doing, it was done so soon.'

'That's the journey you have been away upon?' she quietly remarks.

He glares at her as he smokes; and then, his eyes becoming filmy, answers: 'That's the journey.'

Silence ensues. His eyes are sometimes closed and sometimes open. The woman sits beside him, very attentive to the pipe, which is all the while at his lips.

'I'll warrant,' she observes, when he has been looking fixedly at her for some consecutive moments, with a singular appearance in his eyes of seeming to see her a long way off, instead of so near him: 'I'll warrant you made the journey in a many ways, when you made it so often?'

'No, always in one way.'

'Always in the same way?'

'Ay.'

'In the way in which it was really made at last?'

'Ay.'

'And always took the same pleasure in harping on it?'

'Ay.'

For the time he appears unequal to any other reply than this lazy monosyllabic assent. Probably to assure herself that it is not the assent of a mere automaton, she reverses the form of her next sentence.

'Did you never get tired of it, deary, and try to call up something else for a change?'

He struggles into a sitting posture, and retorts upon her: 'What do you mean? What did I want? What did I come for?'

She gently lays him back again, and, before returning him the instrument he has dropped, revives the fire in it with her own breath; then says to him, coaxingly:

'Sure, sure, sure! Yes, yes, yes! Now, I go along with you. You was too quick for me. I see now. You come o' purpose to take the journey. Why, I might have known it, through its standing by you so.'

He answers first with a laugh, and then with a passionate setting of his teeth: 'Yes, I came on purpose. When I could not bear my life, I came to get the relief, and I got it. It WAS one! It WAS one!' This repetition with extraordinary vehemence, and the snarl of a wolf.

She observes him very cautiously, as though mentally feeling her way to her next remark. It is: 'There was a fellow-traveller, deary.'

'Ha ha ha!' He breaks into a ringing laugh, or rather yell.

'To think,' he cries, 'how often fellow-traveller, and yet not know it! To think how many times he went the journey, and never saw the road!'

The woman kneels upon the floor, with her arms crossed on the coverlet of the bed, close by him, and her chin upon them. In this crouching attitude, she watches him. The pipe is falling from his mouth. She puts it back, and laying her hand upon his chest, moves him slightly from side to side. Upon that he speaks, as if she had spoken.

'Yes! I always made the journey first, before the changes of colours and the great landscapes and glittering processions began. They couldn't begin till it was off my mind. I had no room till then for anything else.'

Once more he lapses into silence. Once more she lays her hand upon his chest, and moves him slightly to and fro, as a cat might stimulate a half-slain mouse. Once more he speaks, as if she had spoken.

'What? I told you so. When it comes to be real at last, it is so short that it seems unreal for the first time. Hark!'

'Yes, deary. I'm listening.'

'Time and place are both at hand.'

He is on his feet, speaking in a whisper, and as if in the dark.

'Time, place, and fellow-traveller,' she suggests, adopting his tone, and holding him softly by the arm.

'How could the time be at hand unless the fellow-traveller was? Hush! The journey's made. It's over.'

'So soon?'

'That's what I said to you. So soon. Wait a little. This is a vision. I shall sleep it off. It has been too short and easy. I must have a better vision than this; this is the poorest of all. No struggle, no consciousness of peril, no entreaty – and yet I never saw *that* before.' With a start.

'Saw what, deary?'

'Look at it! Look what a poor, mean, miserable thing it is! *That* must be real. It's over!'

He has accompanied this incoherence with some wild unmeaning gestures; but they trail off into the progressive inaction of stupor, and he lies a log upon the bed.

The woman, however, is still inquisitive. With a repetition of her cat-like action she slightly stirs his body again, and listens; stirs it again, and listens; whispers to it, and listens. Finding it past all rousing for the time, she slowly gets upon her feet, with an air of disappointment, and flicks the face with the back of her hand in turning from it.

Sleeping it off

But she goes no further away from it than the chair upon the hearth. She sits in it, with an elbow on one of its arms, and her chin upon that hand, intent upon him. 'I heard ye say once,' she croaks under her breath, 'I heard ye say once, when I was lying where you're lying, and you were making your speculations upon me, "Unintelligible!" I heard you say so, of two more than me. But don't ye be too sure always; don't ye be too sure, beauty!'

Unwinking, cat-like, and intent, she presently adds: 'Not so potent as it once was? Ah! Perhaps not at first. You may be more right there. Practice makes perfect. I may have learned the secret how to make ye talk, deary.'

He talks no more, whether or no. Twitching in an ugly way from time to time, both as to his face and limbs, he lies heavy and silent. The wretched candle burns down; the woman takes its expiring end between her fingers, lights another at it, crams the guttering frying morsel deep into the candlestick, and rams it home with the new candle, as if she were loading some ill-savoured and un-seemly weapon of witchcraft; the new candle in its turn burns down; and still he lies insensible. At length what remains of the last candle is blown out, and daylight looks into the room.

It has not looked very long, when he sits up, chilled and shaking, slowly recovers consciousness of where he is, and makes himself ready to depart. The woman receives what he pays her with a grateful 'Bless ye, bless ye, deary!' and seems, tired out, to begin making herself ready for sleep as he leaves the room.

But seeming may be false or true. It is false in this case, for, the moment the stairs have ceased to creak under his tread, she glides after him, muttering emphatically: 'I'll not miss ye twice!'

There is no egress from the court but by its entrance. With a weird peep from the doorway, she watches for his looking back. He does not look back before disappearing, with a wavering step. She follows him, peeps from the court, sees him still faltering on without looking back, and holds him in view.

He repairs to the back of Aldersgate Street, where a door immediately opens to his knocking. She crouches in another doorway, watching that one, and easily comprehending that he puts up temporarily at that house. Her patience is unexhausted by hours. For sustenance she can, and does, buy bread within a hundred yards, and milk as it is carried past her.

He comes forth again at noon, having changed his dress, but carrying nothing in his hand, and having nothing carried for him. He is not going back into the country, therefore, just yet. She follows him a little way, hesitates instantaneously, turns confidently, and goes straight into the house he has quitted.

'Is the gentleman from Cloisterham indoors?'

'Just gone out.'

'Unlucky. When does the gentleman return to Cloisterham?'

'At six this evening.'

'Bless ye and thank ye. May the Lord prosper a business where a civil question, even from a poor soul, is so civilly answered!'

'I'll not miss ye twice!' repeats the poor soul in the street, and not so civilly. 'I lost ye last, where that omnibus you got into nigh your journey's end plied betwixt the station and the place. I wasn't so much as certain that you even went right on to the place. Now, I know ye did. My gentleman from Cloisterham, I'll be there before ye and bide your coming. I've swore my oath that I'll not miss ye twice!'

Accordingly, that same evening the poor soul stands in Cloisterham High Street, looking at the many quaint gables of the Nuns' House, and getting through the time as she best can until nine o'clock; at which hour she has reason to suppose that the arriving omnibus passengers may have some interest for her. The friendly darkness, at that hour, renders it easy for her to ascertain whether this be so or not; and it is so, for the passenger not to be missed twice arrives among the rest.

'Now, let me see what becomes of you. Go on!'

An observation addressed to the air. And yet it might be addressed to the passenger, so compliantly does he go on along the High Street until he comes to an arched gateway, at which he unexpectedly vanishes. The poor soul quickens her pace; is swift, and close upon him in turning under the gateway; but only sees a postern staircase on one side of it, and on the other side an ancient vaulted room, in which a large-headed, grey-haired gentleman is writing, under the odd circumstances of sitting open to the thoroughfare and eyeing all who pass, as if he were toll-taker at the gateway: though the way is free.

'Halloa!' he cries in a low voice, seeing her brought to a standstill: 'who are you looking for?'

'There was a gentleman passed in here this minute, sir. A gentleman in mourning.'

'Of course there was. What do you want with him?'

'Where do he live, deary?'

'Live? Up that staircase.'

'Bless ye! Whisper. What's his name, deary?'

'Surname Jasper, Christian name John. Mr. John Jasper.'

'Has he a calling, good gentleman?'

'Calling? Yes. Sings in the choir.'

'In the spire?'

'Choir.'

'What's that?'

Mr. Datchery rises from his papers, and comes to his doorstep. 'Do you know what a cathedral is?' he asks, jocosely.

The woman nods.

'What is it?'

She looks puzzled, casting about in her mind to find a definition, when it occurs to her that it is easier to point out the substantial object itself, massive against the dark-blue sky and the early stars.

'That's the answer. Go in there at seven to-morrow morning, and you may see Mr. John Jasper, and hear him too.'

'Thank ye! Thank ye!'

The burst of triumph in which she thanks him, does not escape the notice of the single buffer of an easy temper living idly on his means. He glances at her; clasps his hands behind him, as the wont of such buffers is; and lounges along the echoing Precincts at her side.

'Or,' he suggests, with a backward hitch of his head, 'you can go up at once to Mr. Jasper's rooms there.'

The woman eyes him with a cunning smile, and shakes her head.

'Oh! You don't want to speak to him?'

She repeats her dumb reply, and forms with her lips a soundless 'No.'

'You can admire him at a distance three times a day, whenever you like. It's a long way to come for that, though.'

The woman looks up quickly. If Mr. Datchery thinks she is to be so induced to declare where she comes from, he is of a much easier temper than she is. But she acquits him of such an artful thought, as he lounges along, like the chartered bore of the city, with his uncovered grey hair blowing about, and his purposeless hands rattling the loose money in the pockets of his trousers.

The chink of the money has an attraction for her greedy ears. 'Wouldn't you help me to pay for my travellers' lodging, dear gentleman, and to pay my way along? I am a poor soul, I am indeed, and troubled with a grievous cough.'

'You know the travellers' lodging, I perceive, and are making direct for it,' is Mr. Datchery's bland comment, still rattling his loose money. 'Been here often, my good woman?'

'Once in all my life.'

'Ay, ay?'

They have arrived at the entrance to the Monks' Vineyard. An appropriate remembrance, presenting an exemplary model for imitation, is revived in the woman's mind by the sight of the place. She stops at the gate, and says energetically:

'By this token, though you mayn't believe it, That a young gentleman gave me three and sixpence as I was coughing my breath away on this very grass. I asked him for three and sixpence, and he gave it me.'

'Wasn't it a little cool to name your sum?' hints Mr. Datchery, still rattling. 'Isn't it customary to leave the amount open? Mightn't it have had the appearance, to the young gentleman – only the appearance – that he was rather dictated to?'

'Look'ee here, deary,' she replies, in a confidential and persuasive tone, 'I wanted the money to lay it out on a medicine as does me good, and as I deal in. I told the young gentleman so, and he gave it me, and I laid it out honest to the last brass farden. I want to lay out the same sum in the same way now; and if you'll give it me, I'll lay it out honest to the last brass farden again, upon my soul!'

'What's the medicine?'

'I'll be honest with you beforehand, as well as after. It's opium.'

Mr. Datchery, with a sudden change of countenance, gives her a sudden look.

'It's opium, deary. Neither more nor less. And it's like a human creetur so far, that you always hear what can be said against it, but seldom what can be said in its praise.'

Mr. Datchery begins very slowly to count out the sum demanded of him. Greedily watching his hands, she continues to hold forth on the great example set him.

'It was last Christmas Eve, just arter dark, the once that I was here afore, when the young gentleman gave me the three and six.'

Mr. Datchery stops in his counting, finds he has counted wrong, shakes his money together, and begins again.

'And the young gentleman's name,' she adds, 'was Edwin.'

Mr. Datchery drops some money, stoops to pick it up, and reddens with the exertion as he asks:

'How do you know the young gentleman's name?'

'I asked him for it, and he told it me. I only asked him the two questions, what was his Chris'en name, and whether he'd a sweetheart? And he answered, Edwin, and he hadn't.'

Mr. Datchery pauses with the selected coins in his hand, rather as if he were falling into a brown study of their value, and couldn't bear to part with them. The woman looks at him distrustfully, and with her anger brewing for the event of his thinking better of the gift; but he bestows it on her as if he were abstracting his mind from the sacrifice, and with many servile thanks she goes her way.

John Jasper's lamp is kindled, and his Lighthouse is shining when Mr. Datchery returns alone towards it. As mariners on a dangerous voyage, approaching an iron-bound coast, may look along the beams of the warning light to the haven lying beyond it that may never be reached, so Mr. Datchery's wistful gaze is directed to this beacon, and beyond.

His object in now revisiting his lodging is merely to put on the hat which seems so superfluous an article in his wardrobe. It is half-past ten by the Cathedral clock, when he walks out into the Precincts again; he lingers and looks about him, as though, the enchanted hour when Mr. Durdles may be stoned home having struck, he had some expectation of seeing the Imp who is appointed to the mission of stoning him.

In effect, that Power of Evil is abroad. Having nothing living to stone at the moment, he is discovered by Mr. Datchery in the unholy office of stoning the dead, through the railings of the churchyard. The Imp finds this a relishing and piquing pursuit; firstly, because their resting-place is announced to be sacred; and secondly, because the tall head-stones are sufficiently like themselves, on their beat in the dark, to justify the delicious fancy that they are hurt when hit.

Mr. Datchery hails him with: 'Halloa, Winks!'

He acknowledges the hail with: 'Halloa, Dick!' Their acquaintance seemingly having been established on a familiar footing.

'But I say,' he remonstrates, 'don't yer go a making my name public. I never means to plead to no name, mind yer. When they says to me in the Lock-up, a going to put me down in the book, "What's your name?" I says to them, "Find out." Likeways when they says, "What's your religion?" I says, "Find out."'

Which, it may be observed in passing, it would be immensely difficult for the State, however statistical, to do.

'Asides which,' adds the boy, 'there ain't no family of Winkses.'

'I think there must be.'

'Yer lie, there ain't. The travellers give me the name on account of my getting no settled sleep and being knocked up all night; whereby I gets one eye roused open afore I've shut the other. That's what Winks means. Deputy's the nighest name to indict me by: but yer wouldn't catch me pleading to that, neither.'

'Deputy be it always, then. We two are good friends; eh, Deputy?'

'Jolly good.'

'I forgave you the debt you owed me when we first became acquainted, and many of my sixpences have come your way since; eh, Deputy?'

'Ah! And what's more, yer ain't no friend o' Jarsper's. What did he go a histing me off my legs for?'

'What indeed! But never mind him now. A shilling of mine is coming your way to-night, Deputy. You have just taken in a lodger I have been speaking to; an infirm woman with a cough.'

'Puffer,' assents Deputy, with a shrewd leer of recognition, and smoking an imaginary pipe, with his head very much on one side and his eyes rolling very much out of their places: 'Hopeum Puffer.'

'What is her name?'

''Er Royal Highness the Princess Puffer.'

'She has some other name than that; where does she live?'

'Up in London. Among the Jacks.'

'The sailors?'

'I said so; Jacks. And Chaynermen. And hother Knifers.'

'I should like to know, through you, exactly where she lives.'

'All right. Give us 'old.'

A shilling passes; and, in that spirit of confidence which should pervade all business transactions between principals of honor, this piece of business is considered done.

'But here's a lark!' cries Deputy. 'Where do yer think 'Er Royal Highness is a goin' to, to-morrow morning? Blest if she ain't a goin' to the KIN-FREE-DER-EL!' He greatly prolongs the word in his ecstasy, and smites his leg, and doubles himself up in a fit of shrill laughter.

'How do you know that, Deputy?'

"Cos she told me so just now. She said she must be hup and hout o' purpose. She ses, "Deputy, I must 'ave a early wash, and make myself as swell as I can, for I'm a goin' to take a turn at the KIN-FREE-DER-EL!"' He separates the syllables with his former zest, and, not finding his sense of the ludicrous sufficiently relieved by stamping about on the pavement, breaks into a slow and stately dance, perhaps supposed to be performed by the Dean.

Mr. Datchery receives the communication with a well-satisfied though a pondering face, and breaks up the conference. Returning to his quaint lodging, and sitting long over the supper of bread and cheese and salad and ale which Mrs. Tope has left prepared for him, he still sits when his supper is finished. At length he rises, throws open the door of a corner cupboard, and refers to a few uncouth chalked strokes on its inner side.

'I like,' says Mr. Datchery, 'the old tavern way of keeping scores. Illegible, except to the scorer. The scorer not committed, the scored debited with what is against him. Humph! A very small score this; a very poor score!'

He sighs over the contemplation of its poverty, takes a bit of chalk from one of the cupboard shelves, and pauses with it in his hand, uncertain what addition to make to the account.

'I think a moderate stroke,' he concludes, 'is all I am justified in scoring up;' so, suits the action to the word, closes the cupboard, and goes to bed.

A brilliant morning shines on the old city. Its antiquities and ruins are surpassingly beautiful, with the lusty ivy gleaming in the sun, and the rich trees waving in the balmy air. Changes of glorious light from moving boughs, songs of birds, scents from gardens, woods, and fields – or, rather, from the one great garden of the whole cultivated island in its yielding time – penetrate into the Cathedral, subdue its earthy odour, and preach the Resurrection and the Life. The cold stone tombs of centuries ago grow warm; and flecks of brightness dart into the sternest marble corners of the building, fluttering there like wings.

Comes Mr. Tope with his large keys, and yawningly unlocks and sets open. Come Mrs. Tope, and attendant sweeping sprites. Come, in due time, organist and bellows-boy, peeping down from the red curtains in the loft, fearlessly flapping dust from books up at that remote elevation, and whisking it from stops and pedals. Come sundry rooks, from various quarters of the sky, back to the great tower; who may be presumed to enjoy vibration, and to know that bell and organ are going to give it them. Come a very small and straggling congregation indeed: chiefly from Minor Canon Corner and the Precincts. Come Mr. Crisparkle, fresh and bright; and his ministering brethren, not quite so fresh and bright. Come the choir in a hurry (always in a hurry, and struggling into their nightgowns at the last moment, like children shirking bed), and comes John Jasper leading their line. Last of all comes Mr. Datchery into a stall, one of a choice empty collection very much at his service, and glancing about him for Her Royal Highness the Princess Puffer.

The service is pretty well advanced before Mr. Datchery can discern Her Royal Highness. But by that time he has made her out, in the shade. She is behind a pillar, carefully withdrawn from the Choir Master's view, but regards him with the closest attention. All unconscious of her presence, he chants and sings. She grins when he is most musically fervid, and – yes, Mr. Datchery sees her do it! – shakes her fist at him behind the pillar's friendly shelter.

Mr. Datchery looks again to convince himself. Yes, again! As ugly and withered as one of the fantastic carvings on the under brackets of the stall seats, as malignant as the Evil One, as hard as the big brass eagle holding the sacred books upon his wings (and, according to the sculptor's presentation of his ferocious attributes, not at all converted by them), she hugs herself in her lean arms, and then shakes both fists at the leader of the choir.

And at that moment, outside the grated door of the choir, having eluded the vigilance of Mr. Tope by shifty resources in which he is an adept, Deputy peeps, sharp-eyed, through the bars, and stares astounded from the threatener to the threatened.

The service comes to an end, and the servitors disperse to breakfast. Mr. Datchery accosts his last new acquaintance outside, when the choir (as much in a hurry to get their bedgowns off, as they were but now to get them on) have scuffled away.

'Well, mistress. Good-morning. You have seen him?'

'*I*'ve seen him, deary; *I*'ve seen him!'

'And you know him?'

'Know him! Better far, than all the Reverend Parsons put together know him.'

Mrs. Tope's care has spread a very neat, clean breakfast ready for her lodger. Before sitting down to it, he opens his corner cupboard door; takes his bit of chalk from its shelf; adds one thick line to the score, extending from the top of the cupboard door to the bottom; and then falls to with an appetite.

TRIAL OF JOHN JASPER

TRIAL
OF JOHN JASPER

Lay Precentor of Cloisterham Cathedral in the County
of Kent, for the

MURDER
OF EDWIN DROOD

Engineer.

Heard by

MR. JUSTICE GILBERT KEITH CHESTERTON
sitting with a Special Jury, in the King's Hall, Covent Garden,
W.C., on Wednesday, the 7th January, 1914.

Verbatim Report of the proceedings from the Shorthand Notes of
J. W. T. LEY.

LONDON
CHAPMAN & HALL, LTD.
1914

KING'S HALL, COVENT GARDEN
JANUARY 7th, 1914.

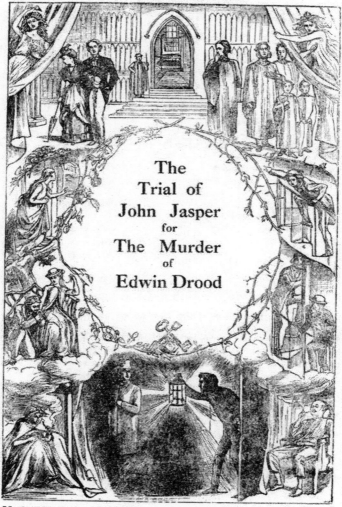

The
Trial of
John Jasper
for
The Murder
of
Edwin Drood

Under the Auspices of The Dickens Fellowship (London Branch)
Frank S. Johnson, *Hon. Sec.*

JUDGE, WITNESSES, COUNSEL AND JURY

JUDGE	Mr. G. K. CHESTERTON
COUNSEL FOR THE PROSECUTION	Mr. J. CUMING WALTERS
	and
	Mr. B. W. MATZ
COUNSEL FOR THE DEFENCE	Mr. CECIL CHESTERTON
	and
	Mr. W. WALTER CROTCH
JOHN JASPER	Mr. FREDERICK T. HARRY
(Lay Precentor at Cloisterham Cathedral)	
ANTHONY DURDLES	Mr. BRANSBY WILLIAMS
(The Cloisterham Stonemason)	
THE REVD. SEPTIMUS CRISPARKLE	Mr. ARTHUR WAUGH
(Minor Canon at Cloisterham Cathedral)	
MISS HELENA LANDLESS	Mrs. LAURENCE CLAY
(Ward of Mr. Honeythunder)	
" 'ER ROYAL HIGNESS PRINCESS PUFFER "	Miss J. K. PROTHERO
(The Opium Woman)	
[THOMAS] BAZZARD	Mr. C. SHERIDAN JONES
(Clerk to Mr. Grewgious)	
THE CLERK OF ARRAIGNS	Mr. WALTER DEXTER
THE USHER	Mr. A. E. BROOKES CROSS
POLICE OFFICERS	Mr. H. H. PEARCE
	and
	Mr. C. H. GREEN

The JURY will be chosen from among the following :

Mr. GEORGE BERNARD SHAW (foreman)	Mr. COULSON KERNAHAN
Sir FRANCIS C. BURNAND	Mr. EDWIN PUGH
Sir EDWARD RUSSELL	Mr. WILLIAM de MORGAN
Dr. W. L. COURTNEY	Mr. ARTHUR MORRISON
Mr. W. W. JACOBS	Mr. RAYMOND PATON
Mr. PETT RIDGE	Mr. FRANCESCO BERGER
Mr. HILAIRE BELLOC	Mr. RIDGWELL CULLUM
Mr. TOM GALLON	Mr. JUSTIN HUNTLY McCARTHY
Mr. MAX PEMBERTON	Mr. OSCAR BROWNING
Mr. G. S. STREET	Mr. WM. ARCHER

Barristers, Reporters and Spectators.

INDICTMENT

of

JOHN JASPER

Lay Precentor of Cloisterham Cathedral, in the County of Kent,

for the

MURDER

of

EDWIN DROOD, *Engineer.*

TRIAL

Holden at the ASSIZES at WESTMINSTER,
on the 7th January, 1914.

ASSIZE COURT
    KING'S HALL, COVENT GARDEN ⎱ To wit :
    County of LONDON ⎰

The Jurors for this trial upon their oath * present, that JOHN JASPER on the 24th day of December in the year of our Lord One thousand eight hundred and sixty in the Parish of Cloisterham and within the jurisdiction of the said Court, feloniously, wilfully, and of his malice aforethought did kill and murder one EDWIN DROOD against the peace of every true Dickensian.

* Or, if one of the Grand Jurors be a Quaker or other person entitled to affirm instead of taking an oath, say instead: " The jurors of Our Lord the King upon their oath *and affirmation* present, &c."

INDICTMENT

WHEREAS, in support of the above Indictment, divers allegations are set forth, as follows, that is to say :—

The accused, JOHN JASPER, aged 26, is Choirmaster at Cloisterham Cathedral, otherwise known as " lay precentor." He lodges over the Gateway of the Cathedral. For some years he admits he has been in the habit of taking opium, and has resorted to an Opium Den in the East End of London kept by an elderly woman known as " Princess Puffer."

The man of whose murder he stands accused was his nephew, EDWIN DROOD, in his 21st year, and by profession an Engineer. The Prisoner, who was likewise Trustee and Guardian of the said Edwin Drood, professed the greatest affection for him, and on the occasion of his visits to Cloisterham manifested every appearance of joy and satisfaction.

The said Edwin Drood was betrothed to one Rosa Bud, this being in fulfilment of a contract made by their respective parents (now deceased). Certain formalities in connection with the confirmation of this engagement, notably the handing of a ring by Mr. Grewgious, solicitor, Staple Inn, legal adviser to Edwin Drood, were witnessed by Mr. Grewgious's clerk, Bazzard. There is evidence to show that they had grown weary of each other, and wished the Contract to be annulled. On the other hand, Jasper, the Accused, was admittedly in love with Rosa Bud, and it is alleged was secretly jealous of his nephew. Miss Bud, on her part, deposes that she not only disliked but " feared " Jasper and avoided his attentions as much as possible. Eventually the engagement between Edwin Drood and Rosa Bud was rescinded by mutual consent ; but the said John Jasper, for sufficient reasons, was not at the time warned of this fact. The circumstance, however, was revealed to Mr. Grewgious.

WITNESSES will be called to prove that in the early part of the year, the Accused, Jasper, accompanied a stonemason named Durdles to the Cathedral and made particular enquiry into the destructive qualities of quicklime. It is also alleged that Jasper applied a drug to this same Durdles, causing sleep, and that he then appropriated his keys, and therefrom made a close investigation of the vaults, especially of the Sapsea vault, which was partly hollow.

There were also residing in Cloisterham an orphan brother and sister, twins, by name Neville and Helena Landless. They came from Ceylon, where they had been subjected to personal ill-treatment, and after staying with Mr. Honeythunder, their guardian, Neville was lodged with Canon Crisparkle, and Helena was sent to Miss

Indictment

Twinkleton's school. Neville Landless is described as "fierce" and hot-blooded, Helena Landless is "almost of the gipsy type." Between her and her brother is a strong bond of affection. In her girlhood she had escaped at times from her cruel step-father by disguising herself as a boy. She is a woman of much daring.

Soon after their arrival in Cloisterham, they met Drood, Jasper and Miss Bud at a party. It will be given in evidence that there was a contention between Drood and Neville, and that Jasper afterwards fomented the ill-feeling and charged Neville Landless with being "murderous." At the same time, Miss Landless was seized with an instinctive hostility towards Jasper, who, she thought, was unduly menacing Rosa Bud. Matters between the two young men were smoothed over to some extent, and on the following Christmas Eve, John Jasper decided to bring them together at a convivial gathering in his own house.

On December 23rd Jasper visited the Opium Den in London. Next day he returned to Cloisterham, and was followed thither by the Opium Woman, who had heard him use threatening language in his sleep towards someone called "Ned" (Jasper's nickname for Edwin Drood).

At night (Christmas Eve) the three men met and dined. It was a night of wild storm. The next morning Jasper hastened to Canon Crisparkle's house shouting excitedly that his dear nephew had disappeared, and that he was convinced he had been murdered.

He plainly indicated that he believed the murderer was Neville Landless, in whose company Drood had left Jasper's house at midnight; and Neville Landless was apprehended, but subsequently released for want of evidence.

On December 26th Mr. Grewgious visited Jasper and informed him that the engagement between Drood and Miss Bud had been broken off. It is in evidence that on hearing this news for the first time, Jasper "gasped, tore his hair, shrieked" and finally swooned away.

Shortly afterwards Canon Crisparkle visiting the Weir on the river, discovered Edwin Drood's watch and chain, which had been placed in the timbers; and in a pool below he found Drood's scarf-pin.

It is in evidence that the accused, Jasper, after a short interval, renewed his attentions to Miss Rosa Bud, and exercised so great a terror upon her that she deemed it advisable to take refuge in London under the supervision of Mr. Grewgious and her friend Miss Twinkleton. Neville Landless also removed to London, where he was visited by his sister Helena.

Meanwhile, a careful watch was kept upon John Jasper by a "stranger," known as Dick Datchery. This person took lodgings opposite Jasper's house and had him under close observation. "Datchery" (which is admittedly an assumed name) interviewed

Indictment

several persons, including Durdles and " Princess Puffer," and kept a private record in chalk marks of all facts thus ascertained. In consequence of the suspicions excited by these circumstances, a warrant was applied for and John Jasper was arrested on a charge of Wilful Murder.

To this he pleads " NOT GUILTY," and this is the issue to be tried.

The following WITNESSES will be called :

ANTHONY DURDLES
CANON CRISPARKLE   By Counsel for the Prosecution.
HELENA LANDLESS

"PRINCESS PUFFER"
[THOMAS] BAZZARD   By Counsel for the Defence.

NOTE

The design on the front page of this Indictment is a reproduction of that on the wrapper of the monthly parts of " The Mystery of Edwin Drood " as originally issued in 1870. It was drawn by Charles Allston Collins, and has been the cause of much controversy and speculation.

CONDITIONS AGREED UPON BETWEEN THE PROSECUTION AND DEFENCE

The three formal witnesses (that is to say, Crisparkle and Durdles for the Prosecution and the Opium Woman for the Defence) shall not in their evidence-in-chief go beyond the book or make any statements not expressly made therein, but in cross-examination they may, in response to specific questions, give explanations not expressly contained in the book.

The two chief witnesses (that is to say, Helena Landless for the Prosecution and Bazzard for the Defence) shall be free both in examination-in-chief and in cross-examination to make statements not made in the book, provided that they are not contradicted therein.

All statements made in the book shall be taken to be true and admitted by both sides, and any statement by a witness contradicting such statements shall be considered thereby proved to be false.

The said two chief witnesses (and no others) shall be allowed to give hear-say evidence.

The Defence having agreed not to call Edwin Drood, the Prosecution agree not to comment upon his absence from the witness-box either in speech or cross-examination, but the Prosecution reserve the right to comment upon the silence of Edwin Drood subsequent to the murder.

Both sides having agreed not to call Grewgious, it is agreed that neither side shall comment upon the fact that the other has not called him.

The Defence agree that the legal point that no conviction can take place since no body has been found, shall be raised only after the retirement of the jury, but the Defence reserves the right to comment upon the absence of a body as part of the general absence of direct evidence of the commission of a murder.

REPORT OF THE PROCEEDINGS

His Lordship having taken his seat, the Prisoner was immediately put into the dock, and addressed by the Clerk of Arraigns in the following terms :

John Jasper, the charge against you is that you did feloniously, wilfully, and with malice aforethought, kill your nephew, Edwin Drood, in the City of Cloisterham, on the night of the 24th of December, 1860. Are you guilty, or not guilty ?

THE PRISONER : Not guilty.

THE CLERK OF ARRAIGNS : Will the gentlemen of the Jury please rise, and sit down as I call their names ? Mr. George Bernard Shaw, Sir Edward Russell, Dr. W. L. Courtney, Mr. W. W. Jacobs, Mr. Pett Ridge, Mr. Tom Gallon, Mr. Max Pemberton, Mr. Coulson Kernahan, Mr. Edwin Pugh, Mr. William de Morgan, Mr. Arthur Morrison, Mr. Francesco Berger, Mr. Ridgwell Cullum, Mr. Justin Huntly McCarthy, Mr. William Archer, Mr. Thomas Seccombe—you shall well and truly try the Prisoner at the Bar, John Jasper, for the murder of Edwin Drood, and a true verdict give according to the evidence.

Mr. George Bernard Shaw was elected Foreman.

MR. WALTERS : I appear for the prosecution, my Lord.

JUDGE : Mr. Cuming Walters, I think, for the prosecution. Is there anyone with you ?

MR. MATZ : I am with him, my Lord.

MR. CECIL CHESTERTON : I appear for the defence, my Lord.

JUDGE : Mr. Chesterton, I think, for the defence. One s, I think. Is anyone with you ?

MR. CROTCH : I am, my Lord.

[THE CASE FOR THE PROSECUTION.]

Mr. Matz then proceeded to open the case for the prosecution in the following speech :

MY LORD AND GENTLEMEN OF THE JURY—

The case to be tried is one of murder—murder which we shall contend was pre-meditated, pre-arranged and carried out in a methodical and determined manner.

The Prisoner is John Jasper, Lay Precentor at Cloisterham Cathedral. The Prosecution will set itself to prove that on the night of the 24th December he murdered in that city his nephew Edwin Drood, an Engineer.

The said Edwin Drood was 21 years of age, and for some years was betrothed to Miss Rosa Bud in fulfilment of a dying wish of their respective parents (now deceased).

To this young lady the Prisoner acted as music master, and admittedly was enamoured of her, although he kept this fact secret from Edwin Drood.

On the evening in question—the 24th December—Edwin Drood and Neville Landless —a pupil of the Revd. Septimus Crisparkle—dined together with the Prisoner in his rooms in the Gate House adjoining the Cathedral.

The night was a terribly stormy one. After leaving the Prisoner, some time about midnight, the two young men took a walk to the river to see the effect of the storm on the water, and returned to the house of the Revd. Septimus Crisparkle in Minor Canon Corner. Here Edwin Drood left his companion, intending to return to his Uncle's lodgings.

Nothing has been heard or seen of him since.

Gentlemen, it is our painful duty to produce evidence to prove that Edwin Drood was murdered by his Uncle, the Prisoner. We contend that Jasper divested him of his watch and chain and his scarf pin, articles the Prisoner had, on another occasion, explained to the local jeweller he knew Drood to possess. The words he used were that he had " an inventory of them in his mind."

We contend that Jasper then cast the body of his victim into a vault in the Cathedral precincts, the key of which, or a duplicate, he had previously become possessed of. There had also been placed in the vicinity a quantity of quicklime, and we submit that Jasper, having made some inquiries into its properties, used this for the purpose of removing all traces of the body in the shortest period of time. We submit that he got rid of the watch and chain and scarf pin in the river, either in the hope of disposing of material which the quicklime would not destroy, or to give the impression, should they be found, that the young man was drowned.

We shall in evidence show that the Prisoner had *motive* for his crime, that he made elaborate preparations for its enactment, and that he succeeded in his terrible deed.

The evidence may be circumstantial only. But circumstantial evidence, I submit, may be extremely strong—as strong indeed as any direct evidence.

We shall show you that all the acts of John Jasper for some time previous to the committal of his atrocious crime were self-incriminatory. Not merely that, but they exhibit his mind working out the very means by which that crime was to be committed. *After* his terrible deed was accomplished, his actions, to those who observed him closely, also indicated clearly his guilt.

The Prisoner, having made up his mind that, for his own selfish ends Edwin Drood must be killed, first chose the spot best suited to his purpose, and laid methodical plans to secure access to that spot. He paid visits to it in the company of one, Durdles, the Cloisterham stonemason, whom he drugged with doctored wine whilst there, in order that he might acquire secretly the key to a certain vault. He knew where quicklime could be procured without loss of time. He interviewed other persons, and timed the hour and everything else so thoroughly that nothing essential for his purpose was overlooked.

Now, gentlemen, it is necessary to refer briefly to some further facts bearing upon the history of this crime.

Neville Landless, upon whom Jasper cast suspicion of being the murderer, and his sister Helena, were both students in Cloisterham : the brother, a pupil of the Revd. Septimus Crisparkle, and the sister a pupil at Miss Twinkleton's Academy in the city. They came from Ceylon, where they had been severely ill-treated, and had made several attempts to escape. On each occasion of the flight Helena " dressed as a boy and showed the daring of a man." Neville, a highly strung and emotional youth, took immediate objection to Drood because of his " air of proprietorship " over Rosa ; whilst Helena instinctively disliked Jasper because she saw that he loved Rosa and that Rosa feared him. It is worth noting as a significant fact that at the earliest stage Rosa appealed to Helena for aid and every assistance was promised to her.

A slight quarrel between Edwin Drood and Neville Landless took place in Jasper's rooms, and undoubtedly Jasper goaded them on by his taunts. On this occasion Jasper gave them some mulled wine which had taken him a long time to mix and compound.

Mr. Matz, Counsel for Prosecution

They drank to the toast proposed by Jasper and their speech quickly became thick and indistinct, indicating that there was a sinister design in the mixing and compounding. Drood became boastful, and Neville Landless resented his tone, and at the height of the dispute, flung the dregs of his wine at Edwin Drood. Although posing as a Peacemaker Jasper actually fomented the hostility of these two young men. He seemed to delight in it and it enabled him subsequently to report to Crisparkle that Neville was "*murderous*." Indeed he went so far as to assert that he "might have laid his dear boy at his feet, and that it was no fault of his that he did not."

The Revd. Mr. Crisparkle talked with Helena and Neville on the latter's rash conduct, and he expressed extreme regret and promised to exercise more caution in future. On another occasion Crisparkle visited Jasper, who read to him passages from his diary expressing fears for Drood's safety. A few days later Drood, at the suggestion of Jasper, wrote and agreed to dine with him and Neville on Christmas Eve at the Gate house, Cloisterham—in order that the two young men should become friends. Their walk after dinner is evidence that this object was fully achieved.

We submit that, the whole plans having thus been prepared, the murder of Edwin Drood took place after the parting of the young men, and that John Jasper and no other was the murderer. In support of this we shall produce evidence to prove that Jasper acted in a highly incriminatory manner.

The next morning whilst great commotion was raging in the vicinity of the cathedral over the damage done by the storm, John Jasper broke into the crowd crying : "Where is my nephew ? " as if everybody knew he was missing, whereas no one but the prisoner had any reason to think he was not in the Prisoner's rooms. He even volunteered the statement that Drood had gone "down to the river last night, with *Mr. Neville*, to look at the storm, and had not been back ? " and demanded that Mr. Neville should be called.

These utterances were made to the Revd. Canon, and showed clearly that the murderer felt so confident that he had executed his deed with perfect thoroughness that no fear of discovery need enter his mind. But knowing his nephew was murdered he tried immediately to fix the deed upon another.

I must direct your attention to one other matter. John Jasper, whether guilty or not of murder, is indisputably a hypocrite, leading a double life. Like most criminals he was also capable of foolish mistakes. Had he not killed his "dear boy," as he called him, he would have made investigations of his whereabouts, he would have refrained from courting inquiries, and would not have excited the hostility of Rosa Bud.

But, gentlemen, most criminals of the John Jasper type, make at least one error in the execution of their crime, which ultimately finds them out. Jasper made his. Having as I have said, divested Edwin Drood of his watch and chain and scarf pin, all the jewellery he was aware Drood had upon his person, he felt safe. But he left, unknown to him, on the person of the young man a valuable gold ring set with rubies and diamonds, and this ring quicklime could not consume. The ring was once the property of Rosa Bud's mother and had been handed to Edwin Drood by Mr. Grewgious, Rosa Bud's guardian, with strict instructions that he should give it to Rosa if he intended to marry her, or return it to Mr. Grewgious should Edwin and Rosa decide, as seemed likely, to break their betrothal.

This was a faithful promise and was witnessed by one, Bazzard, the clerk to the said Mr. Grewgious.

It so happened that on December 24th the young couple did break off their engagement. Therefore if Drood, by any chance, were now alive, that ring would have been

The Trial of John Jasper

returned to Mr. Grewgious, in accordance with his promise. But, gentlemen, it never has been returned, and why ? We say because Drood is no longer alive, but dead, and that where the body was hidden after the murder, there that ring was hidden also.

Jasper knew of all the articles that were on the person of Edwin Drood, except that ring. He did not know of that because it had only been handed to Drood on the previous day.

Nor did Jasper know of the breaking off of the betrothal, else would there have been no object in his committing the murder. Evidence will be given that Drood promised Rosa he would not spoil his Uncle's Christmas festivities by telling him of their decision to part as lovers.

The first time Jasper learnt the fact was on the day following the murder, when he heard it from Mr. Grewgious. He then instantly " gasped, tore his hair, shrieked," swooned and " fell a heap of torn and miry clothes upon the floor." From this we infer that the information was unexpected and a shock to him.

Sometime afterwards the Revd. Canon Crisparkle found the watch and chain and scarf pin, when walking near the weir, and he will be called to give evidence on this and other facts.

Now, gentlemen, let me read to you an extract from the diary of Jasper entered after this discovery. It reads thus—

" My dear boy is murdered. The discovery of the watch and shirt pin convinces me that he was murdered on that night, and that his jewellery was taken from him to prevent identification by its means."

The word " murdered " was frequently in the mind of Jasper at this time, and he made use of it in several phrases in his diary, which clearly demonstrates that he was attempting to create the impression that his nephew was murdered, and, by using the words, hoped to divert attention from himself.

But he became so nervous of what he had written, that he declared to the Revd. Canon that he meant to " burn this year's diary at the year's end " and by so doing, as he evidently thought, destroy all evidence of his guilty conscience.

There is one more phase to touch upon.

It is admitted that John Jasper was secretly addicted to opium smoking and frequented a certain opium den in London kept by a person known as the " Princess Puffer." Whilst under the influence of opium he babbled strangely, moaned, and uttered significant words in the hearing of the opium woman. This woman followed him more than once to Cloisterham and on one of these occasions, the fateful 24th December, she accosted Edwin Drood, and for the price of three and sixpence offered to tell him something. He paid her the money and she asked him first his name, and when he told her Edwin, she wanted to know, "Is the short of that name Eddy ? . . ." Drood answered " It is sometimes called so." " You be thankful your name is not *Ned*," she next replied, " because it is a threatened name : a dangerous name." " Threatened men live long," he assured her. Her reply was—

" Then Ned—so threatened is he, wherever he may be while I am a-talking to you, deary—should live to all eternity ! "

Now, gentlemen, it is a striking and amazing fact that Jasper, and he only, called Edwin Drood " Ned "—the threatened name.

That very night Edwin Drood disappeared, and he has " never revisited the light of the sun."

A few months passed and no trace of the body of the ill-fated young man having been found, Jasper, feeling he had cleared his way effectively, called at the Nun's House

Evidence of Anthony Durdles

(Miss Twinkleton's Academy) one afternoon in the vacation, and taking Rosa unawares made passionate love to her. On being repulsed he vowed vengeance on Neville Landless —the man against whom he had already directed suspicion. So horrified was Rosa, she flew for safety to her guardian Mr. Grewgious at Staple Inn. A strict watch was kept upon Jasper by a person calling himself Mr. Datchery, with the result that he was eventually arrested.

Gentlemen, that is the case put to you as briefly as possible—it is the case you have to try.

We feel confident that the evidence we shall place before you will convince you that the prisoner has committed a foul crime, and that we can safely leave the issue to you. Painful as your duty may be, we look to you to give your verdict faithfully and fearlessly in the interests of justice and your fellow-men.

THE FOREMAN : My Lord, one word. Did I understand the learned gentleman to say that he was going to call evidence ?

MR. MATZ : Certainly.

THE FOREMAN : Well, then, all I can say is, that if the learned gentleman thinks the convictions of a British jury are going to be influenced by evidence, he little knows his fellow countrymen !

JUDGE : At the same time, in spite of this somewhat intemperate observation—— [The remainder of his Lordship's words were inaudible.]

[EVIDENCE OF ANTHONY DURDLES.]

MR. MATZ : Call Anthony Durdles.

USHER : Anthony Durdles ! [That gentleman immediately entered the witness-box.]

CLERK OF ARRAIGNS : The evidence that you shall give before the Court and Jury, shall be the truth, the whole truth, and nothing but the truth.

MR. WALTERS : Your name is Durdles ?

WITNESS : Durdles is my name.

MR. WALTERS : Do you always call yourself Durdles ?

WITNESS : I do ; 'cause my name *is* Durdles.

MR. WALTERS : You are a stone-mason, I believe ?

WITNESS : Ay ; Durdles is a stone-mason.

MR. WALTERS : Would you mind telling us where you work ?

WITNESS : Durdles works anywhere he can, up and down, round about the Cathedral.

MR. WALTERS : Round about the Cathedral. Thank you. Very good. Do you happen to know the prisoner, John Jasper ?

WITNESS : Ay ; I knows John Jarsper.

MR. WALTERS : And did you ever happen to meet him anywhere near the Cathedral ?

WITNESS : Yes ; Durdles met Mister Jarsper near the Cathedral.

MR. WALTERS : Perhaps you met him more than once ?

WITNESS : Twice.

MR. WALTERS : You met him twice. What did you go with him to the Cathedral for ?

The Trial of John Jasper

WITNESS : Well, sir ; he——

MR. WALTERS : Yes : speak up, please.

JUDGE : I must interpose. The witness cannot possibly know what Mr. Jasper went to the Cathedral for.

MR. WALTERS : My Lord, with respectful submission to you, the prisoner might have told him.

JUDGE : But for that purpose you must examine the prisoner in chief.

MR. WALTERS : I think, my Lord, that you will find a conversation took place between Durdles and the prisoner, and that I am perfectly justified in asking what the conversation was.

JUDGE : Yes ; I think so.

MR. WALTERS (to witness) : Let us know what the conversation was between you and Mr. Jasper.

WITNESS : He says to me, " Is there anything new in the crypt ? " and I says, " Anything new ! Anything old, you mean."

MR. WALTERS : Yes ?

WITNESS : Yes.

MR. WALTERS : What happened then ?

WITNESS : We went down in the crypt, and he give me a drink out of his bottle. Fine stuff it was, too.

MR. WALTERS : And what about that bundle which I believe you carried ?

WITNESS : He asked me if he could carry my bundle.

MR. WALTERS : Yes ?

WITNESS : Ay.

MR. WALTERS : What was in your bundle ?

WITNESS : Durdles knows what was in his bundle. Keys, among other things.

MR. WALTERS : Oh, keys. And I suppose you let him carry your bundle ?

WITNESS : I did. Well, I had another drink out of his bottle.

MR. WALTERS : Did you happen on that occasion to see any quicklime lying about ?

WITNESS : Well, there's always quicklime lying about the crypt. Always.

MR. WALTERS : You noticed it. Did Jasper happen to notice it ?

WITNESS : He did. He asked me what it was for.

MR. WALTERS : Oh, he asked you what it was for. And did you tell him ?

WITNESS : Yes ; I told him it 'ud burn anything ; burn your boots, and with a little handy stirring, it 'ud burn your bones.

MR. WALTERS : It would burn your bones with handy stirring. And when he put that curious question to you, did it occur to you there was a reason for it ?

WITNESS : Durdles thinks everybody 'as a reason for everything they says and does.

MR. WALTERS : When he asked you would that quicklime burn, you thought he must have a reason for it ?

18

Evidence of Anthony Durdles

WITNESS : Yes ; so I did.

MR. WALTERS: People use quicklime for quite innocent purposes, I believe, don't they?

WITNESS : Yes.

MR. WALTERS : They use it for cement ?

WITNESS : Yes.

MR. WALTERS : What else do they use it for ?

WITNESS : Bodies.

MR. WALTERS : Did you think, by the way he was making his inquiries, that he wanted to know if it would burn something else besides ordinary stuff ?

WITNESS : I didn't think as 'ow he wanted a heap of quicklime to burn his waste paper with.

MR. WALTERS : What happened next ? You had a drink out of the bottle, and you had a little talk : what happened then ? Did you go home ?

WITNESS : No ; I fell asleep.

MR. WALTERS : Oh, you fell asleep ?

WITNESS : Yes.

MR. WALTERS : Anything else ?

WITNESS : I had a dream.

MR. WALTERS : You had a dream before you woke up ?

WITNESS : Yes.

MR. WALTERS : What was the nature of that dream ?

WITNESS : I dreamt that Mister Jarsper was a-moving around me, handling my keys, and I thought I was left alone in the dark. Then I see a light coming back, and then I found Mr. Jarsper waking me up, saying " Hi ! wake up ! "

MR. WALTERS : Did you wake up ?

WITNESS : Yes.

MR. WALTERS : Did you remember how long you had been asleep ?

WITNESS : A long time. I remember the clock struck two.

MR. WALTERS : And you went in about midnight ?

WITNESS : Yes.

MR. WALTERS : You had two hours' sleep ?

WITNESS : Yes, I suppose so.

MR. WALTERS : Anything else ? Did you notice anything ?

WITNESS : When I woke up, I sees my key on the ground, and I says, " I dropped you, did I ? " So I picks it up, and asks Mister Jarsper for my bundle.

MR. WALTERS : Did he give it to you ?

WITNESS : Yes.

MR. WALTERS : I think you had on that occasion a little conversation about a curious art of yours—tapping the tombs ?

The Trial of John Jasper

WITNESS: Yes; oh, yes—yes.

MR. WALTERS: Would you mind telling the court?

WITNESS: I told him, with my little hammer I could tap and go on tapping, and I could tell whether anything was solid or whether it was hollow. For instance, I says, " Tap, tap, old 'un crumbled up in stone coffin in the vault! "

MR. WALTERS: That's what you said, is it?

WITNESS: Yes.

MR. WALTERS: And what did Mr. Jasper say to that?

WITNESS: He said it was wonderful, and I says, " No; I ain't going to take it as a gift, 'cause it's all out o' my own head."

MR. WALTERS: I understand you told him what you could do by tapping the walls —tell whether it was hollow or solid?

WITNESS: Yes, Durdles can tell whether it's hollow or solid by its tap.

MR. WALTERS: Was he interested in your conversation?

WITNESS: Very much, sir.

MR. WALTERS: Did you happen to notice the Sapsea tomb?

WITNESS: Durdles knows the Sapsea tomb.

MR. WALTERS: There is only one body in that tomb at present?

WITNESS: Yes.

MR. WALTERS: Did you tap the Sapsea tomb with your hammer, and did it sound surprising there?

WITNESS: It sounded more solid than usual.

MR. WALTERS: Since then, you have tapped it lately, and it sounds a little more solid?

WITNESS: Yes.

MR. CHESTERTON: This is contrary to an understanding. This is a formal witness, not to be cross-examined.

MR. WALTERS: Very well, I will go on. (*To witness.*) Did you meet him at another time?

MR. CHESTERTON: This is only formal evidence.

JUDGE: What is the point?

MR. CHESTERTON: You will find before you, my Lord, a document, and you will find there that certain witnesses who are to be cross-examined at length will be free to go beyond certain admitted evidence. The formal witnesses are not to do so.

JUDGE (*after perusing the " Conditions "*): Yes, I think I take your point, Mr. Chesterman—or Chesterton—whatever it is. The point, I understand, is that you are cross-examining this witness as if he were a principal witness of the trial.

MR. CHESTERTON: In the second paragraph I think you will notice——

MR. WALTERS: It is not of great importance to me.

JUDGE: One moment: I will see. (*After reading the paragraph referred to.*) I think you are justified up to the point to which you have gone, but I should recommend you to terminate it with some rapidity.

Evidence of Anthony Durdles

MR. WALTERS : I only want to ask one question. (*To witness.*) You did have a conversation with Mr. Datchery ?

WITNESS : Yes.

MR. CHESTERTON : I ask you to say, my Lord, that the Jury must entirely disregard the statement about the tapping.

THE FOREMAN : How are we to dismiss it from our minds, my Lord ? It is a very difficult point.

MR. WALTERS : I think I shall leave the Jury to draw their own conclusions. All I want to know from Durdles is, did he have a conversation with Datchery ?

WITNESS : Yes.

MR. WALTERS : Thank you. That is all.

WITNESS : Thank you, sir. I'll drink your health on the way home, p'raps twice, and I won't go home till morning.

[DURDLES CROSS-EXAMINED.]

MR. CROTCH : One moment, please.

WITNESS : Oh, beg pardon, sir, beg pardon.

MR. CROTCH : Now, Durdles, you know all about the destructive qualities of quicklime ?

WITNESS : Yes.

MR. CROTCH : Do you say that quicklime will not destroy metals ?

WITNESS : No ; I don't think quicklime will destroy metals.

MR. CROTCH : You don't think it will ?

WITNESS : No, I knows it won't.

MR. CROTCH : Now, Durdles——

JUDGE : I must ask you to address the witness in more respectful terms, such as " Mr." Durdles.

MR. CROTCH : Very well, my Lord.

WITNESS : *Mister* Durdles, sir.

MR. CROTCH (*to witness*) : I understand you were employed round about the Cathedral, and that you know all about the crypt ?

WITNESS : Yes, sir.

MR. CROTCH : Now, tell me what was the state of the windows in 1860.

WITNESS : Ay ?

MR. CROTCH : I put it to you again. In what state were the windows of the crypt in 1860 ?

WITNESS : Do you mean clean or dirty ?

MR. CROTCH : I put it to you they were in a very broken condition ?

WITNESS : Yes, sir ; always broken.

MR. CROTCH : As a matter of fact, they were not only broken, weren't they, but partially boarded up ?

WITNESS : Well, I can't remember, sir.

The Trial of John Jasper

MR. CROTCH : Can't remember! You were constantly in the crypt!

WITNESS : Some of 'em.

MR. CROTCH : How many windows are there ?

WITNESS : I don't know.

MR. WALTERS : I don't suppose the witness is expected to count windows !

WITNESS : Thank you, sir.

MR. CROTCH : Well, now, Mr. Durdles, I will ask you another question. As a matter of fact, have you not on many occasions chased little boys and others out of the crypt ?

WITNESS : Yes, and they've chased me.

MR. CROTCH : Where did these boys find their way into the crypt ?

WITNESS : Ay ?

MR. CROTCH : You don't know ?

WITNESS : No, I don't.

MR. CROTCH : You swear you don't know ?

WITNESS : Ay, I swear I don't know.

MR. CROTCH : You have never seen them creeping through the windows of the crypt ?

WITNESS : Might be : when I've been sober.

MR. CROTCH : That'll do. Now, you tell us that you met Mr. Datchery. Is that so ?

WITNESS : Yes.

MR. CROTCH : Have you ever admitted Mr. Datchery to the Sapsea vault ?

MR. WALTERS : This is going far beyond—

MR. CHESTERTON : If my learned friend will look at the first paragraph he will see that in cross-examination the formal witnesses may, in response to specific questions, give explanations not expressly contained in the book.

MR. WALTERS : Then I must re-examine the witness.

MR. CHESTERTON : Certainly.

MR. CROTCH : Now, Mr. Durdles, have you ever admitted Mr. Datchery to the Sapsea vault ?

WITNESS : Not that I can remember.

MR. CROTCH : If you cannot remember admitting Datchery, do you at any time remember admitting anybody else ?

WITNESS : No ; I can't say as I do.

MR. CROTCH : Thank you, Mr. Durdles.

MR. WALTERS : I won't trouble you to re-examine you, Mr. Durdles.

WITNESS : Well, good day. I'll drink your health on the way home, and I won't go home till morning—I beg your pardon, my Lord.

[EVIDENCE OF REVEREND CANON CRISPARKLE.]

MR. WALTERS : The Reverend Canon Crisparkle.

Evidence of Reverend Canon Crisparkle

USHER : Reverend Canon Crisparkle.

[That gentleman responded to the call, and entering the witness box, was duly sworn.]

THE FOREMAN : May I interpose for a moment ? This gentleman has been called as the Reverend Septimus Crisparkle. I submit to your Lordship that his real name is Christopher Nubbles, a man who was tried before you on the information of a certain Mr. Chuckster, on the charge of being a snob, and you, in one of those summings-up which have made your name famous wherever the English language is spoken, found that the charge brought by Mr. Chuckster was well and truly proved. Now, I contend that Mr. Christopher Nubbles has gone to Cloisterham, become a Minor Canon, taken the name of Crisparkle, and is here obviously a more intolerable snob than ever.

MR. WALTERS : Mr. Crisparkle ; I believe you are a Minor Canon of Cloisterham Cathedral ?

WITNESS : I am, sir.

MR. WALTERS : I believe your identity has never been disputed until this moment ?

WITNESS : Never. I am glad to be able to answer that impertinent reflection.

MR. WALTERS : Do you happen to know John Jasper ?

WITNESS : Very well. He was associated with me daily in the duties of the Cathedral.

MR. WALTERS : Did he ever tell you about his affection for his nephew, Edwin Drood ?

WITNESS : Constantly.

MR. WALTERS : And did he, while in this confidential mood, also tell you of his great affection for Miss Rosa Bud ?

WITNESS : No, I cannot charge my memory that he ever mentioned affection for her.

MR. WALTERS : Well, then, in that matter John Jasper deceived you ?

WITNESS : Well, shall we say deceived ? Guilty of a lapse of confidence to a priest. Theologically speaking it would be deceit, perhaps.

MR. WALTERS : I believe, Mr. Crisparkle, that you have been acting as tutor to Neville Landless ?

WITNESS : Yes.

MR. WALTERS : Do you mind telling the court the opinion you formed of that man's character ?

WITNESS : I should say a very impulsive man, but responsive to influence of any kind.

MR. WALTERS : I think he has a sister ?

WITNESS : Oh, yes : Miss Helena Landless.

MR. WALTERS : Is he under her influence at all ?

WITNESS : Yes, I should say she exercises a good and strong influence upon him.

JUDGE : I should suggest that question is very improper. We are all under the influence of each other to a great extent. I am as much under the influence of the foreman of the Jury that I almost entirely agree with the view that he takes of the situation when he mentions it. But I think it is not quite proper to say " Is he under the influence of his sister ? " Surely ?

MR. WALTERS : But, my Lord, this gentleman knows both parties, and is perfectly acquainted with their relationships.

The Trial of John Jasper

WITNESS : Yes, well.

JUDGE : I——

MR. WALTERS : I will not press the point. I will ask you, Mr. Crisparkle, have you any influence ?

WITNESS : Is that proper, my Lord ?

JUDGE : Quite proper.

WITNESS : I should say I have done my best. I have talked to him from time to time and found him very anxious to profit by any words I was able to say.

MR. WALTERS : You said he was impetuous. Perhaps he has one or two little faults of that sort. Would you regard them as dangerous ?

WITNESS : No, no ; oh no. The faults of an undisciplined boy.

MR. WALTERS : Has he any good qualities ?

WITNESS : Many, which appear to me to far outweigh the others.

MR. WALTERS : Suppose Neville Landless had a little quarrel with another young man. Would you attach much importance to it ?

WITNESS : No, I think not : very little, I think. Hot-tempered youth—soon over. He would be the first to regret it.

MR. WALTERS : Did you know Edwin Drood ?

WITNESS : Yes.

MR. WALTERS : And you heard of a quarrel between him and Neville Landless ?

WITNESS : Yes.

MR. WALTERS : Who told you about that quarrel ?

WITNESS : Well, in the first instance, Neville Landless mentioned it to me when he came back to my house. He said he had made a bad beginning and was sorry. But immediately afterwards John Jasper came to the house, and gave me what I am bound to say was a very different account indeed.

MR. WALTERS : This is the John Jasper who had already deceived you ?

WITNESS : Who had perhaps misled me by suppression.

MR. WALTERS : He was the John Jasper who was Edwin Drood's rival for Rosa Bud ?

WITNESS : It would appear so.

MR. WALTERS : You say he gave a strong account of the quarrel—Is that correct ?

WITNESS : It is more than correct. He said, when he came into the room, that he had had an awful time with him. I said, " Surely not as bad as that ! " and he said " Murderous —murderous ! "

MR. WALTERS : Are you sure he used the word " Murderous " ?

WITNESS : I am absolutely certain.

MR. WALTERS : What did you say to that ?

WITNESS : I said, " I must beg you not to use quite such strong language." He continued to use even stronger terms. He said there was something tigerish in Neville's blood. He was afraid he would have struck his dear boy, as he called him, down at his feet.

24

Evidence of Reverend Canon Crisparkle

MR. WALTERS : You are quite sure those were his words ?

WITNESS : Absolutely.

MR. WALTERS : And I suppose, following on that, you asked for an explanation from Neville ? Did you have any conversation with him ?

WITNESS : Yes, a long conversation with him in company with his sister.

MR. WALTERS : Was Jasper satisfied with the explanation given to him ?

WITNESS : No, I'm afraid not. A few days afterwards, when I was endeavouring to make peace between the two combatants, and arranged a meeting, Jasper took the opportunity to show me his diary, in which he had written his fears and suspicions in regard to his dear boy's safety.

MR. WALTERS : Fears and suspicions ?

WITNESS : That was the phrase.

MR. WALTERS : May we take it then, that this man was always harping on danger and using the word " Murder," and influencing your mind against Neville Landless ?

WITNESS : I am afraid that was the impression which I derived.

MR. WALTERS : Was that the impression left in your mind after the conversation with John Jasper ?

WITNESS : Yes.

MR. WALTERS : I think you know that on the Christmas Eve following, there was a friendly little party ?

WITNESS : Yes ; I was instrumental in arranging it.

MR. WALTERS : Following on that, Neville Landless was, on the following day, to start on a walking expedition ?

WITNESS : Yes.

MR. WALTERS : Did he tell you all about it ?

WITNESS : Oh, yes.

MR. WALTERS : He was quite frank ?

WITNESS : Quite frank.

MR. WALTERS : Did he start to carry out his plans ?

WITNESS : He started.

MR. WALTERS : On the Christmas morning, early ?

WITNESS : Yes.

MR. WALTERS : Do you remember that Christmas Eve ?

WITNESS : Perfectly.

MR. WALTERS : Why ?

WITNESS : Especially because of the beauty of Evensong that day. John Jasper was in splendid voice that day, and I congratulated him when he came out of the Cathedral. I said he must be in very good health.

MR. WALTERS : Very good health : did he say anything ?

WITNESS : He said he *was* in very good health, and that the black humours were

The Trial of John Jasper

passing from him, and that he would have to burn his diary—consign it to the flames—that was the phrase.

MR. WALTERS : He also laughed ?

WITNESS : He went laughing up the postern gate.

MR. WALTERS : Do you mind telling us whether laughing was common with John Jasper.

WITNESS : No.

MR. WALTERS : In short, you thought it an exceptional piece of good humour ?

WITNESS : Yes ; he made that impression on me.

MR. WALTERS : Do you remember what sort of night it was ?

WITNESS : A terrible night of storm.

MR. WALTERS : Let us get on to the next morning. The next morning what happened ?

WITNESS : Before I was about, while I was still in my dressing room, I was aware of a great noise at my gate, and there I saw John Jasper, insufficiently attired, crying very loudly to me in the house. I looked out, and asked what was the matter, and he said, " Where is my nephew ? " Naturally, I said to him, " Why should you ask me ? " and he said, " Last evening, very late, he went down to the river to see the storm, in company with Mr. Neville Landless," since when nothing had been heard of him. And then he said, " Call Mr. Neville." I told him Neville had already started.

MR. WALTERS : When this conversation took place between you and John Jasper, did it occur to you that he was dazed, as if suffering from the effect of drugs ?

WITNESS : No.

MR. WALTERS : Did it strike you that he was particularly clear-headed ?

WITNESS : I think so. Yes : he was very clear-headed.

MR. WALTERS : Was he concise and clear in his remarks ?

WITNESS : Yes, perfectly clear.

MR. WALTERS : If anybody told you he was suffering from the effect of drugs, or was dazed or bewildered, would your observation bear that out ?

WITNESS : No, indeed.

MR. WALTERS : What did you do in respect of Mr. Neville ?

WITNESS : We sent some men after him, and Mr. Jasper and I followed. Directly we came up with him, Jasper said, " Where is my nephew ? " and Neville said, " Why do you ask me ? "

MR. WALTERS : What did Jasper say ?

WITNESS : He said, " He was last seen in your company "—or words to that effect.

MR. WALTERS : When he said that, what sort of impression did it cause on you ? What did you think it meant ?

WITNESS : I am sorry to say I had the unpleasant impression that he meant to suggest that Neville Landless was in some way responsible for Drood's disappearance.

MR. WALTERS : Once more he was suggesting murder ?

Evidence of Reverend Canon Crisparkle

WITNESS : Yes, that was the impression.

MR. WALTERS : And once more suggesting that Neville Landless was the murderer ?

WITNESS : That was so, undoubtedly.

MR. WALTERS : This man, Neville Landless, with this terrible charge hanging over him ; did he come back readily ?

WITNESS : Yes.

MR. WALTERS : Did he answer any questions put to him ?

WITNESS : Quite frankly.

MR. WALTERS : Some time afterwards, you made a discovery, I think. Would you mind telling the Court what it was ?

WITNESS : I was walking along by the river, some two miles above where these young men had gone for their walk—by the weir, in fact,—when I saw something shining brightly. Looking more closely, I thought it was a jewel. I immediately dived in, being fortunately a good swimmer, and found that it was a gold watch and chain. The chain was hanging on the timbers. Later I found in the mud a gold scarf-pin. The watch had the initials E. D. engraved on it.

MR. WALTERS : Did you tell Jasper you had discovered these things ?

WITNESS : At once.

MR. WALTERS : Did he say anything about it ?

WITNESS : Nothing at the time, but a few days later, when we were disrobing in the vestry, he showed me the diary to which I have alluded.

MR. WALTERS : Did it contain any reference to it ?

WITNESS : I cannot charge my memory with the exact words, but something to this effect—" My poor boy is certainly murdered. The discovery of the watch and scarf-pin leaves that beyond doubt. They were no doubt thrown away to prevent identification of the body "—or words to that effect.

MR. WALTERS : One moment, Mr. Crisparkle. Am I right in saying that once more Murder was suggested to you ?

WITNESS : Yes.

MR. WALTERS : And that Neville Landless was pointed to as the murderer ?

WITNESS : Yes.

MR. WALTERS : And so that would be the impression left on your mind by your conversation with Jasper ?

WITNESS : Yes.

MR. WALTERS : Whether it was right or wrong, that would be the impression left ?

WITNESS : Whether right or wrong, that would undoubtedly be the impression.

MR. WALTERS : Thank you, Mr. Crisparkle.

THE FOREMAN : May I ask one question, my Lord ?

JUDGE : Certainly.

THE FOREMAN : Do I understand the witness to say that the prisoner was a musician ?

WITNESS : He was, my Lord.

The Trial of John Jasper

FOREMAN : His case looks black indeed.

MR. CROTCH : Canon Crisparkle, you referred to the night of the preliminary quarrel and the return of Neville Landless. Do you remember accusing Neville of intoxication ?

WITNESS : Quite well.

MR. CROTCH : You said, " You are not sober " ?

WITNESS : I did so.

MR. CROTCH : Do you remember his reply ?

WITNESS : He said, " Yes ; I am afraid that is true, although I took very little to drink."

MR. CROTCH : " Although I can satisfy you at another time that I had very little to drink." I put it, those were the words he used ?

WITNESS : Doubtless.

MR. CROTCH : You said you went down to the weir, which is two miles from the river ?

WITNESS : No ; two miles from the point at which Edwin Drood and Neville Landless went down to watch the storm. It is two miles higher up.

MR. CROTCH : And it was there you found the articles you have described ?

WITNESS : That is so.

MR. CROTCH : What was the position of the watch and chain ?

WITNESS : It was adhering to the timbers. Where two timbers crossed, it had become fixed.

MR. CROTCH : As though somebody had gone down with a hammer and nail and hung it up deliberately ?

WITNESS : No, that I would not say.

MR. CROTCH : Was the pin in the mud ?

WITNESS : In the mud.

MR. CROTCH : This was ordinary loose mud ?

WITNESS : Yes, a kind of sludge.

MR. CROTCH : Did you find anything else ?

WITNESS : No.

MR. CROTCH : Nothing else at all ?

WITNESS : No.

MR. CROTCH : Now, Canon Crisparkle, I have just one question of some delicacy to ask. I hope you won't be offended. Is it not a fact that you are in love with Helena Landless ?

MR. WALTERS : My lord, my lord, I must object. I think this is a secret to a man's breast, and my friend has no right to try to get it out.

WITNESS : My Lord, I have no objection to answer the question. The lady will appear before you shortly, and when you see her you will not be surprised that my heart is a little affected.

28

Evidence of Helena Landless

MR. CROTCH : Thank you, Canon Crisparkle.

MR. WALTERS : Canon Crisparkle, one word please, as to the exact position of the weir. I think you have not been carefully examining the exact position lately ? You could not testify whether it was two miles, one mile, or one and a half miles, and would not commit yourself to an actual distance ?

WITNESS : No ; we are not in mathematics.

MR. WALTERS : If I told you it was a little nearer the Cathedral, you would not dispute it ?

WITNESS : Not for a moment.

MR. WALTERS : Thank you, Canon Crisparkle. That will do.

[EVIDENCE OF HELENA LANDLESS.]

MR. WALTERS : Call Helena Landless.

USHER : Helena Landless !

[That lady was conducted to the witness-box, and duly sworn.]

MR. WALTERS : What is your name, please ?

WITNESS : Helena Landless.

MR. WALTERS : And you have a brother named Neville ?

WITNESS : Yes ; a twin brother.

MR. WALTERS : Is there a great bond of sympathy between you and your brother ?

WITNESS : A very great bond.

MR. WALTERS : Is it so strong that you have an intimate understanding of each other ?

WITNESS : We almost know each other's thoughts.

MR. WALTERS : And I think you are accustomed to exercise influence on him— perhaps to lead him ?

WITNESS : It always has been so.

MR. WALTERS : Where did you live when young ?

WITNESS : In Ceylon.

MR. WALTERS : With your parents ?

WITNESS : No. My parents died when we were young, and a step-father brought us up.

MR. WALTERS : How did he treat you ?

WITNESS : Very badly indeed. He was always cruel and harsh to us.

MR. WALTERS : Ever beat you ?

WITNESS : We were whipped like dogs, and we ran away.

MR. WALTERS : How old were you when you first ran away ?

WITNESS : Seven.

MR. WALTERS : Who suggested running away ?

WITNESS : I did.

MR. WALTERS : And did your brother follow you ?

WITNESS : He always followed me.

MR. WALTERS : You planned everything ?

WITNESS : I always planned.

MR. WALTERS : Weren't you afraid to run away ?

WITNESS : I was afraid of nothing to be free.

MR. WALTERS : What did you do in order to make a flight successful ?

WITNESS : I cut off my hair, and dressed myself as a boy.

MR. WALTERS : That needed a great amount of daring ?

WITNESS : Well, the occasion needed all the daring I could command.

MR. WALTERS : And when it needs all the daring you can command, you don't mind daring ?

WITNESS : No.

MR. WALTERS : As a matter of fact, you did it, I think, not only for yourself, but for your brother ?

WITNESS : I think more for him than for myself.

MR. WALTERS : And you love your brother very much ?

WITNESS : Dearly.

MR. WALTERS : Still ?

WITNESS : Yes.

MR. WALTERS : Would you do as much again, Miss Landless ?

WITNESS : I would ; and more.

MR. WALTERS : As much for anybody else you love ?

WITNESS : If I loved them dearly enough.

MR. WALTERS : You have lately come to England. When you came, tell us where you resided.

WITNESS : I went to Miss Twinkleton's at the Nun's House, and my brother went to Mr. Crisparkle's.

MR. WALTERS : I believe the Nun's House is an Academy ?

WITNESS : Yes.

MR. WALTERS : Other girls there ?

WITNESS : Yes, several.

MR. WALTERS : Miss Rosa Bud there ?

WITNESS : Yes.

MR. WALTERS : Ever meet her ?

WITNESS : Yes.

MR. WALTERS : Ever become friends with her ?

WITNESS : Yes ; very great friends.

MR. WALTERS : Did you form an estimate of her character ?

WITNESS : I thought she was a sweet, lovable girl, but shy and timid.

Evidence of Helena Landless

MR. WALTERS : Not got your daring ?

WITNESS : No.

MR. WALTERS : She was learning music, I think ? Who was her tutor ?

WITNESS : John Jasper.

MR. WALTERS : Do you remember a party at Canon Crisparkle's shortly after your arrival ?

WITNESS : On the night of our arrival.

MR. WALTERS : Who was there ?

WITNESS : Myself, Miss Twinkleton, and Rosa Bud, and Edwin Drood, and John Jasper.

MR. WALTERS : You are sure John Jasper was there ?

WITNESS : Yes ; I noticed him particularly.

MR. WALTERS : Why ?

WITNESS : Because of his strange manner towards Rosa Bud.

MR. WALTERS : How ?

WITNESS : He watched her closely. During the evening she sang to his accompaniment, and his eyes were fixed on her the whole time with a most peculiar expression, and this seemed to trouble Rosa, although she was not looking at him. Suddenly she covered her face with her hands, burst into tears, and said she was frightened and wanted to be taken away.

MR. WALTERS : You don't think it was pure imagination on her part? She was frightened ?

WITNESS : Yes.

MR. WALTERS : When people are frightened there is danger about generally. Did you think there was any danger in his looking at her ?

WITNESS : I thought there was danger in his looks.

MR. WALTERS : Did you ever speak to her about it ?

WITNESS : Yes. She said she was terrified at him ; that he haunted her like a ghost, and that he made secret love to her.

MR. WALTERS : And she didn't like it ?

WITNESS : She begged me to take care of her, and stay with her.

MR. WALTERS : Did you promise to do so ?

WITNESS : I said I would protect her.

MR. WALTERS : Be very careful. If this man frightened her, would he not equally frighten you ?

WITNESS : In no circumstances.

MR. WALTERS : That is because you are a woman of daring ?

WITNESS : I suppose so.

MR. WALTERS : If you promised to shield and protect her, you did not content yourself with words. Did you take any action ?

The Trial of John Jasper

WITNESS : I kept a sort of watch on John Jasper.

MR. WALTERS : Why on Jasper ?

WITNESS : Because I felt that he menaced Rosa's peace and happiness.

MR. WALTERS : You thought he was the source of the danger ?

WITNESS : No one but Jasper.

MR. WALTERS : Had she any enemies ?

WITNESS : No ; she was too sweet and lovable.

MR. WALTERS : And you thought it was John Jasper, and John Jasper alone ?

WITNESS : Yes.

MR. WALTERS : We will leave that for a moment, and come to your brother. You are very intimate with your brother, and he confides in you. Were he and Drood friendly ?

WITNESS : Yes, but they had a little misunderstanding.

MR. WALTERS : Misunderstanding ?

WITNESS : Only a difference of opinion.

MR. WALTERS : Did you think it would lead your brother to make an attack on him ?

WITNESS : The idea is preposterous.

MR. WALTERS : They had a quarrel at the outset ?

WITNESS : My brother did not like the way in which Edwin Drood spoke of Rosa Bud. He thought he was too patronising. John Jasper came up, made a great deal more of it than it warranted, and then insisted on the young men going back with him to have a glass of wine—stirrup-cup, he called it.

MR. WALTERS : What was the effect on your brother ?

WITNESS : Both became flushed and excited.

MR. WALTERS : Was it very usual with your brother ?

WITNESS : No.

MR. WALTERS : Yet a small quantity had this effect on him. Did you suspect anything of the wine ?

WITNESS : I am morally certain the wine was drugged.

MR. WALTERS : I believe after that there was to be a little patching up ?

WITNESS : That was owing to Canon Crisparkle. They were all to meet and shake hands.

MR. WALTERS : Was it to be a large party, or confined to themselves ?

WITNESS : Only my brother and Edwin Drood and John Jasper, who had invited them to his house.

MR. WALTERS : That was on the Christmas Eve ?

WITNESS : Yes.

MR. WALTERS : Did you know anything about your brother's plans for the next day ?

WITNESS : He had planned to go on a walking tour.

MR. WALTERS : You knew all about it ?

WITNESS : Yes.

32

Evidence of Helena Landless

MR. WALTERS : All arranged ?

WITNESS : Yes.

MR. WALTERS : No secret ?

WITNESS : No.

MR. WALTERS : And to the best of your knowledge, he started on that tour next morning ?

WITNESS : Yes.

MR. WALTERS : Now, to get back to the party : you saw your brother just before he went ?

WITNESS : Yes.

MR. WALTERS : Was he happy and jolly going to the party ?

WITNESS : No. He was ready to shake hands with Edwin Drood, but he had a strange dread of the gatehouse.

MR. WALTERS : He did not object to going ?

WITNESS : No ; because he wanted to shake hands with Edwin Drood.

MR. WALTERS : Then the main object of his going was, not to enjoy himself, but to shake hands with Edwin Drood ?

WITNESS : Yes.

MR. WALTERS : And you think that was practically the only motive ?

WITNESS : Yes.

MR. WALTERS : We are told that Neville was fetched back after starting on his journey.

WITNESS : Yes.

MR. WALTERS : Was it a surprise he was fetched back after Drood's extraordinary disappearance was mentioned ?

WITNESS : It was.

MR. WALTERS : But when you heard who had fetched him back, was that a surprise ?

WITNESS : No ; because Jasper had always been his enemy from the first.

MR. WALTERS : You thought he had cast suspicion on him ?

WITNESS : Jasper had hinted in Cloisterham to many people that if anything ever happened to his nephew my brother would be responsible for it.

MR. WALTERS : And so you knew that your brother was under deep suspicion when brought back to Cloisterham ?

WITNESS : Yes.

MR. WALTERS : Did you take that very much to heart ?

WITNESS : I did, indeed, seeing it concerned the one I loved best in the world.

MR. WALTERS : There were two persons you wanted to protect ?

WITNESS : Yes.

MR. WALTERS : Who were they ?

WITNESS : My brother, and Rosa Bud.

The Trial of John Jasper

Mr. WALTERS : You had a double motive, and you thought the danger came from one and the same man ?

WITNESS : I certainly did.

Mr. WALTERS : Who was that ?

WITNESS : John Jasper.

Mr. WALTERS : What did your brother do after all this ?

WITNESS : He was so sad and unhappy that he left Cloisterham, and took lodgings in London.

Mr. WALTERS : You went with him ?

WITNESS : No, I stopped there to live it down.

Mr. WALTERS : That is where your courage came in again ?—But you need not reply. I shall leave it to the Jury to draw their own conclusions. And now, all this time you were watching Jasper ? Did you discover anything about his actions ?

WITNESS : Nothing definite.

Mr. WALTERS : Did you hear of his going here and there ?

WITNESS : Yes ; there were periodical disappearances.

Mr. WALTERS : Did you know where he went on those occasions ?

WITNESS : Yes, he went to London.

Mr. WALTERS : And when in Cloisterham, how did he behave ?

WITNESS : He went about always throwing out hints that he had thought my brother so hot tempered that he was afraid for his nephew to meet him.

Mr. WALTERS : Did he meet Rosa Bud again ?

WITNESS : He made love to her.

Mr. WALTERS : Did she receive him kindly ?

WITNESS : Hated him, loathed him, was terrified at him.

Mr. WALTERS : Did he say anything to her when he discovered what her attitude was ?

WITNESS : He told her that nothing should prevent him from having her himself. No one should stand against him.

Mr. WALTERS : Did he threaten anyone who did stand against him ?

WITNESS : Yes ; he threatened my brother's life.

Mr. WALTERS : You mean, he said to Rosa Bud something which amounted to a threat against your brother's life ?

WITNESS : He said he could place him in the greatest jeopardy and danger.

Mr. WALTERS : Then you thought his danger would increase ?

WITNESS : Yes.

Mr. WALTERS : I suppose you went to London occasionally to see your brother ?

WITNESS : Not often.

Mr. WALTERS : Did you ever see Rosa Bud in London ?

Evidence of Helena Landless

WITNESS : Yes. She fled to London, so terrified was she at Jasper with his desperate love-making. She went to Mr. Grewgious, her guardian.

MR. WALTERS : And you determined to shield her as much as possible ?

WITNESS : More than ever.

MR. WALTERS : Did you ever recall those words, that you would not, in any circumstances, be afraid of Jasper ?

WITNESS : Yes.

MR. WALTERS : Not a mere idle boast ?

WITNESS : No.

MR. WALTERS : You meant it ?

WITNESS : I did.

MR. WALTERS : Six months went by, and no progress made ?

WITNESS : I found out nothing.

MR. WALTERS : Yet the danger remained, and increased ?

WITNESS : I grew more and more anxious.

MR. WALTERS : It was the woman against the man, and the woman was making no headway ?

WITNESS : Yes.

MR. WALTERS : Did you think it was about time to change your course of action ?

WITNESS : I did.

MR. WALTERS : What did you do ?

WITNESS : I remembered how, as a little girl, I dressed myself as a boy, and now I determined to dress myself as a man.

MR. WALTERS : That was the result of recalling what you had done as a girl ?

WITNESS : Yes.

MR. WALTERS : What you had done in the past you could do again ?

WITNESS : Yes.

MR. WALTERS : It was difficult, you realised ?

WITNESS : Yes, it was difficult, but I determined to overcome every difficulty.

MR. WALTERS : You did not shrink ?

WITNESS : Naturally I shrank, but the end was worth all the sacrifice.

MR. WALTERS : You determined to go through with it ?

WITNESS : I did.

MR. WALTERS : Because you had this double motive ?

WITNESS : That is so.

MR. WALTERS : The overpowering motive which overcame everything else ?

WITNESS : Yes.

MR. WALTERS : Very well, now ; if you could have avoided dressing yourself as a man, if some other course had been open to you, would you have taken it ?

WITNESS : If I could have felt sure of success.

MR. WALTERS : But you felt this was the last resource, and determined to do it ?

WITNESS : Yes.

MR. WALTERS : In order to appear as a man, you had to adopt a very complete disguise indeed. Did you remember what you did when you were a little girl ? Did you cut off your hair again ?

WITNESS : No, I thought I could manage.

MR. WALTERS : Miss Landless, I don't want to press you, but was there any particular, personal reason why you didn't wish to sacrifice your hair ?

WITNESS : Am I obliged to answer that question ?

JUDGE : No.

MR. WALTERS : His Lordship says you need not answer that question. I think we may leave it to the Jury, as human beings, to give their own answer. But, at all events, we understand that you did not cut off your hair. Did you whiten your eyebrows ?

WITNESS : No.

MR. WALTERS : You thought you could manage ?

WITNESS : I did.

MR. WALTERS : How did you disguise yourself effectively ?

WITNESS : I put on a large wig of white hair.

MR. WALTERS : To conceal your own luxuriant tresses ?

WITNESS : I bound them well down underneath.

MR. WALTERS : What else ?

WITNESS : I thought, in keeping with a large head of white hair, I had better assume the free and easy manners of an elderly man, and I tried to put a little dash of swagger, and I wore a blue coat and buff waistcoat.

MR. WALTERS : It was not so difficult, after all, in some respects, for you are a rapid and fluent talker—you need not be shy, you are—and therefore, as Dick Datchery, the affable old gentleman, a bit garrulous, you did not find much difficulty ?

WITNESS : No : I did not find it very difficult.

MR. WALTERS : What did you do in Cloisterham ?

WITNESS : I put up at the Crozier Inn.

MR. WALTERS : Where is that ?

WITNESS : In the High Street.

MR. WALTERS : Far from the Gate House ?

WITNESS : No.

MR. WALTERS : Did you try the effect of your disguise on the people in the neighbourhood ?

Evidence of Helena Landless

WITNESS : Yes, at the Crozier I walked in, asked a few questions, and ordered a man's dinner.

MR. WALTERS : You ordered a man's dinner ?

WITNESS : You would not have had me ask for a glass of milk and a Sally Lunn !

JUDGE : What is a man's dinner ?

WITNESS : I called for a fried sole, and a veal cutlet, and a pint of sherry. Something like a man's dinner !

MR. WALTERS : And did you consume this gargantuan feast ?

WITNESS : I think you are an intelligent gentleman, and I will leave it to you.

MR. WALTERS : You may. Now let us come to your inquiries. I suppose you wanted lodgings ?

WITNESS : I asked the waiter if he could direct me to any.

MR. WALTERS : And did he ?

WITNESS : I asked for something old, architectural, and inconvenient.

MR. WALTERS : And he directed you ?

WITNESS : He did.

MR. WALTERS : Very far ?

WITNESS : No ; not far : Mrs. Tope's house.

MR. WALTERS : Did you find it easily ?

WITNESS : No. That would not have done. I wandered about a bit in the wrong direction, and inquired, and at last found it.

MR. WALTERS : The reason for all that ?

WITNESS : I wanted to put everybody off the scent, and tried to act as to the manner born, so that if anybody were watching me they would really take me for the man I wanted to be.

MR. WALTERS : You thought it best to take every precaution, in case you were watched ?

WITNESS : Yes.

MR. WALTERS : And they would think you had lost your way, and were a stranger ?

WITNESS : Yes.

MR. WALTERS : As a matter of fact, you were not a stranger. Did you meet Mr. Jasper ?

WITNESS : I made an excuse, and I went up and asked him if he could tell me anything as to the respectability of the Tope family.

MR. WALTERS : So that you bearded the lion in his den. Did he recognise you ?

WITNESS : No ; he did not know the mouse.

MR. WALTERS : There are other ways of detecting people than by appearance. Jasper is a musician with a very delicate ear. What about your voice ?

WITNESS : Mr. Jasper had only heard it once, and that was months ago, and, besides, I can change it (*changing her voice*)—change the tone of my voice, and speak like a man.

37

The Trial of John Jasper

MR. WALTERS : You can disguise it, Miss Landless, so that people would really think it was a man's voice ?

WITNESS : Yes.

MR. WALTERS : Tell us what you discovered as to Mr. Jasper's movements at this time.

WITNESS : He absented himself from the Cathedral every now and then, and made periodical disappearances.

MR. WALTERS : Where did he go ?

WITNESS : To London.

MR. WALTERS : Were you in correspondence with Mr. Grewgious, the family solicitor, in London ?

WITNESS : Yes.

MR. WALTERS : Did he tell you he had seen Jasper ?

WITNESS : Yes.

MR. WALTERS : So that, between you, you knew all about him ?

WITNESS : Yes.

MR. WALTERS : In the character of Datchery, did you meet people ?

WITNESS : Yes.

MR. WALTERS : Durdles ?

WITNESS : Yes.

MR. WALTERS : The old opium woman ?

WITNESS : Yes.

MR. WALTERS : Mr. Sapsea, the Mayor ?

WITNESS : Yes.

MR. WALTERS : Did you talk to them familiarly ?

WITNESS : Yes. I really knew their idiosyncrasies—everyone of them—so I fooled them to the top of their bent, and got everything out of them.

MR. WALTERS : I have no doubt but that you asked the old opium woman some questions ?

WITNESS : She had been following Jasper to the Gate House, and she asked me, in a whisper, would I mind telling her who he was, his name, and where he lived.

MR. WALTERS : And you said it was John Jasper ?

WITNESS : Yes. She asked, would I give her three-and-sixpence to buy some opium. She said that on Christmas Eve a young gentleman gave her three-and-sixpence, and he said that his name was Edwin. And she said where could she see Jasper ? And I told her in the Cathedral.

MR. WALTERS : Did she go to the Cathedral next morning ?

WITNESS : Yes ; I saw her behind a pillar, shaking her fist at him.

MR. WALTERS : You think she knew something about him ?

WITNESS : Yes ; that she knew more about his character than anybody else suspected.

MR. WALTERS : May I take it that the results of your investigations led you to the conclusions about John Jasper—that they increased your suspicions ?

Evidence of Helena Landless

WITNESS : I had my suspicions from the first.

MR. WALTERS : Did you keep a record of your successes at the time ?

WITNESS : Yes.

MR. WALTERS : How ?

WITNESS : In chalk marks.

MR. WALTERS : Why in chalk marks ?

WITNESS : I like the old tavern way of keeping scores. You may make a little mark, and nobody but the scorer knows what it means : a small mark for a small success, and a big mark for a big one.

MR. WALTERS : Was another reason that you did not wish your woman's handwriting to be discovered ?

WITNESS : That would never have done.

MR. WALTERS : Did you adopt any device to bring Jasper into your presence, or not ?

WITNESS : Yes ; Mr. Grewgious had told me that he had given a ring to Edwin Drood.

MR. WALTERS : And did you use that ring in any way ?

WITNESS : Yes ; it was this ring that I used to lure him.

MR. WALTERS : And then, when you confronted Jasper, you felt that you had sufficient to go upon to accuse him openly of murder ?

WITNESS : I did. His appearance and agitation were sufficient.

MR. WALTERS : And so he was accused of murder ; and your motives throughout were disinterested motives for the protection of Rosa Bud and your brother ?

WITNESS : That is so.

MR. WALTERS : You knew Edwin Drood ?

WITNESS : Yes.

MR. WALTERS : Do you think that if he had voluntarily disappeared while all this trouble was going on, he would have communicated with his friends ?

WITNESS : Yes, he was a kind-hearted lad.

MR. WALTERS : You cannot understand him being silent while Rosa was in danger ?

WITNESS : I am sure he would not be.

MR. WALTERS : You think that, wherever he was, he would have spoken, if alive ?

WITNESS : I do.

MR. WALTERS : Thank you, that will do.

[HELENA LANDLESS CROSS-EXAMINED.]

MR. CHESTERTON : Miss Landless, you say you knew the prisoner to some extent before the disappearance of Edwin Drood ?

WITNESS : Yes.

MR. CHESTERTON : When did you learn that the prisoner was addicted to opium smoking—or have you learned it ?

WITNESS : Mr. Tope told me of a seizure he had in the Cathedral.

The Trial of John Jasper

MR. CHESTERTON : When was that, approximately ?

WITNESS : As far as I can remember, about a few weeks after I came to Cloisterham as Dick Datchery. Rosa told me how frightened she was of him after he had had a dream ; that he used to go into a peculiar kind of dream, and a film came over his eyes, and then she was more terrified of him than before.

MR. CHESTERTON : But you are putting two very different dates. I want to know when you realised he was addicted to opium smoking.

WITNESS : It takes a little time to realise anything. We hear this and that, and we put two and two together.

MR. CHESTERTON : When Rosa gave you that information, did you suspect opium smoking ?

WITNESS : I had a faint suspicion.

MR. CHESTERTON : It occurred to you that it was probably opium. You knew Edwin Drood, Miss Landless ?

WITNESS : Yes.

MR. CHESTERTON : Was he a conspicuous person—a person to notice very much ?

WITNESS : Not very much, with the exception of this : that he was rather patronising, and had the air of a lad who was very much at home with himself.

MR. CHESTERTON : He dressed like ordinary young men ?

WITNESS : Yes.

MR. CHESTERTON : Wore trousers ?

WITNESS : Yes, certainly, I believe so.

MR. CHESTERTON : Do you understand that the ring was found in the quicklime ?

WITNESS : I believe so.

MR. CHESTERTON : Oh ! you believe so !

WITNESS : It was found there.

MR. CHESTERTON : Were any buttons found there ?

WITNESS : No, I believe not.

MR. CHESTERTON : I suppose Mr. Drood would presumably have on either a belt or braces. Was a buckle or a belt or braces found in the quicklime ?

WITNESS : No.

MR. CHESTERTON : Nothing was found in the lime except this ring ?

WITNESS : No.

MR. CHESTERTON : Thank you.

WITNESS : I could throw some light on that.

MR. CHESTERTON : Your Counsel will no doubt re-examine you. Now, I want to know about this disguise of yours. You told us that it was no new thing to disguise yourself, because you dressed up as a boy in Ceylon. Would you kindly tell me how old you were the last time you did it ?

WITNESS : Thirteen.

Evidence of Helena Landless

MR. CHESTERTON : Do you really suggest that a little girl of thirteen dressing up as a little boy—dressing up as a boy of thirteen—is any sort of qualification for a young lady of 21 dressing up as an " old buffer living idly on his means " ?

WITNESS : Yes; the girl is mother to the woman, as the boy is father to the man.

MR. CHESTERTON : Well, now, you have told us, Miss Landless, that in dressing up as Datchery, you wore a white wig, blue coat, buff waistcoat, and so on. Did you do anything to your face ?

WITNESS : No.

MR. CHESTERTON : You did not paint your face at all ?

WITNESS : I always have enough colour in my face without paint.

MR. CHESTERTON : You did not make up your face in any way ?

WITNESS : No.

MR. CHESTERTON : Do you ask the Jury to believe that you had been going about Cloisterham as Helena Landless for more than six months—ever since you came to Canon Crisparkle's—that you had been going about as Miss Helena Landless ; that you did not alter your face in any way, and went about as Dick Datchery, seeing the same people ? Do you ask the Jury to believe that you were not recognised ?

WITNESS : I ask them to believe it, because it is the truth.

MR. CHESTERTON : Very well ; the Jury will decide that for themselves. You say you went to Cloisterham and put up at the Crozier ?

WITNESS : Yes.

MR. CHESTERTON : You also told us that you ordered a certain meal—a fried sole, a veal cutlet, and a pint of sherry. When my learned friend asked you, you said you would leave it to us. I must ask you : did you consume that meal ?

WITNESS : I am a healthy young woman, but I did not eat it all. I had a little of the fish, some of the cutlet, and some of the sherry.

MR. CHESTERTON : How much sherry ?

WITNESS : I had a glass.

JUDGE : It is important to insist whether the glasses were ordinary wine glasses.

A JURYMAN (Mr. EDWIN PUGH) : I think it is not a fair question.

JUDGE : Any question is fair that tends to bring out the truth. We have no reason to suppose that all the people in the Court are not lying—nay, even are not supporting fictitious characters !

THE JURYMAN : But a sherry glass might be a tumbler.

MR. CHESTERTON : Miss Landless, I press you. You say you only drank one glass. The remainder of the pint you left in the bottle.

WITNESS : I did not say that.

MR. CHESTERTON : What did you do ?

WITNESS : If I must say, there were receptacles in the room used by smokers. Some went that way, some I left in the bottle, and some I drank.

MR. CHESTERTON : Were not people present ?

WITNESS : Not all the time. Only part of the time.

The Trial of John Jasper

MR. CHESTERTON : They retired simultaneously ?

WITNESS : No ; there were not many there when I went in. Some left at once ; some finished their dinners and went away.

MR. CHESTERTON : And the fortunate moment arrived when you could pour out the sherry ?

WITNESS : There are such things as fortunate moments.

MR. CHESTERTON : Your taste in food and drink interests me a little. I shall return to the Crozier. But later on, when staying at Tope's, you used to have an evening meal prepared for you, consisting of bread and cheese and salad and ale ?

WITNESS : Yes.

MR. CHESTERTON : Was that the sort of meal you were accustomed to at Miss Twinkleton's.

WITNESS : But, you see, I was not at Miss Twinkleton's.

MR. CHESTERTON: But there would not have been anything eccentric about coffee or tea?

WITNESS : I think it would be a very feminine beverage.

MR. CHESTERTON : Very well. You told my learned friend that you did not really lose your way from the Crozier to Tope's ?

WITNESS : Yes.

MR. CHESTERTON : The truth of your story you are prepared to stake on that being so ?

WITNESS : Yes.

MR. CHESTERTON : Will the Jury look at page 191 of the book ? * There it states "he soon became bewildered, and went boggling about and about the Cathedral tower, whenever he could catch a glimpse of it . . . " (*To the witness.*) You could catch a glimpse of it when you liked ?

WITNESS : Yes.

MR. CHESTERTON : There was no question of catching a glimpse of it. You could go straight to it if you wanted to ?

WITNESS : If you are quoting from the book.

MR. CHESTERTON : We are quoting from something that is admitted as evidence. Every statement made here must be taken as being true.

WITNESS : But that was a blind.

MR. CHESTERTON : I want to carry you further, Miss Landless—" with a general impression on his mind that Mrs. Tope's was somewhere very near it." Is that the general impression on your mind ?

WITNESS : I knew exactly where to go to Mrs. Tope's.

MR. CHESTERTON : And this " general impression on your mind " goes on—" and that, like the children in the game of hot boiled beans and very good butter, he was warm in his search when he saw the tower, and cold when he didn't see it." Is not that a definite statement as to the condition of your mind, and not as to your external actions, and does it not assert that you did not know where Tope's lodgings were ?

* Each Juryman had been supplied with a copy of the book in the 1s. edition.

Evidence of Helena Landless

WITNESS : I take it as a blind.

JUDGE : I draw the attention of the Court to the fact that the conditions of anybody's frame of mind have been paid perhaps too little attention to, and if Miss Landless chooses to say that the original literary person from whom I believe we procured most of this information was not quite accurate, one can only say she has probably gone outside the rules.

MR. CHESTERTON : My Lord, I would direct your attention to the third paragraph of the " Conditions."

JUDGE (*after perusing the paragraph referred to*) : Yes, I see : that is, on the face of it, it is quite clear that a statement does appear to be made to that effect. The rest falls into the deplorable abyss of literature.

MR. CHESTERTON (*to witness*) : Now, after you had been " boggling about " in search of a place which you knew perfectly well already, you met a small boy, I think ?

WITNESS : I did.

MR. CHESTERTON : I need not trouble you with the conversation, but that boy agreed to conduct you to Tope's ?

WITNESS : Yes.

MR. CHESTERTON : Now he brought you to a place from which the arched passage was visible ?

WITNESS : Yes.

MR. CHESTERTON : And you said, " That's Tope's " ?

WITNESS : Yes.

MR. CHESTERTON : And he answered, " Yer lie ; it ain't. That's Jarsper's." Is that so ?

WITNESS : Yes.

MR. CHESTERTON : And you said, " Indeed ? " And you gave a " second look, of some interest." What was the meaning of that ?

WITNESS : Well, of course, I knew it was Jasper's, but when Jasper's house or anything connected with him, was brought to my mind, I always thought it was interesting, and gave a look for that reason.

MR. CHESTERTON : But you knew you were going to Jasper's house ?

WITNESS : Yes.

MR. CHESTERTON : But why did you give it a second look ?

WITNESS : Because I was so interested.

MR. CHESTERTON : You knew it was Jasper's, because the boy said it was Jasper's, and you gave it " a look of some interest " !

WITNESS : We know that dinner is ready, but we look with interest at it before we sit down to it.

MR. CHESTERTON : You knew it was Jasper's, and gave " a second look of some interest " when told it was Jasper's. Now you went to Tope's, and you met, as you told us, Jasper and Mr. Sapsea, and other people. Now you kept your record, you told us, in

43

chalk, and you told us that one of your reasons for doing that was that you must evade discovery of your handwriting?

WITNESS: That is so.

MR. CHESTERTON: Had it not been for the fact that you were a woman, I take it you ask us to believe that you would have written up in ordinary writing all that you thought and speculated about Jasper on the cupboard door?

WITNESS: I do not ask you to believe anything of the kind, for I should not have been so foolish. I could have written some words if I had wished to, but I would not write at all.

MR. CHESTERTON: You used the old tavern way of keeping scores. Where did you learn that?

WITNESS: In Ceylon.

MR. CHESTERTON: What is the Cingalese tavern way?

WITNESS: I have not been brought up in a drawing-room, but among a very rough set of people. My step-father was a low, common man, and frequented taverns, and we children could go inside and outside or anywhere.

MR. CHESTERTON: Are there taverns in Ceylon?

WITNESS: I don't know that they call them taverns.

MR. CHESTERTON: Do you suggest that the phrase "old tavern way of keeping scores" refers to Ceylon?

WITNESS: My chalk marks revert to the time when I was there.

MR. CHESTERTON: How did you keep scores in Ceylon?

WITNESS: I did not keep scores there, but I saw other people.

MR. CHESTERTON: How do you know how they were kept?

WITNESS: I did not say I did know exactly, but I learned that a little mark meant a certain quantity, a bigger mark more, and so no.

MR. CHESTERTON: You like the old tavern way of keeping scores, but do not know how it is done?

WITNESS: I know that a man that had quarts had large strokes, and a man that had pints smaller ones.

MR. CHESTERTON: You swear that was done in Ceylon?

WITNESS: I swear that sort of thing was done there.

MR. CHESTERTON: What sort of drinks do they have there?

WITNESS: I never had their drinks. I saw them drinking, but I did not know what it was. But I saw the scores being kept on the back of the door.

MR. CHESTERTON: Do you know what they were drinking at all?

WITNESS: I took it for spirits, and beer, and so on.

MR. CHESTERTON: So you knew little about the drinking, but a great deal about the scoring?

WITNESS: That interested me as a child. My brother and I used to talk about it.

Evidence of Helena Landless

MR. CHESTERTON : What was the purpose of the scores ?

WITNESS : The tavern keepers would do it to know what was due from Tom Scott, or Jim Price.

MR. CHESTERTON : You told us that you undertook the Datchery impersonation, so to speak, in collaboration with Mr. Grewgious ?

WITNESS : Yes.

MR. CHESTERTON : May I take it you know him well ?

WITNESS : Yes.

MR. CHESTERTON : Frequently correspond with him ?

WITNESS : I correspond with him.

MR. CHESTERTON : Receive letters from him ?

WITNESS : I have had letters from him.

MR. CHESTERTON : You know his profession ?

WITNESS : A lawyer.

MR. CHESTERTON : What sort ?

WITNESS : I don't know.

JUDGE : He is a lawyer, and I think that covers it. He is, indeed, a particular kind of solicitor, but I think a lady might well be excused for not knowing that.

MR. WALTERS : A lawyer covers everything.

JUDGE : I think that is fair.

MR. CHESTERTON : What is he ?

WITNESS : A lawyer.

MR. CHESTERTON : What sort of business does he carry on ?

MR. WALTERS : She doesn't know.

MR. CHESTERTON : I submit she knows nothing about Mr. Grewgious, and that she has not had correspondence with him.

MR. WALTERS : The official record says she did know Mr. Grewgious, and saw him in his Chambers.

MR. CHESTERTON : She might know Mr. Grewgious, but have no correspondence with him. I am asking what sort of business he carries on.

WITNESS : I know he is a lawyer.

MR. CHESTERTON : And nothing more ?

WITNESS : Women don't interest themselves very much in these things.

JUDGE : No, I think that's fair.

MR. CHESTERTON : Now, the next time we hear anything of the official records, Miss Landless, you were back again in London. How was that ?—in your own proper person, and ceased to be Datchery.

WITNESS : I went up in the evening.

MR. CHESTERTON : In the evening ?

The Trial of John Jasper

WITNESS : By the last 'bus and train.

MR. CHESTERTON : What time ?

WITNESS : The 'bus that leaves the Crozier.

MR. CHESTERTON : What time ?

WITNESS : I forget exactly, but I think about six.

MR. CHESTERTON : Had you any reason for going up ?

WITNESS : Yes.

MR. CHESTERTON : What was it ?

WITNESS : I wanted to see my brother.

MR. CHESTERTON : There was no particular reason why that day more than any other day ?

WITNESS : No, I think not.

MR. CHESTERTON : I suppose you will admit you were running a certain risk of discovery?

WITNESS : Yes, there was some, but I thought I should be able to avoid it.

MR. CHESTERTON : Anybody might follow you ?

WITNESS : Might.

MR. CHESTERTON : You were a stranger in Cloisterham. Anybody might have followed you to London. You were running that risk for no particular reason at all ?

WITNESS : Oh ! but I knew my brother was very, very unhappy, and I knew I could cheer him and comfort him, and he was very, very dear to me.

MR. CHESTERTON : Your visit had nothing to do with Rosa's visit to London ?

WITNESS : I did not know she was there.

MR. CHESTERTON : Mr. Grewgious had not written and asked you to go ?

WITNESS : No.

MR. CHESTERTON : No reason ?

WITNESS : Yes ; the reason I have given you.

MR. CHESTERTON : But there was no particular reason ?

WITNESS : Is it not particular to go and cheer one who is closely bound to you ?

JUDGE : I think the witness's remark is quite clear. She says she had an impulse in an avowedly emotional atmosphere to go and see somebody.

MR. CHESTERTON : Very well. (*To witness.*) You met, you have told us, an opium woman ?

WITNESS : Yes.

MR. CHESTERTON : And you had a conversation with her, and afterwards made a mark on your score—your Cingalese score ?

WITNESS : Yes.

MR. CHESTERTON : A moderate mark ; then you saw her, in the Cathedral, shake her fist at Jasper ?

WITNESS : Yes.

Evidence of Helena Landless

MR. CHESTERTON : Then you made a big mark. What was the meaning of that ?

MR. WALTERS : I am not sure that she is bound to answer that question. It is sufficient that she made the mark.

MR. CHESTERTON : I am endeavouring to show that this story is not true, as I shall represent to the Jury, and my motive for asking the question is, that I suggest it was not Miss Landless who made the mark. The witness who did make the mark will be summoned later, and asked why he made it.

WITNESS : You ask why I made the long mark ?

MR. CHESTERTON : Yes.

WITNESS : Because I thought, when she shook her fist at Jasper, and putting with that the fact that she had followed him, I concluded that she knew something against him, and I thought I had scored, and scored heavily.

MR. CHESTERTON : Is that all ?

WITNESS : I had learned more than that. I had learned that Edwin Drood had given her money for opium on Christmas Eve.

MR. CHESTERTON : What did that prove ?

JUDGE : We must not go into what that could prove. The witness has given a perfectly clear and definite account of her proceedings, and I strongly suggest that unless there is some particular point to be made, she should now be released from the witness-box, because the other point whether she knows anything about the scoring at inns, or whether such practices are common in Ceylon, must be left to later discussion.

MR. CHESTERTON : That is not the point I am trying to make ; but that there was no reason why she should make the score, and I asked why she made it. I believe she did not.

JUDGE : But if she replies that she makes long or short chalk marks, in accordance with the ebullitions of her emotional nature——

MR. CHESTERTON : She is entitled to do so.

JUDGE : That would be an answer, and the only answer to which you will be entitled at the moment.

MR. CHESTERTON : If she likes, she may.

JUDGE : She has told you that she made a long stroke because she thought she had made a great score in her own mind against Jasper, and that she made a shorter mark before because she had not made a big score. That is all that could be expected to be got out of her, without a self-contradiction which would amount to perjury.

MR. CHESTERTON : I have very little more to ask, and shall get through very quickly. (*To witness.*) Now, you tell us that your motives were very compelling. You didn't care much about Edwin Drood, did you ?

WITNESS : No, there was nothing particular about him. I thought he was a nice young fellow.

MR. CHESTERTON : You did ? You did not call him " base and trivial " ?

WITNESS : When he acted as he did to my brother, I felt angry, and naturally said things I should not have said.

The Trial of John Jasper

MR. CHESTERTON : Your feelings were not very strong ?

WITNESS : No.

MR. CHESTERTON : Your motive, you say, was care for your brother and for Miss Rosa Bud ?

WITNESS : That is so.

MR. CHESTERTON : Do you consider those motives adequate to induce you to take the course you say you took ?

WITNESS : I do.

MR. CHESTERTON : Enough to make you take all risks ?

WITNESS : Yes.

MR. CHESTERTON : To go all lengths ?

WITNESS : To the risk of my life.

MR. CHESTERTON : Your life ?

WITNESS : He was all I had.

MR. CHESTERTON : Enough to compel you to do anything ?

WITNESS : Anything that was right and true. You can't catch me that way.

MR. CHESTERTON : I put it to you that the whole of your story is a romance.

WITNESS : You put it to me ?

MR. CHESTERTON : I put it to you, in fairness.

WITNESS : Will you please consider that I am here on my oath ?

MR. CHESTERTON (*to Judge*) : Your Lordship knows I am bound to put that.

WITNESS : I can only answer that every word I have spoken is true.

MR. CHESTERTON : Suppose every word you have spoken is true : is there a single word you have spoken that proves that Edwin Drood was murdered ?

WITNESS : I don't know that you have asked questions to elicit that.

MR. CHESTERTON : It is not my business. Is there a word in the whole of the testimony you have given to your own Counsel or to me that proves that Edwin Drood was murdered ? Did you, for example, see Edwin Drood murdered ?

WITNESS : No.

MR. CHESTERTON : Do you know anyone who saw the murder ?

WITNESS : No.

MR. CHESTERTON : Have you seen his body ?

WITNESS : No.

MR. CHESTERTON : Do you know anyone who has seen it ?

WITNESS : I don't think his body could be seen.

MR. CHESTERTON : Then you really have no evidence to produce to prove that Edwin Drood is dead ?

WITNESS : I have the ring.

Evidence of Helena Landless

MR. CHESTERTON : That is all the evidence—your whole case ? I want to press this point very much. On that ring your case rests. Is that so ?

WITNESS : I am not a woman who understands very much about legal proceedings. It is the first time I have been in court. It is a hard thing for a clever man like you to put a question like this to an unsophisticated witness.

MR. CHESTERTON : But you are the person who has worked out the whole scheme against Jasper. Does not the whole case for the death, not for the plan or the undertaking, but for the death having taken place, rest on the finding of that ring ?

WITNESS : Well, perhaps the case for incriminating, bringing it home to Jasper, rests on the ring.

MR. CHESTERTON : And if that ring—the presence of that ring—could be satisfactorily explained—the presence of the ring in the quicklime could be satisfactorily explained in any other way—you would have nothing to produce to show that it was a murder ?

WITNESS : I might have no evidence, but I should be morally certain.

MR. CHESTERTON : You would hold your opinion, we know, but you would have no evidence ?

WITNESS : No.

JUDGE : I think we must be careful not to get into argument.

MR. CHESTERTON : My Lord, I am finishing.

WITNESS : What you and I think is evidence might be two different questions.

JUDGE : That is indeed very probable.

WITNESS : I don't think it fair to ask questions like that.

MR. CHESTERTON : I will take her answer.

MR. WALTERS (re-examining) : It does not require particular affection for any particular person to wish that he should not be murdered ?

WITNESS : No.

MR. WALTERS : Although you might not be violently enamoured of Edwin Drood, you might want to bring his murderer to justice ?

WITNESS : Yes.

MR. WALTERS : It has been suggested that your story is entirely romance. If you had been acting a part, would you not naturally have been disgraced for ever in the eyes of all who know you ?

WITNESS : I should indeed.

MR. WALTERS : Have you not a particular reason at present for wishing to stand high in the esteem of certain people ?

WITNESS : I have.

MR. WALTERS : Don't you think you would forfeit that esteem if you stood there on your oath, and told a tissue of falsehoods ?

WITNESS : I should.

MR. WALTERS : Is there not every reason why you should tell the truth ?

WITNESS : There is.

The Trial of John Jasper

MR. WALTERS : Have you anything to gain by telling lies ?

WITNESS : I have all to lose.

MR. WALTERS : Have you not been working entirely for others throughout ?

WITNESS : Yes.

MR. WALTERS : You would not have taken this part if you could have helped it ?

WITNESS : No.

MR. WALTERS : And when you were making these investigations you did not want to go to everybody and ask his definite business—" What sort of lawyer are you ? " ?

WITNESS : No ; I never thought about it. He was a lawyer, and that's all I knew.

MR. WALTERS : Have you ever written a tragedy that nobody will bring out ?

WITNESS : No, indeed, I have not.

MR. WALTERS : And so you have no particular reason for standing in the limelight and making yourself a heroine. Thank you.

JUDGE : The Court will now adjourn for about ten or fifteen minutes.

The Court accordingly adjourned. On the resumption of the proceedings, Mr. Walters announced that the evidence of Miss Helena Landless had completed his case.

[THE CASE FOR THE DEFENCE.]

Mr. Crotch, in opening the case for the defence, said—

MY LORD, AND GENTLEMEN OF THE JURY—

I am not going to follow the example of my learned friend, but I am merely going to outline the defence as briefly as possible. I am going to say at once that we are not out to attempt to dispute in any way that the prisoner desired the death of Edwin Drood or that he intended to murder him, nor that he planned to murder him, nor that he actually attempted to murder him, nor indeed, my Lord, that at one time, and for some time, he did believe that he had actually murdered him. What we do say, however, is that no murder took place. For any murder there must be, not only a murderer, but a murdered man. Now, granted for a moment that in the prisoner at the bar you have a potential murderer, where is the murdered man ?

MR. WALTERS : This is strictly against all agreements.

MR. CROTCH : I will put my statement in another way, my Lord.

MR. WALTERS : I draw your attention to this fact : it is agreed that the legal point that no conviction can take place since no body has been found, shall be raised only after the retirement of the jury. This ought not to have been introduced at all.

JUDGE : But we may assume, what is apparently the fact, that no murdered body has been found ?

MR. WALTERS : But he went further, and said. " Where is the body ? "

MR. CROTCH : May I placate my friend and say, have we a murdered man ? We say John Jasper did not murder Edwin Drood on the Christmas Eve of 1860. We have every reason to believe that Edwin Drood is still alive, and in that case, of course, it follows that you cannot legally convict John Jasper for murder. Now, it will naturally be asked how, if a murder was admittedly attempted, it can have failed, and still more,

Evidence of " Princess Puffer "

that if it failed, how the supposed murderer could have believed that it had succeeded. Those questions will be probably solved : we hope they will be solved by the evidence which we shall put before you. All I think it is at the moment necessary to say is, that the key to the story will be found in the opium habits to which the prisoner undoubtedly was addicted. My Lord, there is a story told of an Irish priest, who, warning his congregation against the evils of intemperance, said, " What makes you shoot at your landlord ? " And the reply came, " It's the drink." " And begad, what makes you fail to shoot him ? " The same reply—" It's the drink." My Lord and Gentlemen of the Jury, we submit that, in a word, is the story of John Jasper. Now John Jasper is—presumably my friend will admit it—he has tried to prove it—I don't think he has demonstrated much by it—he has tried to get out of his witnesses that this man was an opium smoker. From our point of view that is excellent. We say that John Jasper had, on the night previous to this murderous attack on Edwin Drood, indulged in a gross opium debauch, and because he did, in the midst of the commission of his crime he had one of those sudden seizures to which he was subjected, and that under the influence of opium he failed to complete the crime, but still believed that he had. Because he was under the influence of opium, he completed it in imagination, and then afterwards imagined that he had completed it in fact ; and because his victim—and this is the point that I want to draw your attention to especially—because his victim also was under the influence of opium, having been drugged by Jasper, he failed to give any connected or reasonable and rational account of what had happened in these circumstances. That, I submit, my Lord, and Gentlemen of the Jury, is the outline. The details will be presently filled in by witnesses, who will testify. You will perceive that if it is true—and we shall prove it to be true—then John Jasper, whatever his intention, however great his moral obliquity, cannot be legally convicted of murder.—Eliza Lascar, alias the " Princess Puffer."

[EVIDENCE OF THE " PRINCESS PUFFER."]

USHER : Eliza Lascar, alias " Princess Puffer " !

[The witness entered the witness-box, and was duly sworn.]

MR. CROTCH : Are you sworn ?

WITNESS : Yes, deary.

MR. CROTCH : Your name, I believe, is Eliza Lascar ?

WITNESS : Yes, deary. Oh, my lungs is so weak !

MR. CROTCH : My dear lady !

WITNESS : Oh, my lungs !

MR. CROTCH : You are known as " Princess Puffer " ?

WITNESS : Yes, deary. I got Heavens-hard drunk for sixteen year afore I took to this ; but this don't hurt me, not to speak of.

MR. CROTCH : You keep an opium den in the East End of London, I believe ?

WITNESS : I do ; but business is slack.

MR. CROTCH : Do you know the prisoner ?

WITNESS : Know him ! Better far than all the Reverend Parsons put together know him.

MR. CROTCH : He is a customer of yours, I believe ?

WITNESS : When he first came to me he was quite new to it, but after a while he could take his pipe with the best of 'em, deary.

The Trial of John Jasper

MR. CROTCH : I conclude from that he was a heavy opium smoker ?

WITNESS : He was, deary.

MR. CROTCH : Do you remember his being in your place on the night of the twelfth of December ?

WITNESS : He was, deary. I see him coming to, and I says, deary, " Get him another ready when he wakes, and he will remember the market price of opium is very high."

MR. CROTCH : What was the date he next visited you ?

WITNESS : December 23, my deary dear.

MR. CROTCH : You need not be so affectionate. What happened next day ?

WITNESS : I followed him to his home.

MR. CROTCH : What happened ?

WITNESS : I lost him where the omnibus he got into nigh his journey's end plies betwixt the station and the place.

MR. CROTCH : Did you meet anybody else ?

WITNESS : I met a dear gentleman named Edwin.

MR. CROTCH : What did you say to him ?

WITNESS : I said to him, " My lungs is weak, my lungs is bad "—and the dear gentleman he put three-and-sixpence in my hand.

MR. CROTCH : And when did you next meet the prisoner ?

WITNESS : Oh, my poor head ! In 1861. He comes to me all over like for the want of a smoke. I says, " You have come to the right place. This is the place where the all overs is smoked off."

MR. CROTCH : Then what happened ?

WITNESS : Then what happened, deary ? I follows him to Aldersgate Street, the place where he puts up, and I finds out where he comes from, and I says to my poor self " I missed you the first time, and I swore my oath I will not lose you again, my gentleman from Cloisterham. I'll go there first, and bide your coming." And I did. I goes to Cloisterham, and I waits outside the Nun's House, just where the omnibus goes, and he gets down, and I follows him up a bystreet till he disappears under a archway to the left. I turns round, and he was gone.

MR. CROTCH : Did you see any one ?

WITNESS : A white-haired gentleman who told me that his name was Datchery.

MR. CROTCH : Did you go to the Cathedral next morning ?

WITNESS : I did, deary.

MR. CROTCH : Did you see the prisoner there ?

WITNESS : I see him from behind a pillar.

MR. CROTCH : You recognised him ?

WITNESS : I recognised him, deary.

MR. CROTCH : Did you afterwards meet the white-haired gentleman you have spoken of ?

WITNESS : I did, deary.

Evidence of " Princess Puffer "

MR. CROTCH : Did you tell him you knew the prisoner ?

WITNESS : I told him that I knew him.

MR. CROTCH : Yes ?

WITNESS : I said, " I know him. I know him better than all the Reverend Parsons put together knows him.

MR. CROTCH : Thank you.

[" PRINCESS PUFFER " CROSS-EXAMINED.]

MR. WALTERS : Just one question. When you met Edwin Drood, I think you told him " Ned " was a threatened name ?

WITNESS : Yes, deary.

MR. WALTERS : What did you mean by " threatened " ?

WITNESS : It was a bad name.

MR. WALTERS : Do you think a man threatened is in danger ?

WITNESS : It sounds like it, deary, don't it ?

MR. WALTERS : It does. I want you to agree with me. I think you were in the habit of listening to Mr. Jasper when he had a little opium ?

WITNESS : That is so.

MR. WALTERS : Ever hear him say the word " Ned " ?

WITNESS : I can't recollect. I should think he did.

MR. WALTERS : What made you hit upon the name " Ned " as a threatened name ?

WITNESS : He talked about him in a very unkind way.

MR. WALTERS : You say the man threatened was in danger. Did you think " Ned " in danger ?

WITNESS : I heard what he said. Shall I tell you ?

MR. WALTERS : Not what he said. It doesn't matter. But I want to know that " Ned " was a threatened name.

WITNESS : That's right, deary.

MR. WALTERS : Were you giving warning to anybody of the name of Ned " ?

WITNESS : I told him it was a threatened name.

MR. WALTERS : Did you know he was called " Ned " ?

WITNESS : I asked him.

MR. WALTERS : Did you know who called him " Ned " ?

WITNESS : I don't know.

MR. WALTERS : If I told you that Jasper, and Jasper alone, called him " Ned " ?

WITNESS : I should believe you, deary. I should believe you.

MR. WALTERS : And you would therefore also believe that Jasper was threatening him ?

WITNESS : Yes, deary.

MR. WALTERS : And that he meant it ?

WITNESS : Yes, deary.

53

The Trial of John Jasper

MR. WALTERS : So you think there was murder in the mind of John Jasper ?

WITNESS : I think he wanted to do him harm.

MR. WALTERS : Do you love John Jasper ?

WITNESS : No, I don't.

MR. WALTERS : I suppose you don't love any of your customers ?

WITNESS : I don't care much about 'em.

MR. WALTERS : But you don't turn them away ? When they come to you you take their money ?

WITNESS : Yes.

MR. WALTERS : Do you always follow your customers down to their private residences ?

WITNESS : No.

MR. WALTERS : Why this one ?

WITNESS : He had money.

MR. WALTERS : What ! A poor man in a choir had got money ?

WITNESS : He had money.

MR. WALTERS : It was worth all your while to go all the way to Cloisterham after one customer ?

WITNESS : Yes.

MR. WALTERS : He had such a lot of money ?

WITNESS : Yes ; to me he had. I'm only a poor woman.

MR. WALTERS : He was richer than all your other customers ?

WITNESS : Yes.

MR. WALTERS : You think so ?

WITNESS : Yes.

MR. WALTERS : You don't know where all this money came from ?

WITNESS : No.

MR. WALTERS : You hated him ?

WITNESS : Yes.

MR. WALTERS : And you wanted his money ?

WITNESS : Yes. He was always a-listening.

MR. WALTERS : I thought it was you listening ?

WITNESS : Sometimes I would listen, and once he spoke to me of a hazardous journey, and he said, " I did it a hundred million times ; I did it so often, that when it came to be really done, it was not worth the doing, it was done so soon, and when it comes to be real, it was so short that for the first time it seemed to be unreal. No struggle, no sign of danger, no consciousness of peril ! I never dreamt that before." That's what he said, my deary dear.

MR. WALTERS : Well, he said, when it came to be done it was so short it was not worth doing ?

Evidence of Thomas Bazzard

WITNESS : He said it was not real for the first time.

MR. WALTERS : He talked about a real thing ?

WITNESS : He says, deary, " When it comes to be real it seems to be unreal for the first time," my deary dear.

MR. WALTERS : He said, " when it comes to be real " ?

WITNESS : " It seems unreal for the first time," my poppett.

MR. WALTERS : But when a man says " a real thing," he means a real thing ?

MR. CHESTERTON : My Lord !

JUDGE : There is some element of paradox involved here. I cannot consent to allow the witness to be attacked merely because a criminal says that that which seemed real before it happened appeared unreal when it happened, because I suppose most of us in this room have committed crimes at some time or other, and that is a possible state of affairs.

MR. WALTERS : I will not ask any more questions, my Lord.

MR. CHESTERTON (re-examining) : When you say that you imagined the prisoner was rich as compared with your other clients—they would be Chinamen and sailors and Lascars ?

WITNESS : They was very poor, deary.

MR. CHESTERTON : He was a different class of man ?

WITNESS : He was, my poppett.

MR. CHESTERTON : The other question I want to ask you is this : When you told Mr. Drood that " Ned " was a threatened name, what did Mr. Drood say ?

WITNESS : He says, " But threatened men live long."

MR. CHESTERTON : What did you say ?

WITNESS : " Then," I says to him, " Ned, so threatened is he, whoever he be, while I'm a talking to you, that he should live to all eternity."

MR. CHESTERTON : Thank you. Call Thomas Bazzard.

USHER : Thomas Bazzard !

[That gentleman entered the witness-box and was duly sworn.]

[EVIDENCE OF THOMAS BAZZARD.]

MR. CHESTERTON : Your name is Thomas Bazzard ?

WITNESS : Yes.

MR. CHESTERTON : What is your profession ?

WITNESS : I am a clerk and investigator to Mr. Grewgious, of Staple Inn.

MR. CHESTERTON : Mr. Grewgious is not, as he is wrongfully described I believe, in the indictment, a solicitor ?

WITNESS : No ; Mr. Grewgious is a member of the Bar, but is not practising. He is Receiver and Manager of two large estates.

MR. CHESTERTON : And what sort of work do you do ?

WITNESS : I believe the work that I am at present engaged in is colloquially known as that of a " noser." That is to say, I am engaged partly in collecting the rents, and partly in inquiring what is going on with his tenants—whether they are stealing the game, and improperly dispersing the stock. Largely work of investigation outside the office.

MR. CHESTERTON : When did you enter his employment ?

WITNESS : Ten years ago.

MR. CHESTERTON : Where were you born ?

WITNESS : I am the son of a Norfolk farmer, I am sorry to say.

MR. CHESTERTON : If your employer said, " It would be extremely difficult to replace Mr. Bazzard," that would refer to your inquiry work ?

WITNESS : I think that would refer to my inquiry work.   Yes.

MR. CHESTERTON : Mr. Grewgious treats you rather respectfully ?

WITNESS : Mr. Grewgious is extremely kind to me, and as he values my work outside, he allows a great deal of latitude as to my behaviour inside.

MR. CHESTERTON : Now, when did you first see Edwin Drood ?

WITNESS : I think I saw him—by the way, I should like to point out that Mr. Grewgious was not the legal adviser to Edwin Drood.

MR. CHESTERTON : You might explain that to the Court.

WITNESS : I noticed in the copy of the Agreement that he was the legal adviser to Edwin Drood. So far as I know, that is not the case. I first saw him some time before Christmas 1860, at the office of Mr. Grewgious.

MR. CHESTERTON : Did Mr. Grewgious tell you about Mr. Drood's coming ?

WITNESS : He did. Yes.

MR. CHESTERTON : And what was the general instruction that Mr. Grewgious gave you ?

WITNESS : These instructions : he said he was going to have a private conversation —more or less private conversation—with Mr. Drood, and if I appeared to be very interested in it, it might embarrass Mr. Drood, and that therefore I should not pay any particular attention to it.

MR. CHESTERTON : What did you do ?

WITNESS : What happened was this : I think we all had dinner, and then Mr. Grewgious had the private conversation in question. I understood that what happened was that he admonished Mr. Drood as to his proper feelings towards his future bride.

JUDGE : You did not hear that ?

WITNESS : No ; I didn't hear that. I took the opportunity to have a snooze. Waking up. Mr. Grewgious said to me, " I have handed a ring of diamonds and rubies to Mr. Drood." Mr. Drood handed a case and said, " You see ? " I said, " I follow you both, sir, and I witness the transaction."

MR. CHESTERTON : What was the next occasion you saw him ?

WITNESS : The next occasion I saw Mr. Edwin Drood was Jan. 1st, 1861

MR. CHESTERTON : That was a week after you first met him ?

WITNESS : Yes.

MR. CHESTERTON : Where did you meet him ?

WITNESS : At a hotel in Holborn.

Evidence of Thomas Bazzard

MR. CHESTERTON : Did you hear what happened to him after that ?

WITNESS : After that, I was informed that he was very seriously ill with rheumatic fever, and was sent abroad to the South of France to get his health back.

MR. CHESTERTON : Did Mr. Grewgious ever tell you how he came across Edwin Drood ?

WITNESS : What he told me was this : that on Christmas Eve, 1860, he received very late at night, a letter from Miss Rosa Bud, his ward, to whom he was very much attached, and, if I may be allowed to remark, to whose mother he was very devotedly attached also. This letter was written by Miss Bud immediately following her conversation with Mr. Edwin Drood, which is in the Official Record, I think, and it entreated Mr. Grewgious, in very strong terms, to be with her in Cloisterham on Christmas Day. The letter reached Mr. Grewgious very late in the evening, and owing to the defects of the railway system, some of which, I am glad to learn, have been altered since, it was impossible for Mr. Grewgious to get to Cloisterham except by posting down, which he accordingly did.

MR. CHESTERTON : There was no train after eight o'clock ?

WITNESS : At that time no train after eight o'clock—from Victoria.

MR. CHESTERTON : He posted down, and what do you understand he did when he arrived at Cloisterham ?

WITNESS : He told me that he drove into Cloisterham somewhere about 5.30. Passing the Postern Gate, he stopped his carriage, and asked it to wait a minute.

MR. CHESTERTON : Why ?

WITNESS : He wanted to walk through the gate into the Churchyard, a few yards —some 40 or 50 yards, I think—in order to put some flowers on the grave of Miss Rosa Bud's mother, as I think it is stated in the official documents, he was very much attached to Miss Bud's mother.

MR. CHESTERTON : When he got there, whom did he find ?

WITNESS : He found Edwin Drood lying prone.

MR. CHESTERTON : And what did he do ?

WITNESS : I believe the first thing he did was to pick him up. He then shook him together, begged him to speak to him, and questioned him, and Edwin Drood entreated him to take him out of Cloisterham without any delay.

MR. CHESTERTON : I understand, Mr. Bazzard, from your narrative, that Mr. Drood could give practically no coherent account of what had happened ?

WITNESS : None whatever, beyond the fact that somebody had tried to strangle him, as he thought.

MR. CHESTERTON : When you saw him, what sort of memory had he of that night ?

WITNESS : Vague and unsatisfactory.

MR. CHESTERTON : He could not have sworn that either Neville Landless or Jasper had attacked him ?

WITNESS : He could not swear anything, except that he had been attacked.

MR. CHESTERTON : His sympathies leaned, of course, to Jasper rather than to Landless ?

The Trial of John Jasper

WITNESS : He was very loath indeed to think that his uncle, whom he had cherished with very great respect and esteem, had been concerned in the attempt to murder him.

MR. CHESTERTON : If he could have given evidence then, I take it he would have given evidence rather in favour of Jasper than of Landless ?

WITNESS : That depends on the Jury.

JUDGE : I was going to remark that the question goes a little outside anything the witness is called upon to answer.

WITNESS : He was more inclined to——

THE FOREMAN : On this point the witness has made a very remarkable statement; that Mr. Grewgious shook Mr. Drood together. May I ask how many pieces Drood was in ?

JUDGE : I think the question should be answered.

WITNESS : I was not there, my Lord, at the time. I merely repeat what Mr. Grewgious told me.

JUDGE : You attribute it to a violent metaphor on the part of Mr. Grewgious ?

WITNESS : It is right that I should put the Jury in possession of all matters.

A JURYMAN (Mr. William Archer) : May I ask where Mr. Grewgious is in the meantime ? Met with a violent death ?

MR. CHESTERTON : If the Jury will look at the Official Record——

THE FOREMAN : I am sorry to explain, my Lord, that all our documents have gone, covered with our autographs. (Further copies of the Official Documents were handed to the Jury by the Clerk of Arraigns.)

MR. CHESTERTON : If the Jury have the Document, they will see the last paragraph but one explains the matter. (*To Witness.*) You then saw Mr. Grewgious. What did Mr. Grewgious say ?

WITNESS : What he said was this : that he personally very strongly suspected Jasper, but that Drood's recollections as to what happened on that evening were so confused and incoherent that any testimony he might have to give would not either clear Landless, or incriminate Jasper. He therefore said this : that if Landless were committed for trial it would be necessary to produce Drood, but failing that, he had better keep his continued existence a secret until matters had died down at Cloisterham, and until Jasper thought he was entirely secure.

MR. CHESTERTON : And therefore, what was Mr. Grewgious's plan ?

WITNESS : His plan was this : that if I went down to Cloisterham prosecuting inquiries there, I should detect Jasper.

MR. CHESTERTON : And you did so ?

WITNESS : I did so. Yes.

MR. CHESTERTON : When you went down, how did the case present itself to you as a problem ?

WITNESS : I thought from what Mr. Grewgious told me about the case, that there were three cardinal mysteries. One was why Drood, if he had been murderously assaulted, could give no clear account, as to who had assaulted him ; the second was

58

Evidence of Thomas Bazzard

why, if the prisoner was the author of that murderous assault, he had not effected it; and in the third place, why, having failed to kill Drood, he obviously thought he had killed him.

MR. CHESTERTON : Having put those three things to yourself, you went down to Cloisterham and disguised yourself ?

WITNESS : I went to a costumier.

MR. CHESTERTON : You did not make up your face ?

WITNESS : No.

MR. CHESTERTON : You were not known there ?

WITNESS : As far as I know, no.

MR. CHESTERTON : But there might be an offchance, and so you put on a costume ?

WITNESS : Yes.

MR. CHESTERTON : You went to the Crozier, and ordered a veal cutlet, a mutton chop, and a pint of sherry ?

WITNESS : Yes—and I drank the sherry !

MR. CHESTERTON : And asked the waiter about lodgings ?

WITNESS : I did.

MR. CHESTERTON : You asked for something Cathedrally ?

WITNESS : I thought I ought to get something near the Cathedral, so as to be near to Jasper.

MR. CHESTERTON : They recommended you to Mr. Tope's ?

WITNESS : They did.

MR. CHESTERTON : And you set out to go there ?

WITNESS : I did.

MR. CHESTERTON : What happened ?

WITNESS : I was told I should find the house on the right-hand side. It was so obvious that I went past it. I went on up a lane called Crow Lane, I believe, into the Vineries, and somewhere about there I met the boy named Deputy. I asked him to take me to Tope's, which he did.

MR. CHESTERTON : He took you to within sight, didn't he ?

WITNESS : Yes ; I beg pardon.

MR. CHESTERTON : He pointed out a window ?

WITNESS : Yes.

MR. CHESTERTON : You said, " That's Tope's " ?

WITNESS : Yes ; I thought it was.

MR. CHESTERTON : He said it was Jasper's ?

WITNESS : Yes ; and I looked at it with some interest.

MR. CHESTERTON : You saw Jasper subsequently ?

WITNESS : Yes.

MR. CHESTERTON : You called on him to inquire about the Topes ? You made that opportunity to call ?

WITNESS : Yes.

MR. CHESTERTON : You walked about the Cathedral ; met Sapsea and Durdles ?

WITNESS : Yes.

MR. CHESTERTON : You met Deputy again ?

WITNESS : Yes.

MR. CHESTERTON : And there was a conversation, I think, between you and Deputy, in which you said he was to take you to Durdles's house when you wished ?

WITNESS : Yes.

MR. CHESTERTON : After you installed yourself in the Tope's lodgings, how did you propose to keep a record of your successes ?

WITNESS : I rather amused myself by opening the cupboard door in my room, and chalking it up as is done in taverns which on occasions I have visited in Ceylon—I mean Norfolk.

MR. CHESTERTON : You were brought up as a boy in Norfolk ?

WITNESS : Yes.

MR. CHESTERTON : And they keep chalk scores there ?

WITNESS : They used to chalk it up by means of long or short lines.

MR. CHESTERTON : Generally according to the date of the week ?

WITNESS : The big lines at the end of the week.

MR. CHESTERTON : You kept this record in this fashion ?

WITNESS : Yes.

MR. CHESTERTON : Will you carry your mind back to one evening, I think in July, when Jasper came home comparatively late, and went under the archway, and passed up the staircase ?

WITNESS : Yes.

MR. CHESTERTON : Do you remember an old woman following ?

WITNESS : Yes.

MR. CHESTERTON : What passed between you ?

WITNESS : I asked her if she was looking for anybody, and she, in substance, said that she would like to know the name and address of that gentleman. Then we had some further conversation, and she asked me, first of all for money for her lodgings, and then she asked for money for what she described as opium, which I gave her.

MR. CHESTERTON : She also mentioned an interview with a young gentleman on the previous Christmas Eve ?

WITNESS : Yes, she told me she had been to Cloisterham before on Christmas Eve, and that she had met a youth named Ned, I think it was, who had also given her money. I took it she had been down on the same business as that night—following the prisoner.

MR. CHESTERTON : When you had done that, you went to your score ?

Evidence of Thomas Bazzard

WITNESS : When I had done that, I met Deputy, and he told me that " 'Er Royal Highness the Princess Puffer " was staying at the Travellers' Tuppeny, and that she kept an opium den in the East End of London, and then I had very little doubt that that was the place from which she had followed the prisoner.

MR. CHESTERTON : You told her where she could see the prisoner next morning ?

WITNESS : Yes.

MR. CHESTERTON : She saw him, and shook her fist at him ?

WITNESS : She used dreadful language which is not even in the Official Records.

MR. CHESTERTON : When she came out, did you say to her, " Have you seen him ? "?

WITNESS : I did.

MR. CHESTERTON : And did she say that she had seen him, and knew him better than all the Reverend Parsons put together ?

WITNESS : Yes.

MR. CHESTERTON : You then went to the cupboard door, and what did you do ?

WITNESS : I made a great score.

MR. CHESTERTON : What was its meaning ?

WITNESS : That my interview with, and observations of the opium woman had settled the three main questions as to which I had gone down to Cloisterham to decide.

MR. CHESTERTON : Let us take them seriatim. First, how was it Drood——

WITNESS : From my conversation with her I gathered that Jasper took opium, and having opium, I had no doubt at all that he drugged Drood's wine, and that Drood was so affected as not to be able to give any clear account as to the event.

MR. CHESTERTON : The second question—How was it that, if the prisoner was the author of the assault, he had not achieved his purpose ?

WITNESS : My views as to that also were clear. He had been at the opium den on the night before the Christmas Eve, when she last visited Cloisterham, and I have no doubt at all that he failed because he had an opium seizure—such a seizure as Mr. Grewgious saw him in, and as his nephew Drood saw him in.

MR. CHESTERTON : The third question—How came it, that having failed to kill Drood, he obviously thought he had done so ?

WITNESS : That, I thought, was obvious, because he would have completed the murder in an opium trance, such a trance as, later, the " Princess Puffer " described to me, as Jasper having experienced inside the opium den.

MR. CHESTERTON : We have already heard from the " Princess Puffer " about its being unreal for the first time. That would fit in with your theory ?

JUDGE : I am afraid the witness must have no theory. As soon as the examination has put its main point, we must go on.

MR. CHESTERTON (to witness) : Then, did you get any confirmation of that view from Mr. Grewgious ?

WITNESS : Yes, I wrote to Mr. Grewgious, and he told me of the seizure on Boxing Day—I think it was Boxing Day—when he had an interview with Jasper, the prisoner.

The Trial of John Jasper

MR. CHESTERTON : And also did he tell you that Edwin Drood remembered his uncle in a seizure ?

WITNESS : I remember that also.

MR. CHESTERTON : Did you gather that Drood had had his wine drugged on a previous occasion ?

WITNESS : I gather that from the Official Records.

MR. CHESTERTON : Then, did you claim your promise from Deputy ?

WITNESS : I did.

MR. CHESTERTON : We have been told in evidence that a ring was put in the crypt.

WITNESS : Yes ?

MR. CHESTERTON : Does that surprise you ?

WITNESS : Not in the least.

MR. CHESTERTON : Why ?

WITNESS : Because I put it there.

MR. CHESTERTON : What was your object in pursuing that course ?

WITNESS : This was the ring, I may say, that I had seen pass from Mr. Grewgious to Drood, of the existence of which, I may perhaps point out, it is obvious from the study of the Official Records, Jasper knew nothing at all ; and acting under instructions from Mr. Grewgious, who had received the ring back from Drood, I obtained with the assistance of my friend Durdles access to the Sapsea vault, and therein I placed the ring. My object in doing that was, that subsequently, when Mr. Grewgious offered a reward for the discovery of the ring, the prisoner could be entrapped into a visit to the vault.

MR. CHESTERTON : I take it, Mr. Grewgious would plaster Cloisterham with the description of the ring as believed to be on the person of Edwin Drood ?

WITNESS : That is what he did.

MR. CHESTERTON : It would be a large placard ?

WITNESS : Yes.

MR. CHESTERTON : Rather like this ? (*Handing to the witness a reproduction of the original cover design for the book.*)

WITNESS : Very like the second illustration from the top on the left-hand side.

MR. CHESTERTON : Very well : that was your plan—that Jasper should be caught taking the ring, and thus be convicted of attempted murder ?

WITNESS : Quite.

MR. CHESTERTON : Of which you believed him to be guilty ?

WITNESS : Beyond doubt.

MR. CHESTERTON : It is not my business to ask you what happened, but I suppose somehow or other he got arrested for actual murder. Is that correct ?

WITNESS : Quite right.

MR. CHESTERTON : Thank you.

Evidence of Thomas Bazzard

[THOMAS BAZZARD CROSS-EXAMINED.]

MR. WALTERS (*cross-examining*): I think you have said several times that you come from Norfolk?

WITNESS: I was born in Norfolk.

MR. WALTERS: Is that the country where the dumplings come from?

WITNESS: Some, no doubt.

MR. WALTERS: Where you come from also!

WITNESS: Yes.

MR. WALTERS: Curious coincidence! You are a farmer's son?

WITNESS: Yes.

MR. WALTERS: And very ambitious?

WITNESS: I have not said so.

MR. WALTERS: Don't you want to get on?

WITNESS: I don't think that is very ambitious. I think being very ambitious is more than wanting to get on.

MR. WALTERS: In order to get on you came to London from Norfolk?

WITNESS: A good many people have done that before, I am afraid.

MR. WALTERS: You wanted to give London the benefit of any genius you had?

WITNESS: Thank you very much indeed. I wanted to be usefully employed.

MR. WALTERS: And you became professionally engaged to Mr. Grewgious?

WITNESS: Yes.

MR. WALTERS: And you occupied the responsible and honourable position of " Noser "?

WITNESS: Quite right. The best position I could get.

MR. WALTERS: And he treated you with great respect?

WITNESS: Yes.

MR. WALTERS: Remarkable respect from a barrister to his clerk?

WITNESS: That is due to the fact that he is a man of exceptional graciousness.

MR. WALTERS: And you treated him with great respect?

WITNESS: I worked for him, I think, very hard, and with very great fidelity.

MR. WALTERS: I said you treated him with great respect. I did not ask about your fidelity.

WITNESS: You will forgive my mentioning it, won't you?

MR. WALTERS: Now do you mind replying to the question? You treated him with very great respect?

WITNESS: I hope so.

MR. WALTERS: If you ever gave him a surly answer, would that be respectful?

WITNESS: I don't know. It would depend on the degree of surliness.

MR. WALTERS: And you took his money as a good and faithful servant?

WITNESS: I hope so.

The Trial of John Jasper

MR. WALTERS : And were absolutely devoted to his interests ?

WITNESS : I hope so.

MR. WALTERS : So that on one occasion you fell asleep while he was talking ?

WITNESS : Yes ; but in pursuance to his instructions. He told me that a conversation was going to take place which was no affair of mine, and that he was not particularly anxious for me to overhear it. But he was very anxious that I should witness the transaction at the end of the conversation.

MR. WALTERS : Would it not have been more respectful to walk out of the room ?

WITNESS : I think not. It would place him in an extremely awkward position.

MR. WALTERS : You preferred to fall asleep and snore ?

WITNESS : May I answer ? If I had gone out, Mr. Grewgious would have had to come for me, and to have told Edwin Drood that he required a witness.

MR. WALTERS : You preferred to fall asleep and snore in the presence of a client ?

WITNESS : I had forty winks after dinner.

MR. WALTERS : You had forty winks, as you call it, while your employer was engaged with an important client ?

WITNESS : In a conversation which I was not supposed to hear.

MR. WALTERS : Do you frequently fall asleep ?

WITNESS : No ; I have no desire to slumber at present.

MR. WALTERS : No ; I think we shall wake you up presently. Do you usually sleep when respectable clients enter your office ?

WITNESS : No ; I don't usually receive such instructions.

MR. WALTERS : That was the only respectful way of treating your master and client ?

WITNESS : I have had no remonstrance from Mr. Grewgious for it. I am still in his employment. He thought it was worth his while to go on employing me.

MR. WALTERS : Mr. Bazzard, the story you have told proves to me that you have rather a strong imagination. Am I right ?

WITNESS : If it proves it to you, my good sir, by all means. I prefer to answer questions.

MR. WALTERS : But probably you have also convinced the Jury that you are a gentleman of some imagination ?

WITNESS : It's not for me to say—only to tender my evidence.

MR. WALTERS : I believe you have written a Drama ?

WITNESS : Once, many years ago, when a young man, I did write a Tragedy. A dreadful admission ! I hope no other witness whose veracity is challenged——

MR. WALTERS : What was the name of that Tragedy ?

WITNESS : It is " The Thorn of Anxiety."

MR. WALTERS : Has it ever come out ?

WITNESS : No.

MR. WALTERS : It is, I suppose, a work of great genius ?

WITNESS : I should not like to say.

Evidence of Thomas Bazzard

MR. WALTERS : But all plays are !

WITNESS : Do you think so ! If you would like to read it, I should be delighted.

MR. WALTERS : I don't wish you to be modest. Dramatists usually are not. I suppose there are such things as good dramas and bad dramas ?

WITNESS : There are certainly bad dramas.

MR. WALTERS : Just to give us your opinion : do you think yours was good or bad ?

WITNESS : I don't know. I am naturally impressed in its favour, but several people—some people to whom I submitted it—they rather doubt it.

MR. WALTERS : They don't think there is any " Magic " in it ?

WITNESS : No.

MR. WALTERS : I don't want you to think for a moment that all dramatists are bad people. I only mean that you may possibly have written a bad drama.

WITNESS : There are several dramatists on the Jury, and they can take their impression.

MR. WALTERS : You would not give a reason why it has not come out ?

WITNESS : I don't think it is up to me. If I am asked for a reason, one is I have had very little time to push its merits.

MR. WALTERS : I suppose though, that even bad plays are produced sometimes ?

WITNESS : No doubt.

MR. WALTERS : It's not only the bad ones, though, that are accepted ?

WITNESS : No.

MR. WALTERS : It must be a bad play that does not get accepted in these days ? When a man of genius such as you——

WITNESS : Please ; if you don't mind.

JUDGE : It is not in evidence that this man is a genius.

THE FOREMAN : I respectfully submit that it is in evidence that he has written a play.

JUDGE : Very true.

MR. WALTERS : When a man of your ability, of some little ambition, cannot get his play accepted, he sometimes resorts to other means—other than the ordinary means ?

WITNESS : I could not tell you. I have only tried the ordinary.

MR. WALTERS : You are a legal gentleman ?

WITNESS : No, sir.

MR. WALTERS : You are connected with the law ?

WITNESS : No, sir.

MR. WALTERS : Not connected with a lawyer ?

WITNESS : No, sir.

MR. WALTERS : Know nothing about the law ?

WITNESS : I wouldn't say that. I thought all Englishmen were supposed to under-stand the Statutes under which they live. I am in the office of a barrister who is not acting as a barrister, but as Receiver and Manager of two large estates.

The Trial of John Jasper

MR. WALTERS : And therefore no lawyer.

WITNESS : It is not for me to say that.

MR. WALTERS : Do you think you can give a straightforward answer to any plain question ?

WITNESS : I think I have done so.

MR. WALTERS : You have probably heard that unsuccessful authors and dramatists, when they cannot get their plays or books accepted by ordinary means, adopt little devices ?

WITNESS : I don't think I have.

MR. WALTERS : You have never heard of an actress losing her jewels, or an author pretending to commit suicide ?

WITNESS : I have heard of them actually doing it.

MR. WALTERS : Ever heard of an author saying he has been to the North Pole, and writing a book ? Would it not be absolutely providential if something occurred to you to bring you into notoriety ?

WITNESS : No.

MR. WALTERS : It would not relieve your " Thorn of Anxiety " ?

WITNESS : No.

MR. WALTERS : In other words, would it not rather be to your advantage to be talked about as a hero.

WITNESS : I have never seriously considered the proposition.

MR. WALTERS : You are rather fond of theatricals, are you not ?

WITNESS : No, sir.

MR. WALTERS : Fond of the Drama ?

WITNESS : I am rather too busy to be interested in it. As I have told you, I am too busy——

MR. WALTERS : Yes or no ?

WITNESS : You ought to take my answer. I say I have been too engaged in looking after my livelihood to take a lively interest in the British Drama.

MR. WALTERS : You do take an interest ?

WITNESS : Yes.

MR. WALTERS : Does your employer know it ?

WITNESS : Yes.

MR. WALTERS : He has seen your play ?

WITNESS : Yes.

MR. WALTERS : It rather interested him ?

WITNESS : I think what interested him was my work for him.

MR. WALTERS : He is a keen man, you know.

WITNESS : I know. I can tell you he is not interested in the Drama.

Evidence of Thomas Bazzard

MR. WALTERS : You have a few friends who are interested in the Drama ? Do you meet a few fellow Dramatists ?

WITNESS : No, sir.

MR. WALTERS : But it is in the Official Records that you do !

WITNESS : Then, I must be wrong, and I do. I was told to answer " yes or no." I meet a few people who are interested in the Drama, having attempted plays as I have. I meet them at rather long but happy intervals.

MR. WALTERS : I suppose they would like their plays produced ?

WITNESS : I dare say.

MR. WALTERS : Once more I ask you—and do please give a straightforward answer—

WITNESS : With great respect, I very much resent that.

MR. WALTERS : Do you think it would be to your advantage to be a little famous ?

JUDGE : I must interpose, because I don't think I know any human being in the world who would not think it to his advantage to be rather famous. Also I must remind the Court that two speeches have to be made on both sides, and we are all in high hopes of hanging somebody, and it really ought to be abbreviated if possible. I don't think anyone can say that the answers of the present witness have been such as in any way to expose him to discredit, but if the barrister examining desires to ask a few more questions, by all means let him do so, and then I think we should pass on as quickly as possible.

WITNESS : I could achieve very great notoriety if I were hanged.

JUDGE : Yes : live in hopes.

MR. WALTERS (continuing his cross-examination) : Datchery is rather a famous person at present ?

WITNESS : Yes.

MR. WALTERS : And I suppose you consider it an honour to be considered Datchery ?

WITNESS : I am proud to have worked down there.

MR. WALTERS : You knew a little about the Drood case ?

WITNESS : Yes.

MR. WALTERS : You knew a little of it from Mr. Grewgious ?

WITNESS : I have stated that it was Mr. Grewgious's idea that I should go down there and investigate in character.

MR. WALTERS : It was not a dramatic inspiration ?

WITNESS : The inspiration was Mr. Grewgious's.

MR. WALTERS : When you fell asleep on that occasion, were you pretending ?

WITNESS : No.

MR. WALTERS : You were not preparing for the part of Datchery in advance ?

WITNESS : Datchery never snored, did he ?

MR. WALTERS : You were not preparing a part ?

WITNESS : I had no idea that Mr. Drood was going to be murdered.

MR. WALTERS : You were not pretending, therefore ?

WITNESS : I was not.

MR. WALTERS : You are a man of short sentences, according to the Official Record ?

WITNESS : Yes.

MR. WALTERS : Very abrupt ?

WITNESS : Yes.

MR. WALTERS : Have you given us only two or three words to-night in your sentences ?

WITNESS : I have been answering under some provocation.

MR. WALTERS : Did your Counsel provoke you to your long sentences ?

WITNESS : I trust not.

MR. WALTERS : Were you pretending when you gave those short sentences in Mr. Datchery's character ?

WITNESS : No ; but a man in the witness-box is not a good criterion.

MR. WALTERS : I suppose you can write ?

WITNESS : Yes.

MR. WALTERS : I suppose your professional standing teaches you to keep correct records ?

WITNESS : Yes.

MR. WALTERS : You did not keep the usual records making your investigations in Cloisterham ?

WITNESS : What are the usual records ?

MR. WALTERS : I put it to you that you did not write anything down ?

WITNESS : I did.

MR. WALTERS : Why did you use the chalk marks ?

WITNESS : Merely as a matter for my own amusement.

MR. WALTERS : Were they to be used in any way ?

WITNESS : I should say not.

MR. WALTERS : You valued your time so much that you wasted it by putting chalk marks on a door !

WITNESS : The amount of time would not be much.

MR. WALTERS : You were not going to take the cupboard door to London as evidence ?

WITNESS : No.

MR. WALTERS : It was all a waste of your time ?

WITNESS : Yes ; but harmless. Even a rejected dramatist is entitled to have some hobby.

MR. WALTERS : You know John Jasper ?

WITNESS : Yes.

MR. WALTERS : Did you ever see him take opium ?

WITNESS : Never.

Evidence of Thomas Bazzard

MR. WALTERS : Do you know how long an opium fit lasts ?

WITNESS : No. I imagine it rather depends on the amount of opium taken, and various other circumstances.

MR. WALTERS : Suppose a man was in the habit of having a particular smoke of opium—mixing it in a particular way ; do you think it would be over in a few minutes ?

WITNESS : I could not tell you. Nor do I know whether he had those habits.

MR. WALTERS : You don't think it would take a few hours ?

WITNESS : No idea.

MR. WALTERS : Would it surprise you to know that after an orgy he would be clear-headed in the morning ?

WITNESS : Nothing would surprise me, I think, from the little I have read of their literature.

MR. WALTERS : You know nothing about it ?

WITNESS : As a matter of experience, that is the exhilarating fact.

MR. WALTERS : You never saw Jasper taking opium ?

WITNESS : No.

MR. WALTERS : And you watched him in Cloisterham ?

WITNESS : In the street. He never took any there.

MR. WALTERS : You believe that possibly he made a desperate attack on Edwin Drood ?

WITNESS : Yes, I think so.

MR. WALTERS : He would possibly make an attack on someone else ?

WITNESS : Yes.

MR. WALTERS : Don't you think, therefore, you were in some danger ?

WITNESS : I don't think I was.

MR. WALTERS : You don't think you were in danger from a man who might make an attack ? Are you a man of very great nerve ?

WITNESS : It's not for me to say.

JUDGE : I don't think you have any right to ask him that. That is a matter of personal knowledge. It might be settled in a fight outside.

MR. WALTERS : One or two more questions. Have you a great affection for Edwin Drood ?

WITNESS : I have not.

MR. WALTERS : Nor for Neville Landless ?

WITNESS : No.

MR. WALTERS : No interest in Miss Helena Landless ?

WITNESS : No.

MR. WALTERS : No interest whatever in any of the parties ?

WITNESS : Business interest only.

The Trial of John Jasper

MR. WALTERS : Then, why did you risk your valuable life ?

WITNESS : In the first place, I don't think I exposed my life, valuable or otherwise, to any great risk. Why I went down there was because Mr. Grewgious asked me to do so, and because he had been a very generous and considerate employer to me, and I also thought that if I had good results he would reward me suitably.

MR. WALTERS : Can you give me any explanation, if Drood has disappeared, why he has not communicated with his friends ?

JUDGE : That is surely a point for final discussion in abstract debate ?

MR. WALTERS : I only ask if he can offer any explanation. (*To witness.*) Should you expect a man who has disappeared, and finding all his friends in danger, to communicate with his friends ?

WITNESS : On that hypothetical case, I think I should. But that has no reference to the Drood question.

JUDGE : I think we should confine ourselves as sharply as we can to bringing out the actual facts, and not to abstract argument.

MR. WALTERS (*to witness*) : Can you give us any reason why he should not communicate ?

WITNESS : I cannot : but he has communicated with his friends.

MR. WALTERS : Are you going to produce any evidence ?

WITNESS : That is in the hands of Counsel.

MR. WALTERS : Don't you think the white wig would give you away ?

WITNESS : I can't tell you. I was in the hands of a costumier.

MR. WALTERS : You can go back to Norfolk, Mr. Bazzard.

WITNESS : Thank you, I am going back to the City.

MR. CHESTERTON : I have no intention of cross-examining this witness. That concludes my case.

[SPEECH FOR THE DEFENCE.]

Mr. Chesterton proceeded to address the Court for the defence. He said :

MY LORD, GENTLEMEN OF THE JURY :

I rise to speak in defence of the prisoner in circumstances in many ways difficult and even unfortunate. This is a case which has unfortunately been very much discussed, and very much written about, on which many people have preconceived opinions. I had, indeed, almost thought of appealing to your Lordship to commit at least one well-known man of letters for Contempt of Court, for a very improper article which appeared in yesterday's *Daily Mail*. But, as I say, this is a case which we cannot pretend that any of us comes fresh to. Probably you, Gentlemen of the Jury, have some of you read about it, but I want to point out to you that, situated as you are to-day, you are bound by your oath to give us your decision quite irrespective of any previous opinions which you may have held, quite irrespective of anything that you may have read, or written, or heard ; that you are bound to give your opinions on the evidence, on the evidence which has been offered to the Court to-day. And on that evidence I, without a moment's hesitation, claim an acquittal.

Speech for the Defence

What is the situation ? Now, apart from the formal witnesses, whose evidence is not much disputed on either side, but to whose evidence I shall have to refer in some detail in a moment—apart from this, we have had two principal witnesses in the box to-day. Now it is obvious that one or other of them is not telling the truth. That is clear and unmistakeable. One of the questions you have to put yourselves is, Which of them was telling the truth, and which was telling falsehoods ? You can test that in a good many ways, but whichever way, you will come to the same conclusion—that if there was a witness who was telling the truth it was Thomas Bazzard—if there was a witness who was romancing, it was Miss Helena Landless. What do we know about these two ? Mr. Thomas Bazzard is a clerk in the office of a well-known business man ; Miss Helena Landless is a young lady from Ceylon. Very much, no doubt, comes from there, but we have learned this evening, as one of the most amazing bits of her evidence, that the old English tavern scores come from there !

Now, let us consider first of all, What about the motives ? Here is Bazzard. Bazzard has no motive—no motive whatever—for attempting to secure the release of the prisoner. Miss Helena Landless has admitted in that box on her oath that her hatred of Jasper had nothing whatever to do with the assassination of Edwin Drood. Her hatred of Jasper does not rest on the fact that Jasper has killed Edwin Drood at all. It rests on the fact that Jasper has treated in an unfortunate way her brother, and her friend, Miss Rosa Bud. So there you have her confession that she had a very real motive for hunting down the prisoner. Miss Helena Landless has told her story. She says she was Datchery. What is the first thing that strikes us about that extraordinary story ? I asked her whether she made up her face, and she said she did not. Now, had she said that she made up her face, had she said she had painted herself wrinkles, it might have been just possible to ask a sane man to believe that she could go about Cloisterham, where she was well known, and not be recognised : but how can she have the effrontery to go into that box and ask the Jury to believe that she went about the town where she had been living for nine months, and where she was perfectly well known—round the Nuns' House where she had been at school ; round Canon Crisparkle's house where she had been a visitor ; and round the Cathedral—and that, with her face absolutely unchanged, and merely a white wig and a blue coat ! And she asks you to believe that she did that, and that she called on the people who knew her best, and that they did not recognise her ! Really, after that, can we be expected to believe one word of her evidence ? Really, that is so strong and so monstrous an attempt on our credulity, that I am willing to waive all the other nonsensical parts of her story. There is her way of avoiding suspicion. She wishes to pass as an old buffer. Her idea is to order with a gargantuan meal an enormous quantity of wine and not to drink it ! When I pressed her, she said she poured it away. Is it reasonable ? It is not necessary to the character of an old buffer that she should drink a pint of sherry. But her whole story ! I asked her where she learned to keep tavern scores. Gentlemen, you know what the way of keeping tavern scores means. It is the notorious old English custom of " scoring a man up." As many of you may know, and as Mr. Bazzard has sworn, in evidence, it is a custom particularly of Norfolk. That is a perfectly natural action for Bazzard. Had Miss Landless said a Norfolk man or a countryman had told her, we might have believed her. But she said she learned it in Ceylon ! I am rather surprised she did not say it was an accomplishment taught at Miss Twinkleton's ! Her theory that she could act as an old buffer is so absurd——because when she was thirteen years old she put on her brother's knickerbockers. It is absurd. As if that would help a woman of 21 to pass as

71

an old buffer! So I unhesitatingly ask you to accept the evidence of Bazzard, and reject that of Miss Helena Landless.

Another important aspect of the matter. If you believe the testimony of Bazzard, which is unshaken—it has not been shaken on one point by my learned friend, and not challenged in one single point—if you believe the evidence of Bazzard, you must acquit the prisoner. You must find the prisoner Not Guilty, because Bazzard has sworn that he has seen the alleged murdered man since the attempted murder. If you believe that, you must acquit the prisoner. But it does not follow—and this point I want particularly to emphasise—it does not follow that if you believe the story of Miss Helena Landless you ought to convict the prisoner. As a matter of fact, Miss Helena Landless has not produced, if her story is true, one little rag of evidence in favour of the guilt of John Jasper. She has, indeed, produced a certain amount of evidence suggesting that he planned an attempt on Edwin Drood's life, but the defence admit that. She has produced a certain amount of evidence that John Jasper thought he had murdered him; but she has produced no rag of evidence that the murder took place. I ask you to believe the evidence of Bazzard, and I point out that my learned friend has not challenged the evidence of Bazzard.

I took Miss Landless through the whole of her story. She was a wonderfully good witness, but at every point she had to give some extravagant explanation to cover herself. My learned friend, able Counsel as he is, did not ask Bazzard one question hardly about his story. He devoted the whole of his cross-examination to trying to suggest that Bazzard was a great fool, that he had written a bad tragedy which is not in evidence, and that it has not been produced. Suppose he had produced a bad tragedy, and was vain of it. My learned friend may have heard of Frederick the Great, who was very vain of very bad verses. My learned friend has confined himself to saying that he must be telling lies because he is a fool. That is self-contradictory. We have seen him in the box subjected to cross-examination by one of the ablest Counsel at the Bar, and I ask you who saw him to say whether he is a liar or a fool. If he be lying it is impossible to believe that he is not a man of very remarkable ability. The fact that he is a man of low ability is my friend's only reason for calling him a liar! I ask you to believe the testimony of Bazzard; and you must then acquit the prisoner.

But, as I was saying just now, Miss Helena Landless does not produce any evidence; nor does Durdles; nor Canon Crisparkle; not a shred of evidence to show that the murder took place. I had Miss Landless—an able, determined witness—and I challenged her, could she produce one tittle of evidence, other than the ring, to prove that Drood was murdered? and she had to admit, unwillingly, that she could produce none. She said she still retained her opinions. I am sure she would! We can perfectly estimate the attitude of mind of Miss Landless as one of bitter hatred of the prisoner and readiness to believe anything against him. I have no doubt that if Edwin Drood walked into court, she would still think Jasper murdered him. The only thing she can produce is the ring. If you believe Bazzard's evidence, there is no mystery about the ring. It was put there by him. But suppose you don't believe it: there are a hundred ways by which it might have got there. I could give you half a dozen straight away. Jasper might, in going through Edwin's pockets to take out the watch and chain, have dropped the ring in the trance. Drood himself might have taken out the ring and dropped it. There are a hundred possible explanations of the presence of the ring, but there is no possible explanation of the absence of everything else except the ring. Quicklime will destroy the body, but I do ask whether it is conceivable that Edwin Drood had absolutely no metallic objects about him

Reply for the Prosecution

of any kind. I suggest that he might have had metal trouser buttons—unless he was a member of some extraordinary religious community, or some hygienic body which disapproves of anybody wearing anything of the kind !

My friend has made a great deal of the question of the enormous risks. Miss Landless flouted her enormous risks, and Mr. Walters flouted the enormous risks in Bazzard's face. Mr. Bazzard, who is supposed to be a boaster, did not see that he had run such risks. Nor do I. One of the propositions of the prosecution is that Jasper was an extraordinarily brilliant criminal. Of course, he was the reverse. What is admitted by the prosecution itself is ample for my purpose. We say that Jasper bungled the whole thing and did not kill his man ; but supposing he did kill him, there is no doubt he bungled. Just think. This clever criminal, who kills a man, is content with his own memory that that man had nothing on him but a watch and chain and pin ; drags them out ; never thinks he might have some money, although he is staking his neck, or chance of survival, entirely on the assumption that everything will be destroyed by quicklime. He never takes the ordinary precaution to see if there is anything else. It is so amazingly absurd that it would be incredible if we did not know, as we do know, that he was under the influence of a drug and was not master of his faculties when the crime was being committed.

I conclude by just saying this : I am aware that I appear in one sense at a great disadvantage because I am unable to claim any sympathy for my client. I cannot put it to you that my client has been wronged morally by the accusation. I cannot claim your sympathies for him. Undoubtedly he hated his nephew, and planned his murder ; undoubtedly he is morally guilty of this murder ; but, Gentlemen of the Jury, those things are not within your province. You are not here to judge the soul of John Jasper. You are here to decide whether he has committed the legal crime of murder. Unless that is proved, and proved up to the hilt, you have no right to find him guilty. And I would just say this : if you go beyond your rightful province of pronouncing on that simple matter of fact, you are perhaps thwarting some purpose higher than we know of.

It may not be for nothing that this man has been reserved for this very strange destiny, to have the moral guilt of murder on his head, to have all the remorse for murder in his heart, and yet by a strangely marvellous fate to keep his hand actually free from human blood. Perhaps He who created John Jasper intended for him a destiny more terrible than human punishment, some expiation more terrible than the gallows ; and I ask you to give the benefit of the doubt to the prisoner in the dock. Respect upon his brow the sign of that mysterious immunity. Let Cain pass by, for he belongs to God.

[REPLY FOR THE PROSECUTION.]

Mr. Walters then replied for the Prosecution in the following terms :

May it please you, MY LORD, GENTLEMEN OF THE JURY—

Although this case has many complications, the issue itself is an extremely simple one. Was Edwin Drood killed ? If so, was Jasper the murderer ? The defence has made one amazing, and I think fatal admission. It admits that John Jasper attacked Drood, attacked him with the intention of murdering him, and by that admission it consents that John Jasper's character has gone—that he is a monster, that he is a hypocrite, that he is a man of no moral pretension, that he is a scheming criminal, and that murder was actually in his heart. A stranger defence could scarcely be conceived, and yet there is

73

The Trial of John Jasper

something in it, because it tries to ride off upon a side issue, and says that " Whereas you may convict this man of a certain attempt, we say that half way there he failed." It is our duty, therefore, to try to prove to you that this man must inevitably have succeeded, and that he knew he had succeeded, and acted as if he had. What are the facts that demonstrated to you most conclusively that John Jasper committed the murder, and that Edwin Drood could not escape ? Our contention is that he was the victim of a most carefully and elaborately prepared plot, carried out systematically, arranged most carefully, of such a character that there was no loophole by which he could possibly escape. John Jasper interviewed the right people, chose the exact spot, arranged the very hour when he would have all his material together for the completing of that dreadful task to which he had given himself. He had decided that his rival must be removed—that secret rival who was between him and the great passion, the all-absorbing passion of his life ; having once made up his mind, he was inexorable. He knew nothing whatever of pity ; he was a complete criminal ; and all his acts show that his crime was carried out with a sort of hideous triumph.

But you are asked to believe that he failed, after making all these arrangements, and failed because he was dazed by opium, and only dreamed of the particular act which he thought he had committed. First remember the nature of the attack—the double nature of the attack. It included strangling with a silk scarf, and that was to be followed by the use of quicklime. If Drood escaped the one, surely it was nothing short of a miracle that he escaped the other ? And, in any case, if he escaped why should he obligingly disappear to the convenience of the man who attacked him, and to the very great inconvenience of all the friends who loved him ? John Jasper was a lasting danger to all who remained behind. Edwin Drood could not so entirely disappear from the realms of civilisation that he would not possibly know what was going on in Cloisterham, and yet you are asked to believe, Gentlemen, that this man upon whom a murderous attack had been made, went away at a convenient moment, leaving his friends to the persecution of the man who had assailed him, and leaving the way clear for the assailant to pursue his own evil courses ! I should say it is almost inconceivable—or I should if my learned friend had not so ingeniously conceived it ; but that it is believable I don't think you will for a moment agree.

And what definite evidence has been produced to show that Jasper, who had arranged all this for a definite period—Christmas Eve—was suffering from opium at about that time ? You have the evidence of Canon Crisparkle that on the very morning of that day, when he met him, he was in wonderfully fine voice, clear-headed, cheerful, in a good temper. All this is absolutely proved by the direct and unimpeached testimony of Canon Crisparkle. Where are the traces of opium ? There are no traces of opium. The supreme moment had come, and Jasper was supremely ready for it. There were no traces of opium on him when those two young men departed from his home. He could not have soaked himself in opium during their short absence, and then have recovered in time to make his accusation against Neville Landless by the morning. But you are asked to believe that in that short interval he had time to recover—that he was in a trance so deep that he really thought he had committed a murder which he had not, and yet, early the next morning was so clear-headed, so resolute in purpose, so ready with a connected story which would fix the crime on another person. And why should he have been eager to give the alarm if he had the slightest doubt ? A man risen from a trance of opium might have some doubts : but he had none, and within a few hours he was setting things in motion himself, giving the alarm. He had Neville called back, a course he had decided

74

Reply for the Prosecution

on from the first ; he was going to fix the crime on Neville Landless ; and within those few hours he had carefully and deliberately carried out the entire scheme. Why this immediate suggestion of murder ? Why not a little lapse of time ? Because he was confident that the murder had been committed and that the body would not be recovered ; and therefore he could be resolute and speedy in his actions, and proceed at once to the second part of the crime which had been the motive for the original crime.

What did he do ? Not only did he pursue Neville Landless remorselessly, but he set about persecuting Rosa Bud, whom he could afford to threaten, because he was aware it was safe—that the one rival who had been in his path had been swept out of his way, and that his way was clear. Does a man dazed with opium act in this decisive, rational fashion ? He carefully robbed the corpse of those particular jewels of which he had an inventory. My learned friend makes the point—Why did he not feel in his pockets ? Why did he not do this, that, and the other ? He had inquired of Durdles what quicklime would do. He knew that it would not destroy metal. He had told a jeweller in Cloisterham that he knew exactly what jewellery Edwin had. It consisted of the watch and chain and the scarf pin. It was exactly those things which disappeared and were found in the weir by Canon Crisparkle. What a curious coincidence that the very three things he had an inventory of, and no more, should disappear ! And why did he not seek further ? Coppers and buttons are no means of certain identification ; he could afford to ignore them. Moreover, a murderer does not linger about the body of his victim ; besides, he was already convinced that having removed those three items of jewellery, by which Drood could be identified, he was secure, and the quicklime would do the rest ; then he hastened back, for he had to get home again in order to be prepared for the morning, to make his charge against Neville Landless.

But there was one article about Edwin Drood's person of which Jasper knew nothing —the ring, which Drood was to return if his betrothal was broken off, but which we say Grewgious never received. That ring would hold the murderer, and bring him to his doom. It would not be destroyed by the quicklime, and would be there intact and the means of bringing him to the scene of his desperate crime. Remember, he courted inquiry immediately after Drood's disappearance—a sign of his supreme confidence and his colossal audacity. The man who has the slightest doubt that the murder may not have been completed does not at once set the law into motion, go to the magistrate and bring a charge. But if he knows it is completed and the body has gone, he can afford to do so. Everything he had designed to do, he did. It was only something that he did not know of which caused him to bungle. He was not by nature a bungler. He was one of the completest types of criminals that you can imagine, a man who for months and months had been meditating on the closest details of the crime—been to the crypt, talked with Durdles, spoke to Mr. Crisparkle, started his theory that Neville Landless was the person to be charged—and a man who does all those things cannot be accurately described as a bungler.

Canon Crisparkle told you the part Jasper played in fomenting quarrels between Drood and Landless. It is exactly the course that a calculating murderer would pursue. And you have heard the evidence of Durdles, a man who probably scarcely understood the purport of his own remarks. How valuable his testimony was ! Jasper had spoken to him of quicklime and of tombs, and Jasper had gone with him on a midnight expedition. Was all this vain and useless ? Was the expedition at midnight merely a pleasant little picnic for no particular purpose, or merely for fun ? Not for fun, when we find that it all fits the composite scheme of murder which was carried out

The Trial of John Jasper

My learned friend has spoken about Helena Landless. I say she is a witness entirely beyond reproach. She was the very woman framed by nature to carry out her arduous part. She had every need for her action and the capacity for her daring work—every essential qualification for that difficult part was possessed in advance by Helena Landless. She had had experience ; in her youth she had dressed as a boy, and shown the daring of a man ; she was the leader of her brother, and when everything else had failed, when six months had passed by and she was able to do nothing by ordinary means, she adopted this extraordinary means of disguise in order to carry out her work. We are asked why she did not paint her face. I don't know whether my learned friend wanted her to black her face or what he wanted her to do ; but she was brought up in a warm climate with a rich dark complexion and she chose the part of the " old buffer," which means, if it means anything, something of the sailor type. Her complexion was ready for her. She wore a large white wig to hide her luxuriant tresses. Why Bazzard should wear a large wig I don't know. She had the only effective disguise for her, the disguise of an elderly man, because she had to live up to the white wig to conceal her woman's figure. She was no stranger in Cloisterham and was perfectly equal to the task of conversing with those whom she had already met before.

One word on Bazzard. If you reject Helena Landless, there is only one alternative. You must put Thomas Bazzard in her place. Is this Mr. Bazzard, the man who fell asleep while his employer was discussing crucial matters with a client, one who was likely to appear as the elderly Mr. Datchery in Cloisterham ? This man, who thinks more of his drama than his law work, is he a likely man to have devoted himself to confronting a man already suspected of murder ? You have seen a Mr. Bazzard in the box, and I put it to you that he was specially got up to produce a false impression upon you. The Bazzard in the box was bright and alert and voluble. The official record says that he was " a pale, puffy-faced, dark-haired person of thirty, with big dark eyes that wholly wanted lustre, and a dissatisfied, doughy complexion that seemed to ask to be sent to the baker's." That is the gentleman who was to act the part of the brave and daring Datchery ! I say it is impossible, and that his own vanity has tempted him to claim these honours. He told you he " placed " the ring in the crypt for any passer-by to pick up, and that, knowing Drood was alive, he still allowed Neville Landless to be accused of murder and Rosa Bud to be persecuted by Jasper. This from a man connected with law ! It is an absurd story, and utterly incredible. I ask you to reject it.

Gentlemen, a solemn duty rests on you in this crisis which I am sure gentlemen of your ability and intelligence will faithfully discharge. It is with infinite pain that I have to ask that this man shall pay the penalty of his sin. But John Jasper himself showed no mercy. He fondled the victim whom he intended to butcher ; he lured to his doom one who he had made to feel was his nearest and dearest friend ; he destroyed a life full of promise, a life which might have been fruitful and happy. I do not ask for vengeance, but only for the fulfilment of the law, that justice may be trusted to maintain the sanctity of human life. If you fail in your duty this man will henceforth be free. I charge you, in the name of humanity and human rights, to quit you as men, to act on the facts which have been placed before you. This mystery, Gentlemen, has lasted long enough. It is in your power to-day to elucidate what has seemed to be obscure, to solve this deep and complex problem. Yours is an enviable opportunity, and to-day you may strike a very great blow for the truth. The eyes of the nation are upon you, the whole world is anxiously awaiting your decision. I beg you, Gentlemen, resolutely and earnestly to sweep away all this fantasy which has been placed before you by my learned friend, to

The Judge's Summing Up

forget his extraordinary story of a half murder, which I think I have shown to be impossible, and by one bold and emphatic stroke to solve for ever the Mystery of Edwin Drood.

[THE SUMMING UP.]

His Lordship then proceeded to sum up, as follows :

GENTLEMEN OF THE JURY—

You will not be the first Jury empanelled in this great country who will have to come to your decision with unreasonable speed. The proceedings have been so interesting that I cannot hope to do them justice ; but I will merely go over, as far as I can, the main features of the case, and then my duty will be to leave it to you. First of all, it should be remembered, because it is indeed included in what is referred to as the Official Record——

A SPECTATOR : Louder, please.

JUDGE : I am speaking to the Jury. If you think you can hang that man for us, you are mistaken.—I say it is included even in the Official Record by an indirect admission that we owe a great deal of information that we have heard this evening to a man of letters. I must therefore ask the Gentlemen of the Jury to put themselves for one moment in the position of such a person. You must forget that you are solid and good citizens summoned to decide a serious matter, nay, I must forget that I am an experienced Judge seated on this Bench for many years ; and we must all try to think—both the Jury and myself—try to think we are authors. Supposing that to be the case, it is all the easier, of course, to imagine oneself the author of a crime. I will, therefore, very rapidly divide up the evidence, as I see it, on the two sides, and then leave the matter to you.

I need not tell you how serious is the issue put before you. If it were only the solemnity of ending the Mystery of Edwin Drood it would be almost as solemn as that of ending a human life, but if any doubt exists in your minds at all as to whether the Mystery of Edwin Drood has been solved by the prosecution, you must permit the prisoner in the dock to go forth, even if from a merely personal study of his countenance you think he is going forth to murder other people. Unless the prosecution has convinced you that the Mystery is at an end, you have no right to convict him, and he has the right to the benefit of the doubt.

The next thing necessary clearly to distinguish is the evidence of the two principal witnesses. The others were rather entertainers than witnesses. There were two very genuine witnesses, one of whom perjured himself or herself—that is to say, would have done so had we permitted profanity to enter into these proceedings. I want to say one thing about that. It is a remarkable fact, and in that point the Jury ought to really fairly balance their minds, because there is a case for possible perjury in both instances. So horrible a crime as perjury can only be committed either from a very low or a very high motive. The character of Mr. Bazzard, as revealed by himself with picturesque clearness, appears to me an entertaining and attractive but, shall I say ? not a saintly character, and it appears to me to be arguable that he might possibly tell a lie from general amusement at the absurd way in which the world is run. On the other hand, it is admitted, I think, for Miss Landless that though she would not tell a lie or forswear herself for money, she might conceivably do it as counting religious observance beneath some affection she had for her brother. I therefore put it to the Jury as possible that both are liars. But I should distinguish between their motives if I were writing a spiritual treatise.

77

The Trial of John Jasper

It is tenable in both cases. Undoubtedly if one is telling the truth the other is lying.

About the wearing of a wig, I think the point has been somewhat unduly pressed on one side. I think it is a strong argument for Datchery being Helena Landless, but not a very strong one that she feels the weight of the wig. I suppose there are many of us here this evening who have been not unconscious of the discomfort of wearing a wig when you have too much hair already. So I should not press forward the argument that it must have been a woman's hair—or I should not press it too far. Edwin Drood is represented in the picture as having monstrously long hair—but that does not concern us here. I think it should be conceded as a point, but not a very great point, to the prosecution. We come to the second broad distinction which amounts to this : that very few of the witnesses, and I daresay very few of the Jurymen, are acquainted with the proper use and enjoyment of two substances, one of which is opium, and the other quicklime. Most of us, I conceive, indulge in these things, if at all, in great moderation, but anyhow, a great deal depends upon the operation of these two things ; and it appears to me on that point that the whole of this Court, not having called any expert evidence, either of morphia maniacs, or of persons partially buried in quicklime, (who are, I imagine a select class)—as the trial has not called any kind of technical evidence about the effects of these things, I think it my duty to put it to the Jury that they must reserve their judgment and allow a wide space for human ignorance about the effects of these things. I certainly do not know how quick opium confuses the mind, or how quick quicklime destroys the body, and if the Jury know it, I, in the best traditions of the Bench and Bar, command that they dismiss it from their minds.

We have placed in front of us two allegations. On the one side it is alleged by the prosecution that there is, after all is said and done, a very strong argument for the death of Drood, in the fact that he did not return ; it is alleged by the defence that you have an even stronger argument against any theory of the murder of Edwin Drood, because, again, he did not return, even as a corpse. " If he is dead," says the defence, " where is the corpse ? " " If he is alive," says the prosecution, " where is he ? " That, I think, is a fair summary of the arguments, and it is obvious that if you come to think it out, these two theories depend on those two suppositions. Is it possible for opium to make a person half commit a murder ? or Is it possible for quicklime so to destroy all traces, including buttons, and so that the disappearance of the body is evidence of the murder ? That is the question I shall leave entirely to you—as to whether there is enough of what I may truly call " quicklime evidence " to warrant you regarding Jasper as a real murderer, or enough of " opium evidence " to warrant you saying that it was a visionary or dream murder. Those, I should say, would be the broad lines on which you have to decide. For the rest, you have to be answerable to the highest conceivable Authority as to how you deal with a very fascinating romance. Gentlemen of the Jury, you will retire and consider your verdict.

[The Verdict.]

Immediately his Lordship had concluded, the Foreman of the Jury rose and said :

My Lord,—I am happy to be able to announce to your Lordship that we, following the tradition and practice of British Juries, have arranged our verdict in the luncheon interval. I should explain, my Lord, that it undoubtedly presented itself to us as a point of extraordinary difficulty in this case, that a man should disappear absolutely and completely, having cut off all communication with his friends in Cloisterham ; but

Verdict of the Jury

having seen and heard the society and conversation of Cloisterham here in Court to-day, we no longer feel the slightest surprise at that. Now, under the influence of that observation, my Lord, the more extreme characters, if they will allow me to say so, in this Jury, were at first inclined to find a verdict of Not Guilty, because there was no evidence of a murder having been committed ; but on the other hand, the calmer and more judicious spirits among us felt that to allow a man who had committed a cold-blooded murder of which his own nephew was the victim, to leave the dock absolutely unpunished, was a proceeding which would probably lead to our all being murdered in our beds. And so you will be glad to learn that the spirit of compromise and moderation prevailed, and we find the prisoner guilty of Manslaughter.

We recommend him most earnestly to your Lordship's mercy, whilst at the same time begging your Lordship to remember that the protection of the lives of the community is in your hands, and begging you not to allow any sentimental consideration to deter you from applying the law in its utmost vigour.

MR. WALTERS : I should like to urge that the Jury be discharged for not having performed their duties in the proper spirit of the law. We have heard from the Foreman that the verdict was arranged in advance, and I decline to accept that verdict, and ask for your Lordship's ruling.

THE FOREMAN : The Jury, like all British Juries, will be only too delighted to be discharged at the earliest moment : the sooner the better.

MR. CHESTERTON : I want to associate myself with my learned friend.

JUDGE : My decision is that everybody here, except myself, be committed for Contempt of Court. Off you all go to prison without any trial whatever !

The Court rose at 11.35, the actual hearing having occupied four hours and twenty minutes.

www.vintage-classics.info